PASSION'S GLOW

"Look at me, Nona," he murmured.

When she did, she saw a glow in the depths of his dark eyes that promised more to come. She couldn't deny she craved more. In the darkness, Spencer wrapped his arms around and kissed her. He'd held her gently when they danced but he didn't now. She was crushed against the hard length of his body. Never had she felt so soft, so fragile, and never had a kiss so unsettled her.

"There's no privacy at an Army post. I wish we were somewhere else," he whispered into her ear. "Anywhere else."

His lips traveled past the velvet ribbon at her throat, trailing kisses where no man had ever touched her before and it shocked her to realize she wished he'd never stop. What was the matter with her?

Nona pulled free of Spencer's arms. "I must go home now."

"Considering where we are, I suppose we haven't much choice," he answered, placing her hand on his arm.

Nona started to draw her hand away but thought better of it. Between the darkness and her confused state of mind, she wasn't too sure where they were headed or of anything for that matter, except that it wouldn't be wise to be alone with Spencer Quinlan ever again. . . .

FIERY ROMANCE

CALIFORNIA CARESS   (2771, $3.75)
by Rebecca Sinclair

Hope Bennett was determined to save her brother's life. And if that meant paying notorious gunslinger Drake Frazier to take his place in a fight, she'd barter her last gold nugget. But Hope soon discovered she'd have to give the handsome rattlesnake more than riches if she wanted his help. His improper demands infuriated her; even as she luxuriated in the tantalizing heat of his embrace, she refused to yield to her desires.

ARIZONA CAPTIVE   (2718, $3.75)
by Laree Bryant

Logan Powers had always taken his role as a lady-killer very seriously and no woman was going to change that. Not even the breathtakingly beautiful Callie Nolan with her luxuriant black hair and startling blue eyes. Logan might have considered a lusty romp with her but it was apparent she was a lady, through and through. Hard as he tried, Logan couldn't resist wanting to take her warm slender body in his arms and hold her close to his heart forever.

DECEPTION'S EMBRACE   (2720, $3.75)
by Jeanne Hansen

Terrified heiress Katrina Montgomery fled Memphis with what little she could carry and headed west, hiding in a freight car. By the time she reached Kansas City, she was feeling almost safe . . . until the handsomest man she'd ever seen entered the car and swept her into his embrace. She didn't know who he was or why he refused to let her go, but when she gazed into his eyes, she somehow knew she could trust him with her life . . . and her heart.

Available wherever paperbacks are sold, or order direct from the Publisher. Send cover price plus 50¢ per copy for mailing and handling to Zebra Books, Dept. 2852, 475 Park Avenue South, New York, N.Y. 10016. Residents of New York, New Jersey and Pennsylvania must include sales tax. DO NOT SEND CASH.

MIDNIGHT WHISPERS

JANE TOOMBS

ZEBRA BOOKS

KENSINGTON PUBLISHING CORP.

ZEBRA BOOKS

are published by

Kensington Publishing Corp.
475 Park Avenue South
New York, NY 10016

First printing: December, 1989

Printed in the United States of America

Chapter One

Nona Willard glanced at the dark-haired, dark-eyed man standing next to her at the stern rail of the Missouri River steamboat *Lady Jane* and blinked in surprise at his intent regard. Spencer Quinlan was positively staring at her.

"Is something wrong?" she asked in her school-mistress no-nonsense tone.

His smile lit up his lean, somber face. "When the last of the sun's rays touched your hair, for a moment there it almost seemed your head was afire."

Nona felt for the small porkpie hat and found it still firmly fastened to the top of her head, then ran her gloved fingers backwards to check her chignon. Alas, the wind had undone most of the neat coil of hair—she must look a sight with the free strands blowing every which way.

"Like streamers of flame." His voice was soft.

"Mr. Quinlan, all the Willards have red hair," she said tartly as she tried to gather up her loosened tresses. "I'm no exception."

"All the same glorious shade as yours?"

She raised her eyebrows. She'd tolerated Mr. Quinlan's company since shortly after the *Lady Jane* left St.

Louis, tolerated him because he'd stayed away from the personal.

"Some have darker hair than mine, some lighter. My sister Helen is a strawberry blonde." Her tone indicated this information was really no business of his.

"I prefer your deep auburn. I had a mare once whose coat was the same fine chestnut color. I called her 'Sweetheart'."

A reluctant smile tugged at Nona's mouth. So much for flattery—did Spencer Quinlan really believe women enjoyed being compared to horses? Actually she didn't mind. Her father raised Morgan horses back home in New York State and she and her brothers and her half-sister had grown up with the colts so horses were an integral part of their lives.

Horses were more graceful than any human being and often more attractive. There'd been times she felt the Morgans were even more intelligent than some of the people she met.

"I once had a stallion whose coat was the exact shade of *your* hair, Mr. Quinlan," she countered. "'Black Irish', his name was."

His brows drew together and for a moment his dark eyes glinted in what she thought might be annoyance. Then he threw back his head and laughed long and hard.

"I'll wager Black Irish gave you a bad time," he said when he could speak.

Nona shook her head. "Not a Morgan. Never. They're the sweetest tempered horses alive."

"Perhaps I should take lessons from Black Irish, then." Spencer's voice held amusement.

Thinking there'd been enough of such banter, she didn't answer, staring at the western sky where the setting sun tinted low-lying clouds scarlet and crimson. The paddle wheel below the rail churned the brown water of the Missouri to white froth as the *Lady Jane* chugged up the river. From the west bank a killdeer called plaintively.

So different from the Hudson River Valley in her home state, where mountains thrust up to form highlands and, as the land eased upriver to softer contours, lush green farmlands sloped to the water. Here in the Dakota Territory, the Missouri's banks varied in height from bluffs to low prairie but, except for a fringe of cottonwoods lining the river in the lowlands, the country stretched out brown and barren. Even the cottonwoods were barely in leaf, though it was late April.

"In a few weeks you won't recognize the country," Spencer said, following her gaze. "Everything will be green. Spring is the best time of the year in these parts."

Nona felt the coolness of the evening breeze cut through her brown paletot, through the green moire gown underneath and even through her petticoats, to chill her skin.

"I trust the weather warms up, too," she said.

"In July you'll be sorry you asked."

Her half-sister Helen had complained in her letters that Fort Abraham Lincoln, in the midst of the Dakota Territory, was hot and dusty in the summer and cold and blizzardy in the winter. "I swear the wind not only blows constantly," Helen had written, "but it's never a pleasant breeze—either too hot or too cold."

Helen, Nona was sure, would have been far happier if her husband, Lieutenant Kilby Mead, had been posted to Washington D.C. where there'd have been parties and balls instead of hostile Indians and barren plains.

And Kilby—how did he feel? Nona tightened her lips. What Kilby Mead did or did not feel was really no longer any concern of hers.

"Looks like Captain Ott will be tying up at Fort Rice for the night." Spencer pointed to buildings on the west bank outlined against the red sky.

The captain, though, headed toward a small pier jutting into the water short of the Fort Rice buildings. Soon the *Lady Jane* was roped securely and the gangplank lowered. Several passengers debarked, complaining of the inconvenience of having to ride a wagon to the fort.

"Both the *Ben Johnson* and the *W.B. Dance* are tied up at the Fort Rice docks this very moment," Captain Ott told them. "There ain't room for us and that's a fact. You want to spend the night aboard, I'll set you down there as soon as one or the other of the boats pulls out." He touched his fingers to his cap, wheeled and climbed to the pilot house, where he disappeared.

Nona watched the gangplank pulled back aboard, then turned to Spencer. "If you'll excuse me—"

"I hoped you'd have supper with me," he cut in.

"I don't believe so, thank you."

"You're a hard-hearted woman, Miss Willard, denying a poor, lonely newspaperman the pleasure of your company."

She couldn't see his expression in the gathering dusk but suspected his crooked ironic grin would be in place. It wasn't that she didn't want to dine with him, the problem was she wanted to very much. If she were truthful with herself she'd have to admit she'd enjoyed Mr. Quinlan's company on the upriver voyage from St. Louis more than she should have.

There'd been a moment yesterday evening when she was positive he meant to kiss her and she'd been astounded at her reluctance to avoid that kiss. She'd actually wanted to feel his arms around her, her heart had pounded in anticipation of his lips touching hers. Fortunately she'd had enough sense to move away in time, so nothing had happened.

Nothing would happen; she wouldn't give it a chance. How could she possibly allow herself to be so attracted to

Spencer Quinlan when she loved another man? Loved Kilby Mead.

Even if he was her sister's husband now.

She tried to picture Kilby's green eyes, his longish blond hair and neat mustache but only Spencer's black curls, his mocking brown eyes and sardonic smile came to her mind's eye.

"Goodnight," she said firmly and turned away.

Nona had taken no more than four or five steps when the sharp smack of a hand striking human flesh stopped her in her tracks.

"You damn sneaking squaw!" a man's voice snarled from near the rail amidships. "Where the hell do you think you're headed?"

In the growing darkness, Nona couldn't clearly see either the speaker or the woman he addressed so crudely, but she knew who they were—Paquette, the burly bearded trader who wore buckskins and the Indian woman who traveled with him. She'd overheard Captain Ott speak sharply to him two days ago about the harsh way he treated the Indian woman.

"She's my wife," the trader had muttered. "You've no cause to meddle."

Nona heard soft thudding sounds she couldn't quite identify until the woman moaned. Then she realized with sickening dismay that Paquette was pummeling his wife with his fists.

"Traded a perfectly damn good gun for you, damn your red hide," Paquette growled. "And all the time that bastard knew you had his bun in the oven. I'll get him for that someday."

Nona put her hand to her mouth. So the woman *was* in the family way. She'd been almost certain of it, but bundled in the blanket as the Indian had been, it was hard to tell. She couldn't just stand here and allow Paquette to beat his wife, she just couldn't. Indian or not, the woman

9

was a human being.

"Stop that!" she called sharply. "Do you hear me, Mr. Paquette? Stop it, I say!"

There was a silence.

A lantern flared from the bow, lit by the boatman whose duty it was at night. It cast enough light so Nona could see the woman huddled on her knees beside the rail with Paquette looming over her, his face turned toward Nona.

"You keep out of this, Miss Nosey." Paquette's eyes glinted red in the rays from the lantern. "What I do ain't none of your damn business."

He reached down and grasped the Indian woman's braided hair, yanking her to her feet. She clutched the rail. Paquette's hand slammed across her face, blood trickled darkly from one of her nostrils, she lost her hold on the rail and slid to the deck.

Nona gritted her teeth and advanced on Paquette. He raised an arm threateningly.

"That's enough, Paquette!" Spencer's voice came from behind her, sharp and incisive. He thrust Nona to one side as he strode toward the trader.

Paquette let go of the Indian woman and swung around to face Spencer. Swaying on his feet, the trader put his hands up, fists clenched. "C'mon, I'll take you, never lost a fight in my life," he boasted. "C'mon, you bastard."

"You're drunk, Paquette," Spencer said. "Leave the woman and go sleep it off."

"Like hell I will. Caught her trying to sneak off the boat, always trying to get away. She's mine. I traded for her fair and square."

The thought of trading a gun for a woman sickened Nona. Ducking past Spencer, then Paquette, she crouched beside the woman who huddled on the deck by the rail, arms folded protectively across her distended abdomen.

"Are you all right?" Nona asked softly. "Did he hurt you badly?"

The woman looked up at her with a mute plea in her eyes. Then a hand gripped Nona's shoulder and shoved her sprawling onto the deck.

"Get away from her," Paquette slurred. "You damn interfering bitch. I'd like to—" His words ended in a startled oath as Spencer grabbed him, lifting Paquette off his feet.

Striding to the far side of the boat, Spencer heaved him overboard. With a howl of fear and rage, Paquette splashed into the river.

"That ought to sober him up," Spencer muttered. "Too bad we're so near shore, there's no danger of him drowning."

At the opposite rail, the Indian woman struggled to her feet. Nona scrambled up hastily to help her.

"Good heart—you," the woman said in halting English. "Lakota no forget."

Nona put an arm around the woman's shoulders. "Let me take you to my room. You need to lie down, to rest."

"No stay on boat. Go." Determinedly, she started to climb over the rail.

"Wait, wait, you'll harm the baby!" Nona cried.

"I got a rope ladder here, miss," a man's voice said.

Nona turned. A small crowd had gathered about her and the Indian woman. The man who'd spoken was a boatman holding a ladder. In less than a minute he'd attached the ropes to the rail and tossed the ladder over the side where it unrolled to within a few feet of the dock.

Biting her lip, Nona helped the Indian woman over the rail and onto the rope. "Please be careful," she urged.

"You name?" the woman asked, looking directly into

11

Nona's eyes for the first time.

"Nona, my name's Nona."

"Singing Reed remember Nona. No forget good heart."

With amazing agility for a woman so advanced in her pregnancy, she scrambled down the swaying rope ladder and dropped onto the dock. Moments later she'd melted into the darkness.

"She'll get back to the reservation safe enough, don't you worry," the boatman told Nona as he retrieved the ladder. "Best place for her, that Paquette's a bas—well, he's scum."

"You're not hurt, are you?" Spencer asked from behind her.

Nona turned to him. "I'm fine. Mr. Quinlan, you handled that wonderfully well."

"So did you. Mind you, I don't altogether approve of your foolhardiness—a drunk's liable to do anything."

"That poor woman. She said she was Lakota?"

Spencer touched her arm, urging her away from the gaping spectators and toward the far side of the boat. "They say Dakota or Lakota, we say Sioux. Our word is a corruption of what their enemies, the Chippewa, call them, a word for snake."

"You seem to know a great deal about the Indians." Somehow she was grasping his arm, conscious of the hard muscles underneath the sleeve of his black frockcoat.

"My folks homesteaded in Minnesota and I knew a Dakota medicine man there. Dakota are sort of cousins to the Lakota."

"Singing Reed—do you think she'll find her way to the Sioux—I mean the Lakota—reservation?"

"It's not far from Fort Rice. She'll get there all right, she didn't seem badly hurt despite the beating. Paquette's in no shape to go after her and once he is, I doubt he'll brave her kinfolk to try and get her back. Sounds

12

like he traded for her with another white man no better than himself. She probably was married to the first man—she'd be loyal to him but not to Paquette. Most likely she'll stay with her people for good now."

"What of the man she was married to?"

Spencer shrugged. "I reckon it was an Indian marriage, so Singing Reed's free to say it's over if she believes she's been mistreated. The Lakotas have their own marriage customs, just as we have ours. Personally, I think theirs make more sense. I might find myself interested in marriage if we went by Dakota or Lakota rules. This business of being tied to one woman for life—well, I'm never in one place long enough to keep a wife happy."

Was he warning her? Nona eased her hand from his arm. She certainly wasn't planning to marry Spencer Quinlan, no matter how much she admired the way he'd chastened Paquette.

The only man she'd ever dreamed of marrying had wanted her sister instead. It was difficult to think of Helen with her petite figure swollen by the child she carried. Kilby's child. Nona sighed.

"This is quite an introduction to the Dakota Territory for you," Spencer said. "Now all we need is an Indian raid and you'll be a full-fledged frontierswoman."

"I've been assured the Indians do not attack steamboats between St. Louis and Fort Abraham Lincoln." Her voice was cool.

"They don't. I was teasing. Although the Lakota are unusually restless this spring. Braves have made unprovoked attacks on whites in the Territory."

"Surely not near Fort Lincoln," she said, thinking of Helen so close to delivering her baby.

"No, you'll be safe enough there with Custer's Seventh Cavalry guarding the fort."

"Kilby—that is, my sister's husband, Lieutenant

Mead—believes General Custer is the greatest Indian fighter who ever lived."

"I believe George Armstrong Custer is actually a colonel, Miss Willard. A lieutenant colonel at that. The 'general' is a courtesy title, because he was a brevet major general in the Civil War, only a temporary rank."

"You sound less than enthusiastic about General Custer."

"I don't know about that. Ask me again after I've ridden into battle with him and I'll tell you what I think then."

"Ride to battle? But you're a newspaperman."

"In March I accompanied General Crook when he rode against the hostiles at Powder River. How do you think I get material for my stories on the Indian skirmishes if not by riding with the army? And if you want my opinion of General Crook, he's a fine soldier, somewhat unorthodox, but a sound commanding officer."

Suddenly Nona felt exhausted, as though all her strength had inexplicably drained away. No doubt, she thought, it's a result of one skirmish with that miserable Paquette.

"I believe I'll retire, Mr. Quinlan," she said. "I find I'm quite fatigued."

"And no wonder. I'll see you to your cabin and make certain food is sent in to you."

"Oh, but I can find my way."

"I insist."

In the passageway outside her cabin, before she had time to protest or evade him, he took her into his arms, holding her against him gently but at the same time firmly. The lantern on the wall cast shadows, giving him a Mephistophelean look as he bent to kiss her.

A kaleidoscope of sensations twirled inside her—the warmth of his lips, a warmth that seemed to seep all through her body, the delicious thrill tingling along her

14

nerves, the strange liquefaction of her bones, making her legs so weak she had to cling to him.

When he released her she swayed for an instant, confused by her urge to press close to him, to raise her lips for another kiss. Gathering her wits, Nona reached for her key, thrust it into the lock and opened her cabin.

"Goodnight, Mr. Quinlan," she said, amazed at how cool her voice sounded when inwardly she still felt the flames of the newly kindled fires lit by his embrace.

"For the nonce, Miss Willard."

Inside, she leaned against the closed and locked door. I should have slapped him, she told herself, then shook her head. No. Far too late for such a reprimand once she'd returned his kiss. Any reproof by her, verbal or otherwise after she'd responded to his embrace, would be the height of hypocrisy.

And she'd certainly responded.

Aren't you ashamed? she asked herself.

Her pounding pulse, the fluttering deep inside her, her heaving breasts—all the unresolved residual of the embrace—annoyed and embarrassed her. What kind of woman was she?

"Nona, I swear you're too forward for a lady," her stepmother, Dorothy, had told her before she set off on this trip. "If it weren't for your schoolmarmish ways, I'd worry about you traveling alone, I would indeed. Fortunately, one counteracts the other. I warn you, though, men find neither appealing and you *are* past twenty-one. If only you'll try to be more retiring and at the same time a little softer and sweeter, I'm certain you'll charm every bachelor officer at the fort."

Spencer Quinlan had called her foolhardy for braving the drunken Paquette but apparently hadn't been put off by her schoolmarmish ways. Still, she had only herself to blame for what had happened outside her door—she shouldn't have all but melted in his arms the way she had.

15

That's how it had felt, as though his touch had turned her to molten wax for him to mold however he wished. Such a thing had never happened to her before. In her past there'd been a kiss or two she hadn't been able to avoid and at least one she'd welcomed but none ever had this effect.

Shameful was the right word. Such feelings had nothing to do with love, with the sweet, almost poetical emotion she felt for Kilby. This had to do with the physical and was wrong. Sinful. She couldn't understand how it had happened to her. And with, of all people, a rakish Irish newspaperman.

It certainly would never happen again; she wouldn't allow it to, wouldn't again put herself in a situation where Spencer might kiss her. She'd known the moment she first laid eyes on him that he cut far too dashing a figure in his black broadcloth frockcoat, black silk cravat, black boots and slouch hat. His white linen shirt was the only garment he wore that wasn't black. And he was clean-shaven when every other man she knew sported either a mustache or a beard or both.

Clearly Spencer was different. She now realized he was also dangerous. At least as far as she was concerned. Why had she ever spoken to him to begin with?

Because she was forward, exactly as Dorothy had mentioned. Spencer had begun talking to her just out of St. Louis and she'd answered him, found him well-read and quick of wit. Admit it, she'd enjoyed his company. If she'd cut him off in the beginning and spoken only to Captain Ott and the major and his wife who were traveling to Fort Rice, nothing untoward would have happened.

Yet she thought she'd behaved properly enough. She hadn't flirted with Spencer or even encouraged his company. Apparently he didn't need much encouragement.

16

What had he said? That he wasn't interested in marriage, just temporary liaisons. A man who went from one woman to the next, then, taking but never giving. Such a person wouldn't need to be encouraged.

Though she wasn't in any hurry to marry because of her feelings for Kilby, she definitely didn't intend to be fair game for a man like Spencer. A Casanova. A Don Juan.

Nona crossed the few feet to her bunk and felt for the matches on the washstand, then for the lamp hanging next to the stand. When the lamp was lit, she turned away from the sight of her flushed face in the tiny mirror.

She was well aware she couldn't be called a beauty. Her auburn hair, she thought, was her best feature. Her eyes were hazel and all that could be said about her other features was that they were reasonably normal. Her figure, she'd decided years ago, was too slim and at five seven she was too tall.

Helen was the pretty Willard sister. Strawberry blonde, with blue eyes, she was, as their brother Roger said of Helen as a child, "neat, sweet and petite."

Nona sighed. Roger had been her favorite brother but he'd been killed at Gettysburg. Her older brother, Kenneth, ran the farm with father. In a way, Kenneth was the reason she was on the *Lady Jane* instead of her stepmother.

Dorothy'd been all set to travel west to be with Helen for her confinement when Kenneth's wife, after going into labor unexpectedly early, bore twin girls. Such tiny little babies! The twins required extra special care to survive and Dorothy was badly needed to help.

No one had ever said her stepmother wasn't an organizer, Nona thought. Two days after the twins were born, she'd arranged for the Widow MacKenzie to take over Nona's teaching job in the one-room village school and Nona was packing to leave by train for St. Louis where she'd stay with Cousin Henry and his wife who'd arrange for her trip upriver to Fort Abraham Lincoln.

If it wasn't for the twins coming early, Nona told herself, I'd never have met Spencer Quinlan. Or if Cousin Henry had put me on a later boat. Or if . . .

It was too late for ifs. She *had* met him, he'd kissed her, and now she'd have to form a plan of action. Like a general marshalling his troops for a battle. For a skirmish, anyway. The best plan was to rout the enemy before he knew he was being attacked.

Nona sat on the edge of her bunk. She really was a raw recruit in this campaign, not a general. Spencer was the experienced soldier, he'd fought and, no doubt, won many an engagement. Though maybe engagement wasn't the right word for marriage-shy Spencer.

In any case, he knew more about maneuvering than she did. Her tactics would have to be swift and surprising. Hit and run, never staying within reach where his superior experience might be her undoing.

Lying back on the bunk smiling, she pictured Spencer abject and humiliated. Part of her knew what she was thinking was childish nonsense but she was enjoying the vision of Spencer being bested too much to stop indulging herself.

Someone knocked on her door. For a moment she stared, then sat up and called, "Who is it?"

"Supper," a muffled voice called back.

She remembered Spencer mentioning he'd have food sent to her so she rose from the bunk. Almost to the door, her hand reaching for the latch, she froze.

Spencer was standing outside the door with the supper tray, she knew he was. No doubt smiling crookedly, the way he did, no doubt certain the gullible spinster schoolteacher from back east would never suspect who carried the food tray.

For the nonce, indeed.

18

Nona smiled. This time she'd be one step ahead of Mr. Spencer Quinlan.

Hurrying to the washstand, she peered into the pitcher. Half full. Quickly picking it up, she returned to the door. Luckily the door opened inwardly to her left. She shot the bolt back with her left hand, the pitcher poised in her right. Yanking the door open, she sloshed the water at the man standing in the shadowy corridor, her lips pulled back in a grin of triumph.

That would cool him off for awhile!

He yelled, reeling back, plates, food and silverware sliding from the tipped tray to clatter on the floor.

"God damn it to hell!" he shouted.

About to close the door, Nona held, her eyes widening. That wasn't Spencer's voice. She stared at the drenched face of the man in the dimly lit passageway.

It wasn't Spencer's face. In fact, it wasn't even a man's face. She was looking at the gangly teen-aged youth who was the cook's helper.

Chapter Two

In the morning, Nona ventured from her cabin with trepidation. Giving the cook's helper a twenty-five-cent piece had more than satisfied him but she dreaded to face Spencer, certain he'd heard all about what had happened. Already she could picture his mocking grin.

Whatever had possessed her to act so hastily last evening? In the brightness of morning with the breeze blowing cool from the northwest, the idea of Spencer Quinlan attempting to storm her cabin by the ruse of bringing food seemed ridiculous. If she'd had any sense at all, she'd have realized he was a man who didn't need tricks to gain advantage with a woman. As a matter of fact, she thought it likely he'd scorn such tactics.

She'd never felt so foolish in her entire life.

At least she wouldn't have many more hours on the *Lady Jane*. Though Spencer's destination was the same as hers—Fort Abraham Lincoln—once off the boat she'd be able to avoid him.

If only Kilby and Helen didn't hear about what she'd done. Both of them, she was sure, saw her as prim and proper. Which she usually was. Somehow Spencer brought out the worst in her.

By noon she hadn't yet seen him and decided he must

be avoiding her. Thank heaven, she told herself, trying to ignore the smidgen of disappointment that was mixed with her relief.

When at last, in the late afternoon, the sternwheeler edged alongside the dock at Fort Lincoln, Nona, at the rail, had quite forgotten about Spencer in her eagerness to spot Kilby and Helen among those standing on the wharf.

"I thought I wouldn't finish in time," a familiar voice said from behind her.

Her breath catching and her face reddening, Nona turned to look at Spencer Quinlan.

"I've been cooped up in my cabin all day working on my submissions for the Boston *Globe*," he said. "They wanted a daily journal of the river trip from St. Louis and I'm afraid I've been remiss." He smiled at her. "Your company was much more interesting than scribbling words onto paper."

"I—I noticed you weren't on deck."

"I hope to call on you at your sister's home once you're settled at the fort. Lieutenant and Mrs. Kilby Mead, I believe you said."

She murmured an affirmative, scanning his dark eyes for any sign of mockery.

"That is, if you can find time for me," he added, "once the fort bachelors discover they've been blessed with not only the gift of an unmarried woman visiting but a pretty one to boot."

His gallantry confused her. Had he heard nothing of her dousing the cook's helper?

"I'm sure you exaggerate," she said tartly.

He raised his eyebrows. At the same time she heard a man call her name from the dock.

"Nona! Nona Willard!"

Kilby!

Nona turned her back on Spencer, scanning the faces

21

below. Kilby, in his blue cavalry uniform, hat off, waved to her, green eyes alight with welcome. She stared down at him, waving back, her heart pounding. His blond hair, longer than she remembered, contrasted agreeably with his tanned face and pale eyes to make him appear more handsome than ever.

Belatedly, she looked for her sister but Helen was nowhere in sight. Of course she wouldn't be, Nona admonished herself. Helen was in her last month and shouldn't be in crowds. No, Helen was undoubtedly waiting at home.

So Kilby and I will be alone together for a time, Nona thought, taking a deep breath.

"That's your sister's husband?" Spencer asked. "The blond lieutenant with his hair as long as Custer's?"

She shot Spencer a disapproving glance. There was no need for him to use such a sardonic tone. As if Kilby was imitating General Custer. And even if he had been, what business was it of Spencer's?

"You haven't said I may call on you," Spencer reminded her.

Resenting the fact he was taking her attention away from Kilby, she said, "I understood you were coming here to ride with General Custer after hostile Indians."

"I am. But Custer hasn't yet returned from Washington. The word's out that if President Grant has his way, Custer may never return to Fort Abraham Lincoln."

"I don't know what you mean."

"General Terry's been named by General Sheridan to lead the Dakota column against the Indians. In Custer's place. Knowing how close Sheridan and Custer are, I'm certain the order to make the change came from the top. From the President himself. You don't accuse a President's brother of influence peddling if you want to get ahead. Custer should have had more sense."

"If this is true, then why did you tell me you meant to

ride with Custer when you knew he'd been replaced?"

"Because I don't underestimate Autie Custer. He'll be back in time to go after the hostiles. I don't see how he'll arrange it with Grant gunning for him but I strongly suspect he will. And I'll be here waiting for him."

"One minute you sound as though you don't care for General Custer and the next you're positively admiring."

Spencer shrugged. "He's a man of contradictions. I've only met him once and I didn't care for him. As a cavalry commander he's shown bravery and dash. I want to learn more about the man, to share what I discover about him with others."

"Through the *Globe*, you mean?"

He nodded. "There and elsewhere. I write for other newspapers besides the Boston *Globe*. I'm a free lance, that's how I like it."

Meaning he's bound to no one, she thought. Not a newspaper or to anything else. Anyone else. Not that it mattered to her. She started to turn away but his touch on her arm stopped her.

"If you didn't say no, you must mean maybe at the very least." Spencer grinned and sketched a brief salute. "*Au revoir.*" He turned on his heel and strode off.

Goodbye, Nona was tempted to call after him. Goodbye, certainly not "till we meet again." Instead, she focused her attention on the dockhands who were making fast the *Lady Jane* by looping ropes around the mooring posts. On the dock, Kilby waited for her. Spencer was no more than a chance encounter, one she'd forget inside of a month.

Whereas Kilby belonged to her sister.

Nona sighed. That didn't mean she and Kilby couldn't be friends. She wouldn't dream of letting either him or Helen know she still loved him. A pure love, of course, nothing like the turbulent cataract of emotions Spencer had unloosed in her. Those were inappropriate emotions.

Dangerous ones.

Love was far more than a physical response to a kiss. If Spencer called on her at her sister's house, he'd find her too busy to talk to him.

She watched the gangplank go down, waited until she was sure Spencer had left the boat, then hurried to debark. Kilby greeted her with his hands grasping hers, then leaned forward and kissed her cheek, his blond mustache brushing against her skin.

She wondered why Spencer chose to be clean-shaven. Especially here in the west where all men, it seemed—except, of course, the Indians—sported hair on their faces.

Why on earth was she thinking of Spencer at a time like this?

"Kilby," she murmured, "it's wonderful to see you again."

He held her away from him, his green eyes flicking over her brown traveling dress. "How good you look, Nona. The journey evidently agreed with you."

"I enjoyed the trip. You're very fit yourself. And Helen—how is she?"

"Naturally she couldn't accompany me. She's waiting at home, eager to see you."

Did his mouth tighten a little when he spoke of Helen? Nona couldn't be sure. She did know it must plague her sister to be confined to the house—Helen always liked going places. Her sister hated being excluded from anything, wanted to be in the midst of every activity.

"It's three miles to the fort," Kilby said. "I'm afraid there's no transport except a wagon. I thought of bringing a horse and Helen's saddle for you but I knew you'd have a trunk."

"Dorothy insisted on sending a complete layette for the baby, plus several new gowns for Helen to wear after the baby's born. I'm afraid there's a trunk and two boxes."

He smiled. "That sounds like Dorothy. Frankly, I'm glad you're here instead."

Her heart leaped. She did mean something to Kilby after all.

"I suppose it's natural enough for a mother," he went on, "but Dorothy has always indulged Helen too much. What Helen needs at the moment is a good dose of your common sense, not her mother's petting."

Nona's pulse settled back to normal. He wanted her here for her common sense—what else had she expected?

"I imagine Helen's getting tired of waiting," she said.

"And of everything else." Kilby shook his head. "The weather, the fort, the food, me. There's no end to her list of complaints."

"Oh, I'm certain she's not tired of *you*, Kilby. Once the baby's here, things will be different."

"I don't know, Nona. I hope so."

You chose Helen, she felt like saying. Anyone could have seen she was like a butterfly—beautiful and fragile and constantly flitting. Butterflies aren't meant to face any hardship or inconvenience. Did you really think she'd take kindly to army life?

Remaining silent, Nona pushed away her uncharitable thoughts and looked around. The fort was situated on the west bank of the Missouri with the land rising from the river to a series of bluffs a few miles inland. She could see buildings at the foot of the bluffs and what looked like a guard's tower atop them.

Kilby followed her gaze. "That's Fort McKeen on the top of the bluff. An infantry post. Lincoln's below— we're all cavalry." His tone implied there was no comparison, that the cavalry was clearly the elite.

His uniform—dark blue jacket, lighter blue trousers with stripes down the sides, boots above the calf and a wide brimmed plains hat—was striking. Nona wasn't sure what uniform an infantryman wore but thought it couldn't be as smart as Kilby's.

He helped her onto the seat of the wagon after paying a dockhand to load the trunk and boxes into the wagon bed, then urged the horse into motion. A trio of mounted troopers trotted past them, all saluting Kilby. She knew he was an officer but she'd never actually thought of him as a commander of men. Yet he was.

"Do you still plan to make the Army your career?" she asked.

Kilby's glance held surprise. "Why would I change? Naturally I hope to be posted to Washington one of these days where conditions are a bit more civilized."

And where his connections might be of more use, she thought. His uncle was a full colonel stationed in the capital and he had a cousin who was an aide to General Sherman, now Commander of the Army. Then she shook her head, surprised at her cynicism.

Kilby was every inch a cavalryman, he was intelligent and brave and certainly capable of being promoted on his own merit.

As if to prove she was right, Kilby added, "I wouldn't have missed the chance to come here and serve under General Custer for anything. There's a man worth following. I can't tell you how much I admire him."

"He *is* coming back to Fort Lincoln, then?"

"Why wouldn't he? There's no one as fit to rout the hostiles in the coming campaign."

"I did hear President Grant had him replaced."

"Don't listen to rumors. General Custer *can't* be replaced." Kilby extolled the general's abilities until he paused at the stables to point out Vic, Custer's blooded sorrel with white stockings and blaze, who paced restlessly in the corral.

A fine animal, to be sure, but Nona still preferred Morgans. She decided no mortal man could possibly be as gifted as Kilby seemed to believe his commander was. Furthermore, listening to the paean of praise grew boring.

Beyond the stables, clothes flapped on lines strung between wooden posts. Scattered among them were small frame houses.

"Suds Row," Kilby said. "The families of non-commissioned officers live there and the wives take in laundry." He pointed past the houses to a level plain with log cabins at the far end. "The drill field. The cabins are where our Indian scouts and their families live."

"Sioux—I mean Lakota—scouts?"

"Sioux's the right word. But these Indians aren't Sioux, they're Ree. Arikara. Traditional enemies of the Sioux and friendly to us."

He clucked at the horse to speed its pace. Soon they neared the cluster of buildings at the base of the bluffs and Nona saw they formed a square with a large field between them.

"The parade ground," Kilby told her. "Those long, low buildings are the barracks for bachelor officers and enlisted men." He gestured to the right. "The granary and the guardhouse. The hospital's in back. Opposite are the storehouses and offices."

Nona decided the houses on the remaining side of the square had to be for the officers and their families. That large five-chimneyed one could only be General Custer's.

The Mead house was at the very end of the row of seven white wood-frame married officers' quarters, the smallest of the group. Helen stood on the porch, her swollen figure awkward. As soon as Kilby lifted Nona down from the wagon, Helen threw her arms around her sister.

"Oh, I'm so happy you're here at last," she cried. "You don't know how much I've looked foward to seeing you." She kissed Nona's cheek.

Nona patted Helen's back, then stepped away in surprise when the baby kicked so strongly she felt the thrust against her own stomach.

"You look well," she murmured to Helen.

"I look a fright." Helen's voice was petulant. "I just know I'm never going to have a figure again."

Nona put an arm around her sister's shoulders and guided her toward the house. "That's nonsense," she said sharply. "You're still beautiful and as soon as the baby's here you'll feel differently."

"Will I?" Tears lurked in Helen's voice.

Inside the house, Helen slumped onto a settee in the parlor. Kilby remained outside, Nona could hear him talking to someone about bringing in the trunk.

"Now you can see for yourself how terrible it is here," Helen said. "There's nothing. Just this miserable fort and miles and miles of nothing."

"You said in your letters there was a town called Bismarck across the river."

Helen waved Bismarck away with a flick of her fingers. "It's raw and wretched, not pretty and settled like Newburgh or Kingston back home. I hate the Dakota Territory, I hate it, hate it, hate it!"

Nona eyed her sister. Except for her distended abdomen, Helen appeared much the same, her hair as golden, her eyes the lovely blue they'd always been, her complexion clear and creamy white. Her rosy mouth was drawn into a pout.

"I didn't want to have a baby so soon, either," Helen complained.

"You'll change your mind fast enough once you hold your own child in your arms." Nona hoped she didn't sound wistful. The worst of remaining unmarried all one's life was not being able to have a child.

"I don't feel like a mother."

"You're eighteen now, surely that's old enough to be one. Wait until you see all the baby clothes your mother sent with me. And the lovely blankets Aunt Zelma crocheted."

Helen sat straighter. "What else did you bring?"

"New gowns for you. For after the baby's born."

Helen clapped her hands. "With a bustle? Oh, I can't wait to see them. What color? Did mother send any hats? I've been dying for a Dolly Varden in blue silk."

By the time Kilby entered, followed by the two men carrying the trunk and boxes, Helen was all smiles. After the men were gone, she led Nona upstairs to the guest bedroom and sat on the bed while Nona unpacked, animatedly commenting on every piece of clothing.

"Do you know what this reminds me of?" Helen asked.

Nona shook her head.

"When you were away at normal school. I was so envious I cried for a week. But it was so much fun when you came home on vacation. Remember how we used to talk and talk while you unpacked?"

Nona smiled at her sister. "I remember you asking endless questions, mostly about my social life. I'm afraid my answers disappointed you."

Helen shook her head. "I hung on every word. You'd been somewhere different, seen things I hadn't, met people I didn't know. I made up my mind then and there I wouldn't be stuck in some one-horse town all my life."

"And you won't be."

"I suppose you're right. But who'd ever guess I'd have to start married life in this desolate spot?" Helen grinned as she said it, her ill humor evaporated.

That was one of Helen's charming traits, her bad moods never lasted long. Impulsively, Nona crossed to the bed and hugged her. "I'm glad I'm here with you," she said.

"Me, too." Helen patted Nona's cheek. "You know what we're going to do first?"

"I haven't the slightest idea."

"We're going to transform you. Create a new Nona."

"I'm not sure I like that idea. It sounds alarming."

"No, I insist. I can't dress and go to the dances while

I'm like this—" she glanced down at her abdomen—"but you can go. What fun it'll be gussying you up for a dance. Almost as much fun as going myself." She eyed Nona appraisingly. "First of all we'll change your hair style."

Nona touched her chignon. "What's wrong with the way I wear my hair?"

"It's old-fashioned. And too severe. Like a schoolmarm."

"That's what I am."

Helen shook her head. "Not here. At Fort Abraham Lincoln you're going to be the beautiful unmarried Willard sister from back east. No, don't you frown at me. If you dressed differently and fixed your hair right you'd be quite pretty. I've told you that ever since we were little but you never would listen. Well, now you have to. Because of my condition I have to be humored, you know."

Helen grinned teasingly and lay back on the bed, propping a pillow under her head. "That's settled. You can tell me all about home; I wasn't ready to listen before. When I feel bad I can't bear to think about New York and the farm."

Nona began with Kenneth's twin girls and went on from there. After she'd talked for awhile she noticed Helen's eyes had closed and she was breathing deeply and evenly, sound asleep. Nona tiptoed about, finishing her unpacking, then went quietly downstairs to begin supper.

Yes, it was clear Helen needed her. And Kilby? What did he think of her being in his house?

Neither she nor Kilby had ever referred in any way to that moonlit night years ago by the Hudson River when they both thought she'd be the one he'd ask to marry him.

Nona had hoped Helen would forget her plan to "redo"

30

her sister but, if she had, the invitation to the Saturday night dance reminded her.

"You can wear the apricot gown with the black overskirt mother sent me," Helen insisted. "Luckily she didn't have it hemmed, so the skirt will be long enough. That darling ruffled underskirt and the bustle so cunningly draped is the very latest style. You must have a choker with you—I have one if you don't—to wear with grandmother's old locket. We'll put your hair in rags all day so it'll curl around your face. Oh, Nona, I can hardly wait to see how marvelous you'll look when we finish."

The last thing Nona wanted was to be done over but she hadn't the heart to dampen her sister's enthusiasm. By Saturday afternoon she found herself almost as caught up in the preparations as Helen.

"I hope the results will be worth all this work." Nona fingered one of the rags wrapped about a tress of her hair. "What if we find I'm the same old me, no matter what?"

"Don't be silly. You'll be the belle of the ball." Helen shook a finger at Nona. "That means you have to act like a belle, mind you."

"And how does a belle act?"

"You smile graciously at compliments, you gaze at each man as though he's the one you've been waiting for all your life, you don't say much, listening is more important—"

Nona held up a hand. "Enough. I'll never be able to manage more than that. Or even that much. Listening is easy enough but I'm not certain I know how one looks at a man to persuade him he's that special someone. And what happens to the gracious smile if there aren't any compliments?"

"Don't worry. You'll be so gorgeous you'll grow tired of hearing about it before the night's over."

Nona gazed at Helen's flushed, excited face, wondering if that had ever happened to her sister, if she'd ever

31

grown bored with compliments. It certainly wasn't anything she herself had experienced and she doubted she would tonight.

"I wish you were going instead of me," she said. "You're the truly beautiful Willard sister."

Helen shook her head. "I wouldn't go looking like this. Men don't like to see women in my condition. Even Kilby—" Her words trailed off and she bit her lip. "You know, Nona, sometimes I get the strangest feeling I'm never going to look any different than I do right now, that I'll be fat and ugly forever."

"Now you're the silly one. Every baby has to be born sometime. Otherwise where would we all be?"

Helen's smile was small and reluctant. "I keep thinking—what if Kilby has to march against the hostiles before my time comes? And what if something happens to him?"

"Kilby won't be going anywhere until General Custer returns. And nothing's going to happen to him."

Helen sighed, her expression troubled. Then she shrugged and her face grew animated once more. "You're sure to meet Tom Custer tonight, he's the general's bachelor brother. What a coup if you bowl him over, as I'm sure you will. Tom's a captain and commands one of the companies of the Seventh Cavalry. Oh, Nona, wouldn't it be wonderful if you and Tom—?"

"You've moving far too fast for me. I haven't even met Captain Custer yet. We may loathe one another on sight."

Helen laughed. "Everyone likes Tom."

"Well, at least don't go marrying me off before I've even been asked to dance."

Later, when she was seated before the dressing table with Helen arranging her hair, Nona began to see that she was going to look quite different from her usual self and her stomach knotted in apprehension. Up until now it had been a game to amuse Helen but soon she'd have to leave Helen behind and be on her own.

"Why don't you come along and sit on the sidelines?" she asked, catching at Helen's hand.

"Kilby wouldn't want me there. It isn't proper." Helen didn't meet Nona's eyes.

"But at home women in your condition attend socials."

"They're country women, Kilby says, and don't know any better. I can't go, Nona; I don't even want to. I wouldn't feel right. You and I, though, maybe we'll have a picnic when the weather turns warmer, just the two of us. We won't invite Kilby." Her face brightened. "Yes, that's what we'll do, we'll have a picnic like we used to on the farm."

"It sounds like fun." Privately Nona wondered where they'd go for a picnic. Kilby had shown her all over the fort and, outside of a few sickly cottonwood saplings in the yard of General Custer's house, there wasn't a shade tree on the grounds. What was a picnic without a shade tree?

"You have to remember every word anyone says to you tonight," Helen told her. "And every single thing that happens because I expect to hear all about the dance. Everything. Who you danced with, what was said, how you liked each partner. Promise you'll try to remember every detail."

"I have a pretty fair memory."

"And don't be a coward. You're only allowed one dance with Kilby, after that you have to mingle."

What if I admitted I'd like to dance every dance with Kilby? Nona wondered, knowing she'd never say such a thing to her sister. Her heart ached for Helen who had to spend the evening alone when it was clear that, despite her protests, she longed to be at the dance.

I never knew Kilby was so priggish, she thought, then

33

chastised herself for being unfair. He'd been raised in Baltimore, not the New York countryside. City people had different ideas of what was right and proper.

When Helen finished the last tiny curl, she whisked the drape off Nona's shoulders and began fastening the black velvet choker around her throat. Nona swallowed, staring in total disbelief at her image in the mirror. Her auburn hair had been coaxed into a myriad of curls around her face and strands were caught up in the back so they cascaded in a froth of curls over her shoulders.

Grandmother's tiny gold locket settled in the hollow of her throat, its black velvet band making her skin appear even whiter than it was.

The hair style somehow changed her face. Instead of the rather pleasant looking Nona she was used to, she saw a haughty, attractive stranger. Even her ordinary hazel eyes glowed a golden amber. Perhaps it came from the apricot of the dress, she wasn't accustomed to wearing such a lively color.

Or a dress with so many furbelows. The decolletage wasn't immodest but neither did she usually show quite so much of her upper chest and shoulders. Silk flowers decorated the neckline, the sleeves were gathered organdy and very short, the bodice fit snugly. The black net overskirt partly covered an apricot underskirt that was ruched, gathered, pleated and ruffled to a fare-thee-well, even over the bustle.

"I fear I'm overdressed," she murmured.

"Nonsense. Wait until you see how some of the officers' wives get themselves up. The dances are the only place we can show off. I'm showing you off tonight in my place." Helen clasped her hands together, gazing at Nona in the mirror. "You're a credit to the Willards, whether you think so or not. Even I didn't believe you'd turn out to be so lovely. It's a shame you don't take more pains with yourself. No wonder—" She stopped abruptly.

Nona knew what Helen had been going to say. "No wonder you aren't married yet." Helen didn't realize that fancy clothes and cunning curls could never attract the only man Nona had ever wanted to marry. It was too late.

As she preceded Helen down the stairs, Spencer Quinlan's face flashed across her mind. What would he make of her if he was at tonight's dance? He hadn't come calling as he'd threatened to do, perhaps she'd discouraged him as she'd meant to. Of course, she'd only been here four days. It would be interesting to see his surprise when he looked at this new Nona.

Kilby appeared in the parlor doorway, gazing up the stairs. He blinked several times as if he couldn't believe she was Nona, then held out his hand, his eyes on hers.

Helen pushed past Nona to take her husband's arm. "Isn't she magnificent, Kilby? The gown is one my mother sent me, I can hardly wait until I can wear it. I wondered about that color with her auburn hair but I needn't have." She chattered on, breaking the moment when Nona had felt something crystallizing in the air between her and Kilby.

It was just as well. She certainly didn't want to cause trouble between them. Not in any way. Her love for him was a secret she'd never reveal and never do anything about, either. Helen was her sister and she wouldn't hurt her for the world. Despite the fact, she'd have been far better suited to be Kilby's wife than Helen.

The dance was held in a rickety-looking frame building Kilby told her the men had built as a theater. Inside, the seats and benches had been pushed to the walls and an orchestra tuned up on a small stage.

"They're part of the Seventh's band," Kilby said, steering her toward a dark-haired officer, then pausing in front of him. "Major Reno, our post commander," he said. "Major, this is my wife's sister, Miss Nona Willard."

"Delighted to meet you," the Major said, his eyes bright with admiration. "Apparently New York State produces a bonus crop of pretty girls."

Nona smiled, as Helen had told her to.

When they moved beyond earshot of the Major, Kilby said, "Of course Major Reno's only the temporary commander in General Custer's absence. The general was Fort Lincoln's commander from the time it was built three years ago."

Nona nodded a bit absently. A tall man had entered the room and, for a moment before she saw the uniform, she thought it was Spencer.

The orchestra struck up a waltz and Kilby led her onto the floor. "As soon as you've introduced me to a few more people," she said, "I want you to go back to the house. I'll not enjoy myself if I think of Helen all alone there. You can come back for me later."

Kilby nodded, rather reluctantly she thought, and put one arm about her waist, his other hand holding hers, their arms outstretched. She hadn't been this close to him since those long ago days at West Point and she held herself stiffly, afraid of the contact. Soon, though, she relaxed, swaying to the rhythm of "The Blue Danube" as Kilby turned her in precise circles.

Nona closed her eyes, happy to be in his arms, but she soon found herself glancing at the crowd and realized with dismay she was searching for a head of curly dark hair, a clean-shaven face.

When the waltz ended, blue-coated officers surrounded them. Nona looked from one set of masculine eyes to another, seeing admiration in every pair. As Kilby introduced her to one after another of the men, she smiled and smiled until her lips felt positively numb, the men's names and faces blurring into one another.

"If I might have the honor," a captain with a small brownish beard said.

36

Kilby handed her over to him and couples formed for a quadrille, Nona and her escort among them. As the music began, she was whirled from his arms to those of other men in the set, and back. When she caught her breath, she said to him, "Captain, with so many names to remember, I'm afraid I've misplaced yours."

"Tom. Tom Custer. I'll wager you won't forget it again." His smile was confident.

Good heavens, she thought, the general's brother. Helen will kill me for not paying attention.

Tom Custer gave her up, with marked reluctance, to a Captain King for the next dance. Unfortunately, Captain King had a tendency to step on her toes. After him came a series of lieutenants but Tom was back to claim her when the orchestra paused to rest, escorting her to the refreshment table. She drank lemonade but suspected from his flushed face and expansive gestures, as well as the faint scent of whiskey on his breath, that Tom had found something stronger.

He brought her to a short, plump, bright-eyed woman, smartly dressed in olive-green taffeta, who turned out to be the general's wife.

"Don't let this bad boy monopolize you," Mrs. Custer told Nona. "I can see how eager our lonely bachelors are for a dance with you."

Nona would have been only too happy to comply with this advice but Tom had other ideas. He swung her into the next waltz, scowling fiercely at Captain King when he tried to cut in, swirling her away possessively, his arm alarmingly tight around her waist.

"Captain Custer," she protested, "that was unfair."

"All's fair in love and war." Did he slur his words ever so slightly?

"This is neither." Her words were as tart as a quince picked out of season.

Tom paid no attention and Nona looked around for

37

Kilby, confident he'd rescue her if she could catch his eye. He was nowhere in sight and she realized he must have taken her suggestion and gone home to Helen. Nona tried to ease herself away from Tom's tight grasp, hoping one of the other bachelors would try to cut in.

None did and she thought she understood why. Tom Custer had made it clear he wasn't about to give her up without an argument and no one cared to make a scene. Neither did she. Yet she definitely didn't want to dance any longer with Captain Custer.

"If you don't mind, sir," a familiar voice said firmly. She was plucked from Tom's grasp and whirled off in Spencer Quinlan's arms.

"Undeniably lovely," he murmured, his amused brown eyes gazing into hers, "but I much prefer the way you looked on the *Lady Jane*."

Chapter Three

Nona twirled across the floor in Spencer's arms, her heart racing and her mind in a giddy spin from the wild tumult within her. Why did this man have such a devastating effect on her? She wanted to pull away from him and flee yet at the same time longed to press closer to him while the band played on and on forever.

Ths whisper of his breath against her temple sent a tingle racing through her and there was nothing ladylike about the way her body pulsed and simmered from the touch of his. Everything faded from her awareness but Spencer.

He smelled of tobacco and soap, mixed with something unique, something she found increasingly exciting—his male scent. The warmth of his hand at her waist burned through her gown until it almost seemed he was touching her bare skin, giving her sensations that took her breath away.

"Look at me, Nona," he murmured, his voice resonating through her very bones.

When she did, she saw a glow in the depths of his dark eyes that promised more to come. She couldn't deny she craved more. No man had ever made her feel this need before; when she was in his arms she hovered on the edge

39

of losing control of her own will.

"If we stay here," he said, "Captain Custer's sure to try to reclaim you—I see him glowering from the sidelines. I don't mean to let him."

Nona believed him. Heady though it was to think that two men might actually come to blows over her, she didn't intend to embarrass Kilby and Helen by causing a fracas. Still in a partial daze, she allowed Spencer to fetch her evening cape and spirit her away from the dance.

The cooler outside air brought back some of her sanity and she might have recovered completely if Spencer hadn't almost immediately led her off the walk. In the darkness he wrapped his arms around her and kissed her. He'd held her gently when they danced but he didn't now, she was crushed against the hard length of his body. Never had she felt so soft and fragile, never had a kiss so unsettled her.

Her dazzled mind had no words for the wonderful way he tasted, or for the springy feel of the hair on his nape under her fingers. She only knew she'd never forget this moment.

"There's no privacy at an Army post—I wish we were somewhere else," he whispered into her ear. "Anywhere else."

His lips traveled past the velvet ribbon at her throat, trailing kisses where no man had ever touched her before and it shocked her to realize she wished her gown wasn't there to bar him from her breasts.

What was the matter with her? She couldn't allow this to happen, she'd never in her life behaved like a wanton.

Nona pulled free of Spencer's arms. "I must go to my sister's," she said. Her words sounded weak and breathless to her own ears but at least she'd been able to speak, she hadn't been certain she could.

"Considering where we are, I suppose we haven't much choice." He placed her hand on his arm and led her

40

through the night.

Was she to suffer this tingling every time she touched him? Nona started to draw her hand away but thought better of it. Between the darkness and her confused state of mind, she wasn't too sure where Helen's house was. Or of anything else except it wouldn't be wise to be alone with Spencer Quinlan ever again.

When they reached the house, Nona let go of Spencer's arm and quickly climbed the porch steps, taking no chances. Who knew what he might do? Or what she might let him do if he kissed her again? Before she reached the door—to her surprise—it opened.

"I've been watching for you," Helen said.

Since her sister was still dressed, Nona felt obligated to invite Spencer in and introduce him.

"I'm so sorry Kilby missed you," Helen told Spencer. "He just left to return to the dance and collect Nona—you must have taken another way here." She smiled and cast a teasing glance at Nona. "You two must have gotten acquainted on the riverboat—am I right?" She didn't wait for an answer. "How romantic! Maybe we should invite Mr. Quinlan along on our picnic, Nona."

"I'd be delighted," Spencer said at once. "Just name the day and I'll make sure I'm available. If you'll excuse me now, ladies, I'll say goodnight." He smiled at Helen, a smile that changed when he glanced at Nona, becoming slightly challenging, as though he knew how unsettled he'd made her.

Once the door closed behind Spencer, Helen turned to Nona. "You've always been so close-mouthed," she complained. "You didn't say a word about meeting the handsome Mr. Quinlan on your trip."

Nona did her best to sound casual. "I didn't consider meeting him important."

"A man like that is always important."

Nona looked at Helen in surprise.

41

"He positively crackles with energy," Helen continued. "Nothing would ever be dull with Mr. Quinlan present."

"You can't say Kilby is dull."

"I wasn't disparaging my husband, I was only thinking of you. I can't imagine you marrying anyone ordinary, that's all."

Nona didn't argue although she wasn't completely sure her sister hadn't meant something else.

"You didn't stay long at the ball," Helen said. "Come upstairs and I'll help you undress while you tell me all about what happened and who you met. What was Libbie Custer wearing?"

"An olive-green taffeta, if I recall correctly," Nona said as they started up the stairs. "Captain Custer introduced us. She was very pleasant."

"So you *did* meet Tom Custer."

Nona nodded. "I danced with him, a Captain King and several lieutenants whose names I don't remember."

"You didn't dance with Mr. Quinlan?"

She'd been in Spencer's arms for much more than a dance but she didn't mean to admit it. "I danced with him, yes. He rescued me from Captain Custer who, I'm afraid, was three sheets to the wind and in danger of forgetting his manners."

Helen frowned. "Shame on Tom. But Mr. Quinlan may have made an enemy. Tom Custer tends to hold a grudge."

Nona shrugged, not seeing what possible difference it would make if he did. After all, Spencer wasn't in the Army and, likely as not, in the morning Captain Custer wouldn't even recall what happened. Overindulging made for a bad memory.

In Nona's room, Helen chattered as she undid the buttons of the apricot gown. Nona let her run on until Helen said, "Having Mr. Quinlan along on our picnic will be great fun."

"I thought the picnic was just for the two of us," Nona protested.

"I meant I didn't want Kilby along. He always makes such a fuss when I appear in public so far along. It's best if we keep our plans secret so he won't order me to stay home."

Nona wasn't certain she approved. On the other hand, it wasn't fair of Kilby to confine Helen to the house.

Helen giggled, pointing to the mirror where she could see Nona's image. "Disapproval's written all over your face. I can imagine what you're thinking—there goes Helen getting me into trouble again, just like she did in the old days."

Nona smiled at her. "You always were a little minx. I've never forgotten the ruckus over Mrs. Leatherby's tulips."

"You *did* try to stop me from picking every last one of them."

"No one has ever succeeded in stopping you from what you have your heart set on—least of all me." Nona spoke lightly while mentally castigating herself for equating Helen's "picking" of Kilby with the long-ago tulips. The flowers had been a childish whim but Helen was truly in love with Kilby. Wasn't she?

Nona carried the question to bed with her. But it wasn't Kilby's face she saw when she closed her eyes, not his touch she relived over and over as she tried to fall asleep. She couldn't forget the excitement Spencer's kiss had been. If he were with her now she knew his lips would be laying a trail of fire along her throat to the valley between her breasts. Her nightgown had a tie at the neck, how easy to . . .

What was she thinking? Disturbed by her own imagining, Nona turned onto her side, resolving to rout Spencer from her mind.

Black Irish. How she'd loved that stallion. She hadn't really lied to Spencer, Black Irish was a dear. Though he'd had a temper and refused to suffer fools or careless riders—he'd thrown more than one. Never her. Black Irish loved her.

But Spencer did not. Spencer had no room in his life for love and marriage—hadn't he said so? She'd be a fool not to keep that in mind. How he made her feel was a purely physical sensation. Lust? The word made her uneasy when applied to herself. Nona Willard, prim and proper schoolmarm, lusting for a man? Never!

Yet what she felt surely wasn't love. She knew what love was—didn't she love Kilby? Love made you glad to be with someone but it didn't kindle an inner fire that melted your bones. Love was realizing the nobility and fine character of the beloved, not longing for a kiss that seared into your very soul. Love was poetry, not the intoxicating tang of a man's mouth.

Obviously there *was* a physical side to love or there'd be no babies. But the wild tumult Spencer induced in her had nothing to do with wanting a child. Children were the product of love and marriage. Like Helen's coming baby.

The Sioux woman on the boat had also carried a child within her. Paquette didn't love Singing Reed, neither had her previous man, the one who'd sold her to Paquette. Love and marriage? Nona shook her head. Not necessarily.

Men took advantage of women, with or without the woman's consent; she knew that was true. Babies could come whether or not the woman had consented. Nona sighed. What had started her thinking about babies anyway? A baby of Spencer's would have dark curls and laughing brown eyes, she could picture his child in her mind. In her arms. . . .

Nona gritted her teeth. Enough! She did *not* intend to become further entangled with Spencer Quinlan. Why on earth should she be thinking of holding his child in her arms? Because she certainly never would.

The following week Helen and Nona were invited to an afternoon tea at Elizabeth Custer's—Libbie, as everyone called her.

"I can't go, of course," Helen said regretfully.

"Why not?" Nona asked. "We'll be all women, won't we?"

"Kilby would be angry if I went after he's told me to stay inside until the baby's born. Besides, likely as not, Tom will contrive to drop by to say hello to Libbie's guests before the day is out. I wouldn't be surprised if that isn't why Libbie's giving the tea—she's fond of Tom and must know he was taken with you. Actually he's not so bad. And he *is* the General's brother."

Nona shrugged. She didn't care whose brother Tom Custer was, she hadn't enjoyed his behavior at the dance. "I'd as soon stay home with you," she told Helen.

Helen's eyes widened. "You can't! Kilby would be furious. You don't understand the Army. When the post commander's wife invites you anywhere, you go."

"But you're not going."

"Libbie doesn't really expect me to—my condition exempts me. I was invited purely so she could ask you. She'll be expecting you and so you must go. You can wear another of the gowns my mother sent and—"

Nona held up her hand. "No. Oh, I'll go, if it means so much to you, but I'll wear my own clothes."

Helen made a face but Nona's mind was made up. Trying to dress as the belle of the ball had brought troubles that plain schoolmarm Nona, in her practical, no-nonsense gowns, had never experienced and didn't care to again.

On the appointed afternoon, wearing a periwinkle

45

serge princess with navy blue braid trim, a white ruffle at the throat and a modest bustle, Nona walked along the row of seven officers' houses until she came to General Custer's larger house, set apart from the others, but by no means a mansion. Fort Abraham Lincoln had no mansions.

Unlike the others, the Custer house had several spindly cottonwood saplings growing in the front but this meager greenery did little to mitigate the starkness of the fort. In the Dakota Territory, it seemed, trees grew only along the rivers and streams.

Nona found the gathering of women little different from a social tea in Kingston, New York, except that the conversation concerned the current hostile Indians and the upcoming summer Army campaign against Sitting Bull and the Sioux.

"My heart sank when I heard the news about the campaign," Libbie Custer said. "Much as I miss the General, it troubles me to think his return from the East will mean he'll be leading the Seventh against the Sioux once again. The only comfort I take is that the General has always been victorious in his Indian campaigns."

Nona knew General Custer commanded the Seventh Cavalry, but her knowledge of Indian Territory tribes was scant. "Aren't any of the Indians living off the reservations friendly to the Army?" she asked.

"The Crow in the Wyoming and Montana Territory have long been our friends," Libbie told her, "but the non-reservation Sioux and their allies, the Cheyenne, are not only enemies of the Crow but also our enemies. Worse, this Sioux leader, Sitting Bull, encourages those of his people living peaceably on reservations to once again follow the warpath. The General will soon put a stop to all this and bring Sitting Bull to heel."

The chorus of agreement from the officers' wives included enthusiastic praise for General Custer's military genius. Kilby, Nona realized with a shiver, would be a part of the coming campaign. She wondered if Spencer would ride with the Seventh when they set out, and decided he would. Not as a soldier but as a roving correspondent, reporting on the rigors of Indian campaigning so people safely east of the Mississippi could read about Indians on the warpath. Spencer would be in as much danger as Kilby.

I don't care to see Spencer again, she thought, but I'd hate to see him wounded. Or worse. I hope General Custer is as capable an Indian fighter as everyone claims.

She remembered her Uncle Joe, who lost his left leg below the knee at the Battle of Gettysburg, remarking to her father on General Custer's fearlessness and luck. "In that hell at Gettysburg," Joe had said, "most of the troopers in his unit were killed or wounded. Custer—riding in front of his men, as always—didn't get a scratch."

Her recollection of her uncle's words didn't reassure her— Custer's luck apparently didn't apply to the men he led. Nona's musing was cut short when one of the wives sat at the piano and began playing a sprightly tune. Libbie smiled and the others applauded.

"It's 'Garry Owen'," a captain's wife told Nona. "The Seventh's own song. The General chose it himself."

When Nona returned to her sister's house, Helen was eager to hear about the tea.

"But first I have news of my own," Helen said with a secret smile. "You'll never guess who called while you were out."

"I know it wasn't Tom Custer," Nona told her. "He came in just as I was leaving the General's."

"Didn't I tell you he would? What did he say?"

Nona shook her head. "Your news first."

"Well, while you were having a wonderful time at the Custers, Mr. Quinlan and I planned the picnic." Helen gave her a sly look. "He promised not to tell Kilby."

Nona eyed her sister severely. "You're up to something, I can tell."

"You're wrong. I simply don't want Kilby to prevent me from enjoying an outing. And, if he hears about the picnic, he will. I must say my condition didn't seem to embarrass Mr. Quinlan one bit. He even teased me, as though I was still slim and pretty instead of being a fat cow."

Nona couldn't deny she disapproved of Kilby restricting Helen to the house, but she disliked being a party to deceiving him.

"Don't frown at me so!" Helen cried. "You make me feel like a naughty little girl."

"It's just that I thought we'd be alone on our picnic."

"But we need a man to arrange for a wagon and to drive it. I don't fancy walking."

Helen's perfectly aware I can drive a wagon, Nona told herself. Why is she so determined to bring Spencer with us? If she's trying a spot of matchmaking, she's picked the wrong pair, and the sooner I tell her, the better.

Before Nona had a chance to speak, Helen burst into tears. "I was so glad when I heard you were coming," she sobbed. "I never dreamed you'd be on Kilby's side."

Comforting her sister, Nona sighed inwardly. Helen hadn't changed. As a child, if one ploy didn't work, she'd try another and another until she got what she wanted. Though Nona knew very well the tears were meant to persuade her, she couldn't bear to see Helen weeping.

"I'll put up with Spencer Quinlan this once," she told Helen, "but please don't invite him again without first asking me if I want to see him. Because I don't."

Helen dabbed at her wet cheeks with a tiny lace-edged handkerchief. "I promise, I truly do. I had no idea you didn't want him along."

Never mind that I told her, Nona thought tartly.

Helen gave her a speculative glance from tear-bright eyes. "If I might express an opinion without upsetting you—*I* think you're afraid of Mr. Quinlan. Afraid you might be attracted to him. Or maybe you already are and that's why you're scared. The trouble with you is you've got the mind of an old maid."

Nona opened her mouth for an indignant reply, thought better of it and said nothing. Maybe she did have an old maid's mind. Wasn't that better than being added to Spencer's collection of women he'd made love to and then left behind?

The sun rose bright and warm on the morning of the picnic. Spencer came by shortly after Kilby left the house.

"I'm terribly sorry to beg off," he told Helen and Nona, "but Major Reno's invited me to ride to Fort McKeen and I can't very well refuse, since I *am* here to write about the Army."

Nona knew Fort McKeen was the infantry post on a bluff to the northwest of Fort Abraham Lincoln and she understood why Spencer would want to go there with the Major. What she didn't understand was her unexpected pang of regret that he wouldn't be coming with them.

"If you'll postpone the picnic for a day or two, I'd be delighted," Spencer went on. "I was looking forward to—"

"I'm sure we'll survive without you," Nona put in tartly, more annoyed with her own disappointment than with Spencer.

He frowned. "I'd advise waiting."

"Why of course we will," Helen cooed. "Don't you worry, you go right ahead with your plans."

Spencer gave her a suspicious glance but apparently Helen's big blue eyes convinced him she was speaking the truth. Strange, Nona thought, how men could be fooled by an innocent face when she well knew what a devious mind Helen concealed behind her wide-eyed expression.

When at last Spencer left, Nona waited, certain Helen had something more than waiting for another day in mind.

"I'm sure if you asked Tom Custer," Helen said finally, "he'd be more than happy to arrange for the wagon and drive it for us."

When Nona got over her initial surprise, she said, "I'm convinced he must have duties to attend to. In any case, I don't want him along."

"Well, but you didn't want Spencer along either. Don't you like men?"

I like Kilby just fine, Nona was tempted to say but bit her tongue. She chose her words carefully, not wishing to start her sister crying again.

"Why don't we have our picnic in the back yard?" she asked. "We can pretend we're back on the farm and—"

"No! The yard is so ugly. This entire post is ugly. I hate it. If you refuse to ask Tom, then you'll have to drive the wagon yourself. What you do is, you go to the stables. They're outside the garrison, past the sentries. Everyone knows who you are by now, so if you say you want a horse and wagon for Mrs. Mead—you don't have to say why— they'll give you one down at the stables."

"Helen—"

"Please, Nona. I've so looked forward to this day, I can't bear not to have my picnic as I planned. Is that asking so much?"

Nona had to admit it wasn't, even if she did feel awkward about commandeering Army property. And guilty over keeping their picnic a secret from Kilby.

With some trepidation, she set off from the Row, as she'd learned the seven houses that quartered the officers and their families were called. The fort had no palisades or guard towers, in fact, no walls at all. Kilby claimed it was because the nearby reservation Indians were tame and stockades were no longer needed.

The buildings of the fort clustered in a square around the parade ground—barracks for the unmarried officers and enlisted men, the granary and guardhouse and the hospital. Suds Row, where the married enlisted men had their cottages, was outside the garrison, as were the stables and huts where the Indian scouts lived.

Nona passed the sentries after telling one of them where she was going. She wore her black merino riding skirt, no longer in fashion but still serviceable with its practical cuirass basque. Last year's black felt hat with its turned-up brim was firmly pinned onto her head. It was now past ten and the day so warm she didn't need a wrap.

At the stables, troopers grooming their horses turned to watch her approach. Six hundred horses were quartered here, Kilby had told her, many of them blooded animals from Kentucky chosen by General Custer himself. To look at the horses meant facing the stares of the men, so Nona kept her eyes straight ahead.

She saw a grizzled, bow-legged man who, though he wore a blue bandana around his neck, didn't seem to be in uniform. He wasn't grooming a horse but sat on the top rail of a fence, giving advice to the groomers. Nona walked up to him.

"Excuse me," she said. "I'm Mrs. Mead's sister and she sent me to ask for a horse and wagon. A small wagon."

The man turned to face her. "You come to the right place. We got horses and we got wagons."

"Tell her I'll drive the wagon, Ned," one of the troopers called.

Ned paid no attention as he walked into the stables with Nona following. Her attention was immediately caught by a magnificent sorrel horse with four white feet and a white blaze. She stopped to admire him, remembering that Kilby had shown her the horse before.

"That there's Vic, the General's mount," Ned told her.

Nona's estimation of General Custer rose. If nothing else, he was obviously an excellent judge of horseflesh.

After Ned hitched a swaybacked buckskin to a wagon with a five-foot bed, the smallest in the stables, he wasn't too happy to hear she planned to drive it herself.

"I grew up on a farm and helped with chores," Nona explained. "A horse farm."

Ned was still reluctant until he saw how she handled the buckskin. "Reckon you'll do all right," he said grudgingly, his words all but drowned out by the troopers' calls offering help when they saw her alone on the wagon seat.

Ignoring the men, she drove into the garrison and down the road along the Row to Helen's house where she halted the horse and climbed down. If Helen had hoped she'd attract less attention in the wagon than on foot, Nona thought, she'd made a misjudgment. Everybody gawked at the wagon as it passed, no doubt because a woman was driving. She said as much to her sister as she helped Helen up to the seat after putting the quilt and picnic basket in the wagon bed.

"Oh, but I couldn't possibly walk all the way to the hill where the bluebells grow," Helen said as she settled herself onto the plank seat. "Not in my condition."

This was the first Nona had heard of such a place. "Where is this hill?" she asked, climbing onto the wagon. "I haven't noticed any hills on the post."

"It's not far. Within earshot of the sentries."

"But outside the garrison."

Helen nodded. "There's absolutely no spot on the post pretty enough for a picnic—surely you can see that."

"Is it safe to go off the post alone?"

"Goodness, yes, the men would never harm either of us."

"I was thinking of Indians. Unfriendly Sioux."

"The hostiles? They're miles and miles from here, they steer clear of the fort. Besides, we'll be only a hop, skip and a jump away from the sentries." Helen's expression turned sulky. "Don't tell me you're going to spoil our picnic by worrying over hostiles."

"I want to be certain it's safe, that's all."

"Safe? You know what a coward I am. If there were any risk I'd be home behind locked doors and hiding under the bed." Helen grimaced as she smoothed the cloth of her voluminous gown over her swollen stomach. "If I could fit under the bed, big as I am."

Nona eyed her sister. Helen spoke the truth—she was timid. On the other hand, since she'd made up her mind to this picnic, she might refuse to recognize danger.

"You went outside the garrison to the stables," Helen went on. "Did you see any hostiles? Of course not! We're not going any farther than the stables, not really, just in a different direction."

Perhaps she was being overly protective of Helen.

"I'll simply die if you change your mind about going," Helen threatened, tears in her eyes.

Hadn't Kilby himself said the fort was without walls because the nearby Indians had been tamed? Nona asked herself. And Libbie Custer had mentioned the General's march against the hostiles would take the Seventh into the Montana Territory—truly far away. Apparently she was behaving like a typical tenderfoot by overestimating the possible danger.

Nona decided she'd be a spoilsport to back out now and clucked to the buckskin to get him moving. She did love picnics but she wasn't at all sure she'd enjoy this one.

Chapter Four

The sentries let the wagon pass with a warning to Nona not to travel out of their sight.

"No use taking a chance, miss," the younger soldier told her. "Injuns is Injuns, that's what I always say, and you can't trust a one."

Helen shrugged and pointed toward a rise several hundred yards south of the garrison. "We're only going to Bluebell Hill."

"See that you stay in sight, ma'am," the sentry warned.

Nona steered the buckskin in that direction and he ambled slowly toward the hill. The late April breeze carried a sweet but elusive scent and, though an underlying coolness remained, the warm rays of the sun and the green of the grass sprouting everywhere proclaimed spring's arrival. Nona's spirits lifted; she was glad she'd agreed to the picnic.

"We won't go beyond the hill, no matter what," she warned Helen in case her sister had some farfetched notion of disobeying the sentries.

Helen smiled but said nothing, so Nona turned her attention back to the buckskin since the horse tried to turn back to the stables if she slacked up. With the hills greening, the countryside didn't look so barren, despite the absence of trees. A flock of red-breasted birds flew toward the river and, as the wagon continued on, a rabbit leaped across the horse's path. Luckily, the buckskin was too phlegmatic to be spooked.

"It must be wonderful to be free like the birds and that rabbit," Helen said.

Free? Nona cast a quick glance at her sister, wondering exactly what she meant.

Helen caught her look. "I've begun to feel like a prisoner." Her voice held an unaccustomed edge. "You don't know what it's like to be married. I wouldn't trade Kilby for any other man but sometimes I remember how free I felt before I married him." She sighed and patted her abdomen. "And before I got like this."

"If marriage is so tiresome, why do you keep hinting I should find a husband?"

"What else can a woman do? Surely you don't mean to teach school all your life and never have a home of your own."

"I don't yet know what I mean to do with the rest of my life, but I'll never marry just to be married. You didn't, you married for love. Or so you told me." Nona's voice had taken on an edge, too.

Helen blinked indignantly. "Of course I love Kilby! Love has nothing to do with what I'm talking about." In one of her quick changes of mood, she giggled. "Poor Nona, I'm upsetting you. You always did think Kilby was far more wonderful than he really is."

Her sister's words jarred Nona. Did Helen suspect her feelings for Kilby were more than a sister-in-law should have?

"But let's not think about him—or any other man," Helen went on. "Today's just for us, for you and me."

That suited Nona. She didn't care to talk about either Kilby or Spencer. The buckskin plodded up the rise and she halted him at the top. Looking down she saw a shallow depression between the hill they were on and the next hill and she caught her breath in pleased surprise. The tiny valley was carpeted in blue flowers—there were hundreds, perhaps thousands of bluebells nestled among the spring green of the grass.

"This is Bluebell Hill," Helen said softly. "Isn't it a perfect picnic spot?"

"Beautiful," Nona agreed, climbing from the wagon and helping her sister out.

Helen was all for descending the gentle slope into the vale and spreading the quilt among the bluebells, but Nona shook her head. "We promised we'd stay in sight and, besides, I don't trust this horse to stay put."

As if to give her the lie, the buckskin lowered his head and began to graze, seeming perfectly content with his surroundings.

Helen glanced from the horse to Nona, lifted her eyebrows, plucked the quilt from the wagon bed and started down the slope with it over her arm. Nona had no choice but to trail after her carrying the picnic basket.

"Heavens, we're not that far from the post," Helen said as she arranged the quilt on the blue carpet of flowers, then lowered herself carefully onto it.

Surrounded by the delicate blue of the blossoms, inhaling their faint sweetness, Nona found it difficult to imagine any danger. Kneeling on the quilt, she opened the basket. They'd brought ham, cheese, bread and tarts made from some of the dried apples Nona had brought with her from New York.

After they'd eaten their fill, all the while reminiscing about growing up on the farm, Helen unpinned and took off her hat, eased down onto her back and lay staring up at the sky. "Look, there's a hawk circling above us," she said. "No, I'm wrong, I see two. Are they mates, do you think?"

"If they are they must be searching for food for their young."

"I wonder what it'll be like to hold my baby in my arms." Helen's voice was plaintive. "Sometimes I have the feeling I never will."

Unease trickled along Nona's spine. This was the second time Helen had said these same ominous words to her. Helen's mother, Dorothy, claimed she had second sight and had predicted that Kenneth's wife would have girl twins months before the babies were born. Did Helen have some sort of premonition? Nona shook her head. More than likely all mothers-to-be sooner or later grew tired of waiting and came to feel they'd never give birth.

Before she could find the right words to reassure her sister, Helen said, "Remember how we talked for hours the night before you left for normal school? I told you I wanted to marry a Crown Prince so I could sit on a throne and wear purple velvet trimmed with ermine."

Nona smiled. "I thought the prince was a great improvement. Two years before you decided you'd marry a circus trapeze artist so you could wear spangles and swing through the air."

Helen made a face. "I'd forgotten that. But I do recall what you told me. You wanted, you said, to marry a man who wrote books. An author like Sir Walter Scott. Isn't it strange that way out here in the Dakota Territory you've actually met a man who writes?"

"Spencer Quinlan is a newspaper correspondent, not an author."

"How do you know he won't write a book someday?"

"He may. But he's not any more interested in marriage than I am."

"*I* think he's sweet on you." Helen smiled drowsily. "And I think you like him, even though you claim you don't. I could tell from the way you looked that you let him kiss you on the way home from the dance."

Her sister's words brought back the thrilling moments she'd spent in Spencer's arms. Once more Nona relived his embrace, the magic of his kiss melting her bones all over again and making her tingle with desire. She struggled to free herself of memory's spell and by the time she had her thoughts under control again, she noticed Helen's eyes had closed and she was dozing.

After casting a glance at the buckskin and seeing he hadn't moved, Nona quietly rose to her feet. She stepped into the bluebells, then knelt to pluck some of them. Like all wildflowers, they'd probably wilt quickly but she couldn't resist.

A flick of brown among the blooms caught her eye and she held, watching. Moments later a baby rabbit jumped away from her. She smiled as her gaze followed his wild dash up the hillside toward the wagon but her smile faded when she noticed the buckskin's head turned toward her, ears pricked forward in attention. Because of the rabbit? It seemed unlikely. What then? The hair rose on her nape as she started to turn.

An arm snaked around her throat from behind, cutting off her breath. A hand clamped over her mouth, stopping a strangled scream. Before she could make any attempt to struggle free, she was yanked from her feet and slung roughly over a man's naked shoulder. An Indian's shoulder, she realized with mounting horror. He ran, carrying her upside down, and the jolting flight jarred her so badly she couldn't scream.

She caught blurred glimpses of another running Indian with the quilt thrown over his shoulder. When she realized Helen could be wrapped inside the quilt, despair numbed her.

The jolting ceased, she was flung onto a black pony. The Indian leaped up behind her, jerked her into a sitting position and wrapped an arm around her waist. She screamed as loudly as she could. The Indian cuffed her

58

hard across the side of the head. Her mind blurred and shining dots danced at the edge of her vision.

When she could think clearly again, the pony was galloping along a defile between two hills. Nona gathered what remnants of courage remained and looked around for her sister, hoping she'd been wrong about Helen being abducted, too. She couldn't bear to think of Helen being hurt.

A pinto pony galloped to the left. On his back was an Indian brave in breeches and moccasins, naked from the waist up. His black hair was long and braided, his dark face without expression. One arm clutched Helen, who sat in front of him, Grandma Willard's star quilt still half wrapped about her. Her head dropped to the side as though she'd fainted. God grant it *was* only a faint, Nona prayed.

Her own situation was desperate enough but what terrified her the most was what might happen to her sister and the baby she carried. Recalling ghastly tales of the suffering of Indian captives, bile rose in her throat as horrific visions of torture and mutilation darkened her mind.

Spencer found Fort Abraham Lincoln in an uproar when, in the late afternoon, he rode in from Fort McKeen with Major Reno and their escort of five troopers. With mounting apprehension he listened to the Major being briefed.

"The horse and wagon was in the sentries' sight the whole time, sir," Captain Ames said. "They had no idea anything was wrong till the horse decided to return to the stable and they saw the women weren't in the wagon. I rode out myself with ten men. Lieutenant Mead accompanied us, seeing as how it was his wife and sister-in-law."

"Nona!" The name escaped Spencer before he realized it.

Captain Ames's eyes flicked to Spencer and back to the Major. "We found Mrs. Mead's hat just over the rise where the wagon was, sir, so I sent a man to fetch one of the Ree scouts. From the sign the scout worked out that two Sioux crept into that little vale where the bluebells grow, made off with the women, carried them over the far hill to where they'd left their ponies and rode west with them."

I should never have trusted that wide-eyed little blonde's promise, Spencer thought. She's the kind who never tells the truth. But I expected Nona to have better sense than to go picnicking without me.

"Why did the sentries let the women leave the garrison alone?" he demanded.

Captain Ames glanced at Major Reno before answering. "Women aren't restricted to the garrison, Mr. Quinlan. They go back and forth to Suds Row every day. Lieutenant Mead says he had no idea what his wife and sister-in-law were up to."

Major Reno gave Spencer a level look. "The sentries aren't at fault. We've had no raids by hostiles in months and the Ree scouts haven't reported any Sioux near the fort."

"Yet there were at least two." Spencer's tone was curt.

He knew it was as much the fault of the women for going by themselves as it was the sentries or the Ree scouts, but anger roiled by fear simmered in him. He knew all too well what happened to women taken captive by the Sioux.

Every brave in the village took his turn with a captive woman. If she survived, a brave might make her his wife. If not, she remained a slave to the desires of the men and a servant of the squaws—who could be even crueler than the braves.

"In my opinion, the two Sioux were scouting the fort and happened on the women," the Major said, his voice cool. He turned to Captain Ames. "Are the Rees following the trail?"

"Yes, sir. Two Ree scouts. One's to keep on the trail and the other reports back here tonight to guide a search party if that seems advisable."

Spencer clenched his fists. Advisable? Damn it, why hadn't soldiers been sent with the scouts instead of waiting? As he started to ask, the Major forestalled him.

"As a civilian, Mr. Quinlan, you aren't familiar with Plains Indian tactics. One trick we've come to expect from Sioux and Cheyenne is for them to entice small parties of troopers into ambush and massacre every last man. Perhaps you remember how Crazy Horse lured Lieutenant Fetterman and all his men to their deaths." The Major spoke calmly enough, but anger threaded through his words.

"Ten years ago come December, that was. The only way we can be sure the women weren't captured as a lure to draw the Seventh into ambush is to send Rees ahead to scout."

Spencer still wondered why the Ree scouts couldn't have been part of a contingent of troopers, but realizing it wouldn't help matters to antagonize the Major any further, he struggled to keep his thoughts to himself.

"I've heard of the Fetterman disaster," Spencer acknowledged. He glanced at Captain Ames. "Where's Lieutenant Mead?"

"I believe he went home," the Captain replied.

Home? Spencer fought his urge to shout the word aloud. Mead went home when his wife was in the hands of the Sioux? What was wrong with the man? Damn it, if he'd been Mead he'd have gone with those Ree scouts and to hell with Army rules and regulations.

"When the search party rides out, I want to be part of

it," Spencer said.

Major Reno eyed him for a long moment. "Sorry," he said at last. "No civilians allowed."

Spencer opened his mouth to argue and then shut it. Don't ram your head against a stone wall of regulations, Quinlan, he advised himself. Find another way. You know damn well you work best alone.

"If you'll excuse me," he said to the Major, "I'll stable my horse." Without waiting for a reply, Spencer swung onto Kaintuck, the Army chestnut gelding he'd ridden to Fort McKeen and back.

He passed the sentries and turned the horse toward the stables, though he had no intention of going there. His destination was the Ree village by the river.

Three Crows wore a buckskin shirt over blue army trousers, a red bandana tried over his hair, and moccasins instead of boots. As a rule the Arikara, the Rees, were smaller and stockier than the Lakota but Three Crows was tall and slim. Spencer guessed him to be about twenty.

He'd paid the Ree to guide him, to find the trail of the Lakota who captured the women and to follow it. Three Crows hadn't wanted to start so late in the day but the sight of the gold coin had convinced him.

Spencer's chestnut loomed large beside the Ree's buckskin pony as they trotted side by side toward the setting sun. I suppose the Army will never forgive me for making off with one of their horses, Spencer thought with a shrug. To hell with the Army and its damn regulations; Nona was more important than all the armies in the world. And her sister, of course. But it was Nona he feared for. Helen Mead was so big with child that one of the Lakota women might sympathize and offer her protection. Nona would have no protection whatsoever.

Nona, with her sunset hair and soft, fair skin, was lovely. At the dance she'd been so beautiful it took his breath away. Any man would want such a beautiful woman, but he wanted more than beauty. He'd been speaking the truth when he'd told her he preferred her dressed as she'd been on the boat. That was the Nona he savored, that woman of independent spirit and quickness of mind.

Spencer gritted his teeth. Her independence wouldn't help her now. The more she resisted, the more savagely she'd be treated. If she did survive, she'd no longer be the Nona he knew. Women captives rescued from the Indians were never the same afterward. The shock of what had been done to them was a mark they bore forever, even after their physical injuries had healed. All the same, he meant to find her and save her—or die trying.

"Many ponies leave tracks here," Three Crows said, jolting Spencer from his unhappy musing.

"Braves with the ponies?" Spencer asked.

"Men. Women. Children. Dogs."

"A whole village moving?"

"You speak true. See, marks of travois. Many villages pass this long ago." He held up four fingers. "Trail of two men we follow lays over others."

Spencer tried to make sense of what he'd heard. More than one entire village of Lakota had traveled west four days ago. Headed where? To camp along what the Lakota called the Greasy Grass River in the Montana Territory, he figured. As a boy in Minnesota he'd heard from old Dancing Coyote about the Greasy Grass with its good hunting. He'd learned about the Lakota, as well as the Dakota, from the ancient medicine man—their language, their beliefs and how they followed the buffalo.

Dancing Coyote, old and sick, had been left behind to die when the Army forced his people to leave Minnesota in 1863 after scores of settlers were killed by rampaging Dakota. Spencer's father, a frontier doctor, rescued the medicine man, restored him to health and allowed him to pitch a tipi on Quinlan property. He cared for Dancing Coyote for the seven years the old man lived.

Spencer, fascinated by the Indian living practically in his back yard, had spent all the time he could with Dancing Coyote. The medicine man was a natural teacher and he and the boy became so close that he allowed Spencer to call him grandfather.

Spencer knew the Sioux called themselves Dakota or Lakota, depending on their tribe. Dancing Coyote had been Dakota; the Sioux in the Dakota Territory were Lakota. But the language was similar and all the tribes understood one another. Because of Dancing Coyote, he could talk with any of them.

Despite his fury at the braves who'd abducted Nona, Spencer knew his chances of rescuing her were greater if he didn't use force. He was handy enough with a gun—and with his fists, too, for that matter—but he wasn't a warrior and likely Nona's captors were. Three Crows had made it clear he'd lead Spencer to the Lakota but not fight them. Spencer was well aware the Ree meant to hightail it home the moment any Lakota were near at hand. Alone, the odds were against him in a fight.

He hoped to bargain with Nona's captors and ransom her and her sister. But if the two Lakota braves joined others of their people before he caught up with them, he'd have to change his plan. Two Lakota were one thing, an entire village another. If he retrieved every crumb he'd ever learned from Dancing Coyote and mixed that knowledge with the Irish guile he'd inherited from his father, he stood a slim chance of surviving the first crucial minutes in a Lakota village. Only then could he begin to plan how to rescue Nona.

If she still lived.

After enduring mile after mile of the jouncing ride astride the Indian pony, Nona at last slumped, exhausted, against the Sioux brave who held her in front of him. Her dazed mind could no longer fret over Helen's fate nor fear what awaited her. At first she'd expected the cavalry would ride to their rescue but by the time the long shadows of evening slanted over the hills, she lost all hope.

The country seemed to be nothing but hills, endless hills, though once or twice she'd caught glimpses of trees, indicating a stream ran nearby. Darkness was settling over the land by the time they neared a dozen conical shapes her sluggish mind belatedly identified as tipis. A Sioux village.

Their captors halted and the brave who held her called to someone she couldn't see. A man's voice replied and their pony walked to the nearest tipi and stopped. Her captor slid off, yanking her with him. When her feet touched the ground she gasped with pain. Her thighs were chafed raw and every bone in her body ached. Before she'd recovered enough to look for Helen, she was shoved so roughly toward the open flap of the tipi that she stumbled and fell to her knees.

Cruel fingers dug into her shoulder, jerking her upright, then forcing her into the tipi. A tiny fire glowed in the center of the circle formed by the bottom of the hide dwelling, and the smell of smoke permeated the air. An Indian woman crouched by the fire stared up at them.

Nona turned toward the open flap in time to see Helen's captor carry her inside and dump her on a mat beside the fire. Helen moaned but her eyes remained closed. Nona dropped to her knees beside her sister. Outside the tipi a man's voice called sharply. The two braves glanced at one another and, without a word, left the dwelling.

"Helen," Nona whispered, chafing her sister's hand. Helen gave no sign she heard. To her horror, Nona noticed a large bloodstain on her sister's gown.

Desperate, she glanced at the Indian woman and saw for the first time that the Sioux was also far along with child. Something about her looked familiar. Not daring to believe she could be right, Nona asked, "Singing Reed?"

The Sioux woman's dark eyes narrowed as she scrutinized Nona's face. "You Nona," she said at last. "Good Heart."

Nona all but collapsed with relief. Pointing to Helen, she said, "My sister bleeds."

Singing Reed rose to her feet and came around the fire to where Helen lay. Squatting beside her, she lifted her skirts. Nona gasped in dismay. Her sister's muslin drawers were soaked with blood.

"No can see," Singing Reed said, pulling at one of the ties.

Hesitantly, not knowing what else to do, Nona untied the drawers and, with Singing Reed's help, slid them off. She bit her lip as she watched the Sioux woman spread Helen's thighs and examine her sister.

"Baby not come yet," Singing Reed said when she finished. "Bad she bleed."

Nona touched Singing Reed's arm. "Can you help her?"

Singing Reed turned up her hands in a gesture Nona understood. Who could tell?

"Give medicine," the Sioux women said. "Maybe stop blood."

Nona pulled down her sister's skirts as Singing Reed prepared some kind of potion by the fire. Outside she

66

could hear men's voices, she wasn't certain how many. Though she couldn't understand what was said, she was sure they were arguing.

"What will happen to her?" Nona asked. "And to me?" She motioned toward the flap. "What will they do?"

"Your sister safe in my tipi. Like me, she not ready for men. You—" Singing Reed paused. "My brother need wife."

Nona drew in her breath. "Please, no," she whispered.

"Wife—one man. Not wife—many men. No good."

Forcing her tired mind to interpret Singing Reed's words, Nona blanched when she finally understood. "Oh, dear God," she gasped.

"Better you Sky Arrow's wife," Singing Reed said. "My brother good hunter, brave warrior."

Tears burned in Nona's eyes. If she understood correctly, and she feared she did, either she gave herself to one Sioux warrior as his wife or any and all of the men could take her any time they wanted.

"How soon?" Nona's voice quivered.

Singing Reed gestured toward the flap. "Painted Dog tells men he see buffalo, they hunt next sun. You marry after buffalo feast. Maybe this long." She held up three fingers.

Nona tried to pull herself together. For Helen's sake she had to be strong. She shuddered to think of what she must face but at least it wouldn't be immediately. She could still hear the men outside but their raised voices didn't sound as though they were discussing a hunt.

"The men sound angry," she said.

"We travel west after hunt. Lean Bear no want white women with us."

Nona took her sister's hand in both of hers. "What does Lean Bear want to do?" She hoped against hope he might decide to send her and Helen back to the fort.

"He say kill you."

Nona clutched her sister's hand convulsively. "Kill us?"

Singing Reed smiled reassuringly as she crouched beside Helen with the potion she'd mixed. "Sky Arrow no let you die. He need wife. I keep your sister safe. I tell Lean Bear she belong to me."

Nona held up her sister's head as Singing Reed dribbled the medicine between Helen's lips. "Swallow, Helen," Nona ordered. "Swallow."

Though her eyes remained closed, Helen swallowed at least some of the liquid Singing Reed had prepared. The Sioux woman stroked Helen's blonde hair when she was through.

"Her name Yellow Bird," she said.

So they weren't to keep even their names. "What about me?" Nona asked.

"You Good Heart."

Despite her fear and exhaustion, Nona tried to smile at the Sioux woman. God knows their situation was desperate, but she shuddered to think how much worse it would be without Singing Reed to intercede for them.

Helen's eyes fluttered open and she moaned. "Mama?" she said plaintively. "Mama, my stomach hurts real bad."

Nona leaned over her. "I'm here, Helen."

Helen's eyes filled with tears. "I don't want you, I want my mama," she wailed.

"She make much noise," Singing Reed told Nona. "Tell her be quiet or maybe men come. Lean Bear."

Helen turned her head toward the Sioux woman and her eyes widened in shock. Her mouth opened and Nona's hand over it was barely in time to muffle Helen's scream.

"Helen, you must keep still." Nona spoke rapidly, keeping her hand over her sister's mouth. "We're in a

Sioux tipi but this woman is my friend. Your friend. We must do what she says or we'll be in worse trouble. Nod your head if you understand what I'm saying."

Helen, her eyes dark with panic, slowly nodded. Nona took her hand away.

"I thought it was a nightmare," Helen whispered. Her hands clutched at her swollen abdomen. "It hurts inside here, Nona. Help me, please help me."

Chapter Five

When Helen dropped into a restless sleep, Nona eased her hand from her sister's and looked around the tipi. Skin rugs, with the hair side up, covered the ground, making a warm floor. Helen rested on one of these hides, the quilt over her and a buckskin pillow under her head. Similar pillows, some fancifully decorated with beads and quills, rested on two pallets at either end of the tipi.

Two tripods made of sticks and adorned with tassels and feathers sat at the foot of the pallet-beds. Nona puzzled over them until she realized they must be back rests. Decorated buckskin containers of various sizes hung on the tipi's yellow walls.

On her knees, Singing Reed tended a kettle set on a tripod to the side of a small fire crackling in a pit in the center of the lodge. Smoke rose to an opening above. As Nona watched, the Sioux woman used wooden tongs to lift a fist-sized rock from the blaze and drop it carefully into the kettle. The liquid contents sizzled and steam rose while Singing Reed stirred the contents with a horn spoon. The savory smell of cooking meat filled the tipi.

Nona's stomach rumbled and she wondered how she could possibly be hungry in such perilous circumstances. She'd heard that Indians ate dogs—God knows what kind of meat was in the kettle.

Singing Reed's loose buckskin tunic was stretched tightly across her distended abdomen, reminding Nona the Sioux woman was as far along with child as Helen.

There was little point in dwelling on any plan to escape, for even if she were clever enough to get away undetected, Helen couldn't possibly ride a horse in her condition. Nona would never leave her sister alone in the hands of Indians. Besides, she hadn't the slightest notion how to find Fort Lincoln even if Helen could travel.

Cool evening air drifted in through the open flap of the tipi. Was the Sioux woman leaving the flap up for her brother? Nona shivered, more from apprehension than from any chill, as she eyed the two pallets with increasing anxiety. One must be Sky Arrow's. Would that pallet be her marriage bed?

"Does your brother speak the white man's tongue, as you do?" she asked Singing Reed, seeking even a small crumb of reassurance.

"He no speak *wasichu,*" Singing Reed said. "He have bad heart for white man."

"If he hates my people, why would he want me for a wife?"

"He no fight white *woman.*" Singing Reed's tone made it clear women were a species apart as far as her brother was concerned.

Nona sighed in despair. How was she to prevent herself from becoming Sky Arrow's wife? If the Seventh Cavalry didn't come to rescue her and Helen soon, it would be too late.

With no warning sound, a man pushed through the tipi opening, dropped the flap into place and loomed over the frightened Nona, his naked brown chest gleaming in the firelight. With his long black hair confined in two braids and his dark, hawk-nosed face, he looked every bit the rude savage he was. Sky Arrow, beyond doubt. Nona

71

forced herself not to shrink away as he leaned down and touched her hair, muttering words she didn't understand.

"My brother says you take off hat," Singing Reed told her.

Nona, who'd forgotten she wore one, reached up with shaking fingers, pulled out the pearl-headed pins that held the hat to her hair, inserted them into the hat brim and lifted the hat off her head. Sky Arrow plucked it from her fingers and turned it over in his hands, examining every inch.

The hat, far from new, was made of black felt with a brim bound in black velvet and edged with steel galoon. Sky Arrow pulled the single ostrich feather from the gray velvet and surah ribbon trimming and tossed the hat across the tipi onto one of the beds. He thrust the feather into his hair so it curled, white and incongruous, over one ear. Instead of making him look ridiculous, the inappropriate adornment made him appear more menacing than ever and the tipi suddenly seemed much too crowded.

Nona, repelled, did her best to conceal a shudder. How could she possibly spend the night in the same lodge as this savage? Bile rose in her throat when she thought of him forcing her to be his wife.

Nodding his head toward Helen, he spoke to Nona in his own language. She glanced helplessly at Singing Reed.

"He asks about your sister," she told Nona. "Blood of women bad medicine."

"He must know I don't understand a single word he says. Why doesn't he ask you instead?"

"Lakota brother and sister no can speak."

How strange, Nona thought. And inconvenient.

Not looking at her brother, her eyes fixed on Nona's face, Singing Reed rattled off a string of unintelligible words.

72

"What did you say?" Nona asked when she finished.

"Your sister's young one ready to jump down, maybe take two suns."

Nona realized she must mean the baby would be born in two days. How could Singing Reed be sure?

Apparently Sky Arrow was satisfied, for he paid Helen no more attention and squatted beside the fire well apart from where she lay. Singing Reed hurried to heap meat from the kettle on a wooden plate and handed it to her brother.

Nona watched in horrified fascination as Sky Arrow grasped a long strip of meat in his fingers and brought it to his mouth. Holding the meat in his teeth, he yanked a bone-handled knife from a buckskin sheath and cut it into bite-sized pieces. Grease dripped onto his chin as he ate. Whatever slight appetite she might have had, disappeared as she fought not to show her distaste.

When he finished the helping, Singing Reed filled the plate again and Sky Arrow made short work of the contents. After he was done, he belched loudly and rose.

How can I bear to have such a man touch me? Nona asked herself in horror. Because she didn't know what might happen next, she stared openly at him as he crossed to the pallet where he'd thrown her hat. Only when he began to remove his leggings did she realize he was undressing. Quickly she averted her gaze.

Hugging herself, she pressed close to Helen's side, waiting helplessly while the slow moments crept past. Would he claim her tonight? Singing Reed had told her it wouldn't be until after the buffalo hunt, but what if Sky Arrow had decided not to go hunting?

"You eat?" Singing Reed's words made Nona start. She looked up to see the Sioux woman offering her a wooden plate of food. Apparently the women ate after the men were fed.

About to refuse, Nona had second thoughts. She had to remain strong for Helen's sake; she must eat to keep up

73

her strength. She thanked Singing Reed and accepted the plate. Fastidiously picking at the chunks of meat with her fingers, Nona forced herself to swallow all she could. Whatever the ingredients, the stew tasted surprisingly good, she'd try to get some of the broth down Helen when she woke.

Singing Reed ate very little and Nona noticed she frequently put a hand to her back as though it pained her. No sound came from Sky Arrow's pallet and Nona fervently hoped he'd gone to sleep.

After they'd finished eating, Singing Reed offered Nona a skin robe from a stack between the pallets and a pillow from her bed. Nona took them and stretched out beside Helen. Though she was determined not to close her eyes, her exhausted body demanded sleep and, fight as she would, her eyelids drooped shut.

The next Nona knew, the tipi was filled with early morning light filtering through the hide walls. Beside her, Helen moaned. As Nona started to sit up and tend to her sister, she saw a dark figure crouched above her. A hand touched her shoulder. In her terror, Nona's scream emerged as a choked gasp.

Spencer woke to the gray of predawn. Three Crows was already saddling the horses, so Spencer sprang up and began rolling his blanket. They'd traveled through the early part of the night, even though the Ree disliked riding in the dark without a medicine man along to protect him. Like the Lakota, he believed evil spirits roamed at night, lying in wait for the unwary traveler.

Around midnight Spencer had agreed to camp, mostly to rest the horses, but he regretted the time lost. He forced his thoughts away from what horrors Nona might be facing—there was nothing he could do to help her until they reached the Lakota village Three Crows claimed lay somewhere to the west.

Chewing on a chunk of pemmican the Ree shared with him, Spencer swung onto Kaintuck and set off again on the travois trail Three Crows was following. All the women of the Plains Indian tribes used travois to transport tipi poles and buffalo hides for the tipi walls. The crude poled carriers dragged by horses left tracks even Spencer could identify.

"They camp by Many Rabbits Creek," Three Crows said.

Spencer decided there was no use asking the Ree how he knew the Lakota had chosen that site. Like most scouts, Three Crows would likely find it impossible to explain the way he read sign.

"How far's the creek?" he asked instead.

Three Crows' fingers made the motions that meant the sun would be past the meridian before they reached the stream. Afternoon. Spencer damped down his impatience and let the chestnut set his own pace. If he urged Kaintuck into a gallop to get there sooner, nothing would be gained. He'd wind up with a lathered, tired horse and still have to wait till dark to chance entering the village.

"Longhair spends many suns in Great White Father's village," Three Crows said after a time.

Knowing he meant General Custer, Spencer held up all his fingers to indicate the number of days. "He'll be back from Washington in about a week."

"Sioux camp on Many Rabbits Creek on way to far hills." Three Crows gestured westward. "Sioux swarm in far hills like bees."

"When he returns, Custer leads many bluecoats against them," Spencer said. "The Sioux can't hold out against troopers and cannon."

Three Crows looked far from convinced. "Sioux make powerful medicine in far hills. Cheyenne come. Arapaho come. Stand with Sioux."

Spencer glanced at Three Crows, uncertain what to say. The Ree's expression was unusually somber; he was obviously worried and unhappy about the large gathering of the Sioux and their allies in the far hills. Perhaps 'far hills' meant along the Greasy Grass in the Montana Territory.

"I don't ride against the Sioux in the far hills," Spencer said finally. "I only intend to find the women and bring them back to the fort."

Three Crows grunted. The sound could mean anything, but Spencer interpreted it as the Ree doubting the success of such a risky mission. He wondered about it himself.

Nona stared up at the figure standing over her, belatedly recognizing Singing Reed. The Sioux woman made the universal sign for silence, a finger across her lips.

"We take your sister from tipi," Singing Reed whispered as Helen moaned again.

Nona rose; when she and Singing Reed lifted Helen, she heard her sister cry out in pain. Nona glanced apprehensively toward Sky Arrow's pallet and saw the brave turn over. She needed no urging to hurry her quilt-wrapped sister through the flap. Supporting Helen between them, Nona and Singing Reed made their way through the early dawn toward the sound of running water.

"Where are we going?" Nona kept her voice low.

"My little one jumps down this sun," Singing Reed told her as they approached a gurgling stream. "Your sister make much noise in tipi, turn my brother's heart bad toward her."

"Your baby's coming?" Nona asked. "Now?"

Singing Reed grunted as though in pain and stopped

walking, abruptly released her hold on Helen. Nona, unable to bear the full weight of her sister, was forced to ease Helen down onto the grass near the bank of a gurgling stream. Kneeling beside Helen, Nona watched Singing Reed enter a crude brush shelter in a small grove of cottonwoods. Once inside, the Sioux woman let down a hide cover to block the entrance.

A birthing lodge? Nona wondered, recalling Singing Reed saying her brother believed woman's blood was bad medicine. With the Sioux woman gone, Nona looked around fearfully. No one was in sight and the new leaves of the trees and the brush hid the circle of tipis from her view.

Helen moaned. Nona leaned over her sister.

"I'm here, dear," she murmured. "Nona's here."

Helen's eyes fluttered open. Weakly, she pushed aside the quilt and placed both of her hands over her swollen abdomen. "It hurts," she whimpered. "I can't stand the pain any longer."

Was Helen's baby coming? How could she tell? Nona bit her lip, glancing toward the brush lodge. She couldn't expect any help from Singing Reed. She and Helen were on their own.

What could she do? She knew nothing at all about birthing babies. She'd seen foals born, but Helen wasn't a mare and she doubted if human babies came out the same way as foals. They certainly weren't ready to stand on their wobbly little legs minutes after being born. This baby wasn't supposed to arrive until next month. Would it survive if born this early in these primitive surroundings?

"Let me look, dear," Nona said, hesitantly pulling up Helen's skirts and easing her legs apart as she'd seen Singing Reed do. She bit back a gasp of horror as blood gushed from between Helen's thighs, soaking through the quilt to the ground beneath. So much blood! Too much? If only she knew more.

Because she couldn't think of anything else to do, Nona covered her sister and sat beside her, holding Helen's hand and squeezing it in sympathy each time Helen moaned.

Tears came to Nona's eyes as she recalled a rainy day in spring when she and Helen were little and they were playing with their dolls in the front parlor. Helen sat in the Windsor rocker cuddling Amanda Jean, her favorite doll with long golden curls and blue eyes that opened and closed.

"When I get married and have a baby she'll look just like my Amanda Jean," Helen said.

"You don't always get to pick," Nona reminded her. "Like Mrs. Travers. Remember how she told Mama Dorothy how bad she wanted a girl baby 'cause she already had three boys? All she got was another boy."

Helen glared at her. "I won't have a boy baby, I won't, I won't, and you can't make me!"

Nona blinked back her tears. If only the two of them were at the farm now where Dorothy, who knew all about birthing, could help her daughter. Instead, they were outside a Sioux village, in the midst of savages.

Why didn't the Seventh ride to their rescue? Nona closed her eyes and tried to picture Kilby galloping toward them, leading his troopers. But it wasn't Kilby's blond hair and green eyes she saw in her mind.

"Spencer," Nona whispered. She could see him riding, dark eyes flashing, saber in hand, slashing through a horde of howling warriors, letting nothing stop him as he fought to save her.

Camp noises—dogs barking, women calling to children—roused Nona from her dream of rescue. She opened her eyes, facing bitter reality. Neither Kilby nor Spencer was here to save her and Helen. For all she knew the Sioux village was so well hidden no one could find them. She huddled next to Helen, expecting Sky Arrow or some other equally frightening brave, to stride through the trees at any moment and wrench her away from her sister.

The sun was well above the eastern hills when Singing Reed emerged from the birth lodge carrying a small, hide-wrapped bundle. Her baby? Nona watched uncomprehendingly as the Sioux woman walked to the nearest cottonwood sapling, wedged the bundle into a high crotch, then turned away.

Nona leaped to her feet. "Your baby—he'll fall!"

"He travels Path of Spirits." Singing Reed's voice was choked and, as she neared, Nona saw tears in her eyes.

She must mean her baby's dead, Nona thought, belatedly realizing she hadn't heard a sound from the brush lodge the entire time Singing Reed was inside, not even a baby's cry.

"I'm sorry," she murmured.

Singing Reed knelt beside the moaning Helen and felt her distended abdomen. "We take your sister to birth lodge," she said. "Little one ready to jump down."

Inside the brush shelter, they eased Helen down onto the blood-stained quilt and Singing Reed dropped the hide to close the entrance. Light slanted in through the many cracks and crevices, so it wasn't as dark as Nona had expected.

"She kneel," Singing Reed ordered, trying to pull Helen up.

Helen screamed.

"She's in too much pain to move," Nona protested.

"You help," the Sioux woman ordered Nona, persisting in her effort to force Helen into position.

Certain that Singing Reed knew more about birthing than she, Nona decided that, pain or not, Helen would have to kneel if that was the way babies were born.

"Your baby's coming, Helen," she said. "Singing Reed's trying to help you. Do as she says."

Between them, they managed to bring the whimpering Helen onto her knees. "No move!" Singing Reed warned Helen. "Open mouth, do like me." She demonstrated taking deep breaths through the mouth.

Nona coaxed Helen into trying to imitate the Sioux woman. When Helen was breathing to suit Singing Reed, the Sioux picked up a peeled stick about three feet long and just the right size for a woman's hands to close around.

"You hold," she told Helen, offering the stick horizontally. "When hurt come, pull hard on stick." After adjusting Helen's hands so they were about six inches apart, she ordered Nona to kneel facing her sister and grip the stick outside her sister's hands. "She pull—" Singing Reed gestured the way Helen would pull—"you pull." The Sioux gestured in the opposite direction. "No let go."

"It hurts so," Helen muttered.

"No talk," Singing Reed ordered, as she crouched beside Helen. "Breathe."

"I can't stand the pain," Helen cried. "I can't!"

An old memory came back to Nona and she decided to talk to Helen about what she remembered. It might distract her sister from the pain.

"It's supposed to hurt," she told Helen. "And you *can* bear it. All women do. Don't you remember holiday dinners when we were young, how the women would shoo us from the kitchen when they wanted to gossip? We used to creep under the dining room table where the tablecloth would hide us and listen to them, hoping to hear what we weren't supposed to.

"One Thanksgiving, Mrs. Pennyworth went on and on about her lying-in. I can still hear her going on about

80

'those blamed labor pains' while we giggled ourselves silly. You're having labor pains, Helen. Birthing a baby is work. But if addle-pated Henrietta Pennyworth managed it, you certainly can."

Helen answered with a groan. Soon her groans changed to grunts and she pulled so hard on the birth stick that Nona had to exert all her strength to keep the stick taut. She was concentrating so hard that the mewling cry of a newborn baby took her by surprise. At the same time, Helen let go of the stick and slumped onto her side. Taken off balance, Nona rocked back on her heels.

"Get feather," Singing Reed ordered over the baby's wails.

Nona rose to her feet and looked into the buckskin containers where two hawk feathers rested next to leather thongs and a flint knife. She brought one to Singing Reed.

"Put feather in her mouth," the Sioux woman said and gagged, creating a retching sound to show what she wanted Nona to make Helen do.

Helen was now lying on her back with the crying baby on her stomach. Blood trickled in a steady stream from between her thighs where a cord stretched from somewhere inside her to the baby. Nona saw the child was a girl. Despite her worry and fear, she smiled as she knelt beside her sister.

"You've birthed Amanda Jean," she said softly. "You have a daughter."

Helen's eyes opened and stared blankly up at Nona.

"A daughter," Nona repeated.

"Use feather!" Singing Reed's voice was sharp.

"Please open your mouth," Nona urged Helen. She repeated the request four times before Helen seemed to understand what she wanted.

Nona thrust the feather deep into Helen's mouth,

81

forcing her sister to gag convulsively.

"It comes," Singing Reed said.

Nona watched a dark red mass slide from inside her sister. Of course, she thought, the afterbirth. I should have remembered; it's the same with mares. Singing Reed tied a thong tightly around the cord an inch or so from the baby and severed the cord between the tie and the afterbirth. Nona was relieved to see that Helen's bleeding had slowed.

Singing Reed stood and folded back the hide covering the opening. Light poured into the shelter. The Sioux lifted the baby and left the lodge, walking toward the stream.

What did she mean to do? Nona wondered, staring after her. When Singing Reed knelt on the bank, bending forward with the child in her arms, Nona sprang to her feet and ran toward her.

"No!" she cried, unsure whether the Sioux meant to drown the baby or simply immerse her in water far too cold for a helpless infant.

Singing Reed continued to bathe the baby in the stream despite Nona's protests. When she finished, she wrapped the child in a buckskin robe and cuddled her until the girl stopped crying. Looking at Nona, she said, "Wash your sister."

Later, when the four were back in Singing Reed's tipi, the Sioux woman suckled the child. Amanda Jean nursed greedily, her fair skin contrasting sharply with the brown of Singing Reed's breast.

Looking from the baby to Helen, who lay sleeping next to the fire, Nona wondered when her sister would regain enough strength to nurse her daughter herself. She brushed a strand of hair from Helen's forehead. Her sister's face was a ghastly white, drained of all color. Bloodless. She wasn't even certain Helen knew she'd given birth to the girl she'd always wanted. A girl with

82

blue eyes and golden hair.

"My sister's so weak," Nona said, trying to keep the fear from her voice.

"Much blood lost," Singing Reed told her. "No good."

Nona felt completely helpless. There was nothing she could do to help Helen recover quickly.

"Soon my brother kills buffalo," Singing Reed added. "We feed her buffalo blood, make her strong."

Nona struggled to hide her grimace. Singing Reed meant well but she couldn't imagine Helen swallowing the blood of a buffalo. Mention of the buffalo hunt sent a cold arrow of fear down her spine. When Sky Arrow returned with his kill, he'd claim her as his wife.

It was mid-afternoon before Three Crows pounded up to where Spencer waited beside Kaintuck. When they neared the Sioux, he'd made Spencer stay behind while he scouted ahead for sign. Sliding off his pony, the Ree pointed toward a line of straggling green in the distance.

"Plenty Rabbits Creek," he said. "Sioux camp there. Two men bring women to camp. This many tipis." He held up both hands, then two fingers.

Spencer frowned. Twelve tipis. A fair-sized village. As he'd suspected all along, guile was his only possible weapon against so many braves.

"Sioux wolves," Three Crows said, showing two fingers. "I come back quick, they no see me."

Wolves meant scouts and the two guarding the village had frightened the Ree away. Spencer knew the Ree, taking no chances of being trapped by enemy warriors, meant to turn back here, leaving him to go on alone. He couldn't complain, since Three Crows had done what he promised—guided him to the women.

"I go." Without another word, Three Crows mounted

his buckskin and turned the pony to the east.

Kaintuck stomped and snorted, tugging against the reins in his eagerness to follow the pony home. "You won't see your stable for awhile yet," Spencer advised the chestnut.

As he calmed the horse, he stared westward to the distant greenery bordering Plenty Rabbits Creek. Somewhere in those trees was a village of twelve tipis. That would mean at least twelve warriors and more probably twice as many. Spencer Quinlan against twenty-four hostile Lakota.

No, not Lakota. "Sioux." Spencer hissed the word, making it sound like what it meant—a Chippewa term for snake. Sioux was an enemy word and the men living in those tipis were his enemies till he convinced them he was a friend. To do that he had to outwit the wolves and reach the village alive.

He sure as hell wouldn't be any help to Nona dead. Damn, he'd been trying all day to keep himself from thinking about her. An image of her face rose before him—clear hazel eyes, fair skin, and that lovely hair.

She hadn't impressed him at first. "Miss Prim and Proper," he'd dubbed her when he saw her board the *Lady Jane* at St. Louis. Then he'd caught a glimpse of auburn hair under her severe black bonnet and decided she might be worth cultivating despite the drab clothes and her don't-come-near-me expression. Besides, he enjoyed a challenge.

He was intrigued by the discovery that Nona had an inquiring mind and a lively intelligence and he began striving to induce the sparkle that glinted in her hazel eyes when a topic interested her. The more he talked to her, the more attractive he found her and, ah, that hair was gorgeous. When he started to imagine it spread like silken fire over his pillow, he pulled back on the reins.

He liked his life just as it was; no entanglements. Even

if he didn't shy away from the very idea of marriage, Nona Willard would never fit into his roving life. And she wasn't the type for a casual affair. But he'd been damned if he was going to part from her without at least one kiss for his trouble.

There's where he'd made his mistake. That one simple kiss had seared through him like plains lightning and scared him to hell and gone. Steer clear of this one, Quinlan, he'd warned himself, or you'll get burned.

He'd tried and he might have succeeded if he hadn't gone to the dance—but then, he'd gone solely because he knew she'd be there. Once he waltzed her in his arms, he knew he had to have her and damn the consequences. When and how wasn't clear, but have her he would. He had his campaign well-planned.

Until some bloody Sioux brave interfered.

Chapter Six

Spencer waited until dusk to tie pieces of cut blanket around each of Kaintuck's hoofs. The wool padding blurred the distinctive track of iron-shod Army horses, as well as muffling the sound.

As soon as darkness settled over the hills, Spencer mounted the chestnut and rode west toward Plenty Rabbits Creek. He planned to cross well downstream from the village and approach from the west side of the creek because the wolves would expect danger to arrive from the east—bluecoats from the two nearby forts, Lincoln and Rice. To the west, the forts were hundreds of miles away in the Montana Territory and so was the village of the Crows, the nearest Indian enemies of the Sioux.

He had to reach the village before the moon rose and exposed him to the scouts, so he urged Kaintuck into a trot. Despite cover of darkness, Spencer felt exposed crossing the hilly ground as he rode toward the trees lining the creek. Though he realized the Sioux wolves were handicapped by the dark, he half-expected a silent, swift arrow to pierce through him at any moment.

When Spencer neared the trees, he heard spring peepers calling and slowed Kaintuck to a walk. He slipped off the horse as soon as greenery closed about them. Threading through the rampant growth along the stream, he led Kaintuck toward the sound of running water. He'd almost reached the creek when an owl hooted five times. Spencer froze, placing a silencing hand over the chestnut's nose.

Dancing Coyote had taught him how the Dakota used bird calls to signal one another—an owl's mournful hoot was one of the easiest to imitate. Had he been spotted? Spencer waited, tense with apprehension.

The small grove of cottonwoods and willows seemed abnormally silent. Where were the frog songs and the rustlings of small night animals? The owl cry came again, five hoots, closer this time. An answering signal?

Something white flashed across his path and he grabbed the butt of his holstered Colt before he realized what he'd seen. A real owl in soundless flight. No wonder the grove was so quiet—the night animals knew the big bird was hunting and had gone to earth. Or had the owl been startled into flight by the hooting of nearby Sioux scouts?

After long moments, the frogs began singing again and Spencer decided the hunting owl had done the hooting. He removed his hand from Kaintuck's nose and inched slowly toward the creek.

Nona's first intimation that Sky Arrow hadn't left camp to hunt buffalo came near sundown when Singing Reed handed the sleeping Amanda Jean to her and began adding meat and unfamiliar-looking roots to the kettle by the fire.

"My brother hungry after sweat lodge," Singing Reed said. "Too bad he no can eat my food."

Nona stopped marveling at how quickly the Sioux woman had regained her strength after the birth of her

87

baby and tensed. "Sweat lodge?" she echoed. "I thought all the men were buffalo hunting for the next two days."

"He hunt after sweat lodge cures bad medicine," Singing Reed explained.

The bad medicine of woman's blood, Nona supposed. "Where is the sweat lodge?" she asked, hoping it was many miles away.

"Downstream from camp."

Too close. "But won't he find bad medicine in the tipi if he returns tonight? My sister still bleeds a little." Nona thought Singing Reed must be bleeding, too, but didn't say so.

"He no can come to my tipi. He eat and sleep in friend's tipi," Singing Reed said. "You take his bed."

"No! I'll sleep next to my sister in case she needs me." Nona didn't mean to go near Sky Arrow's bed unless forced to.

Her raised voice startled the baby into whimpering and Nona rocked her back and forth in her arms, trying to comfort her. Amanda Jean was larger and much prettier than Kenneth's twins, who'd also been born early.

"Lakota baby no cry." Singing Reed said. "I teach Light Of Sun no cry."

It took Nona a moment or two to realize the Sioux woman meant Amanda Jean. Light Of Sun. The name fit the fair-skinned, fair-haired baby but Nona was disturbed that Singing Reed had chosen a Sioux name for her. Helen's daughter was certainly not an Indian! Glancing at her sister's motionless form, Nona sighed. Earlier she'd tried to feed Helen a bit of broth, but hadn't been able to coax her to swallow.

At least Helen's face wasn't so pale; she was regaining her color. Or was she? Nona frowned. Was what she saw normal color or a flush? She shifted the baby into one arm and leaned over to touch Helen's forehead. When she felt the heat under her fingers her heart sank.

"My sister has a fever," she told Singing Reed. "Can you help her?"

"I fix fever medicine," the Sioux woman said.

Most of the potion Singing Reed prepared ran from the corners of Helen's mouth, no matter how hard Nona tried to get her sister to swallow. Afterwards, Nona sat beside her sister feeling the heat from her body without touching her. The fever was worse.

Recalling how Dorothy used to bathe her with cool water to bring down a fever when she was sick, Nona decided to try bathing Helen and she told Singing Reed, who was nursing Amanda Jean again, what she planned.

"Need more water," Singing Reed said, gesturing toward what Nona recognized as the skin water bag. "You get from creek."

When Nona, bag in hand, opened the tipi flap, she saw night had crept into the Sioux village. A passing dog, now used to her scent, paid her no attention. She stood for a moment outside the tipi, looking at the other Sioux lodges, noticing some had a horse tethered outside. Illuminated by the fires inside, the tipis were as colorful and alien as Chinese lanterns.

Darkness had never intimidated her and she knew the way to the creek, but the thought of meeting one of the men unexpectedly at night unsettled her. Yet she had to bring down her sister's fever. Taking a deep breath, she began walking determinedly toward the sound of running water.

Hearing the frog chorus made a lump rise in her throat as she thought of past spring nights on the farm, both she and Helen safe with their family. Would either of them ever be safe again?

Reaching the bank, she knelt. Though the moon hadn't risen, stars shimmered in the dark creek and Nona wished there was some curative magic in starlit water. She started to lower the skin bag into the stream and suddenly held. The stars had disappeared, blotted out. After a moment she frowned at her nervousness—a cloud must have passed. She filled the water bag, retied the thong at the top and rose to her feet.

A hand clamped over her mouth, she was yanked backward against a man's hard body, lifted off her feet and carried into the trees.

"Don't scream when I let you go," a voice whispered in her ear. "It's Spencer."

Nona sagged against him, limp with relief. She was in Spencer's arms, not those of a villainous Sioux. Spencer had come to save her, just as she'd pictured him doing.

He removed his hand from her mouth, turned her toward him and hugged her close. "I'll take you to my horse," he whispered. "You wait there while I steal a horse for myself. There's no time to lose."

She tensed. "Helen," she whispered.

"Where is she?"

"In Singing Reed's tipi."

"Too risky. We'll be caught. Come on." He tried to lead her toward the creek.

She resisted. "I can't leave Helen."

"The troops will be here in a couple days. They'll—"

"You mean Kilby's not with you?" she asked.

"I'm alone. I've seen what happens to white women held captive by the Lakota so I didn't wait for the troopers. I can get you out of here, but if I try to rescue Helen all three of us may wind up dead." Again he tried to urge her toward the creek.

She desperately wanted to go with Spencer, to flee from the Sioux and from the threat of Sky Arrow, but in her heart she knew that no matter what happened to her, she couldn't desert her sister.

Nona laid a restraining hand on Spencer's arm. "You don't understand. Helen had her baby. She's too ill to be moved. I can't leave her. I won't leave her."

"Helen's safe enough—the warriors will leave her alone because of the baby. But you're in deadly peril. I'm damned if I'm leaving without you."

"I can't go without my sister," she repeated. "Now I must get back to the tipi with the water before Singing Reed begins to wonder where I am."

Spencer muttered something too low for her to hear.

If only he knew how she dreaded returning to the tipi! Yet she had to.

As she started to move away from him, he gripped her hand. "Wait. Do you know how many men are in the village?"

"Some rode west this morning to hunt buffalo. I'm not certain how many are left. I think the rest mean to follow tomorrow."

"Did you hear the names of any of the men?"

"Singing Reed told me two names. Her brother is Sky Arrow and there's Lean Bear, who might be a chief. You remember Singing Reed—she was on the boat with Paquette."

"I'll be damned!"

Nona glanced around apprehensively, fearful for Spencer. If he was caught, surely he'd be killed. "You must go," she urged. "Hide and wait for the troopers."

"Come with me."

Tears filled her eyes. "I can't."

Spencer kissed her quickly. "If you see me, don't let on you know me," he warned enigmatically before melting into the night.

After removing the tattered strips of blanket from the horse's hoofs, Spencer stood beside Kaintuck on the west bank of the stream, waiting to make certain Nona had time to reach Singing Reed's tipi while cursing her under his breath for her stubborn insistence. He understood why she couldn't bear to desert Helen, he even admired her loving loyalty to her sister, but she sure as hell irritated him. He'd been momentarily tempted to fling her over his shoulder and carry her away with him, but without her cooperation, they didn't stand a chance of escaping.

It had been a stroke of pure luck to find her at the stream. They could have been long gone before anyone realized she was missing, both he and Nona safe and sound. But, even if he'd tried, he'd never have been able to convince Nona that if Helen must be left behind, the Sioux men wouldn't bother her for at least a month. With luck, the Seventh would rescue her before then.

Nona had her mind made up not to go without Helen. And now there was a newborn infant to further complicate things. Plan Number One had failed, through no fault of his. Since he didn't mean to leave this camp without Nona, he had no choice but to come up with another scheme.

Evidently Nona didn't realize a buffalo hunt also involved the women. Since Plenty Rabbits Creek was a temporary stop for the Sioux on the way to the far hills and the buffalo were also moving west, he had little doubt the Sioux would pull up stakes tomorrow and transport the tipis closer to both buffalo and the valley of the Greasy Grass. When the cavalry arrived, most likely the day after tomorrow, the tipis would be gone. Along with Nona and Helen. And what would happen to Nona before the Seventh located the new camp? Helen might be safe from the Sioux men but Nona wasn't.

All right, Quinlan, he told himself, she's had plenty of time to reach the tipi. Get cracking.

He swung onto the chestnut and splashed through the water toward the tipis, making no attempt to be quiet.

"Ho," he called loudly in Dakota, "a friend comes to Lean Bear's village."

Barking dogs rushed from the tipis, flaps were thrown back in two lodges and four men emerged, each carrying a rifle. Three of them raised their guns, aiming at him.

Spencer ignored the threat. "A Dakota friend visits the Lakota," he called as he rode Kaintuck through the pack of dogs. "I seek Lean Bear." He stopped three yards from the nearest tipi and raised both hands in the gesture of peace. He gave the men time to answer; when none did, he looked directly at the one man who hadn't raised his rifle. "Do the Lakota welcome all friends so warmly?" he asked scornfully.

"Who seeks Lean Bear?" the man he'd addressed demanded.

Heavy Foot was Spencer's Dakota name, given to him as a boy by Dancing Coyote who'd despaired of ever teaching him to move quietly through the woods. Dancing Coyote would have been proud of him tonight.

The name would mean nothing to these Lakota and he had no intention of letting any of them take the initiative away from him. "You ask this of a man who passed your wolves without being challenged?" Spencer countered. He'd come to the conclusion none of the four was Lean Bear and decided to risk his belief. "Is it you fear strangers when Lean Bear's not among you?"

"Sky Arrow fears no one!" The response came from the man who hadn't aimed his rifle.

"I, too, have a strong heart," Spencer told him. "A strong heart and powerful medicine. I will prove my bravery tomorrow at the buffalo hunt." He noticed two of the other men glance at one another, mention of the hunt evidently surprising them, as he'd hoped it would.

Sky Arrow gestured to the others and they lowered their rifles. "You are welcome in this Lakota village," he said.

Spencer promptly dismounted. Another of the men, Burnt Dog, invited him into his tipi and he accepted. Sky

Arrow came, too. Spencer was motioned to seat himself at one of the rear back rests and Sky Arrow took the other. Burnt Dog sat to the right, marking him as the host, honoring his guests by seating them to his left, or heart side.

So Sky Arrow, who'd rushed out of this tipi when Spencer rode into the camp, was also a guest. Did this mean he usually lived with Singing Reed and had to leave his sister's tipi because of Helen having her child? The thought of Sky Arrow in the same tipi with Nona made Spencer's jaw clench.

A young woman, no doubt Burnt Dog's wife, ladled meat and broth from a kettle to a wooden plate and offered it to Spencer. Since he was hungry, he had little difficulty finishing the serving—luckily, because it was an insult to the host if a guest left even a morsel on his plate. Aware of good Lakota manners, he belched as loudly as he could, thus assuring the host he'd enjoyed the food.

A pipe was lit and passed to the left to be smoked ritually. After he'd taken the required puffs, Spencer passed the pipe back and relaxed a little. He'd been fed and they'd smoked with him so he was safe for the moment. They'd accepted him and the Lakota didn't kill their guests.

The three men sat in silence for some time. One of the lessons Spencer had learned from Dancing Coyote was not to speak first if you could avoid it.

"You are Dakota," Sky Arrow said finally.

Spencer knew this was more than an observation. Sky Arrow wanted more information about him but was reluctant to be impolite enough to ask questions of a guest. They'd noticed he rode an Army horse, but strayed and stolen Army horses weren't uncommon as Indian mounts. It was obvious he didn't look like an Indian. But with his dark eyes and hair they couldn't be sure he

94

wasn't part Dakota.

Spencer allowed a few moments to pass before replying, "I dreamed of Lean Bear's village, of a buffalo hunt and of a white buffalo. I rode here." He hoped mention of a dream, combined with the sacred symbol of the white buffalo, would convince the men he was on a vision journey and therefore not to be interfered with. He needed to seize every advantage.

"At the next sun we travel west," Sky Arrow said.

"Toward the buffalo," Spencer agreed. "I will travel with you. I will hunt with you."

Burnt Dog spoke up. "You have no rifle. You have no bow."

They'd seen he carried a Colt, so there was no need for Spencer to mention he'd be using it in the hunt. "My medicine is strong," he told them, keeping his tone confident when in reality he knew he'd be lucky to survive the hunt.

The closest he'd come to hunting buffalo was listening to Dancing Coyote's stories of how it was done in the days when great herds of *pte*, the buffalo, covered the plains. "The spirit of *pte* must enter a hunter," the old medicine man had said. "A strong-heart hunter hears what *pte* hears, sees what *pte* sees, thinks like *pte*—he becomes *pte*."

Powerful medicine. Dancing Coyote had shown him how to follow such paths but he hadn't tried in years.

"We will see," Sky Arrow said.

Spencer looked at him appraisingly. He'd noticed when they were standing that he and the Lakota were the same height, but Sky Arrow had a few pounds advantage. Not that he planned to fight the brave, though he was getting the feeling Sky Arrow took his words about powerful medicine as a challenge. Did the Lakota mean to prove him wrong at the hunt?

Spencer's eyes narrowed. If she was living in his

sister's tipi, Sky Arrow must be Nona's captor. In that case, Nona was his to claim. Had Sky Arrow already forced her? Spencer took a deep breath, forcing himself to appear calm.

He'd passed a sweat lodge downriver. Most likely the men had been purifying themselves for the hunt and that meant they couldn't bed a woman. He sure as hell hoped he was right.

Wait, he cautioned himself. Your only chance to get Nona and her sister back to the fort is to play out this game, and to play it well. Dancing Coyote taught you all you need to know. The question is, can you remember enough to succeed?

Singing Reed woke Nona at dawn. "We travel west," she said.

Nona, her mind clogged with sleep, stared up at the Sioux woman in confusion.

"Hurry," Singing Reed urged, handing her a buckskin tunic and leggings. "Put on Lakota dress, better to ride horse."

Nona sat up, looking toward her sister. She'd spent much of the night trying to coax Helen to swallow water—to no avail. Helen, feverish and weak, didn't even open her eyes.

Rising to her feet, Nona said, "My sister can't travel."

"She ride on travois." Singing Reed turned away and Nona saw Amanda Jean, strapped to her back in a cradle board.

Certain Helen's condition would be worsened by being dragged on a travois, Nona tried to argue but got nowhere. The camp was moving and they were moving with it. Resigned, she discarded her dress and petticoats for the Indian clothes and found the buckskin soft and comfortable, despite its odd style.

Where was Spencer? Did he realize what was happening? She didn't know. In any case, he couldn't help.

While Nona changed her clothes, Singing Reed dragged Helen, on a hide rug, out through the flap. By the time Nona hurried to join her sister, the Sioux woman was pulling up the pegs holding the buffalo walls of the tipi in place. Quickly she removed some of the poles, then folded the walls into a triangle, eased them to the ground and rolled them into a compact bundle.

Singing Reed lashed the poles and the buffalo-hide walls to a travois attached to a waiting pony. She asked Nona's help to shift Helen onto a second travois that also held household belongings, then tied Helen onto the carrier. Noticing other women dismantling tipis and loading travois, Nona realized shifting camp must be a woman's job for there wasn't a man in sight.

In less than half an hour, the entire camp was moving west, men riding in front, women and children to the rear. Nona, mounted on the pony pulling Helen, looked back from time to time to make certain the thongs holding her sister to the travois hadn't loosened, before she finally decided Helen was as secure on the carrier as Amanda Jean was riding in the cradle board on Singing Reed's back.

Spencer had said the troopers were coming but Nona saw no signs of pursuit. Would he hide near the old camp and wait to direct the soldiers or would he follow her?

"Where are we going?" she asked Singing Reed finally.

"We follow buffalo. Men hunt, women cut up kill. You. Me."

Nona grimaced. On the farm, she'd watched her father and brothers butcher hogs and steers, happy to leave the bloody business to them. Skinning and gutting rabbits was as close as she'd ever come to butchering and she hadn't much cared for that. Helen had flatly refused to have anything to do with meat until it was ready for cooking.

"What kind of farm wife will you make?" Dorothy would scold.

"I'll marry someone rich," Helen had insisted, "and have servants to do the work."

Poor Helen. She not only never had the servants she craved, but when she recovered her strength, she'd be forced to be a servant herself, Sioux fashion.

The queue of men, women, children, ponies and dogs, straggled along slowly as the sun climbed the sky and warmed the day. Occasionally, Nona stopped her pony and dismounted, checked Helen, then walked alongside the horse as it plodded on. Children ran up to look at her and giggle, but fled quickly if she tried to speak to them. The Sioux women nearby stared at her speculatively.

"Stranger rides with my brother," Singing Reed said when they paused to try to give Helen a few sips of water.

Nona paid little attention. One Indian was as strange as another to her.

"He rides Army horse," the Sioux woman added.

Nona glanced at her and found Singing Reed watching her intently. Why? Kilby had told her the Sioux often tried to steal horses from the Army and were sometimes successful. Was it so unusual for one of these stolen horses to be ridden by a brave?

Helen choked on the water and Nona forgot Singing Reed's stranger in her anxiety. "Please try to swallow," she begged Helen, but her sister either would not or could not.

"I can't help cut up dead buffalo when we camp," Nona told Singing Reed. "My sister needs me."

"Old grandmother watch her. You help women. Learn Lakota way."

"I don't want to learn Lakota ways, I want to stay with Helen!"

"No can do." Singing Reed remounted her pony and started off again.

Unless she wanted to be left alone in the middle of nowhere, without food, water or shelter, Nona had no choice but to get on her pony and follow.

The sun was low over the western hills by the time the men chose a new camp site near a stream. Again, putting up the tipis was woman's work and Singing Reed told Nona how to help her set up the poles. The Sioux woman finished the rest of the tipi by herself while Nona tended to her sister. Sooner than Nona believed possible, Singing Reed dug the fire pit, spread the hide rugs in place and started a small blaze.

"Fetch water," the Sioux woman ordered.

Nona picked up the skin bag and left the tipi. Other women were filling their water bags at the stream but none spoke to her, although they watched her every move. She waited until they were finished before kneeling on the bank to fill her bag. By the time she rose to her feet, they'd returned to their tipis.

As Nona walked toward Singing Reed's tipi, three men rode into the camp, Sky Arrow leading, and the brave who'd carried off Helen behind him. The third man was partly blocked from her view but she saw he wasn't wearing buckskins, nor was his hair in braids so she decided he was Singing Reed's stranger. Curious, she slowed long enough to get a good look at him.

Nona almost lost her grip on the water bag. Spencer! He didn't seem to be a prisoner—what was he doing with the Sioux braves? He didn't even glance her way and she recalled his parting words—"don't let on you know me."

She'd heard someone ride into camp last night calling out in the Sioux tongue but she'd never dreamed it could be Spencer. Suddenly aware her gawking might jeopardize whatever he had in mind, Nona ducked into the tipi. As she did, she realized why Singing Reed had watched her so intently when she first mentioned the stranger. The Sioux woman must have seen Spencer and recognized him from the *Lady Jane*.

Would she ruin Spencer's plans by telling her brother?

What shall I do? Nona asked herself. I can't pretend not to know Quinlan when she's well aware I do.

She placed the water bag in its supporting willow framework and sat down by the motionless Helen, her mind in a turmoil. Singing Reed sat on the opposite side of the fire nursing Amanda Jean.

"I saw the stranger," Nona said finally.

"You know him." Singing Reed's words weren't a question.

"I met him on the boat, yes. I don't know him well."

"He claims he Dakota, his name Heavy Foot."

Nona's eyes widened, her surprise real. Heavy Foot? She spread her hands to show she had no idea what he was doing in the Sioux camp. Which was true enough. She couldn't imagine what Spencer hoped to accomplish all alone in a camp of hostiles.

"He hunts with men next sun," Singing Reed said. "You no speak to him."

"I won't say a word to Mr. Quinlan—Heavy Foot, I mean," Nona hastened to assure her. After all, Spencer had told her not to talk to him.

Helen whimpered and Nona turned to her, leaning over her sister anxiously.

Helen's eyes fluttered and opened. "Nona," she whispered "I saw Grandma Holmes."

Grandma Holmes was Dorothy's mother and she'd died six years ago.

"You're feverish, dear," Nona said.

"I really did see her." Helen spoke weakly but the words coming from her fever-cracked lips were clear. "There was a shining light all around grandma and she held out her hand and said, 'Helen, listen to me. Nona will take care of the baby, it's time for you to come with me.'"

"Your sister see true," Singing Reed said. "See the path ahead."

Chapter Seven

Nona hovered over her feverish sister. Was Singing Reed right? Was Helen's insistence she'd seen her dead grandmother a vision of what was to come? Nona shook her head violently. No matter what Singing Reed thought, Helen had only been dreaming, that's all.

Helen's fever seemed to be subsiding and she was able to swallow a little water. Didn't that mean she was improving ever so slightly? Hopeful, but still worried, Nona refused to leave her sister's side.

After dark the drums began, their throbbing beat insistent and disturbing. What did the drumming mean? Nona sent covert glances toward Singing Reed, but for a long time the Sioux woman paid no heed. Finally she gestured Nona away from Helen.

"Buffalo dance," Singing Reed announced. "You go with Pretty Shield."

Nona frowned. "I can't leave my sister. What if she needs me?"

"I watch her."

"You don't understand. She's my sister. I must stay with her. What if—?" She couldn't finish.

"I name Great Spirit *Wakan Tanka,* you name Great Spirit God Jesus Christ," Singing Reed said. "One, same.

Great Spirit say live, Great Spirit say die. Not you say, not me say."

Nona, momentarily distracted from her worry over Helen, stared at Singing Reed.

"I hear your sister say spirit Grandmother call her," the Sioux woman reminded her. "You no stand in way, no try hold your sister here. Bad medicine."

"Helen isn't going to die!"

As soon as she's spoken, Nona wanted to call back the words. She hadn't let herself dwell on the possibility Helen wouldn't recover, but saying the word "die" forced her to face what might happen and she couldn't bear it.

"Helen would be all right if that brave hadn't captured her." Nona's voice raised in accusation. "She wouldn't have bled, the baby wouldn't have come early—it's his fault she's so sick. Why can't your people leave us alone?"

"Your people no leave us alone." Singing Reed spoke flatly. "Bluecoats ride through my village seven winters ago, kill women, children, burn tipis. Why?"

Nona, taken aback, couldn't answer. "Two wrongs don't make a right," she said finally. "Your brother brought me here against my will. I don't want to be his wife; I want to go back to the fort, to my own people."

"Sky Arrow good man."

"I don't care! I don't want him!" Nona burst into tears.

Amanda Jean began to wail too but her cries stopped so abruptly that even in her misery Nona noticed and was alarmed, wiping the tears from her eyes with her fingers. To her horror she saw Singing Reed pinching the baby's nostrils shut.

"She can't breathe," Nona protested. "You'll suffocate her."

"No hurt Light Of Sun," Singing Reed told her. "I

teach not to cry. Lakota baby no cry."

About to say Amanda Jean wasn't an Indian baby, Nona held her tongue. If she, Helen and the baby didn't escape, it was all too likely Amanda Jean would be raised as a Sioux.

Never! she vowed. All the same, Nona saw that Singing Reed spoke the truth. The baby hadn't been harmed by having her breathing temporarily cut off and she didn't resume crying as the Sioux woman cuddled her in her arms. If mothering the baby were all that counted, at the moment Singing Reed had charge of Amanda Jean. Nona meant to see that change as soon as Helen was able to nurse.

God only knew when or if the troops would find the Sioux village in its new location. Spencer was their only hope of getting away soon. Nona had no idea what he was up to, pretending to be a Dakota and hunting buffalo, but she didn't see how he, one man alone, could help them even if Helen was well enough to travel. Surrounded by savages, he'd be lucky to stay alive.

Someone scratched at the door flap and Singing Reed called out in Sioux. A middle-aged Sioux woman came into the tipi—her escort, Pretty Shield, Nona decided. The last thing in the world she wanted to do now was watch a mob of howling savages dance.

"You go," Singing Reed said to her. "You no go, my brother send for you."

So either she went quietly with Pretty Shield or someone else—she was afraid to ask who—would come and force her to go.

"Pretty Shield braid your hair," Singing Reed announced.

Resigned, Nona undid the knot she'd twisted on top of her head so it spilled in tangles over her shoulders and down her back. With a bone comb, Pretty Shield untangled the snarls, carefully parted her hair in the center and braided it into two neat plaits that she fastened with thongs decorated with tiny feathers and colorful beads. When she was finished, the Sioux woman said something to Singing Reed.

"She says your hair like sunset," Singing Reed told her. "A good sign."

Not for me, Nona thought as she bent to kiss her sister's forehead before reluctantly following Pretty Shield from the tipi.

Spencer, sitting in the guest place in Lean Bear's tipi, took a puff, then handed the pipe back to his host. Outside in the darkness, drums called to the hunters, called them to the *pte* dance. Lean Bear, older and shrewder than Burnt Dog and Sky Arrow, was head man of the village and Spencer knew the chief viewed him with more skepticism than the younger men.

"You say you'll kill *pte* with a pistol." Lean Bear smiled sardonically. "Never have I seen a man bring down *pte* with a small gun."

"If a man seizes the spirit of *pte*, what difference the weapon he uses?" Spencer kept his voice even and calm.

Lean Bear grunted.

"The gun doesn't matter," Spencer went on, deciding to push for what he did need, "but the horse does. I ask for the use of a *pte* pony. And moccasins, for the pony's sake."

"It is true your bluecoat horse is useless in a herd of *pte*. I will give you a pony. I will give you moccasins to ride him. And then I will watch you and *pte* and I will see about this medicine of yours."

Lean Bear tapped the pipe's ashes into a neat little pile on the offering place beside the fire, then laid the pipe aside and rose. "We go to the dance," he said.

At least he didn't dump the ash on my boots, Spencer told himself, so whether or not he believes I can kill a buffalo, he doesn't wish me bad luck. Thank God I know the buffalo dance or I might well be exposed as the imposter I am.

Before they left the tipi, Lean Bear's wife offered Spencer a new pair of beautifully quilled and beaded moccasins. He thanked her and, after admiring her fine workmanship, yanked off his boots and put on the buckskin shoes, finding them a somewhat snug fit. They'd probably been made for Lean Bear, and Lakota men, though as tall as whites, usually had smaller hands and feet. But, since moccasins were made to adapt to the wearer's feet, Spencer knew they'd soon be comfortable.

Two drummers squatted to one side of a fire kindled near the stream, their rhythmic beats calling the hunters. Lean Bear, a buffalo head mounted atop his own, began the shuffling, circling dance and, one by one, the hunters joined in mock chase. The words of the dance song were simple; the steps hardly more complex. But each syllable sung, each movement made, added up to the success or failure of the hunt.

Spencer, the last hunter to join the dancers, tried not to scan the ranks of the women who sang in high-pitched ululations as they stood watching. If Nona was among them, the sight of her would only distract him from the dance.

"Understand the dance hunt is as real as stalking and killing *pte* himself," Dancing Coyote had taught.

Spencer had tried but never felt this reality when the old medicine man, after showing him the steps, had pounded his medicine drum while Spencer danced. Would it be any different here in the Dakota Territory? And did it matter? He was afraid it would.

106

He fixed his gaze on Lean Bear's buffalo head and made an attempt to go within himself. He could almost hear Dancing Coyote repeating, "To understand, you need a quiet mind, grandson. A quiet mind."

Against his will, Spencer's gaze shifted to the women as he circled past. Nona stood among them, dressed as a Lakota woman, her auburn hair braided. The mutinous set of her chin told him she didn't want to be here. She glanced at him and looked quickly away. He had a crazy impulse to dash from the circle of dancers, grab her, flee to the horses and gallop away. He didn't, well aware they'd be caught in minutes.

Spencer danced on, his gaze firmly fixed on the buffalo head. He'd do neither Nona nor himself any good by losing his head. Since he couldn't seem to free his mind of all thought, he began deliberately thinking of *pte*—his massive head with small cruel horns, humped back under a shaggy brown coat, and slender, delicate legs ending in sharp hoofs. *Pte*, who roamed the plains in freedom. *Pte*, whom he hunted tomorrow.

Slowly, so slowly Spencer wasn't aware of how it happened, the constantly repeated words of the song took on a depth of meaning, becoming a mystic chant guaranteeing success in the hunt, while the figure of Lean Bear changed into that of a four-footed animal, becoming the real *pte*, to be stalked and killed. Spencer was the stalker, the hunter and yet he was also *pte*, the prey. He lived the blood-hot rapture of the kill and, at the same time, entered the cold, black maw of death. . . .

The following morning, when an aged and wrinkled Sioux woman came into Singing Reed's tipi, Nona realized she must be here to look after Helen.

"How can I leave my sister?" she demanded of Singing

Reed. "If she needs anything, that old woman won't understand a word she says."

Singing Reed gestured at Helen, lying motionless by the fire. "Look. She no move, she no speak, she not know who stay with her."

"But what if she does wake up? What if she wants me?"

Singing Reed gazed at Nona with sad eyes. "Your sister no wake in my tipi. You be strong-heart and follow buffalo hunters with me."

No matter what Singing Reed says, I won't believe Helen's dying, Nona told herself. Her fever's down, she could simply be in a deep sleep. "I want to stay with her," she insisted.

"No can do. Need many hands for kill."

"I won't go!"

"My brother want you at kill. You go there."

The implied threat in Singing Reed's words wasn't lost on Nona. As it had been with the dance last night, she could either go along of her own will or she'd be forced. No matter what, she wouldn't be allowed to remain in the tipi with her sister.

She had no choice; she had to follow Singing Reed, but as a last-minute act of defiance, Nona pinned her braids into a coronet instead of wearing them hanging down as the Sioux women did. Singing Reed, she saw, carried Amanda Jean on her back. Two other women also carried babies. Evidently Sioux babies went everywhere with their mothers.

All the ponies the women rode, including Nona's, dragged empty poled carriers. Coming back, she realized, the travois would be loaded with butchered meat and hides. Since the hunters had left the village earlier, only a few toddlers watched by old men and women remained in the village. And Helen. Pray God her sister wouldn't need her while she was gone.

The ride was short. Before the sun was halfway up the sky, they halted at the top of a flat-topped hill and dismounted. Bellows and shouts and the crack of rifles came from below. Clouds of dust made it difficult to separate the hunters on their ponies from the great-headed beasts they hunted. Nona, who'd never seen a buffalo except in pictures, stared in fascination at the shaggy animals.

Singing Reed, next to her, pointed. "Cows and calves there. No kill." She pointed again. "Bulls."

The female buffalo stood grouped together, guarding their long-legged babies while the males scattered with hunters in pursuit.

"There must be at least fifty buffalo down there," Nona exclaimed.

"Small herd." Singing Reed kicked open an ant hill with her moccasin and hundreds of black ants swarmed from the exposed nest. "Long ago many more buffalo, like ants. All Lakota bellies full. Now buffalo hard to find. Lakota go hungry."

"The government feeds the Sioux on the reservations," Nona pointed out. "They don't go hungry."

"Lakota no belong in cage. You no like I say go here, do this. Lakota no like *wasichu* tell them how to live." Singing Reed turned away to watch the hunt below.

Nona's gaze sought Spencer among the mounted men chasing buffalo. As she looked for him, she mulled over what the Sioux woman had said. For an Indian, was a reservation like being put into a cage? Nona decided it might be, considering the way they liked to travel from one camping spot to another.

There was no hunter with a hat; no hunter wearing a shirt. Spencer must have taken his off, Nona thought. His face, tanned from the sun, was almost as dark as a

109

Sioux; his chest and back must be tanned, too, because there seemed to be no difference in skin color among the hunters and they all rode Indian ponies.

Compared to the men on their ponies, the buffalo looked huge and dangerous but Nona spotted four fallen buffalo—kills—and glanced apprehensively at Singing Reed, hoping the women wouldn't be expected to begin butchering while the hunt was still on. She had no desire to go any closer to live buffalo.

"Sky Arrow." Singing Reed pointed to a hunter, bow in hand, chasing a bull.

Nona deliberately looked away and her attention was caught by the sight of a man so close to a buffalo that the pony and bull were touching. As she watched, the pony stumbled and she gasped when the man leaped from the falling horse onto the back of the bull. He carried no bow or rifle. From this distance nothing distinguished him from the other hunters but somehow she knew he was Spencer.

Her intake of breath was echoed by the gasps of the women surrounding her. They murmured admiringly in Sioux.

"Stranger is strong-heart," Singing Reed muttered grudgingly.

Certain Spencer would be tossed off the buffalo's back and killed, Nona clutched her hands together tightly. "Don't die," she whispered. "Live. Live. Live."

Singing Reed glanced at her curiously and Nona realized that without intending to, she'd begun to chant the word aloud. "Live!" she shouted defiantly.

She heard a shot and suddenly the bull Spencer rode paused in midstride. As the buffalo slowly toppled, Spencer leaped free, landing in a crouch. He turned and knelt beside the fallen buffalo, bending his head as though whispering in the animal's ear. Barely in time, Nona caught back the shout of "Bravo!" that leaped to her lips, belatedly afraid she'd already said enough to endanger Spencer.

He spoke to his brother, *Pte*, in apology for killing him. The bullet that shattered *Pte's* heart he'd felt in his own heart, for they were kin, they were one and the same, he and *Pte*. So he could survive, *Pte* had to die at his hands.

"Ho!" someone called.

He turned and blinked up at the mounted man. At first he didn't recognize him but gradually he understood this was Lean Bear.

"Buffalo Rider, I bring you a fresh pony," Lean Bear told him.

Spencer stared, confused, for ten heartbeats, then realized the chief had given him a new name. *He* was Buffalo Rider. He swung onto the pony, still dazed and unsure of his surroundings, still not quite certain he was a man and no longer one with *Pte*. The noise of bellowing bulls, the crack of rifles, the pounding hoofs all came to him through a veil that muted sound.

He looked toward the sky and, seeing the slow spiral of an eagle, wondered if the spirit of Dancing Coyote had been watching over him.

"Old Grandfather, you taught me better than I knew," he said in Dakota.

Lean Bear grunted in approval; the Lakota understood it was right to thank a helping spirit. "We will honor you at tonight's feast," the chief said.

Spencer took a deep breath, gathering his wits. Nona. He had to save Nona. The women would butcher the kills. Would she be assigned to his? More likely she'd help Singing Reed with Sky Arrow's kill. He'd draw a widow or an eligible maiden not being courted by any of the men. But he had to find a way to talk to Nona and make her understand how urgent it was for them to flee the camp.

Sky Arrow had announced before the hunt that he planned to marry after the buffalo feast. Marry the white woman his sister had named Good Heart. Marry Nona.

Spencer cursed. Never!

Helen was sleeping when Nona and Singing Reed returned from the buffalo hunt. The old woman told Singing Reed that Helen hadn't roused or taken any water. She offered to stay in the tipi and watch both the baby and Helen while Singing Reed and Nona bathed, and Nona, unable to stand being drenched in buffalo blood, agreed.

Following other women downriver, Nona and Singing Reed stripped off their bloody clothes and washed themselves in the creek. Nona scrubbed herself with the soap root she'd been given, scouring every last trace of blood and the scent of raw buffalo meat from her skin and hair. She tried to ignore how the others stared at her, aware they were merely curious about the pale color of her skin.

On the bank, Singing Reed had laid out a new tunic and leggings for her, a beautiful soft white buckskin with a pleasing design of dyed porcupine quills. The garments felt wonderfully good against her skin. Perversely, though, she wished she could put on her own dirty, torn clothes.

She was Nona Willard, not Good Heart, and she always would be. She was not a Sioux; she refused to become one.

When they approached the tipi, Nona's breath caught in alarm when she saw the old woman's head thrust through the flap, obviously watching for them. Nona began to run. Once inside, she threw herself on her knees beside Helen. Relief swept over her when she saw that her sister was smiling, but almost immediately she realized the glassy look of Helen's eyes wasn't normal.

"Helen!" she cried, clutching her sister's shoulders, dimly aware of the old woman chattering to Singing Reed. A word caught her attention.

"Gra-ma," the old woman repeated.

"She say your sister open her eyes, smile, say, 'Gra-ma,'" Singing Reed told Nona. "Then her spirit fly away."

"No!" Nona cried, stroking Helen's face and chafing her hand. "No, she's not dead!"

"You know your sister walks Path of Spirits with her grandmother. She tell you last sun."

Tears streaked Nona's cheeks. "She can't be dead, she can't be."

Singing Reed lifted her, forcing Nona to stand. "Green Woman and I, we make your sister ready for scaffold." She walked Nona to one of the back rests supported by the tripods and sat her there. Lifting the sleeping Amanda Jean from her hide blanket near the fire, she laid the baby across Nona's lap. "You hold Light of Sun."

Nona looked down at the baby and gently touched the fair curls. So like Helen's. "You're here," she murmured through her tears. "Part of Helen still lives." She lifted Amanda Jean into her arms, cuddling the baby to her breast while she crooned to her.

Helen, I promise you, she vowed silently, *that I'll take care of this child as long as I live.*

When dusk came, Nona watched and wept as Sky Arrow and another brave hoisted Helen's body wrapped in a buffalo robe into the branches of a cottonwood. When the men left, Nona stayed behind. Singing Reed tugged at her arm but Nona resisted.

"I can't leave Helen all alone," Nona sobbed.

Singing Reed put an arm around Nona's shoulders. "Your sister's spirit no alone. Spirit with grandmother."

Nona knew she spoke the truth, but it still seemed

wrong to leave Helen's body resting in the branches of a tree in this alien wilderness. Reluctantly, she allowed Singing Reed to lead her back to the tipi.

"We no go buffalo feast," Singing Reed told her.

Nona was too numbed by grief to feel relieved. How could her little sister be dead? If only she'd mentioned Helen's picnic plans to Kilby. Or insisted on waiting until Spencer could go with them. If only she could go back and do it over.

Yet it wasn't all her fault. Sky Arrow and the other Sioux braves were the ones who'd truly killed Helen, as surely as if they'd pierced her heart with an arrow. Hatred dried Nona's tears. Sky Arrow was her enemy, now and forever.

Once he heard of Helen's death, Spencer tried to think of a way to see Nona alone. He couldn't. Nor could he avoid the buffalo feast, since he, as Buffalo Rider, was to be the guest of honor. There was no appropriate excuse, and if he didn't appear, they'd search for him. He had to go.

The feast would be long, everyone would eat too much, and most of the hunters would make speeches—but that wasn't the problem. Afterward was. Sky Arrow would claim Nona—and what the hell would he do to prevent it? He had until the end of the feast to come up with a plan.

First, he couldn't overeat. He couldn't afford to stuff himself and suffer the lethargy that followed. He needed his wits about him. Yet if he refused food he'd insult the hunters who'd provided the meat and the women who'd cooked it. Leaving food on his plate was also impossible. Fortunately the feast was outdoors so there was one possible solution.

He left Lean Bear's tipi and strolled through the camp, lifting several strips of meat from drying racks on the way. Near the stream he finally found the ally he was looking for—a half-grown brown and white pup near starvation, every rib showing through his hide. Spencer crouched and coaxed the dog to his side where he fondled his ears, told him in Dakota that his name was Friend, then fed him a meat strip.

He rose to his feet and the pup trailed after him. Spencer stopped and fed him a second strip. He did this until the meat was gone. By that time Friend was ready to follow him anywhere.

Later, when Spencer sat with the men at the feast, he took care to choose a spot where the pup could reach him without getting kicked for annoying the others. As he'd hoped, eventually Friend slunk up behind him and sat waiting hopefully. By judicious "accidental" spilling of food from his plate that the dog immediately gobbled down and by surreptitiously slipping him chunks of meat, Spencer was able to feed Friend at least half of what he was served.

Friend, who'd never had so much to eat at one time in his short life, fell asleep during the speeches and Spencer couldn't help but envy him.

When it came his turn to speak, he rose and said, "My spirit ally, Dancing Coyote, flew to me during the hunt. It was his powerful medicine that enabled me to kill *pte*. I will honor him with offerings after the feast."

The grunts of approval showed him the men either appreciated what he'd said or were happy because he'd said so little. But he'd accomplished his purpose— they'd expect him to go off by himself afterwards.

When at last the gathering began to break up, the men drifting away one by one, Spencer rose and strode toward the stream. Friend, his belly distended by food, trotted after him. As quickly as he could, Spencer retrieved Kaintuck from where he'd tethered the chestnut apart from the pony herd. He led the horse into the trees without attracting attention.

The pony Lean Bear had given him was tethered outside the chief's tipi and Spencer saw no way to collect him undetected but he put that worry aside for the moment. At least he had one horse ready and waiting. But it had taken him longer than he thought.

What was happening to Nona? Would he be too late?

Chapter Eight

As darkness deepened, Nona looked across the fire at Singing Reed, who was nursing Amanda Jean. Her grief had been temporarily set aside by her terror over what was in store for her at Sky Arrow's hands. She kept herself from glancing again at the screen formed by buffalo robes thrown over the two back rests, placed at the foot and side of Singing Reed's pallet, effectively cutting off the Sioux woman's view of the rest of the tipi. The meaning of that screen was all too clear.

I can't bear to have that savage touch me, Nona told herself. Would it be any use to defend herself with the knife she'd used to butcher the buffalo? Regretfully she shook her head. Even if she were able to kill Sky Arrow, and she doubted it, she'd still be a Sioux captive and be punished.

If only she could find a way to make Singing Reed understand how abhorrent the very idea of her brother was.

"Did you wish to be married to Paquette?" Nona asked finally.

"He bad heart. He no my husband, he trade gun with my husband for me. I no stay with Paquette."

Nona didn't think much of a man who'd trade a wife

for a rifle and evidently her expression showed her disgust because the Sioux woman sighed, her eyes sad.

"My husband no can help what he do. He trade everything for firewater, we hungry, no have gun. Paquette have gun, want me. He give my husband firewater. I no like Paquette, no want him. He give gun, my husband say go with Paquette." Singing Reed turned up her free hand in a gesture of helplessness. "I go."

Nona couldn't help feeling sorry for Singing Reed. How awful to be carrying a child and have your husband force you to leave with another man, one you detested. Surely, though, the woman ought to be able to understand Nona's hatred of Sky Arrow.

"Paquette say I leave he come after me, kill me," Singing Reed added. "Take long time me get away."

"You're safe now. I wish I was safe." Nona took a deep breath and went on. "I know you must love your brother, but I can't. I feel about him as you felt about Paquette—I don't like him; I don't want him. I'm not a Sioux and I never will be, yet I'm being forced to be his wife. By you as well as Sky Arrow."

"He good man. No like Paquette."

"Don't you understand?" Nona cried in desperation. "I hate Sky Arrow for killing Helen. I can never forgive him. Why are you forcing me to marry him?"

Singing Reed gazed at her in astonishment. Before she could respond, the tipi flap lifted and Nona's heart sank when she saw Sky Arrow enter. Now nothing could save her.

Without a word, Singing Reed rose and carried Amanda Jean with her to her pallet, disappearing behind the screen. Nona remained frozen where she sat, facing Sky Arrow in terrified defiance.

He said something to her and held out his hand. She ignored the gesture. He frowned, leaned down and grasped her shoulders, yanking her to her feet. She jerked away from him.

"Don't touch me!" she cried, knowing he didn't understand her, but also knowing that words wouldn't stop him.

Evidently her actions spoke clearly enough, for his frown deepened to a scowl. As he reached for her again, a scratching came at the flap and a second later a brown-and-white puppy tumbled into the tipi.

Sky Arrow muttered angrily at the cowering dog and took a menacing step toward him. As he did, the tipi flap pushed open and, to Nona's shock, Spencer stepped inside. Ignoring her, Spencer pointed at the dog and spoke to Sky Arrow in Sioux, sounding extremely apologetic.

Sky Arrow gave a short, unamused laugh and replied curtly.

Spencer reached down, picked up the dog and started to turn away. Suddenly he whirled and pitched the animal into Sky Arrow's face, sending him staggering back. Before the Sioux could recover, Spencer rapped him sharply on the head with the butt of his pistol and Sky Arrow sagged to the ground, unmoving.

"Let's get out of here," Spencer said to Nona, keeping his voice low.

Singing Reed appeared from behind the screen with the baby in her arms, startling Spencer, who evidently hadn't known she was in the tipi.

"Don't give the alarm," Nona begged as Spencer strode toward the Sioux woman. "Let us go."

"My brother?" Singing Reed asked.

"He's not dead, he'll come around." Spencer eyed her warily.

"I no stop you," Singing Reed told Nona.

"I want Helen's baby," Nona said. "Amanda Jean's my sister's baby. I have to bring her to her father."

Singing Reed's eyes shone with tears and for a moment

Nona thought she meant to refuse. "I put Light of Sun in cradle board," she said at last.

Spencer and Nona left the tipi minutes later, with the baby in the cradle board and carrying a buckskin container with a buffalo cow's udder full of milk that Singing Reed had salvaged from the day's kills. The Sioux woman held the frightened puppy so he wouldn't follow them. From a stake near the tipi, Spencer untied the pinto pony Nona had been riding and led him along with them.

Nona shivered with apprehension, expecting they'd be spotted at any moment, that a cry would go up and she'd be dragged back to Sky Arrow. Spencer had taken a terrible risk to save her; what would happen to him if he were caught didn't bear thinking about.

At last they reached Spencer's tethered horse among the trees and Spencer helped her onto the pinto, offering to carry the baby. She refused. The cradle board—stiff rawhide covered with soft buckskin—wasn't heavy and she found it comfortable enough on her back.

Spencer mounted his horse and she kept her pinto on the bigger horse's heels, following him through the woods along the stream, her heart still hammering with fear. She longed to talk to Spencer, to pour out her gratitude, but she knew she must be as quiet as possible. She wouldn't say a word until he told her it was safe.

Luckily Amanda Jean was sleeping. If she began to cry the sound would give them away. That's why Singing Reed had insisted on training the baby not to cry, Nona realized. The Sioux, fearing bluecoat raids, knew a crying baby revealed the location of a village.

They were miles from Lean Bear's village with no outcry or other sign of pursuit behind them before Spencer finally spoke. "Thank God the wolves were too full of buffalo meat to be alert."

"Wolves?" She had no idea what he meant.

"Lakota scouts who guard the camp."

"If you hadn't come for me when you did—" she began.

He cut her off. "I wanted to tell you what I meant to do, but I couldn't take the risk of being seen talking to you. I'm sorry about your sister."

Tears gathered in Nona's eyes. If Helen hadn't died she would have been too weak to escape with Spencer. Would I have refused to go with him a second time? Nona asked herself. Would I have stayed behind with Helen? Recalling her terror and hatred of Sky Arrow, she shook her head uncertainly.

"Are we safe?" she asked, afraid they weren't, but wanting to be reassured.

"For the moment. If Singing Reed doesn't give the alarm, we have until Sky Arrow regains his senses and realizes what's happened. Even then, I don't think they'll come after us at night; it's too hard to follow sign. In the morning they may decide chasing us isn't worth the risk of running into troopers."

"Will we? Run into troopers, I mean."

"I certainly hope so. Then we're safe for sure."

"You ran a terrible risk pretending to be a Dakota," she said. "And that buffalo hunt! It scared me to death when your pony fell and I saw you leap onto one of those beasts. I was so upset I lost my head and screamed at you not to die but to live."

"With you and Dancing Coyote on my side, how could I lose? The only thing I regret is betraying Friend's trust by tossing him at Sky Arrow."

"Friend? Oh, you mean the puppy. He didn't seem to be hurt."

"I hope not. That was the second tight spot he helped me out of."

"Maybe Singing Reed will adopt the dog. She'll be lonesome. It was hard for her to give up Amanda Jean—I wasn't sure she would. Her own baby died at birth and I know she loved Light of Sun, the name she gave Amanda Jean. I hated every moment in that Sioux village and sometimes I even hated Singing Reed. But I'm going to miss her."

They rode in silence for a time, Nona grateful she was wearing leggings and tunic since she had to sit astride, and thankful the pony was familiar. Twisted Ear was what Singing Reed called him, because his left ear was crooked. She remembered the strange name the Sioux woman gave Spencer.

"Why do the Sioux call you Heavy Foot?" she asked.

He chuckled. "That was my boyhood name. I never did learn to creep through the woods silently enough to suit Dancing Coyote. Lean Bear rechristened me Buffalo Rider today but, for all I know, he may change it to Man-Who-Runs-Off-With-Good Heart."

Nona smiled for the first time since she and Helen had been taken captive.

As they rode on, the elation of escaping gradually faded and Nona began to realize how tired she was. She'd been up since early morning and had butchered dead buffalo for hours—she grimaced just thinking about the bloody mess. Singing Reed had told her the hunters only killed bulls but she'd seen two cows and a calf lying dead. She wondered if the udder they'd brought along came from one of those cows and prayed that buffalo milk would agree with Amanda Jean.

"Is the baby all right?" Spencer asked, as though reading her mind.

"I think she's still asleep. Usually she doesn't cry unless she's hungry."

"We'll have to stop and rest the horses soon. Maybe you'd better feed her then."

Obviously Spencer didn't know much about babies. Nona had already learned from watching Amanda Jean that she nursed when she was ready no matter how inconvenient the time. Still, she could try to coax the baby into taking some of the buffalo milk.

Because she was eager to put as many miles as possible between them and the Sioux village, Nona fought her fatigue, not telling Spencer how exhausted she felt. When at last he called a halt, dismounted and helped her off the pony, her knees threatened to give way and she clung to him. He held her gently for a moment or two, then eased the cradle board straps from her shoulders.

"Don't lie down," he warned. "We can't risk sleeping yet." He hung the cradle board carefully on a low cottonwood branch, and after tethering the horses, put his arm around Nona and drew her to him while he braced his back against the trunk.

She leaned her head against his chest and closed her eyes. She was safe with Spencer, safe and protected. He'd rescued her; he wouldn't let anything bad happen to her. His heart beat under her ear, steady and reassuring, his strength supported her, his warmth comforted her.

The next she knew he was shaking her gently. "You fell asleep on your feet," he said, holding her away from him. "I hate to wake you, but we must keep moving. It's not safe to stop long. Are you going to feed the baby?"

By the scant light of the waning moon Nona lifted down the cradle board. She remembered Singing Reed telling her the Moon of Buffalo Making Fat was dying and the Moon of Ripening Chokecherries would soon be born. More by intuition than by sight, Nona decided Amanda Jean was still asleep.

"I don't want to wake her," she told Spencer. "Maybe she'll be content until we stop again."

"How about you? Can you go on? I don't want you falling off your pony, sound asleep."

"I'll stay awake." She had to; her life depended on it. But she didn't argue when Spencer insisted on strapping the cradle board onto his own back.

The rest of the night passed in a blur as she dozed, jerked half-awake when she slumped forward, then dozed again. Shortly before dawn Amanda Jean's wails roused her.

Spencer let the baby cry until he found a stream, by which time the baby was red-faced. He settled Nona, Amanda Jean and the container with the buffalo udder under a cottonwood before taking the horses to the stream.

Nona, no stranger to milking a cow, had little difficulty coaxing milk from a buffalo teat but it was much harder to induce the baby to accept such a strange nipple. Amanda Jean howled in frustration and hunger and milk sprayed over both her and Nona before she finally mastered the knack. Even then she sputtered and choked as she gulped the milk.

"She makes a whale of a racket for such a little shrimp," Spencer observed when he finished with the horses and returned to where Nona sat under the tree.

"She's a beautiful baby," Nona informed him.

"If you say so. I don't know much about the breed, be they boy or girl." His tone suggested he didn't care to learn, either.

Nona frowned at him. His dark hair was wet and dripping as though he'd ducked his head in the creek to keep himself awake. For the first time, she realized Spencer must be as worn out as she was. She'd butchered buffalo but he'd hunted them and survived a ride on the back of the bull he'd killed.

"Why don't you rest for awhile?" she asked. "I'll stay awake and keep watch."

He hesitated, glancing around the grove of cottonwoods along the stream. "I reckon I will," he said finally. "I'm dead on my feet. Wake me after an hour." He ambled away and returned with an army blanket, spread it on the ground next to her and stretched out. His eyes closed immediately.

When Amanda Jean seemed satisfied, Nona stopped squirting milk into her mouth. She lifted the baby up on her shoulder as she'd seen Singing Reed do, feeling awkward and unsure.

I'm doing my best to bring your daughter to her father, Helen, she said silently. I promise I'll help to raise her, I'll do everything I can for her.

After a time she laid the now quiet, drowsy baby on the edge of Spencer's blanket so she could clean the cradle board. Sioux babies didn't wear diaper cloths, or any clothes, though soft rabbitskin was wrapped around the upper half of the baby for warmth. Dried sweetgrass was stuffed inside the bottom of the carrier and changed often. The problem was she didn't have anything to replace the wet and soiled grass she removed.

The only possibility was the crumbly, dried leaves the trees had shed last fall. Nona gathered enough to put inside the bottom of the carrier. The leaves didn't have the softness nor the sweet fragrance of the grass but they'd have to do.

Kilby won't know how to take care of Amanda Jean, Nona thought as she replaced the baby in the cradle board. *I'll have to stay to help him.* Unbidden, it crossed her mind that Kilby might well assume she'd marry him. Would she? She shot the sleeping Spencer a quick look, feeling inexplicably guilty.

Immediately she took herself to task. What business was it of Spencer's what she did? He may have risked his life to rescue her but he'd more or less told her by the creek in the Sioux village that he'd have done the same for any white woman captive. His rescue of her didn't mean he'd changed his mind or his ways. *He* certainly wouldn't ask her to marry him.

Not that she wanted to. But she continued to watch

125

him. His black hair, drying as he slept, sprang into curls that, for some reason, she was tempted to wind around her finger. Perhaps it was because when he was off guard he looked so much younger, letting her see traces of the boy he'd been.

Had it been an hour? She wasn't sure but she hated to wake him. Did he know his upper lip was a perfect cupid's bow? She smiled. No doubt he'd prefer a Sioux—no, Dakota—bow. He spoke of the old medicine man of his boyhood with great affection; he and Dancing Coyote must have been very close.

Spencer woke abruptly, his arrow-sharp senses telling him someone watched him. He stared into wide hazel eyes. Nona!

Without thinking, he did what he'd been longing to do, reached for her and drew her down to him, close to him. His hand cupped the back of her head, bringing her lips near enough for him to kiss. They were yielding and warm, exciting him as they parted under the pressure of his.

She belonged in his arms, she was his woman, not any other man's—definitely not Sky Arrow's. He'd gone after her, he'd found her, rescued her and he meant to make her his.

The Lakota dress she wore was soft and smooth under his hand but her skin was softer still; nothing could rival its smoothness. He wanted her lying naked on the blanket with him, her glorious hair unwound and spread out for his fingers to tangle in. He wanted to touch all of her, to feel her respond to his caresses.

She wanted it too; he could tell by the way she pressed closer, by her sighing breath, by the way the pulse in her throat throbbed and fluttered.

An unfamiliar sound intruded and Spencer felt her

tense. He identified what he heard as she pulled away.

"The baby's fussing," Nona said, confirming what he'd already suspected.

He'd forgotten about the baby. Forgotten how precarious their safety was. Forgotten everything but how good Nona felt in his arms. Spencer sat up and shook his head as though that would clear his mind.

First things first, Quinlan, he reminded himself. Get the three of you back to the fort before you even think about anything else. And keep your hands off her or you may never get there.

"Time to move on," he said, rising to his feet while he did his best to ignore what his body continued to demand. He couldn't have her now, no matter how great his need. Staying alive was more important. It was never wise to underestimate the Lakota.

Why do I lose my wits every time Spencer kisses me? Nona asked herself as they rode from under the trees into the full glare of the sunlight. When he takes me into his arms I behave like a wanton; that's all there is to it. A wanton. She slanted a furtive glance at him. He'd insisted on carrying the baby and, despite her anger at herself and annoyance at him, she had to smile. How incongruous it looked. He was the last man in the world anyone would expect to have a cradle board strapped to his back.

Her smile faded as she remembered how quickly she'd dismissed Amanda Jean from her mind when he pulled her down against him. Nothing in the world existed at that moment except Spencer and the tingling thrill of his embrace. How could she have done such a terrible thing as forget Helen's daughter? Motherless little Amanda Jean depended on her for everything; the baby must come first, no matter what.

I won't let him touch me again, she told herself firmly.

It's far too dangerous.

They rode until the sun was high overhead, when Spencer suddenly halted and slid off the chestnut. Surprised and alarmed, Nona checked Twisted Ear. What was wrong? Spencer leaned against his horse and lifted Kaintuck's right front leg, grimaced and let it go.

"I felt him going lame," he told her. "He's got a swelling below the knee. We'll have to camp." He jerked his head. "Back at that last stream."

With Spencer leading Kaintuck, they retraced their trail until they reached the ever-present line of trees along the creek. Spencer hung the cradle board on a low branch and examined Kaintuck's leg again. Nona slid off the pony, glad of the excuse to stop. She was so tired it was an effort to walk over and make certain Amanda Jean was all right. Seeing the baby slept, she crossed to Spencer and Kaintuck. The chestnut's leg was badly swollen.

"He can't travel on that," she said.

"Even if I tried to make him we wouldn't get far," Spencer agreed. "He stumbled a few times in the night, but I didn't see any damage when we stopped before."

Nona touched the swelling with gentle fingers. "We can try binding the leg with wet willow leaves—there's nothing else available. But even if the compresses do help, it'll take days before you can ride him. Maybe weeks."

"We don't have days, much less weeks." Spencer scowled. "Damn those troopers—where are they?"

"In the first Sioux camp you told me they were two days behind you at the most."

"That's what I thought. I don't see how we could have missed them—I found the travois trail at daylight and we've been following it ever since. That's the trail they'd be on. Unless—"

Nona waited for him to go on and when he didn't she

prompted him. "Unless?"

"They might have found the first camp deserted and turned back. I left sign for the Ree scouts so they'd know I was trailing the Lakota, sign that would tell them you and Helen were with the Lakota. It's true the Lakota turned off the travois trail before they located this last village, but I don't see how an Indian scout could have missed the sign and I'm sure the troopers would have at least one scout along."

Watching him, Nona saw his jaw clench and he muttered something she couldn't hear.

"What did you say?"

He shook his head. "Never mind. It doesn't bear repeating. But I think we might as well face the fact we're on our own. We can't count on the Seventh being anywhere closer than Fort Lincoln."

She drew in her breath sharply. "How far are we from the fort?"

"With two horses, maybe three days, if we slept at night. With one horse, twice that or more."

"We can do it!"

He twisted his mouth into the travesty of a smile. "We have to because we sure as hell can't stay here and wait for Kaintuck to heal. We do have a few other problems. No food, for one. I tried to bring some from the village but I couldn't. I hoped we'd be lucky enough to be eating Army rations by tonight, but I was wrong."

Nona hadn't mentioned her growing hunger because she knew there was nothing to eat. "I guess you'll have to kill another buffalo," she said lightly, trying to boost his spirits as well as her own.

He grinned. "I'd have to find one first. Rabbits are easier to locate. I used to be able to set a fair rabbit snare. We won't starve. And the baby has milk."

Not for the first time, Nona wondered how long the milk in the buffalo udder would stay sweet. She hadn't really worried over it until now because she'd expected the Army to come to their rescue. She'd have to do what she could to preserve the milk as long as possible.

"I'll put the container with the udder in the creek to keep it cool," she said. "And if you can trap a rabbit, I know how to cook it without a kettle."

Despite their danger, Nona's heart lifted when Spencer smiled at her. It made her feel that as long as they were together, everything would work out, that they'd be all right.

"First of all, we'll camp farther off the trail," Spencer said.

Once they'd moved a half mile or so upriver, Spencer disappeared among the trees to set up rabbit snares and Nona poulticed Kaintuck's leg as well as she could with wet willow leaves held on by thongs. Then she set about kindling a fire—making it small; large fires meant a lot of smoke and smoke might mean discovery.

Amanda Jean, in her cradle board, hung from a nearby limb and the horses grazed within sight. Nona wondered why she felt a peculiar contentment. Considering the circumstances, she should be apprehensive and alarmed. Maybe it was because it was impossible for her to stay frightened continuously. For the moment, at least, they were safe and whatever danger might lie ahead she couldn't foresee.

Or perhaps she didn't worry because she was with Spencer. He was brave and resourceful. Hadn't he outsmarted an entire Sioux village to rescue her? He was a man any woman would feel safe with. She certainly did. Unless he touched her. Nona paused in her careful feeding of twigs into the tiny fire and sat back on her heels.

Each time he kissed her, the need inside her grew stronger and more urgent. She'd never given herself to a man, but that didn't mean she wasn't aware of what it felt like to want to. Spencer made her want to.

Kilby had never made her feel this way. With a start, Nona realized it had been a long time since she'd thought about Kilby at all.

The caw of a crow brought her back to her surroundings. She glanced to her left at the big black bird perched in a tree and involuntarily shuddered as Grandma Willard's old saw surfaced in her mind:

"One crow for sorrow . . ."

She didn't believe in omens and God knows Helen's death had been more than enough sorrow, but nevertheless, her spirits were dampened and she sighed with foreboding.

Would they ever reach Fort Lincoln and safety?

Chapter Nine

Kaintuck snorted. Startled, Nona looked up from her small cooking fire and was horrified to see Twisted Ear splashing across the creek. She leaped up and raced after the pony. Once he reached the west bank, he broke into a lope and Nona realized she had no chance to catch him. Even if she mounted Kaintuck, the lame chestnut was in no condition to run down the pony.

She stopped on the stream's east bank and stared after the runaway pinto until he disappeared into the trees— no doubt on his way back to the Sioux village. "Damn!" she muttered, tears of angry frustration in her eyes. The loss of the pony was as much her fault as Spencer's— she'd forgotten Singing Reed's warning that Twisted Ear often slipped free of his tether.

She'd thought it was bad enough when Kaintuck went lame; now he was their only horse. One disabled horse, one helpless baby, no food, and miles of wilderness between them and the fort. The situation could hardly get any worse. Walking slowly back to the fire, she imagined Spencer's shock when he came back from trapping rabbit and discovered what had happened.

How long did it take to set snares? He hadn't been gone long, yet all of sudden she felt terribly alone. The snap of a twig somewhere under the trees downriver made her tense with apprehension. Sioux warriors creeping up on her? She quelled a frantic impulse to shout Spencer's name and edged toward where he'd tossed Kaintuck's saddle.

When she reached the Army saddle, she crouched and slipped her hand inside the saddlebag where Spencer had stored the knife and sheath Singing Reed had given her at the buffalo hunt. Looking fearfully around her, she slid the sheathed knife under the tie of her leggings. No more twigs cracked, no savages rushed from the trees to overwhelm her, and after a moment, Nona rose. Her imagination must be working overtime. Just the same, she felt better with the knife pressed against her thigh.

Kaintuck was once again cropping grass; surely he'd let her know if someone was nearby. Relieved but still wary, she began to search for more small branches to add to the fire. She gathered an armful and was returning to the fire when Kaintuck's head came up. He stared at her, ears pricked forward.

"It's only me," she told him. Her voice sounded abnormally loud, making her wish she hadn't spoken.

The chestnut continued to look at her. The hair on Nona's nape prickled. Was Kaintuck watching her or did he see something behind her? She whirled around.

A black-bearded man stood less than a foot away. A man she recognized. She gasped. Paquette! Before she could move, he leaped forward and grabbed her, one hand cutting off her scream. Nona squirmed and kicked, trying to free her right arm so she could reach for the knife.

"No woman cuts Paquette," he snarled, tugging the sheathed knife free and tossing it away. His fingers closed around her throat.

Unable to breathe, Nona struggled to pry loose his hands, but failed. Blackness gathered at the edges of her vision, coalesced, and she collapsed. The next she knew she was on the ground, her wrists behind her back, bound with a leather thong. Paquette knelt above her, one knee thrust between her thighs.

He grinned down at her. "Ran out on your buck, didja?"

She opened her mouth to scream. He slapped her before any sound emerged.

"Paquette likes his women quiet. Yell and I'll use my fist next." His expression told her he'd enjoy beating her into silence. "Yelling ain't gonna do no good nohow with only your lame horse to hear."

Nona didn't know how he'd missed seeing the baby, but she kept her eyes resolutely away from the cradle hanging on a branch in the shade of a large cottonwood. Except for Kaintuck's saddle, Spencer had thrust the rest of their gear into the broad crotch of the same tree. Obviously Paquette hadn't noticed that, either.

"You ain't the kind to tie up with no Sioux buck on purpose," he said.

"He—he captured me," she whispered.

"Me, I got you now. 'Most as good as catching up with that sneaking squaw you helped get away from me." Paquette fumbled with the thongs of her leggings. "We got some unfinished business, you and me." His gloating smile left little doubt what he meant.

Nona tried to writhe away from his searching hands. "No!" she cried. "No, don't!"

He backhanded her so hard she saw stars. His rank smell and his fingers on her bare flesh gagged her, sending bile to burn her throat. She'd loathed Sky Arrow's touch but Paquette's was ten times worse, bringing her perilously close to vomiting.

He thrust her thighs brutally apart and, terrified, she tried futilely to squirm away. Closing her eyes against the expected blow, she screamed as loudly as she could.

The blow never came. Nona heard a grunt, her eyes flew open and she found herself staring at Spencer as he dragged the struggling Paquette away from her.

She scrambled awkwardly to her feet as the two men rolled on the ground, pummeling each other. Try as she might, she couldn't free her hands from the thong, so she looked frantically around for her sheathed knife and saw it lying on the ground several yards away. Before she reached the knife, Amanda Jean woke and began to wail.

Spurred on by the crying baby, the thud of fists and grunts and curses of the fighting men, Nona struggled to work the knife free of the sheath and position it so she could slice through the thong binding her wrists, all the while keeping her eyes glued to the men.

Paquette reached down and yanked a knife from his boot. "Watch out, he's got a knife!" she shouted to Spencer as she thrust her own blade desperately at the thong.

Paquette's knife rose and fell. "No!" she moaned as blood stained Spencer's buckskin shirt.

Spencer's hand pinned Paquette's wrist above his head, squeezing it until he forced the knife from Paquette's fingers. Abandoning her struggle, Nona hurried toward them, kicked Paquette's knife out of his reach, then backed away. With her hands bound, she was helpless to aid Spencer. Since she wore moccasins, kicking Paquette wouldn't hurt him and she feared if she tried to arm Spencer with one of the knives, Paquette might grab it instead.

Amanda Jean sobbed piteously, but Nona didn't dare to so much as glance at her, afraid to take her attention from the men, watching as Paquette squirmed and shifted to free his hand again.

"He's going for your gun!" she cried to Spencer as Paquette's fingers snaked toward the holster. Spencer

135

wrestled with Paquette as the pistol pulled free. They rolled over so she couldn't see whose hand grasped the gun. A shot rang out. Nona caught her breath in terrified apprehension.

Paquette thrust himself free of Spencer and started to rise. Nona stared at him numbly, certain he'd shot Spencer. Then she saw blood smearing Paquette's fingers as, clutching his abdomen with both hands, he stumbled into the trees.

A long-buried memory of her father surfaced, of him saying to one of her brothers, "You gut-shoot a deer, you're honor-bound to track him and put him out of his misery. Gut-shot's a hard way to die."

She could find no pity for Paquette.

Spencer propped himself on one elbow, the gun in his hand. "Got to go after the bastard." His voice was alarmingly weak. "Kill him. Before he gets to his rifle."

Nona dropped to her knees beside Spencer. Blood trickled from the knife wound in his chest.

"Help me up," he ordered.

"I can't." She showed him her bound hands.

"Knife. Hurry."

Nona brought him her knife and he cut the thong. With her steadying him, he got to his feet and started after Paquette. Nona followed.

"Listen!" she urged, hearing what sounded like a horse crashing through the undergrowth, then splashing across the stream. "He's riding away," she added, relieved.

"Bastard'll come back. Got to—"

"He's wounded," she said.

Spencer blinked at her. "Where?"

Nona put a hand over her abdomen.

"He tried to pull my gun," Spencer muttered. "Went off."

"I know, I saw what happened. At first I thought the bullet hit you." Looking at the blood oozing from his chest, she winced. "We must stop that bleeding."

"Got to get Paquette first. Kill him. Take his rifle."

"He might not have a rifle. He traded one for—"

"A man's a fool to ride in this country without a rifle, I found that out. Odds are he's not that much of a fool. Help me on the pony."

"The pony ran away. There's only Kaintuck."

Spencer stared at her, his face pale. "We need Paquette's horse as well as his rifle then," he said finally, crossing to the chestnut.

"You're hurt," she cried. "You can't go after Paquette."

Spencer paid no attention. Untying Kaintuck, he led him to a fallen log. Stepping onto the log, he struggled onto the horse's bare back and urged Kaintuck toward the stream. As he splashed through the water, he heard, over the screaming of the baby, Nona pleading with him to come back. Though he felt weak as a winter fly, he went on. If Kaintuck could make it, he could.

When the hobbling Kaintuck left the trees, Paquette's horse was nowhere in sight. Dismayed, Spencer halted the chestnut. Was the bastard sneaking back through the trees with his rifle? Stalking Nona? Spencer cursed.

As he started to turn the horse back, he noticed something dark lying on the ground some yards away. Because there seemed to be a shifting veil obstructing his vision, he couldn't be sure what he saw. Checking the turn, he rode forward, fighting to keep his mind clear.

A white spirit buffalo shimmered before his eyes. "A man who kills his brother, pte, must die in turn," the spirit buffalo told him.

He knew the vision spoke truth, yet he couldn't die now, he couldn't leave Nona alone and unprotected. Was it *pte* who lay dead on the ground before him? It couldn't be.

Kaintuck stepped sideways unexpectedly and Spencer

137

almost slid off his back. The effort to remain on the horse brought him back to his senses. A man's body sprawled in the dirt. Paquette. Knowing he'd never have the energy to remount Kaintuck if he got off to examine the body, Spencer stared down at Paquette until he was satisfied the bastard was dead. If he hadn't been sure, the vultures already circling overhead would have convinced him.

As Spencer started back to the camp, he clutched at Kaintuck's mane as his remaining strength ebbed. "Grandfather," he whispered, "if I die, two others die as well. Show me how to stay alive."

Nona, Amanda Jean's sobs echoing in her ears, watched from the bank of the stream as Kaintuck hobbled through the water toward her, Spencer swaying with each step the horse took. She held her breath until the chestnut reached dry ground. Spencer looked down at her, squinting as though he couldn't see clearly.

"Paquette's dead," he mumbled. "Horse gone." He slurred the words so she scarcely understood them. She cried out in dismay as Spencer slid off Kaintuck and lay motionless on the ground beside her.

She flung herself to her knees and cupped her hand over his nose and mouth. When she felt the faint breath of life, she closed her eyes momentarily in thankful relief. Taking her hand away, she bit her lip as she saw blood oozing from his chest. The bleeding, she had to stop the bleeding or he'd die.

They had no medicine, nothing. She glanced around in desperation at the willows and cottonwoods surrounding her. Willow. Willow bark was an astringent. And, back at the farm, hadn't Dorothy always bound a bleeding cut tightly?

Nona pulled her knife from its sheath and cut into the bark of a willow, peeling it away from the pith of the

138

trunk as quickly as she could. When she had several strips, she set them aside and cut two wide strips from one of their blankets.

She pulled up Spencer's buckskin shirt and pressed the inside of the willow bark over the knife wound, then struggled to tie the bark in place with the blanket strips, shoving and pushing at Spencer's limp body to wrap them around his chest. When she finished, she realized he was too close to the stream; if he turned over, he'd be in the water. After removing his pistol and holster for his comfort, she exerted all her strength to roll him onto the mutilated blanket, and pulled him, inch by inch, until he was near the fire. There she covered him with the uncut blanket.

Amanda Jean's wails had diminished to exhausted sobbing, but Nona knew she had to take care of Kaintuck and make sure he was tethered before she tended to the baby. When at last she took down the cradle, Amanda Jean gave only short, shuddering cries as Nona lifted the baby into her arms.

"Poor little girl," Nona soothed, half her attention on the baby, the other on Spencer. How was he?

As she coaxed buffalo milk into Amanda Jean, Nona tried to order her thoughts. Paquette was dead; they were safe from him. But the Sioux could well be tracking them. And they had only the lame Kaintuck. Even if the horse was sound, Spencer couldn't ride in his condition. How long was it safe to stay here? The buffalo udder was almost empty. What would she feed the baby when the milk was gone? And how long could she and Spencer live without food?

The rabbit snares. When she finished tending to Amanda Jean she must go upriver and try to find the snares. If by chance a rabbit had been trapped, at least there'd be food.

Once the baby was sleeping in the cradle again, Nona

bent over Spencer to examine her makeshift bandage. She was encouraged to note the bleeding seemed to have stopped, but when she called his name softly, he didn't respond and that frightened her. A bad sign. She hated to leave him and the baby, but soon it would be too dark to look for the snares, their only chance for food. She cast more branches on the fire and reluctantly started upriver.

Long shadows of evening were darkening the woods when Nona returned to the camp carrying two dead rabbits. These weren't the first rabbits she'd skinned and cleaned so she made short work of the job, skewering the meat onto sharpened sticks and propping them to cook over the coals of her fire. Despite the terrors of the day and her worry over Spencer, the tantalizing smell of cooking meat made her realize how hungry she was.

Though Nona tried her best to rouse Spencer to eat, she couldn't. After she'd eaten all she could, she wrapped the rest of the rabbit meat in damp leaves and thrust it into a saddle bag. She lifted Amanda Jean's cradle from the tree and, holding the baby next to her, she lay down next to Spencer, the holster and gun within easy reach, and pulled the blanket over her and the baby. She tried to lay apart from him, but the May night was cool and she found herself edging closer and closer to his warmth.

Nona woke sometime in the night and realized from the heat of his body that Spencer must have a fever. Since there was nothing she could do about it, she finally fell asleep again but soon he began tossing and muttering in delirium.

"Grandfather," he said. "Save her, grandfather."

Nona sat up, the baby on her shoulder. "Spencer," she said.

"Buffalo Rider," he mumbled. "Brother *pte.*"

"Spencer, it's Nona," she whispered.

Amanda Jean began to whimper and Nona rocked the

baby in her arms.

"Nona," Spencer muttered. "Pretty Nona."

"We're camping in the wilderness," she said. "You've been hurt."

He was quiet for a moment. "Water," he said finally. "Thirsty."

Earlier Nona had rinsed out the Army canteen and filled it with water from the stream. She laid the fussing baby on the blanket and reached for the canteen. Spencer was so weak she had to hold his head up for him to drink from the container. His skin felt fiery hot against her arm. By the time she finished with Spencer, Amanda Jean was wailing.

"Baby?" he asked weakly.

"We have Helen's baby with us," she told him.

He mumbled something that sounded like "poor baby."

Nona retrieved the buffalo udder and fed Amanda Jean with the last of the milk. Poor baby was right. What was she to do the next time Amanda Jean cried for milk?

The sky had begun to gray while she fed and cleaned the baby, so Nona didn't dare try to sleep any longer. She put Amanda Jean into the cradle and stood looking down at the restless Spencer. With him so ill and the baby out of milk, she couldn't stay here—but how could she go on?

A travois, she thought. If she had a travois to hitch to Kaintuck, the horse could pull Spencer while she walked alongside carrying the baby. A travois was nothing more than poles tied together—why couldn't she make one?

Before the sun was halfway up the sky, Nona had fashioned a crude travois from willow branches bound together with the rope she had found with the Army gear. She saddled Kaintuck and, using leather straps she'd cut from the reins and the stirrups, hitched the travois to the saddle.

She roused the feverish Spencer, persuaded him to drink some water. By patiently repeating how she wanted him to move, she got him onto the travois. Kaintuck was willing to walk despite his swollen leg, so, with the cradle on her back, Nona set off wearing Spencer's wide-brimmed black hat and his gun and holster, strapped around her waist, an unfamiliar weight as she paced beside the horse. The grass-covered hills stretched endlessly in front of her, one looking much like the next. She had no idea where Fort Lincoln was but she knew if they traveled east they'd eventually come to the Missouri River and could follow it north to the fort. She refused to think of how long the trip might take or how they were going to survive.

Shortly past midday, she stopped to rest herself and Kaintuck. She offered Spencer water but he only swallowed a mouthful.

"*Pte,*" he muttered, followed by what was gibberish to her. She suspected he was rambling in Sioux.

Though his eyes were open he didn't recognize her. He tried to struggle off the travois, but she'd tied him to the carrier with a rope and he was too weak to free himself. Nona worried that his efforts would make him bleed again.

"Lie still, everything's all right," she said to him as she would to a child, laying a hand on his hot forehead. "Nona's here; you're all right."

Whether he knew her or not, her words seemed to penetrate and he quieted.

As Nona started off again, Amanda Jean began to whimper, then cry, but there was nothing to feed her. "Hush," Nona murmured over and over. Finally, in desperation, she began to sing:

> "Bye baby bunting
> Daddy's gone a-hunting

> To fetch a little rabbit skin
> To wrap the baby bunting in."

Over and over she sang the lullaby, her words blending into Amanda Jean's sobs. As she sang, her mind drifted back to the farm and little Nona watching Dorothy rock baby Helen while she sang to her. She stopped singing and sank deeper into her reverie of the past when she and Helen were safe and secure on the farm.

Kaintuck snorted and veered to the right, startling Nona into alertness. She glanced apprehensively around her but saw nothing that could have alarmed the horse. Noticing a distant green line to the right, she realized the chestnut must have scented water and was heading for it. Aware she couldn't walk much farther without collapsing, she followed Kaintuck, planning to camp for the night beside the stream.

It seemed to take forever to reach the trees lining the water. The baby had cried herself into exhaustion and didn't rouse when Nona lifted the cradle from her back and hung it on a limb. She eased Spencer, blankets and all, from the travois until he lay flat on the ground. She longed to stretch out and rest, but first Kaintuck had to be unsaddled and seen to.

The sun was halfway down the sky by the time Nona finished with the horse. She'd no sooner knelt beside Spencer to see how he was when Amanda Jean began to wail. Pushing herself to her feet, she took the baby from the cradle and cleaned her. Having nothing else to give the hungry child, Nona tried water. Amanda Jean sputtered and choked but Nona patiently persisted, hoping to coax enough water down the baby to satisfy her temporarily.

The realization that the child wasn't baptized crept into her mind. Afraid to admit to herself that Amanda Jean might die, Nona did her best to banish the thought.

There was plenty of time to have the baby baptized when they reached the fort.

If they reached the fort.

With Spencer delirious and no food for the baby, what were the chances that any of them would survive?

Forced to face the possibility of failure, Nona reached for the water, sprinkled a few drops on the baby's forehead and traced a cross.

"I baptize thee Amanda Jean Mead in the name of the Father, the Son and the Holy Ghost," she murmured.

Spencer roused to the wails of a baby. Confused, he tried to raise his head and found it a tremendous effort.

An auburn-haired woman with a tiny baby in her arms sat beside him. He knew the woman but couldn't quite grasp her name. Thoughts flitted through his mind like a flight of birds and he tried to capture one or two as they fluttered by.

Nona. Nona with her sister's baby. "Paquette!" He said the word aloud, tensing in alarm.

Nona turned. "Paquette's dead," she told him.

Spencer relaxed and became aware he ached all over with the worst pain in his chest. Looking down at his shirt he saw the rusty stains of old blood. Paquette's knife? It hurt his head trying to make sense of what had happened, but he persisted. Water gurgled nearby; new green leaves formed a canopy overhead. He glanced to his left and saw Kaintuck cropping grass. The last he remembered they'd camped and he'd been setting rabbit snares when he heard Nona scream. Then he'd fought Paquette.

He thought he recalled traveling after that but it could have been a fever dream.

"Where are we?" he asked finally.

"A few miles east of where we were last night," Nona told him.

144

To Spencer's relief the baby's wails had diminished to whimpers. The high-pitched crying had pierced through his skull, seeming to lodge in his already fuzzy brain, making it hard to think at all. Now he could order his thoughts.

"Travois," he said. "Kaintuck pulled me on a travois."

"Would you like something to eat?" Nona asked as she propped the baby up on her shoulder. "There's leftover roast rabbit."

Spencer's stomach roiled uneasily at the idea. "I'd better stick to water." He tried to sit up but couldn't.

"Take it easy," she warned. "You'll start bleeding again."

Muttering under his breath, Spencer subsided. Weak as he was, he didn't have much choice but to do as she said. He watched Nona clean the cradle and stuff leaves inside it before putting the baby in.

"Paquette must have been following Singing Reed," he said when Nona finished.

When she shuddered, he remembered how Paquette had attacked her and cursed himself for reminding her. If only he could take her in his arms, hold her close and comfort her, but it was all he could do to lift his hand and cover hers.

Nona clutched his hand in both of hers, gazing at him through shining tears. "Oh, Spencer," she cried, "I thought you were going to die."

He did his best to smile reassuringly, all the while feeling like death warmed over. Dimly he recalled a white buffalo talking to him; he must really have been out of his head. What a courageous woman she was, packing him onto a travois—one she must have made herself—and setting off on foot with the cradle on her back.

He must force himself to eat; he needed to regain his strength quickly. "I'll try a few bites of the rabbit," he said. "If you'll join me."

He managed to swallow a few mouthfuls washed down with water before exhaustion sapped what little strength he had. Despite his attempt to stay awake, his eyelids dropped shut.

It was dark when he woke. The baby was crying again, seemed to be wailing directly in his ear. Someone stirred and he realized Nona was beside him.

"What's the matter with the baby?" he asked as she sat up.

"She's hungry." Nona spoke above the baby's howls. "We ran out of buffalo milk last night and she's had nothing but water all day."

No wonder the poor little thing cried so piercingly, he thought. What the hell were they going to do with her? God knows how far they were from the fort. Or even where they were—Nona would hardly be able to keep to a trail. He could only hope Kaintuck had instinctively struck out for the fort.

He'd probably be too weak to walk tomorrow, so he'd have to ride the travois again. They wouldn't get far with Kaintuck still lame. Spencer clenched his jaw. They had to reach help soon or the baby would die.

"What are you doing?" he asked Nona as she was getting up from the blanket with the baby.

"Listening to her tears my heart out." Nona spoke hoarsely, as though she, too, had been crying. "I have to do something. My stepmother used to fix sugar tits for Helen to suck when she was a baby. I don't have any sugar but I'm going to try tying a piece of buckskin with a thong to make a nipple for Amanda Jean to suck on."

The contrivance finally pacified the baby and she fell asleep cuddled against Nona. Aware of Nona's warmth, Spencer turned onto his side and reached for her. If she'd resisted he couldn't have pulled her to him, but she slid closer with a sigh, settling her head on his shoulder when he eased onto his back once again.

He was too feverish and weak for the hot fire of passion to stir inside him but the feel of Nona next to him warmed his heart. He didn't mind that the baby lay between them; he hoped the poor tyke was as comforted as he by Nona's touch. No matter how desperate their circumstances, for the moment, with Nona's head on his shoulder, he had everything he wanted.

Chapter Ten

The caw of a crow woke Nona. She opened her eyes to see, through the screen of cottonwood leaves, a pale sky streaked with dawn pinks and golds. She recalled falling asleep with her head on Spencer's shoulder and the baby between them and how warm and safe she'd felt. Apparently they'd shifted in the night because they now lay back to back with Amanda Jean cuddled in Nona's arms.

By some miracle the baby still slept and Nona hated to move lest she disturb her. Yet she couldn't lie here all day, so she began to ease her arm from under the baby very quietly and carefully.

The crow cawed again from a nearby tree and Nona glanced toward the sound. She stiffened when a flicker of motion between two cottonwoods caught her eye. Was the crow's caw a warning? If so, of what? Hardly daring to breathe, she watched the trees but saw no more movement. At last she decided she'd been mistaken and slowly pulled her arm free of the baby.

The crow burst from one of the cottonwoods in a great flapping of big black wings. It flew toward the stream, cawing. Nona, startled by its sudden flight, froze again. A second later something brown moved between the trees.

A deer? She fervently hoped so. The baby made a tiny whimpering sound, and Spencer shifted his legs. She held her breath. Though uncertain what it was, her instinct told her there was danger between the trees, and if the baby began screaming or Spencer moved enough to prove himself awake, doom would follow.

The brown in the woods moved again, drifting out of her line of vision as it began to circle them, apparently heading for the stream. Nona swallowed to ease her dry throat. She didn't believe it was a deer; she'd spent hours as a girl in the fall woods of New York spotting deer runs for her brothers, and this creature moved all wrong. Besides, she hadn't heard a single twig snap as twigs did under a deer's hoofs. And a crow wouldn't be likely to warn of a deer's passage.

What she'd seen was a man. Spencer had assured her Paquette was dead so it couldn't be him. Anyway, only an Indian could creep through the woods so silently. Terror gripped her.

The Sioux had found them!

Nona bit her lip to stop her involuntary cry of denial. She didn't dare move. Still lying on her side, she apprehensively scanned the woods. Nothing moved. If Sioux warriors were surrounding them she ought to see something. Was it possible there was only one man, possible that Sky Arrow had come after them alone?

She fought down her surge of terror at the thought of becoming Sky Arrow's captive again. If he *was* alone, it meant they had only one man to fear. But Spencer couldn't fight; he was all but helpless.

I can fight! she told herself firmly. I *will* fight!

The pistol, what had she done with the pistol? Cautiously and very slowly, she turned onto her stomach and propped her chin on the blanket. The holstered gun lay partly inside the baby's cradle, within reach if she stretched out her arm and pulled the cradle closer.

He'll see me, she thought. He must have his rifle with him. He'll kill Spencer before I have the Colt in my hand.

The more she thought about it, the more certain she was that the stalker in the trees *was* Sky Arrow and that he was alone. If there'd been more Sioux, by now she, Spencer and the baby would have been surrounded and captured. She could easily imagine Sky Arrow setting off by himself, determined on revenge. She didn't fear her own death at Sky Arrow's hands, she feared Spencer's. The Sioux meant to kill Spencer, she was sure. Unless she found the means to prevent him.

She scanned the woods from her new position and finally a tiny flicker of brown told her Sky Arrow was almost in position to shoot Spencer without harming her. She couldn't delay any longer; she had to take the chance he wouldn't see the cradle moving and realize she was awake. Otherwise they had no chance at all.

Inching her hand toward the cradle, she prayed she'd remember every detail her brothers had taught her about a Colt, how to cock the hammer, how to aim. She'd never checked the gun to see if it needed reloading, an oversight that frightened her. What if there were no bullets in the cylinder?

Her fingers touched, then closed around the decorative fringe of buckskin on the cradle. Keeping her eyes on the woods, she inched the cradle closer. It seemed an eternity before she felt the leather of the holster under her fingers. Hoping her actions were hidden by the cradle, she eased the Colt from the holster and held the pistol concealed under the blanket.

Now she had to turn toward Spencer and toward the death waiting for him. As she carefully changed her position, the crow cawed again from near the stream, locating Sky Arrow for her. Hidden behind Spencer, Nona quickly checked the pistol. Loaded. She hunched herself so she could move in a hurry.

"Ho!" Sky Arrow's shout, his sudden leap from concealment, took her by surprise, even though she'd known approximately where he was. He called more words in Sioux, obviously a challenge, his rifle aimed directly at Spencer.

Nona cocked the Colt's hammer as Spencer jerked awake, tried to lunge to his feet and fell to his knees. She leaned to his right, aimed at Sky Arrow and pulled the trigger of the Colt, one, two, three times. Mixed with the roar of the Colt, she heard the crack of Sky Arrow's rifle. Spencer fell onto his side. Sky Arrow staggered, toppled forward and didn't move. Amanda Jean began screaming.

Terrified she'd shot too late to save Spencer, Nona bent over him, crying his name. She could hardly believe it when he pulled himself into a sitting position and she saw he wasn't even wounded.

"Thank God you're all right!" she cried.

After a wary glance at the fallen Sioux, Spencer eased the Colt from her tense grip. "Help me up," he ordered.

With Nona's aid he walked to Sky Arrow, kneeling and turning the limp body onto its back. Nona grimaced when she saw the three bloody holes in Sky Arrow's bare chest. She felt sick rather than triumphant. She, who'd never shot so much as a squirrel in her life, had killed a man.

Spencer looked up at her. "Where'd you learn to shoot like that?" he asked.

"Bottles on f-fence p-posts." Her voice quivered and broke on the last word. A shattered bottle was nowhere near the same as a dead man.

Spencer pushed himself to his feet and put his arms around her. "You saved my life," he murmured. "You hit him before he fired and that spoiled his aim. His rifle bullet came so close I heard the zing."

As Nona tried to concentrate on her relief that Spencer

was alive, rather than being devastated over killing Sky Arrow, she finally became aware of Amanda Jean's wailing. Easing from Spencer's comforting embrace, she hurried to the baby.

"Is she hurt?" he asked.

"She's hungry." Tears welled in Nona's eyes and she blinked them back as she bent to pick up Amanda Jean. She had no time to cry, she must do her best to quiet the baby by feeding her water, since there was nothing else.

"I'll look for Sky Arrow's pony," Spencer told her, belting on his holster and sheathing the Colt. His movements were slow and careful. He wasn't back to normal by any means, but it lifted Nona's spirits to see he was recovering.

As she tried to coax water from the canteen down Amanda Jean's throat, Nona realized she couldn't have borne it if Sky Arrow had killed Spencer. Something within her would have died, too. An intangible bond linked her with Spencer, and though she had no idea how and when it had formed, nor exactly what it meant, she sensed the bond was there.

The water managed to calm the baby. When Amanda Jean refused to swallow any more, Nona encouraged her to suck the leather nipple. She cleaned the baby, put her into the cradle and was hanging it from a stout branch when Spencer returned.

"The Lakota train their war ponies well," he said, shaking his head. "Sky Arrow left his horse untethered and the pony would have waited hours for his master's return, but he got one whiff of a stranger and took off for home before I could get anywhere near him. I found no sign other Lakota were with Sky Arrow—he came alone."

He eased onto the blanket and propped himself onto his elbow. She noticed his strained face and her heart sank. On foot, Spencer wasn't going to be able to travel far, if at all.

He sighed. "Have to admit I'm pretty well done in. Kaintuck's leg isn't healed, he can't take me far. It's safer to stay here rather than take a chance on me breaking down where there's no water or trees to make camp."

"Kaintuck pulled you on the travois yesterday," she reminded him. "We could try that again."

"Kaintuck and I will both be the better for one more day here," he said. "We have a rifle now and I'll hunt for food. There are deer tracks on the stream bank—I could be lucky enough to bag a deer. We need to eat and the juice from the meat might nourish the baby."

Nona, thinking about traveling without food and with nothing for Amanda Jean, nodded. Spencer was right.

"First we have to bury Sky Arrow, Lakota fashion," he said.

With Nona's reluctant help, Spencer hoisted Sky Arrow's body into the crotch of a tree. After they finished, Spencer chanted a few words in Sioux and Nona couldn't hold back her tears.

"I hated him," she sobbed, "but I wish I hadn't been forced to kill him."

Spencer put an arm around her and drew her close. "You're the most courageous, most resourceful woman I ever met," he told her. "Don't blame yourself for what you had to do to save us both."

"What—what did you say in Sioux?" she asked, pulling free to look into his face. "Was it a prayer?"

"I asked *Wakan Tanka*, the Great Spirit, to set his dead grandson's feet on the spirit path. Who knows, someday I may meet Sky Arrow's spirit there myself."

Nona stared at him. "You don't really believe that, do you?"

Spencer shrugged. "I believe in a Great Spirit, yes, and what Dancing Coyote taught me makes as much sense as anything I learned from Father Kennedy, the traveling parish priest in Minnesota."

As they walked slowly back to their campsite, Nona pondered Spencer's religious views, feeling she couldn't accept them. Singing Reed had insisted the Sioux *Wakan Tanka* was the same as God, as Jesus, but— Nona stopped dead, her hand flying to her mouth. Beside her, Spencer swore and halted, too.

Singing Reed herself stood beside a tree, facing them, bow drawn, arrow nocked.

Addressing Spencer, the Sioux woman spoke in her own tongue.

"Speak so I can understand!" Nona begged, terrified Singing Reed would let the arrow fly. If she did, Spencer hadn't a chance.

"He killed my brother, he dies," Singing Reed said, her gaze fixed on Spencer.

"I shot Sky Arrow!" Nona's voice rose. "I killed your brother."

"I kill Buffalo Rider." Singing Reed didn't so much as glance at her and Nona realized the Sioux woman didn't believe her. Would never believe her, even though she spoke the truth.

"Wait!" Nona pleaded, frantically asking herself how she could save Spencer. "Paquette was after you—this man killed him. You're free of Paquette."

Singing Reed shrugged off Paquette. "Buffalo Rider killed my brother, he dies."

"I offer a trade," Nona said desperately, not knowing what she meant to say until the words came out of her mouth. "Light of Sun for his life."

For the first time the Sioux woman shifted her gaze to Nona. "You give me Light of Sun?"

"Yes, yes. If you don't kill Buffalo Rider."

For a long moment Singing Reed didn't move, the arrow aimed at Spencer's chest. Then she released the pressure on the bowstring and thrust the arrow into the quiver on her back. Spencer's hand hovered over the handle of his Colt but didn't draw the gun.

Singing Reed turned her back on them and strode toward the cradle hanging from a tree branch. She lifted out the whimpering Amanda Jean, and pulling aside her tunic, held the baby to her breast.

Tears ran down Nona's face as she watched the baby nurse eagerly. Would she ever see Amanda Jean again? What had she done?

Spencer stared from the weeping Nona to Singing Reed and the baby, torn between the honoring of a promise and the reality of losing Nona's niece to the Lakota. Singing Reed was no longer a threat; he could easily kill her. If he could bring himself to such a dishonorable act. For Nona he could. He would if she wanted him to.

His life in exchange for the baby. Nona loved Amanda Jean, how could she have made the sacrifice to give up the baby forever? God knows he wasn't worth it. His fingers touched the butt of his Colt as his gaze met Nona's.

She shook her head. "I promised," she sobbed. "I gave my word."

His hand dropped away from the gun.

Singing Reed paid neither any heed until the baby was through nursing. After she packed the child tenderly into the cradle and positioned it on her back, she turned to them. "I follow my brother when he hunt you," she said. "His pony find me, I know what happen. Now pony carry him home."

Spencer realized Singing Reed meant she'd recovered the war pony. Knowing she must have ridden her own pony to get here, he decided to try bargaining.

"We have a travois," he said in Dakota. "You have two ponies. If we give you the travois, you won't need two ponies."

Her gaze was impassive as it swept over him, over Nona, Kaintuck and the makeshift travois. Finally she spoke.

"You take Twisted Ear from my tipi, he come back. I give him to you. Someday he come back to me."

Aware now of Twisted Ear's talent for escaping his tether, Spencer thought it quite possible she was right—a horse determined to escape, usually does. Just the same, he was grateful for her offer to return the pony to them. Though he wasn't sure he had enough energy left to help her lift Sky Arrow's body from the tree to the travois, he meant to try.

Later, when he was sure Twisted Ear was firmly tethered next to Kaintuck and Singing Reed had left the camp with her brother's body and the baby, Spencer collapsed onto the blanket.

"Sit beside me," he urged Nona.

After she did, he handed her a strip of pemmican. "Singing Reed shared her food with us," he said and began to chew hungrily on his chunk of dried meat and berries.

"Why would she do that?" Nona asked. "I don't understand Indians."

"The Lakota share with friends. We're her friends. You erased the blood feud between Singing Reed and me when you gave her the baby."

Nona ate without saying any more, finishing her pemmican almost as quickly as he did. He offered her a drink from the canteen and took one himself when she was through.

He set the canteen aside, reached for her hand and brought it to his lips. Even if he hadn't been so damn tired, he couldn't have found words to tell her how he felt about what she'd done for him. In the Dakota tongue he'd say that she'd touched his heart and the words would have a deep and true meaning, but in English they

156

sounded false and insincere, words a man might use to try to seduce a woman. At the moment, seducing Nona was the farthest thing from his mind.

With her hand locked securely in his, he dropped into a deep sleep.

Nona looked down at Spencer's sleeping face, covered with a week's growth of black beard, and sighed. Amanda Jean might not have been hers to trade but what was done was done. She'd had no choice. She'd saved Spencer's life by giving the baby to Singing Reed and may well have saved the baby's life as well—but she hadn't made the trade for the baby's sake. She'd done it because she wanted Spencer alive and she knew she'd do everything she could to keep him that way.

She had no idea how she'd ever explain to Kilby why she'd given the baby away. Helen might have understood but Kilby, never. He seemed a distant dream; she could hardly remember him being a part of her life. But he had been and would be again when she returned to Fort Lincoln. As Amanda Jean's father, he had every right to rage and refuse to forgive her. She could hardly forgive herself.

Nevertheless, she'd do it again if she had to.

Carefully, not wanting to disturb Spencer, she freed her hand from his grasp and was upset to see a smear of dried blood on her wrist. Certain it had come from Sky Arrow's body, Nona felt bile rise into her throat.

Determined to wash her hands, she rose and hurried to the stream. Once there, she decided she needed to clean more than her hands and face—she hadn't had time to bathe since she'd escaped from the Sioux camp. Spencer had thought it safe here for another day, so she'd take this chance to scrub herself free of Paquette's touch, as well as any trace of Sky Arrow's blood.

Moving upstream until bushes screened her from the sleeping Spencer, Nona unwound her braids from the coils atop her head and unbraided her hair. She stripped off her moccasins, tunic and leggings and waded into the cool water. Though she had no soap root such as Singing Reed had given her at the camp, she sat in the shallow stream, splashing water over herself and rubbing her hands vigorously over her skin. How good it felt to be clean again! A yellow-throated bird lit on a willow branch overhanging the stream and cocked its head to eye her, then warbled a long trill.

"I take it you approve of bathing," she said to the bird.

She was bending over sluicing water through her hair, when a tingling along her spine warned her she was no longer alone and that it wasn't a bird watching her. Tensing, she straightened and glanced quickly around.

Spencer leaned against the trunk of the willow. "You're the most beautiful woman I've ever set eyes on," he told her.

Nona gasped and quickly sat down in the water, crossing her arms over her breasts, both relieved and annoyed. Thank God it was Spencer and not some new threat. On the other hand, he should have whistled or called out or something to let her know he was awake.

"A gentleman would turn his back," she said severely, uncomfortably aware she was blushing.

He smiled at her. "I think we agreed aboard the *Lady Jane* that I was no gentleman." As he spoke he pulled off his buckskin shirt.

Nona was distracted for a moment when she saw he'd previously removed her makeshift bandages and that the knife wound had started to heal. She realized she was staring, not only at the healing gash, but at the thatch of curly black hair between his tiny nipples, so she hastily averted her gaze—only to see him kick off his moccasins and begin unbuckling his belt. Her eyes widened in disbelief.

"Spencer!" Her voice rose indignantly. "You aren't thinking of bathing while I'm here!"

"Why not? I'll be glad to turn my back so you can wash it."

Tossing modesty to the warm May breeze, she sprang to her feet and hastily splashed to the bank where she grabbed up her clothes and held them in front of her, watching him warily.

He continued to undress and finally she fled into the trees. He didn't follow her. As she yanked on her clothes, she heard him splashing in the stream. Nona wrung the water from her hair, listening to him whistle a marching tune she recognized as one the Seventh Cavalry Band played. Just because they were alone together, he needn't think she'd abandoned all notions of propriety.

Admit it, she told herself, you wanted to stay there and watch him finish undressing. You wanted to see him as he'd seen you. Naked. You wanted to be in the water with him, wanted. . . .

Nona compressed her lips. Yes, maybe so, but she knew better than to give way to any such crazy impulses. While she couldn't deny the bond between them, that didn't mean he had the right to invade her privacy.

Spencer Quinlan was no gentleman.

And you don't care if he isn't, she admitted. You even hope he won't be. He's the most exciting, fascinating man you've ever met. He's not merely Spencer Quinlan, he's Buffalo Rider, dashing and brave and wild.

Did he really think she was the most beautiful woman he'd ever seen?

Spencer left his chest bare to the sun and the air as he returned to the blanket. He needed rest, the effort to wash himself had sapped all his strength. He was a damn

159

fool to go haring down to the creek when he woke, found her gone and then heard her splashing but he couldn't resist the chance to see her nude. God, she was lovely. He wanted that woman like he'd never wanted another, and if he wasn't so exhausted, he'd damn well do something about it.

"Nona!" he called.

She walked from between the trees, stopped short of the blanket and stood looking at him, her expression wary. Scared her, he thought. Or maybe she was pretending to be scared because she thought she ought to be. He'd not had much experience with schoolmarms and never one from New York.

"Wake me at dusk so I can hunt," he said to her and she nodded.

The deer would come to the stream at dusk and he'd be waiting. How different it was to plan the killing of a deer now that he'd slipped into thinking like a Dakota again. A hunter had to be clean, had to enter into the spirit of the hunt, knowing the deer's life was as important as his own, equal to his own, and the only reason to take the deer's life was to sustain his. This is what he must tell the deer when he apologized for killing it—the reason why.

Would he be as open and honest with the beautiful and elusive Nona when the time came to take her? He closed his eyes and imagined her as she'd been in the stream, washing her glorious hair and, tired as he was, desire stirred within him. Soon, he thought. Soon. . . .

Sleep grasped him with eagle talons and whirled him away from the familiar into the strange. When the eagle spoke, he understood Dancing Coyote's spirit was in the bird.

"Grandfather," he said, *"I thank you for my life."*

"I did not save you," the eagle said, *"you saved yourself by recalling what you learned as a boy. Why do you forget the other lessons you were taught as a child? Why do you*

160

forget you must be a man with a brave and strong heart instead of a weak and foolish heart?"

His words reminded Spencer of an oft-repeated boyhood story: Two young Dakota men went out searching for buffalo and met a strangely beautiful young woman singing alone on the plains.

"We will overpower her and enjoy her," one said.

"We must not, she looks like a spirit woman who should be respected," the other warned, though he, too, desired her.

The first man paid no attention. Overcome by his lust, he forced the woman to the ground to have his way with her. Suddenly a great mist blotted out earth and sky alike and, when it lifted, the foolish man lay dead under the hoofs of a white buffalo. The stronghearted man returned to his people with a sacred pipe, the gift of White Buffalo Woman.

"I remember the story of the white buffalo, grandfather," Spencer said.

The eagle examined him with a fierce yellow eye. *"Then you know why you still walk the earth instead of treading the spirit path with Sky Arrow."*

But Spencer did not know why.

The eagle released him and Spencer floated down and down until he stood on the ground with brown hills stretching to every side. He waited but the eagle was gone and there was nothing to see except the hills, so he began walking. No matter how far he walked the hills remained the same. He met no one, no animals, no birds. There were no trees, no streams. He was alone and he despaired.

A thin mist settled over the land, thickened, and in its midst he thought he glimpsed a white buffalo. He ran toward it but the mist receded as he approached, always the same distance away.

"Grandfather," he begged, *"help me."*

A voice spoke to him from the mist but it was not the voice of Dancing Coyote, it was a woman's voice.

"What do you see?" she asked.

161

"*A white buffalo.*"

"*Your eyes are closed. You will never see truly unless you open them,*" the woman said.

The misty image of the white buffalo began to fade.

"*Wait!*" he begged. "*Help me.*"

"*Wake,*" she urged, "*and you will need no help. Wake.*"

Chapter Eleven

Nona, standing over Spencer, called to him three times, telling him it was time to wake up. When he didn't rouse, she reached down to shake his shoulder. Before she touched him, Spencer's eyes opened and he stared up at her as though she were a stranger. Nona drew back her hand quickly.

"Spencer," she said. "It's dusk. You asked me to wake you."

He blinked and recognition warmed his eyes. "Nona." Though he said her name softly, almost caressingly, she couldn't interpret his expression. He yawned, stretched and winced slightly as he sat up. She knew it must be because of the healing chest wound.

Having been raised with two brothers, she also knew enough not to ask if his chest hurt. Men hated to admit to pain.

"I walked upstream and found a spot with dozens of deer tracks on the bank," she said. "And deer droppings nearby."

He rose to his feet, pulled on his buckskin shirt and picked up the rifle before he spoke. "How far upstream?"

"I'll show you. Don't worry, I've gone deer hunting before and I learned the hard way not to move a muscle or

163

utter one word while waiting."

"An older brother?"

"Two."

He grinned. "That's a good enough recommendation." His smile faded. "I want you with me, anyway. We've had too many unpleasant surprises."

Nona grimaced, remembering Paquette.

"It didn't cross my mind Singing Reed might follow her brother," Spencer said. "I might have known she'd be concerned for you."

"For me?" Nona was astounded.

"You're her friend. Singing Reed expected Sky Arrow to kill me and she wanted to prevent him from mistreating you."

Nona shuddered. It had come so close to happening that way, Spencer dead and she a Sioux captive again. Such a small thing had saved them—a crow's caw.

"I never really appreciated crows before," she said and told him why she'd changed her mind about the birds.

"Dancing Coyote raised a pet crow from a fledgling," Spencer said. "The bird used to sit on a lodgepole of his tipi and warn of visitors long before they came near the lodge. Dancing Coyote claimed the crow also foretold the weather. They're smart birds. If you shoot one of a flock of crows, forever after every crow that saw the shooting will recognize a gun and not come near a man who carries one."

"It's lucky crows sleep at night or we might never get near a deer," she said.

Nona led Spencer upriver to the deer watering place and sat quietly beside him in the gloom under the trees. After a few moments the frogs who'd fallen silent at their coming resumed their evening song. From a branch somewhere above, a sleepy bird called once and fell silent. Stars glimmered in what Nona could see of the sky's deep blue. The stream gurgled past and a damp cool breeze stirred the leaves, bringing the smell of moist earth and a faint, unidentifiable fragrance.

In New York the apple blossoms would be filling the orchards with sweetness and the promise of the harvest to come. In New York, Dorothy did not yet know her daughter was dead and her grandchild lost forever. Nona tried to swallow but there was a lump in her throat.

Beside her, Spencer, on one knee, cradled the rifle, waiting. The sky darkened. Small rustlings around them betrayed the comings and goings of the little animals who foraged at night. The distant hoot of an owl floated across the stream. A twig snapped somewhere behind them and Nona resisted the urge to turn and look.

Even with the snapped twig to warn her, the deer appeared so suddenly they seemed to materialize like brown ghosts beside the stream—four of them, no, six; she hadn't at first seen the two fawns. They dipped their heads to drink and Spencer's rifle cracked. One of the adult deer staggered forward into the stream and dropped. The other five bolted into the darkness under the trees.

Spencer rose, handed her the rifle and walked to the fallen deer. He bent his head as though whispering into the animal's ear, just as he'd done with the buffalo.

"We'll drag him closer to camp," he said, turning to her, "build a fire for light, then gut and butcher the carcass Dakota-fashion. We'll cook and eat what we can and save some for drying. I'll haul the rest across the stream and leave it a long way from camp. I haven't heard any wolves or coyotes near us or seen any sign, but I don't want to take a chance."

Until that moment, it hadn't occurred to Nona to worry about wolves or coyotes. Back home in New York she'd never had to. Wolves were confined to the mountains and New York didn't have coyotes.

The thin moon rode high by the time they finished

165

eating the chunks of venison roasted over the fire. Never had meat tasted so good to Nona. She watched Spencer hoist what was left of the meat high into a tree downriver from camp.

"Out of the reach of wolves?" she asked nervously as they walked back to the dying fire.

"A precaution, that's all."

Nona didn't care to dwell on the possibility wolves might prowl through these woods at night, so she changed the subject. "What did you say to the deer after you shot him?"

"I told his spirit why I shot him and thanked him for giving his life to help us live."

He sounded perfectly serious. Taken aback, Nona said nothing. When she'd met Spencer on the *Lady Jane* he'd seemed no more than a brash, if attractive, newspaper correspondent. He was, she'd discovered, far more than that. At times, though, his Indianness made her uneasy. He wasn't, after all, really a Dakota—he was as white as she was.

The coals of the fire watched like red eyes when they finally stretched out on the bedraggled blanket she'd mutilated for bandages. Nona pulled her share of the second, intact blanket over her and lay with her back to Spencer, taking care not to touch him in any way. She'd shared these same blankets with him before. Why did it seem so different tonight?

Because the baby wasn't here for her to worry and fuss over? Thinking of Amanda Jean made the tears start, as hard as she tried to hold them back. She attempted to stifle her weeping, not wanting to disturb Spencer.

"I'm sorry about the baby," he said after a time. "Even I miss her."

His sympathy undermined her control and she broke into great wrenching sobs, hardly aware, in her misery, of Spencer's hands turning her and urging her into his arms. She wept on his shoulder while he stroked her back and murmured soothingly, his breath stirring her hair.

Some of his words penetrated her grief.

". . . wanted and loved . . . best of care . . ."

Yes, Singing Reed loved Amanda Jean and Nona knew the Sioux woman would care for the baby as if she were her own daughter. It was small comfort for the baby's loss but it was all Nona had.

No, not all. Spencer was alive. Nona's sobs quieted as she admitted to herself she'd make the trade again to save his life.

Snuggled close to him she felt safe and protected; she didn't even worry about prowling wolves.

"You taste nicely salty," he told her, and she realized his lips were touching her wet cheek.

Now was the time to free herself, to turn her back to him again, give up the warmth and comfort he offered. Nona didn't move. How could she, when of its own volition, her hand was reaching to caress his dark curls? How could she possibly turn away when his lips were blazing a fiery path along her throat, kindling tiny flames inside her?

His mouth claimed hers. He tasted of venison, wild and delicious; his scent surrounded her, compellingly male. His kiss intoxicated her, making nonsense of all the reasons why she shouldn't be in his arms. She tingled all over with wanting more of his touch.

Her lips parted under the insistent pressure of his, and his tongue, hot and exciting, invaded her mouth, sending tiny arrows of delight to bury themselves deep within her. His hands slid under her tunic, caressing the bare flesh of her back, making her body ache with the need to feel his touch everywhere.

Their surroundings faded; she and Spencer inhabited a world of their own where nothing mattered except his kisses and caresses. Nothing existed for her except him.

"Nona." His husky whisper was a snare, trapping her, making her weak with longing.

Spencer would teach her what she'd always been afraid to learn—the wonder a man could bring to a woman. His embrace made her eager to discover the secrets he knew and she did not. He was the only man who could ever be her teacher in this old-as-time but new-to-her art.

Her body knew more than she did; it throbbed and tingled in places she'd never before realized needed a man's touch. When Spencer's fingers brushed over her nipple and his hand covered her breast, she moaned in yearning pleasure.

She heard Spencer catch his breath, knew he wanted what she did and was thrilled to realize she had the power to make him feel the same eager passion surging through her with every heart beat.

A distant sound flicked at her attention, boring a tiny hole in the enclosed world-for-two she and Spencer inhabited. The noise grew louder, more insistent, until she was forced to recognize what she heard.

Howling.

Nona tensed. She pulled free of Spencer's embrace and sat up. "Wolves!" she gasped.

He didn't move. "Coyotes. They've found the carcass."

She clutched his arm, listening to the sounds change to snarling yips. One of the horses stamped and snorted. Until that moment she hadn't given a thought to the horses. Why didn't Spencer leap to his feet and grab the rifle?

"How can you tell the difference?" she demanded.

"Coyotes don't sound the same as wolves. They've got a different pitch. Coyotes won't bother us or the horses; they'll feast on what's left of the deer, that's all. Don't worry."

Nona eased back down onto the blanket, but the

intrusion of the coyotes' howling had shattered their separate world beyond repair.

How could she have behaved with such reckless abandon? she asked herself, huddling away from Spencer. He seemed to sense her withdrawal for he made no move to touch her. Perhaps she ought to appreciate his understanding but, perversely, she half-wished he'd sweep her back into his arms, pay no attention to her protests and whirl her away again up and up into the dangerous heights of passion.

Restless, Nona listened for the coyotes, but they made no more noise. She was disturbed by an unsatisfied ache inside her, an unfamiliar ache and one she realized only Spencer could assuage. Yet he, she was sure from his deep and regular breathing, had fallen asleep almost immediately. How could he?

What he'd told her aboard the *Lady Jane* came back to haunt her. There was no place for marriage in Spencer Quinlan's roving life. She'd been brought up to believe love between a man and woman led to marriage.

Love? She stared up at the stars through the lacework of the leaves. Was what she felt for him love? She'd imagined herself in love with Kilby, but that feeling seemed a pale and thin emotion compared to her overwhelming need for Spencer.

Once she'd labeled her attraction to Spencer as lust and had been ashamed of it. Nona bit her lip. She'd killed a man and traded away her helpless little niece so Spencer might live. Not so he'd love her or marry her but just to keep him alive. If he died her world would never be the same; she couldn't bear to think of a world without him. No matter what he felt for her—lust, passion—she loved him. And always would.

But she had to face the fact that marriage was not in his plans. No matter how she longed to melt into his arms, she didn't dare to. Sooner or later he'd leave her behind, whether or not she surrendered to her passion. Wouldn't it be easier to bear if she hadn't made love with him?

Nona sighed. Her mind urged caution but her body longed to throw caution to the winds and take whatever he offered. Wasn't half a loaf better than none? To love to the full as long as it lasted?

And then what? She fell asleep with the question unanswered.

The morning sky was overcast, gray with the threat of rain.

"We've been lucky," Spencer said as he roasted the remaining chunks of venison over a smoky fire. "Good weather never lasts."

Nona, feeling as sullen as the sky, muttered, "Does anything?"

He slanted her a look before giving her one of his mocking smiles, something he hadn't done since Fort Lincoln. Looking off into the trees, he spoke slowly—as though, she thought, he was translating from another language:

> "The eagle dies and the buffalo,
> The pine grows, falls and dies
> The corn is harvested and eaten
> I, too, will die—and you
> Only the sun is forever, and the moon
> Only the earth lives on . . ."

Moved in spite of herself, Nona lost her urge to remind him he wasn't Dakota. No doubt there was good in the Dakota way, but there was also bad. As there was in the ways of the white man.

"Flowers don't last long either," she observed, a bit of tartness creeping into her tone. "Are you advising 'gather ye rosebuds while ye may'?"

"Why not?" Again the mocking smile.

How she hated that smile. You won't gather me, she vowed.

After they ate, she rolled up the blankets while Spencer saddled the horses.

"You ride Kaintuck," he told her. "It'll be less weight for him to carry."

Nona examined the chestnut's foreleg and found the swelling down but not completely gone. "We shouldn't push him," she warned.

"I wasn't planning to. We're moving on because it's not wise to camp in one place too long, even though I think we're fairly safe except for being too far south. There may yet be Lakota riding west from the reservation near Fort Rice—going to join Sitting Bull at the Greasy Grass—the Little Bighorn River—like the band we were with."

Sitting Bull? Where had she heard the name before? Kilby? Libbie Custer? "Who is this Sitting Bull?" she asked. "An Indian warrior?"

Spencer shook his head. "A Lakota medicine man. They respect the power of his visions. I'd like to meet him and talk to him."

"Aren't you *persona non grata* in Sioux camps now?"

"In some of them anyway. But I may get to meet Sitting Bull when I ride with Custer and the Seventh."

Nona had almost forgotten Spencer's reason for coming to Fort Lincoln—to report on General Custer's campaign against the hostile Indians.

"We'll ride north," he said. "It'll start raining soon, so we'll camp early."

When the rain began they were once again in the middle of nowhere, as Nona termed it. Low hills, green with spring grass, stretched in every direction. Without the sun as a guide, she had no idea how Spencer knew they were headed in the right direction for he didn't have a compass. Still, she trusted his ability.

A sideways glance showed her his black curls were soaked and rain trickled down his face. Her head was relatively dry, thanks to his hat that he'd insisted she go on wearing, but it wasn't fair of her to keep the hat in the rain.

"Would you like your hat back?" she asked, the first she'd spoken since they rode from the camp.

"No, you keep it." He didn't look at her.

Nona felt like hurling the hat at him. She was wet and getting chilled and she was miserable. The least he could do was talk to her.

"Maybe you've missed General Custer," she said to prod him. "Maybe he's already gone after the hostiles with the Seventh."

"I doubt it. He isn't due back at the fort from Washington for another couple of days. If then."

"What do you mean, 'if then'? I thought you believed he'd succeed no matter who opposed him."

"Custer went to Washington to try to improve conditions at the Indian agencies. He knows, as anyone who knows anything about it does, that there's a good bit of graft at the expense of the Indians, but Custer's up against the fact that President Grant's brother may be mixed up in the cheating at the agencies. Custer's in the right; there's no doubt of it, but I don't imagine the President's happy with his testimony. Grant may not allow Custer to return to Fort Lincoln, no matter how many strings Custer has to pull."

She stared at him. "You don't really think General Custer might not come back, do you?"

"I'd lay odds he does—though he might be delayed. Autie Custer's a hard man to keep down. I'm looking forward to riding with him and the Seventh."

"I don't understand you. One minute you're an advocate of Indian life and the next you're eager to be a part of a campaign against them."

172

"I'm neither an Indian nor a trooper. I'm an observer. A reporter."

"You mean you don't take sides?"

Spencer didn't reply immediately. "I try to write an unbiased account of what I see," he said finally, "but I guess I mostly belong in the Indian camp. Not that I admit it when I ride with soldiers. How can I when they're being killed by Indians?"

Nona wasn't surprised, she'd known he was on the side of the Indians. Well, *she* certainly wasn't.

"Why did you bother to come to my rescue if you're such a friend of the Sioux?" she challenged.

"You know why."

She shrugged. "Because white women captives are cruelly mistreated by the warriors and you don't approve. I think you said."

He shot her a dark look. "Sky Arrow had no right to you." Anger edged his voice. At her? At the dead Sioux? "You belong to—" He stopped abruptly. "To another people," he finished lamely.

Was it possible he'd intended to say she belonged to him? What nerve! She belonged to no one but herself. Certainly not to Spencer Quinlan, whatever he might think. Even if he *had* rescued her. But she was too dispirited by the continuing rain to maintain her anger.

They rode in sodden silence until Spencer pointed left. "We're coming to another creek," he said. "We've pushed Kaintuck enough for one day. We'll camp."

Nona didn't argue, she could hardly wait for the comfort of a fire—providing they could manage one, as wet as everything was. She'd never thought to wish for a tipi but if they'd been dragging one on a travois they'd have a warm, cozy shelter. Instead, all they could hope for was to huddle under the branches of a cottonwood with no more than leaves to protect them from the rain.

When they pulled up the horses by the tree-bordered

173

creek, she dismounted and started to unsaddle Kaintuck, but Spencer stopped her. "Just tether the horses for now," he told her.

Nona shrugged and tied Twisted Ear securely to a sapling before tethering Kaintuck. Spencer, she saw, was cutting branches.

"I wish pine and cedar grew in the Dakota Territory like they do in Minnesota's Big Woods," he said. "Evergreen branches are better for lean-tos."

Cheered to realize they'd have a shelter of sorts, Nona pulled her knife from its sheath and helped him, almost forgetting her misery as together they weaved cottonwood and willow branches into a makeshift lean-to against a broad tree trunk.

When they finished, Spencer unsaddled the horses and lugged the saddles into the tiny shelter where he turned them upside down, dry side up. He removed the blankets—dry because he'd stuffed them into the saddlebags before they set off—and handed her one, saying, "Get out of those wet clothes and wrap yourself in this." Without waiting to see if she obeyed, he began stripping.

Nona hastily turned her back, reluctant to take off her clothes in the enforced intimacy of the tiny shelter. Yet if she didn't she'd remain wet and chilled. Finally deciding comfort was more important than modesty, she pulled off her tunic. With the blanket draped over her shoulders, she removed her leggings. It was wonderful to be rid of the wet garments.

Clutching the blanket around her, she turned warily to face Spencer and found him perched on Kaintuck's inverted saddle, folded into his blanket. A giggle took her by surprise.

He raised his eyebrows.

"You look so odd," she explained.

He grinned. "You're not exactly a fashion plate

yourself. Unless this year's Paris styles feature Army blankets."

"What day is it?" she asked abruptly. "I know it's May, but I've lost track of the days."

Spencer thought a moment. "I figure it's the seventh. Why?"

Nona eased herself onto the other saddle, keeping the blanket carefully in place, acutely aware of how close they were in the tiny brush shelter and desperately certain her only safety lay in talking. "Your tactful comment on French fashions reminded me that before I knew I was coming to Fort Lincoln, I planned to visit Philadelphia to see the Centennial Exposition. It opens in three days."

"So it does. I admit I'd quite forgotten."

"You aren't interested in the Centennial?"

Spencer scowled. "I don't feel at home east of the Mississippi."

Nona stared at him. Was he actually admitting to a flaw?

"Folks back east are good at what you're doing right this minute," he continued, "looking down their noses at others. I never took to snobbishness."

"I am *not* snobbish!"

His gaze wandered over her, from the coils of her damp braids to her bare feet. "Pretty hard to be, given the circumstances, yet there it is."

She refused to acknowledge the heat his appraisal generated deep inside her. Instead, she glared at him.

He offered his mocking smile. "You couldn't be a true snob if your life depended on it, Miss Willard. For one thing, your mind's too inquisitive. For another, Singing Reed named you right, you have a good heart. Even if you do look down your nose at me from time to time for my uncouth ways."

It was far safer to keep talking than to think about how

naked they were under their respective blankets. If he wanted home truths, she had a few ready for him. "Uncouth's the wrong word. Exasperating is the one I'd choose. I dislike being mocked."

Spencer sobered. "Not guilty," he insisted.

"Then just what does that lopsided grin of yours mean?"

"I mock myself."

His expression was so serious she had to believe him. "What on earth for?" she asked after a few moments.

He shrugged, either unable or unwilling to explain. "What did you most want to see at the Exposition?" he asked, obviously changing the subject.

Nona lifted her chilled feet higher on the saddle, wishing she could sit Indian-fashion and tuck them under the blanket. The Philadelphia Exposition seemed as far away as the moon, but afraid of silence, she tried to think what had most interested her.

"I heard there was an instrument called the telephone a person can speak into and be heard by another person miles away," she told Spencer. "Doesn't that sound fascinating? Almost like magic? At the Centennial, its inventor, a Mr. Bell, is to demonstrate how the machine works."

He raised his eyebrows. "What, not Paris fashions? Miss Willard, you're a constant surprise and delight."

Was he mocking her, despite his disclaimer? Nona wasn't sure. "Am I to go back to calling you Mr. Quinlan?" she asked lightly.

He didn't smile and his dark gaze caught hers, trapping her so she couldn't look away. "I'm afraid we've come much too far to take any steps backward."

He was, she knew, referring to last night. All day they'd both pretended nothing had happened, but at last he was challenging her to face what lay between them. She could refuse, she could go on chattering, but all the words in the world wouldn't put out the smoldering fuse that sparked and sputtered in her. She was certain he was affected in the same way. Their feelings threatened to set off an explosion she both feared and desired.

"Do you know what your eyes tell me?" he demanded.

She shook her head, certain her eyes revealed far too much.

"Shall I show you?" His voice had grown husky, undermining what meager resolve she'd been able to muster.

"I—I'm afraid," she managed to whisper.

"I'd never hurt you."

Not deliberately, she knew that. But he would, all the same. Hadn't he warned her aboard the *Lady Jane*?

His arm eased free of the blanket and it slid from his broad shoulders. Nona sucked in her breath as she stared at his bare chest. Why was it so exciting to look at him now, so different than it had been when she'd dressed his wound? She longed to touch him, all she could think of was how wonderful his skin would feel under her hands.

Slowly he reached toward her until his fingers rested over her fingers clutching her blanket. His hand was warm and forceful as he loosened her grip on the gray wool. As her blanket fell away he stood and pulled her to her feet, his glance caressing her nakedness.

When he looked into her eyes again the passion and longing she saw made her heart pound like a Sioux drum summoning her to his embrace.

Chapter Twelve

In the dim light of the small enclosure, the luster of Nona's fair skin reminded Spencer of his mother's pearls—opalescent and beautiful. When he touched Nona she'd be warm like the pearls—no, warmer, much warmer. She'd be vibrantly alive in his arms. He ached to hold her.

"Your hair." He spoke hoarsely. "Take down your hair for me, Nona."

Her eyes never left his as she lifted her arms to release the coil on her head, her graceful movement raising her breasts so provocatively a tremor ran through him. Not from chill but from need. Her fingers undid her long braid and her wonderful chestnut hair rippled over her shoulders.

With a quick shove, he thrust the two saddles apart and flung one of the blankets onto the relatively dry ground between them. He stood facing Nona, so close he could see the pulse in her neck fluttering like a trapped bird. He held out his hand.

Nona put her hand in his and he urged her sideways until they both stood on the blanket. Then he brought her hand to his lips as he'd done when he was weak and ill. At that time the feel of her fingers against his lips had

178

been comforting. Now every fleeting touch of her skin roused him further. He kissed her palm and tasted it with his tongue. She drew in her breath.

He placed her hand on his shoulder and released it, slid his hand down along the curve of her hip and drew her into his arms, where she belonged. She sighed when she pressed closer, as though agreeing.

How soft she was. Because she was tall for a woman, her body fit against his as though she'd been made for him. He lowered his head to her lips, to taste again the potent sweetness of her mouth. She'd learned to part her lips so his tongue could enter and the awareness he'd taught her sent a thrill of possessiveness through him. His, she was his; she belonged to him and to no one else.

He trailed kisses along her throat and down to the upper swell of her breast. She clung to him, moaning as he took her nipple into his mouth and his desire mounted until he had to fight to control himself. When he felt her tremble in his arms, he eased her down until they both lay on the blanket. Holding her to him with one arm, he reached his hand for the other blanket and pulled it over them.

The rain pattered on the leaves above the shelter and from somewhere inside he heard a drip-drip-drip that told him the lean-to wasn't completely waterproof. It didn't matter. Nothing mattered as long as Nona was in his arms.

He knew she was inexperienced, that he'd be the first man for her, and he meant to be as gentle as his increasing need would allow. She trusted him. Giving her pleasure was as important as fulfilling himself. More important.

Her breasts were so lovely, her skin so smooth. She tasted of the rain and of herself, her taste and her scent drugged him until he couldn't think, he could only make love to her, on and on, forever.

179

She moaned in pleasure as he caressed her thighs, his fingers probing the fragile petals between. She clung to him, pressing closer, offering herself with the passion he'd sensed within her from the first.

He murmured to her, telling her how beautiful she was, how much he wanted her, meaning every word but finding words inadequate to say everything he meant. He kissed her mouth, her breasts, felt her writhe in need beneath him and knew he couldn't hold back much longer. He parted her thighs and rose over her.

She was warm and moist to his gentle probing and she arched to him, pulling him to her until, in his frenzied need, he forgot to be gentle and plunged deep within her.

"Oh!" she cried and tensed.

Spencer stopped. He hadn't meant to hurt her. He never wanted to hurt her. His lips sought hers, offering an apology with kisses. When he tried to withdraw she clung to him, refusing to let him go. Soon her fingers began caressing his back and he moved again, stroking in a slow rhythm. He felt her start to move with him and an exultant thrill shook him.

Her soft whimpering murmurs of pleasure increased his own pleasure, igniting a fierce and all-consuming passion that took him out of himself and sent him soaring on eagle wings. With Nona, always with Nona. Together they flew higher and higher until they were consumed by the golden radiance of the sun.

Drowsy and happy, Nona lay with her head on Spencer's shoulder, his arm nestling her against him. From his even breathing, she thought he must be asleep. She was almost alseep herself.

Though her need for Spencer's embrace had driven her to make love with him, she hadn't known what to expect beyond the kisses and caresses. She closed her eyes and breathed deeply, smelling the wet leaves and damp earth of their shelter, and mingling with these odors, the strange and wonderful scent of lovemaking. Their lovemaking, hers and Spencer's.

Trying to recall every precious second of joining with him was like trying to describe ecstasy. Impossible. It had to be experienced, not described or memorized. She'd often wondered in secret exactly how men and women came together—surely not like stallions and mares!—and what she and Spencer had done together amazed her. If she hadn't been so caught up in the doing, so enthralled and rapturous, she'd have been able to learn more about the how. For one thing, she didn't know exactly how Spencer looked nude. Though she blushed to admit it, she was tempted to pull away the blanket and see what was usually hidden under his trousers. Just thinking about what she might see made her feel warm and tingly all over.

The only adult male animal she was completely familiar with was a stallion. Was Spencer built—scaled down to human proportions, of course—like a stallion?

Why shouldn't she satisfy her curiosity? After all, he'd seen her nude. Nona flushed, remembering how shamelessly she'd stood before him naked, taking down her hair, thrilled and excited by the admiration and the need glowing in his dark eyes. Even thinking about it excited her all over again.

If only she had the nerve to fling back the blanket and look. But that was sure to wake him and how could she explain? Was it possible she could slide her hand down and touch him without rousing him? That would give her some notion of his—his maleness.

Spencer lay on his back with Nona snuggled against his side, her right arm draped across his chest. Slowly and carefully, she angled her arm until her fingers were inching downward. She paused when she reached his

181

navel, her breath quickening. When he didn't move, Nona gathered her courage and crept on.

Her fingers encountered a nest of crinkly hair, far more than on his chest. She slipped lightly over the hair, continuing down and suddenly there it was under her touch, hard and hot. Involuntarily, her fingers closed around it and she felt a throbbing. At the same time, Spencer groaned.

"I thought you'd never get there," he said huskily.

Startled, Nona tried to snatch her hand away but his hand closed over hers, trapping her.

"Don't stop," he begged.

"You mean you—you like being touched?" she managed to ask.

He made an inarticulate sound of pleasure and took his hand from hers.

Greatly daring, Nona slid her fingers up and down, satisfying her curiosity as to size and shape. But she still wasn't sure of one thing and she supposed she never would be unless she asked point-blank.

She swallowed and cleared her throat. "Uh, does it retract?"

"What do you mean?" Spencer asked.

"Like, uh, well, a stallion's?"

He gave a great shout of laughter and rolled over, pinning her half-beneath him. "No, my inquisitive little schoolmarm," he said. "Flattering as it is to be compared to a stallion, I don't work the same way."

Nona could feel the heat of the embarrassed flush that seemed to cover every inch of her body.

"When the most beautiful and desirable woman in the world isn't in my arms," he continued, "that part of me is considerably smaller but it doesn't retract like a horse's."

"Oh." Nona could hardly push the word out.

Spencer kissed her, speaking between kisses. "You are the—most curious—most wonderful—woman I've ever—met."

His tongue stroked inside her mouth, sending delicious tingles all over her, making her forget her embarrassment, forget everything but his lips and his touch and the arousing warmth of his body.

His hand closed over her breast, his thumb caressing her nipple until she throbbed with such inner need she thought she'd go mad if he didn't satisfy it. When he took her nipple into his mouth her desire burgeoned, spreading to every part of her. She moaned, holding him to her, half out of her mind with pleasure and longing.

His fingers found her secret place with velvet soft caresses.

"Do you like it when I touch you?" he murmured.

She could only murmur wordless assent.

"I feel this way when you touch me," he said hoarsely.

Nona, hardly able to think, was thrilled to realize she could bring him the same intense pleasure he gave to her. But right now she wanted him inside her, she'd die if he didn't satisfy her desperatē need.

"Please," she gasped, doing her utmost to pull him to her.

He rose over her, thrusting deeply, awakening a fiery surge of passion that enabled her to match his rhythm without trying, a passion that seared through her until she flared into flaming ecstasy.

When Nona woke, sun was slanting into the lean-to and Spencer was propped on one elbow, watching her. She smiled shyly, tucking the blanket more closely around her.

"I guess the rain's over," she said when he didn't speak or return her smile.

"What comes next?" he asked.

She didn't know what he meant. "After the rain?"

"After we reach the Fort," he corrected.

Nona blinked, wondering what he was getting at. "I'm

not looking forward to telling Kilby what happened to Helen and Amanda Jean," she answered finally. Just saying her sister's name depressed her. "He'll be terribly upset."

"You're fond of Lieutenant Mead, aren't you?"

Nona, detecting accusation in his words, frowned and bristled. "Why shouldn't I be—he's my brother-in-law."

"That's not what I mean. I heard what you said about him before the *Lady Jane* docked and I saw how enthusiastically you greeted him when the boat docked."

Nona, indignant, started to sit up, remembered she had no clothes on and clutched the blanket to her. "What's wrong with admiring a Seventh Cavalry trooper? Kilby's a fine, courageous man."

"Known him a long time, have you?"

"As a matter of fact, I met him before Helen did—if that's any business of yours."

"That's what I thought."

"You thought it wasn't any of your business? You're right."

"No, that you knew him before he met your sister."

Nona stared up at him, growing progressively more upset. What was wrong with Spencer? Why was he asking such questions? The way he was acting it seemed unbelieveable how close they'd been only a short while before. She refused to lie here and be cross-examined like a hostile witness in a courtroom.

She yanked the blanket off Spencer and sprang to her feet, wrapping the gray wool around her.

"Hey!" he protested. A moment later he stood facing her, the other blanket around his waist.

She paid no attention to him, reaching for her discarded clothes. His hand clamped onto her wrist.

"Are you in love with Mead?" he demanded.

Nona, taken aback, gaped at him.

"Answer me!" he insisted.

184

She glared at him, too hurt and furious to tell him anything about her feelings for Kilby. "That's none of your business either," she snapped.

He let her go. She picked up her clothes and ducked out of the shelter, marching to the stream where she washed, and slipped, shivering, into her damp buckskins. If he watched she didn't know—or care.

Once he was dressed, Spencer strode under the dripping trees. Damn women, anyway! He'd never met one who could give a straight answer to a simple question. Why had he expected Nona to be any different? He muttered to himself as he set rabbit snares and gathered wood dry enough to start a fire.

When he woke before Nona and watched her sleeping, his heart had gone soft with tenderness. How lovely she was with her chestnut hair glowing on the gray blanket. She'd given herself to him with such perfect trust it frightened him to think about it. She was too trusting; she believed the best of everyone. She was his woman; he'd see that nothing ever harmed her.

When they got back to the Fort he'd make certain she'd be safe while he was off with Custer and the Seventh. . . .

It was then he'd remembered where she'd be staying. In the Mead house. Alone with her sister's husband—at least until the campaign began. The more he'd thought about it, the more angry and upset he'd become. By the time she roused, he couldn't control himself. But, hell, he'd only asked a few simple questions. Why hadn't she answered them?

She couldn't possibly be in love with the lieutenant. She'd called Mead brave. Brave? Then why hadn't he ridden after his wife instead of waiting for Reno to decide to send a search party?

A fine man? Mead might cut a dashing figure, but he was imitating the real thing—Autie Custer. However he felt about the General, Spencer would never deny Custer's personal bravery. If Libbie Custer had been captured by Indians, Custer would have ridden after his wife alone, if need be—to hell with waiting around.

Any man in his right mind would want Nona; Mead would be no exception. No doubt the lieutenant would be genuinely grieved by his wife's death, but he wouldn't put it past Mead to play on Nona's sympathies. Alone in the house with her. At night.

Spencer cursed. He could hardly insist that Nona ask Libbie Custer or one of the other wives to take her in when she had her own room waiting for her at Mead's. And if he did ask her she'd refuse, if for no other reason than believing it to be her duty to be near at hand to comfort Mead. He couldn't bear to think of her putting her arms around another man, even in sympathy. Besides, he didn't trust Mead, not where Nona was concerned.

He trusted Nona but doubted that she realized she belonged to him. Damn these independent eastern schoolmarms.

Once they returned to the Fort, he'd have difficulty finding a time and place to be alone with her, much less make love to her. The only bright spot was that he and Mead would both ride out with the Seventh.

Never mind Mead, how does Nona feel about me? Spencer asked himself.

She wasn't one of those languishing women who breathlessly confess their love after the first kiss. Such women had no idea what the word really meant. Hell, he wasn't sure what it meant himself. He'd never told any woman he loved her. Why should it be disturbing that Nona hadn't told him? He didn't want any permanent entanglements.

But he wanted Nona here and now. He wanted more from her, he wasn't ready to give her up and he damned well wouldn't until he *was* ready. And no fair-haired, blue-coated lieutenant was going to push him aside.

Mead has the advantage of longer acquaintance, Spencer told himself, but he doesn't know her the way I do. I have the edge, the advantage.

Spencer's musing stopped short when he caught a glimpse of white to his left. He whirled, hand on the butt of the Colt. Nothing stood between him and the tangled willow thicket, nothing white, nothing at all. For an instant he thought he heard a voice in his head whispering, "Wake."

"White Buffalo Woman?" he demanded.

His own words mocked him. There was nothing to see or hear. Nona was right, he was getting too Indian for his own good.

After setting the snares, he sat on the stream bank upriver and stared at the rippling water. He'd thought he understood women pretty well, but he was far from sure he knew enough about Nona. Making love to her hadn't sated him—just the opposite. An hour apart, and he wanted her in his arms again.

Birds called to one another from the trees overhead and flitted back and forth across the stream. The lowering sun warmed the damp earth, slanting through the leaves to warm him as well. She should be here by his side, her head on his shoulder, nestled in his arms. Instead she'd gone off to sulk simply because he'd asked a few simple questions. Questions which she hadn't answered.

Wasn't it his right to know if she was in love with another man? With Mead?

The sun was setting when Spencer made his way back to camp carrying four dead rabbits. A small fire near the lean-to greeted him, but there was no sign of Nona. His heart leaped in alarm.

"Nona!" he shouted, dropping the rabbits.

"I'm here," she called, stepping from the shadows under the trees with the blankets folded over her arm.

Because he was so relieved to see she was all right and because he couldn't help himself, he strode to her and wrapped his arms around her, gathering her to him. She stiffened at first, but then leaned against him, burrowing her face into his neck. When her lips touched his skin, he was as shaken as if struck by plains lightning.

"I'm starving," she murmured. "I hope you caught lots of rabbits."

He was hungry, too, but he needed her more than food. Tipping up her face, he kissed her, long and deeply, savoring her taste and the welcoming warmth of a mouth inviting him to take more. God knows he wanted to. But their joining would be all the sweeter for waiting until after they'd eaten. Reluctantly he released her.

"Four rabbits," he said. "Two apiece."

She smiled at him and he noticed she hadn't rebraided her hair; instead, she'd caught it back loosely with a thong so that it hung over her shoulders. He touched the fine chestnut strands and they clung to his fingers, reminding him of the way Nona clung to him when he made love to her and increasing his arousal until he felt ready to explode.

Her fingertips touched his lips. "Spencer?" she asked huskily, her eyes aglow with desire.

"If you don't stop looking at me like that, we'll never get those rabbits cleaned, much less eaten," he warned her. She made a face at him and turned toward the fire.

Nona helped him skin and gut the rabbits, and by the time evening's long shadows darkened the camp, they sat side by side in companionable silence as the meat roasted over the fire.

"I've almost forgotten what it's like to sit at a table and

eat," she said. "I'm not sure I'll remember how to use a fork or a napkin when we get back to Fort Lincoln."

"I wish we'd never get back." His vehemence took him by surprise.

She raised her eyebrows. "I've been told the Dakota Territory gets awfully cold in the winter."

"I could shoot enough buffalo to make a tipi. Of course, you'd have to clean the hides. That's woman's work."

He expected her to grimace, to show her distaste for such a task. Instead she sighed and stared into the fire.

"When we skinned the rabbits," she said, "I couldn't help remember the rabbitskin covering Singing Reed gave Amanda Jean to keep her warm." Nona turned to him. "Oh, Spencer, how am I ever going to explain to Kilby what I did with his daughter? He'll never understand."

He pictured her with Mead, telling him that Spencer Quinlan's life was so important to her that she traded away her niece to keep him alive. A quiver ran along his spine. Was it true? It must be, since that's what Nona had done. For him alone? Or would Good Heart Nona have done the same for Mead in the same circumstances?

Spencer sought the right words. "I don't suppose anyone can understand except you and me and Singing Reed."

"I know." Her voice was sad.

Would you do it again? he wanted to ask, but quashed the impulse. The trade preyed on her mind enough without him making it worse. He didn't want her to dwell on her loss now, so he searched for a way to distract her.

"When I was setting the snares this afternoon," he began, "I decided you were right to tell me I'm in grave danger of turning Indian."

She stared at him, obviously curious.

"When a man starts seeing things that aren't there, it's

time he thought about changing his ways, wouldn't you say?"

"What did you think you saw?" she asked.

"A white buffalo. No, not exactly—White Buffalo Woman. Sometimes she's a white buffalo, sometimes a beautiful woman. I even heard her speak to me, but of course, it was all in my head. Probably brought on by a strange dream I had the other night. If I were truly Dakota I'd say it was a vision dream, showing me or warning me what was to come."

"Do the Sioux really believe dreams come true?"

Spencer nodded. "They believe in vision dreams. The trick is to decide which dream is truly a vision. Dancing Coyote told a story about a Dakota man in Minnesota who mistook an ordinary dream for a vision. In the dream he was flying over the water; so, believing after he woke that he'd be able to fly, he spread his arms like wings and leaped from a cliff above Big Muddy River. He dropped like a stone and very nearly drowned before his wife pulled him out."

Nona smiled—a bit sadly, he thought. "Sometimes it's difficult to know what's real and what's not."

"It's not the first time I've seen the white buffalo," he admitted. "Or imagined I had."

"Back home on the farm, I saw a white deer once," she said. "They're albinos. I suppose white buffalo could exist."

He shrugged. "So they say. I've never seen one in a buffalo herd. Anyway, I don't think mine is real."

Glancing at her, he found her gazing at him, a question in her eyes. What was she asking? He didn't know. Disturbed, wishing he hadn't brought up his dreams or what was real and what wasn't, he looked back to the fire where the rabbit chunks sizzled and popped on their wooden skewers. That was real enough.

"The meat's done," he said.

Nona watched Spencer as they ate. The discussion of what was real and what was not had unsettled her. She knew she loved him; there was no doubt in her mind about how she felt. But what did he feel for her? What did their lovemaking mean to him? Was it real at the time but to be as easily dismissed as the wrong kind of dream once they returned to Fort Lincoln?

Why had he asked the questions about Kilby earlier? Did he hope she was in love with Kilby? Why? So he could turn her over to him and be relieved of any responsibility?

Much as she loved Spencer, she wondered if she was closing her eyes to the truth, like the man who'd jumped off the cliff expecting to fly. She hoped not, for she had no one to pull her from the river's depths.

Later, in Spencer's arms, her unanswered questions didn't matter. With his lips on hers and the heat of his body flaming through her, how could she care about what might happen once they returned to the Fort?

"Nona," he whispered, his hands tangled in her hair, "you are so beautiful, so very lovely. All of you." His lips caressed her breasts and skimmed along her stomach, then lower until they were pressed against that part of her she'd hardly known existed until Spencer's teaching.

Nona gasped in wondering surprise as she felt the warm moistness of his tongue. Shivery thrills arrowed deep inside her and, as he continued, she began to thrash her head back and forth, moaning with a pleasure so exquisite she didn't know how long she could bear it.

"Spencer!" she cried, caught in a throbbing, whirling magic.

She felt him come into her, rocking her in the pulsating, glorious rhythm of joining, making her a part of him as he was a part of her. Together they rose above the earth, leaving behind the real world for their own private paradise.

Afterward, she fell asleep in his arms, secure and content.

She drifted serenely in a void, floating happily in nothingness. Gradually she began to drop lower and lower, but she wasn't frightened until she suddenly realized she was falling. She flung out with her hands, desperately searching for something to hold onto, but found nothing.

As she opened her mouth to scream, she plunged into water and choked. Thrashing and floundering, she sought to rise above the water. But she could not. Despite her frantic struggle, she was caught in a whirlpool and carried deeper and deeper . . .

"Nona!" Spencer's voice.

Darkness. His arms were close around her, holding her. She clutched him, breathing his familiar scent. There was no water; she was here in Spencer's arms and she was safe.

"What's the matter?" he whispered into her ear. "You were choking, like you couldn't breathe. Are you all right?"

"I dreamed," she said, shuddering, the shards of nightmare lurking in her mind. "I dreamed I was in water so deep there was no bottom. I was caught in a maelstrom; I was drowning."

"I'm here," he murmured, his warm breath reassuring in her ear. "Don't worry, I'm here and you know I'd never let you drown."

── FREE ──
B O O K C E R T I F I C A T E

ZEBRA HOME SUBSCRIPTION SERVICE, INC.

YES! Please start my subscription to Zebra Historical Romances and send me my free Zebra Novel along with my first month's Romances. I understand that I may preview these four new Zebra Historical Romances Free for 10 days. If I'm not satisfied with them I may return the four books within 10 days and owe nothing. Otherwise I will pay just $3.50 each; a total of $14.00 (a $15.80 value—I save $1.80). Then each month I will receive the 4 newest titles as soon as they come off the press for the same 10 day Free preview and low price. I may return any shipment and I may cancel this arrangement at any time. There is no minimum number of books to buy and there are no shipping, handling or postage charges. Regardless of what I do, the FREE book is mine to keep.

Name _____
(Please Print)

Address _____ Apt. # _____

City _____ State _____ Zip _____

Telephone (___) _____

Signature _____
(if under 18, parent or guardian must sign)

Terms and offer subject to change without notice.   12-89

**MAIL IN THE COUPON
BELOW TODAY**

To get your Free ZEBRA HISTORICAL
ROMANCE fill out the coupon below and send
it in today. As soon as we receive the coupon,
we'll send your first month's books to preview
Free for 10 days along with your FREE NOVEL.

Zebra Historical Romances Make This Special Offer...

IF YOU ENJOYED READING THIS BOOK, WE'LL SEND YOU ANOTHER ONE

FREE

a $3.95 value

No Obligation!

—Zebra Historical Romances Burn With The Fire Of History—

Chapter Thirteen

In the morning, Spencer examined Kaintuck's foreleg and announced the swelling was gone. After looking at the chestnut, Nona agreed.

"He ought to be able to hold my weight now, so we'll go on," Spencer said.

She nodded, wondering why she was so reluctant. She certainly wanted to get back to the Fort. Didn't she? The sun warmed her face, birds sang in the cottonwoods, the May breeze teased the leaves and caressed the loose strands of her hair. A beautiful spring day, perfect for traveling. Of course they must go on.

Smoothing her tangled hair with her fingers, she began to braid it while Spencer watched, saying nothing. When she finished, he handed her his hat.

"I'm afraid my face is already sunburned," she said.

He touched the tip of her nose with his finger. "Maybe a new freckle or two." Though he smiled, his eyes were shuttered and dark, the glow gone. After setting his hat on her head, he turned away and began saddling Kaintuck.

Why was he shutting her out? she wondered as she busied herself with Twisted Ear. Did he regret their lovemaking?

"It's a good thing you didn't find a way to slip your tether and strand us again," she said softly to the pinto, at the same time wishing the pony had done just that if it meant another day here with Spencer.

But she knew they'd have gone on, even without the pinto. This camp was only a temporary Eden.

She cast one lingering look back at the branch shelter as they rode away.

Neither spoke as they left the trees behind and started across the endless low hills. Spencer seemed concerned about Kaintuck for awhile, but when he satisfied himself the horse's gait was normal, withdrew into himself.

Nona tried to think of something light and airy to say, but nothing came to her. It was difficult to pretend to be cheerful with such a heavy heart. They rode in silence until the sun climbed well up the sky.

"When we reach the Fort, let me do the talking," Spencer said finally.

"Will we get there today?" she asked.

"I'm not sure. I think we might. Unless we make it a short day's travel." He glanced at her and his eyes gleamed for a moment, hinting he'd like to stop early and camp yet again.

Her spirits rose as she decided he was just as reluctant to see their traveling together end. She wanted to tell him to stop at the next creek, but instead, she controlled her urge to grin from ear to ear in pure joy and said as soberly as she could, "We shouldn't tire Kaintuck."

He nodded solemnly. "You're right."

They rode in silence until he asked, "Did you really have a horse named Black Irish?"

"Yes. He's getting on, but old as he is, my father claims he's the best stud on the farm."

Spencer grinned. "Is Black Irish the stallion you compared me to?"

Nona reddened not having foreseen where Spencer was leading her. Refusing to let herself be embarrassed by his teasing, she slanted him a glance and murmured, "Black Irish is one of a kind and so, Mr. Quinlan, are you."

"I'm not quite sure how to take that."

"No fishing allowed," she said with mock sternness. "As Hank Ainsley, one of our hired hands, used to say about the horses, 'Them as got it knows it, them as ain't got it don't know from diddley.'"

"I'm not sure I understand Mr. Ainsley. Which makes him a true philosopher."

She laughed. "My father always claimed it took horse sense to understand Hank and that's why only the horses knew what he meant."

"Sounds like I'd get along with your father just fine."

Nona sobered, for the first time picturing Spencer meeting her still vigorous white-haired father. "Yes," she said slowly, "he'd like you."

But, of course, they'd never meet.

"I got on with my own father even though he didn't have much time for me," Spencer said. "He was a good man, but being the only doctor for at least fifty miles in any direction, kept him busy. And tired. My mother died when I was eleven. Dancing Coyote was the one who was always there."

"You had no brothers or sisters?"

Spencer shook his head. "After my father died I kept the Minnesota property to use as a home base, but I haven't been back in a couple of years—I'm too much of a rolling stone, I guess."

"Why?"

He shrugged. "There's a lot to see, to try to understand and to share with others. You easterners don't know beans about the west; that's one reason I enjoy writing for the eastern papers—I like to think I'm educating them. Besides, the *Globe* pays me more than any other newspaper."

Nona supposed he was right about the ignorance of

many easterners. She considered herself fairly well-educated but she'd learned a lot since her arrival in St. Louis. In some cases, more than she cared to know.

"Even rolling stones eventually come to rest," she said.

"That won't happen till I'm six feet under."

Nona wondered if she imagined the edge of defiance in his voice. Did he think she meant to try to hogtie him so he couldn't roam? He ought to give her credit for knowing better.

"What about you?" he asked. "No doubt you'll be returning to New York soon."

She'd planned to stay through the summer to help Helen with the new baby before returning east in time to take up her teaching job in the fall. But poor Helen was beyond anyone's help and Amanda Jean was lost forever.

"I'll have to talk things over with Kilby," Nona said. blinking back tears. "I'll stay as long as he needs me."

Spencer started to say something but clamped his mouth shut before any words emerged. He glowered at her instead. For some reason the mere mention of Kilby's name infuriated him.

Nona scowled back at Spencer but he'd ceased to look at her and was staring ahead, shading his eyes with his hand. Kaintuck's ears were pricked forward, and when she glanced at her pinto, his one good ear was, too. Nona peered ahead.

"Something's moving up there!" she cried apprehensively, uncertain whether what she saw was buffalo or men on horseback. "Is it Sioux?"

Spencer pulled the rifle from its saddle scabbard. "I hope not." His voice was grim.

"They aren't riding from the south like you said the Sioux would."

He grunted in reply, his attention fixed on the approaching riders. Nona glanced around and saw there was no place to hide. Spencer must already know this, for he didn't check their pace. Whatever came at them, he intended to ride to meet it.

Minutes later, Spencer thrust the rifle back into the scabbard. "Troopers," he said.

Nona couldn't see how he knew and said so.

"The sun's reflecting off metal. Indian gear has little metal, troopers's gear a lot."

Staring at the oncoming riders, Nona saw bright flashes now and again and nodded in understanding, easing out her breath in relief. She and Spencer were safe.

As the riders drew closer, Nona recognized the man who led them. "That's Kilby!" she told Spencer.

He grunted and muttered something too low for her to hear. Nona ignored him, taking off her hat and waving it. Minutes later she and Spencer were surrounded by blue-coated soldiers.

"Thank God you're all right," Kilby said. His eyes asked what he did not.

"Oh, Kilby, Helen's dead," Nona said hastily, wanting the telling of the terrible tragedy over and done with. "She—"

"Unfortunately, I arrived too late to save your wife," Spencer cut in, his gaze on Kilby. "I was able to rescue Miss Willard, but regret to say I was forced to leave your newborn daughter behind."

Nona stared at him. Is this why Spencer wanted to do the talking—so he could lie to Kilby?

"But Amanda Jean is alive and well," Spencer went on, his voice matter-of-fact. "An Indian woman adopted her."

"Amanda Jean?" Kilby echoed.

"I—I named the baby." Nona wanted to say more but her throat closed with grief.

"Helen's dead." Kilby spoke numbly.

197

"We'd best save the explanations for later," Spencer said. "Miss Willard isn't up to answering questions. We must get her to Fort Lincoln as quickly as possible."

Kilby drew in a deep breath and gave a curt order to the ten men with him. Escorting Spencer and Nona, the troopers swung their horses toward the Fort.

Nona rode in a daze for a time, hardly able to believe it was all over—the abduction, the escape, the time with Spencer. Without protest, she listened to Spencer continue lying to Kilby. Though she had no desire to regurgitate all the horrors of the captivity she and Helen had endured, or dwell on how Paquette and Sky Arrow had died, she would have told the truth, grim as it was. Why hadn't Spencer let her?

"Miss Willard wasn't seriously harmed in any way," Spencer told Kilby, "but naturally she's badly shocked by what's happened. Adding to that is exhaustion—we've been pushing the horses and ourselves for days without enough food or rest. I hope you know some dependable woman who can take care of her until she's herself again."

He's making it sound as though we rode here straight from the Sioux camp, she thought. Without anything happening in between. No Paquette. No Sky Arrow. No Singing Reed. And no lovemaking in a leafy shelter.

She'd certainly appreciate a good meal, a bath and a comfortable bed but she didn't need a nursemaid. Before she could gather her wits to say so, Kilby was assuring Spencer he knew just the person.

"I expected troopers to find us long before you did," Spencer said.

"I've ridden out every day since the women were abducted." Kilby sounded offended. "We found an abandoned Sioux camp but had no idea where to go next."

"I left the Ree scouts a message at that campsite telling

198

them," Spencer said.

Kilby shrugged. "They either didn't find it or couldn't read your sign. We'd given you up for dead by then."

Nona could see by the bunching of muscles along Spencer's jaw that he was holding back angry words. "I'm hard to kill," he said tersely.

"Evidently." For some reason Kilby didn't seem particularly pleased Spencer was alive.

Remembering how close Spencer had come to dying, Nona bit her lip, not wanting to think about it. Yet she knew he'd deliberately provoked Kilby, so she could hardly blame her brother-in-law for being annoyed. Didn't Spencer realize poor Kilby must be suffering agonies over Helen's death and the loss of the daughter he'd never seen?

Apparently Kilby had had enough of Spencer for the moment because he rode ahead to speak to the lead rider. Spencer immediately dropped back to ride alongside her.

"Don't contradict my story." He spoke so low she hardly heard him and she doubted any of the troopers did. "Believe me, it's best to leave things the way I've told them."

Perhaps it was. Nona could no longer be certain of anything. Just the same, she wouldn't promise. "I'll think it over," she said tartly, "providing my nursemaid doesn't insist thinking's too strenuous."

His lips twitched into a reluctant smile. But he didn't look at her, and a moment later, dropped back even farther until he brought up the rear. Nona urged the pinto ahead, catching up to Kilby. Once riding next to him, though, she couldn't find anything to say.

"Did she suffer?" he asked finally.

Helen had suffered a good deal of pain having the baby, but Nona didn't intend to tell him that. Anyway, that wasn't what he meant. "No, Helen died quite peacefully," she said, telling him how her sister had believed her dead grandmother had come for her. And how, at the end, Helen hadn't been afraid or in pain.

"A Sioux woman called Singing Reed watched over us," Nona explained. "She kept anyone from—from bothering Helen and me."

"Thank God!"

"She's the woman who has Amanda Jean. Singing Reed lost her own baby."

"That's no reason she should have my child!"

No, of course it wasn't. Nona tried to screw up her courage to admit exactly how Singing Reed acquired Amanda Jean, but found she couldn't. He'd be even more upset than he was. How could she add to his grief?

"Why did you choose such an odd name for my daughter?" Kilby asked.

"Helen always wanted a daughter called Amanda Jean."

"She never once mentioned it to me. I'd chosen my mother's name, Martha, for a girl, and Helen agreed." His fingers tightened on the reins. "Oh, my God, I can't believe Helen's dead."

Tears sprang to Nona's eyes. Poor Kilby. She, too, had loved Helen; she understood how he felt and she made up her mind then and there to stay at the Fort as long as he needed her.

Nona *was* exhausted when they finally reached Fort Lincoln at dusk and made no fuss when a plump middle-aged woman wearing a white apron over her calico dress arrived at Kilby's house.

"My name's Rose Grady," she told Nona, looking her up and down. "I'll be bound 'twas never your choice to wear such heathen garments. Let's get them off you and you into a tub. 'Tis plain to see, child, you're plumb wore out."

As though she were the child Mrs. Grady called her, Nona allowed herself to be led to a zinc tub of hot water where she bathed. After toweling herself dry, she slipped into the nightgown Mrs. Grady held for her and was tucked into bed.

"You won't be wanting to keep these," Mrs. Grady said, rolling the buckskins into a bundle.

"Don't throw them away," Nona said drowsily, closing her eyes. The Sioux garments were a part of her time with Spencer, but she could hardly explain that to Mrs. Grady.

Nona barely had time to wonder when she'd see Spencer again before sleep whisked her away on dark wings.

Morning lightened the room when Nona roused and she stared up at a round-faced girl looking at her from eyes as bright blue as Mrs. Grady's.

"Ma sent me with tea," the girl said, setting a tray on the small table beside the bed. "Want me to pour you a cup?"

"Please." Nona propped herself onto pillows. "This is a luxury. I don't remember ever having tea served to me in bed."

"Ma says after what you been through you need to rest." The girl examined her curiously before pouring dark tea into a willow ware cup.

"What's your name?" Nona asked.

"Mary Katherine Grady, only they mostly call me Katy. You want sugar and milk?"

"Just plain, please."

Katy handed cup and saucer to Nona. "I'd like to of died if it'd been me the Sioux captured," she said.

"I was scared," Nona confessed, taking a cautious sip of the strong, hot brew.

"What did they—?" Katy began, then stopped abruptly, reddening.

Nona raised her eyebrows questioningly.

"Ma said she'd smack me silly did I ask you what happened and all," Katy confessed. "I ain't supposed to be dawdling, so I better go bring you up some hot water."

After Katy's precipitous departure, Nona sipped her tea and thought about her. She'd taught girls much like her. Katy looked to be about sixteen—plenty old enough to be interested in boys. Though not pretty, she was plump and lively, with curly dark hair, a girl sure to have admirers among the soldiers. Katy, young and curious, was dying to find out if Nona had been forced to lay with a Sioux brave.

Nona shuddered at how close she'd come to such a terrible fate. Mrs. Grady was right; what had happened to her was none of Katy's business. On the other hand, if she said nothing, Katy would imagine the worst. And wouldn't others, too? Katy's mother, for example. Distasteful and painful as it was to talk about her Sioux captivity, Nona realized she might have to.

Katy reappeared with hot water for Nona to wash with. "Ma says will you be wanting me to bring up a tray for your breakfast?" she asked.

"No, I'll come down as soon as I'm dressed. It's very kind of you and your mother to wait on me, Katy. I do appreciate it, but I feel quite rested now."

Kilby was seated at the table when Nona came into the dining room wearing her drabbest gown—the only black dress she owned. He rose immediately and seated her, saying, "Are you certain you're well enough to be up?"

Nona frowned. This was Spencer's doing, making out that she needed to be taken care of. One good night's rest had gone a long way toward restoring her and she was completely capable of waiting on herself.

"Don't contradict what I've said," Spencer had warned her. Nona took a deep breath. She hated lies.

"I'm quite well," she told Kilby, dismayed at the edge in her words, because she hadn't meant it for him but for

202

the absent Spencer.

"I'm happy to hear that," Kilby said, as Mrs. Grady appeared with fried ham, bread and cheese.

"I was hoping for eggs," Mrs. Grady said, "but the hens ain't laying none too good."

"The food looks wonderful to me," Nona assured her. "Thank you for sending Katy with the tea."

"I've made up my mind," Kilby said when Mrs. Grady returned to the kitchen. "I'm going after my daughter. No matter what Major Reno says, I mean to search for her."

Nona, who'd never heard him speak so positively, was impressed. But she'd given Amanda Jean to Singing Reed and Kilby didn't know that. Eyeing the determined set of his jaw, she decided that, even if he did, he wouldn't change his mind—Amanda Jean was his daughter, his by right.

Still, she must tell him what she'd done. Spencer had tried to shield her by concealing the truth, but Kilby must know the truth, grim though it was.

Twisting her hands together in her lap, she took a deep breath. "Kilby," she said.

He held up a hand to cut her off. "Don't try to change my mind. I know I've chosen a dangerous path, but it's my choice to make and no one can stop me."

"But you don't understand—"

"Do *you?* That baby girl is all I have left of Helen and I'm damned if I'll leave her in the hands of savages."

Dear God, how could she tell him it was her fault Amanda Jean was with the Sioux? Somehow, she had to, even if he never forgave her.

"I gave Amanda Jean—" she began again.

"Don't use that name! Good God, Nona, back in Maryland we had a Negro cook named Amanda. My daughter will be called Martha Helen."

"I'm—I'm afraid I baptized her Amanda Jean," Nona

confessed. "I didn't know what might happen, so I thought it best to be sure she was baptized."

Kilby waved his hand. "I'm sure you did what you thought best at the time. But once she's safe with me, I'll have a priest do it properly and give her the name I've chosen."

Nona said the words silently. Martha Helen. A perfectly appropriate name. Yet somehow it didn't fit Helen's daughter as well as Amanda Jean. Or even Light of Sun.

I must remember she's Kilby's daughter as well as Helen's, Nona admonished herself.

She'd forgotten he'd grown up in Maryland and his family had Negro servants, some of whom had been slaves before the War.

"I'll never be satisfied until Martha Helen is home with me, where she belongs," Kilby said.

"You can't ride out alone in search of your daughter," Nona said, momentarily distracted from her confession. "Won't you need Major Reno's permission to take troopers with you?"

"To hell with regulations! I'll go alone if I must."

Though impressed with Kilby's determination, Nona wondered if in his anguish he was being foolhardy rather than brave. She must dissuade him.

"You can't go alone," she said firmly. "What good would it do Amanda—uh, Martha—if the Sioux kill you?"

"Quinlan rode into the Sioux camp alone. Do you think I have less courage?"

"Mr. Quinlan speaks their tongue."

Kilby stared at her. "He does?"

She nodded, considering it unnecessary to explain why.

"Maybe I should ask him to help me," Kilby said.

Nona bit back instinctive denial. Spencer couldn't go;

he'd be killed. But surely he knew that and would refuse if Kilby did ask. Besides, Spencer was aware that she'd traded Amanda Jean to Singing Reed and that the Sioux woman would never give up the baby.

"Why don't you speak to Major Reno first?" she suggested.

"Good advice. Always go through the proper channels before proceeding." Kilby smiled at her, but his smile faded almost immediately. "I can't get used to the idea I'll never see Helen again. She was so young to die."

"I blame myself. If I'd realized the danger, I'd never have agreed to the picnic."

"It's not your fault. I know how headstrong poor Helen could be. Much as I loved her, she was sometimes a trial." He sighed. "If only she had listened to me." Tears glistened in his eyes but he blinked them away. "Thank God you're safe and that those damned savages didn't harm you." He speared a chunk of ham and brought it to his mouth, chewing carefully and neatly.

It disturbed her that Kilby could speak of his grief over Helen's death, yet go right on eating. For some reason it reminded her of Sky Arrow's hearty appetite, the meat juice running down his chin while on the other side of the tipi fire Helen lay dying. Unable to swallow another bite of food, Nona set down her fork, her appetite gone.

He looked at her, his knife suspended over his plate. "They didn't, did they?" Kilby's voice rang falsely casual.

It took Nona a moment to realize he was asking if the Sioux braves had forced her. She hadn't expected the question and it hurt.

"Mr. Quinlan's rescue was timely," she said frostily and excused herself.

After Kilby left the house, she wandered into the kitchen. Neither Katy nor her mother was in sight, but Nona heard someone giggling on the back porch and

205

opened the door. Katy whirled to face her, hastily dropping the hand of the young soldier standing on the steps.

"Mike—uh, Private Jakes—is just bringing the water," Katy said.

Nona already knew there were no wells here and that water from the Missouri River was delivered to the Fort daily and stored in barrels. She glanced at Private Jakes, as red-faced as his hair. "Hello," she said.

"Pleased to meet you, miss," he mumbled.

Obviously Mike was one of Katy's admirers. Nona smiled at them both and retreated inside. Minutes later Katy followed her in.

"You won't tell Ma, will you?" Katy begged. "Mike and me, we wasn't doing nothing wrong, but Ma don't like me to talk to him. Or to any soldier. She says she don't want me to tie up with no Army man. It's on account of Pa got killed by the Sioux six months ago. He was a sergeant. They let us stay at our house on Sud's Row on account of Ma's the best laundress at the Fort."

"I won't say anything," Nona assured her.

Katy smiled her thanks. "I really do like Mike a whole lot. I just can't help it. No matter what Ma says."

Nona sighed inwardly, understanding better than Katy could realize. When it came to Spencer, she couldn't help herself any more than Katy could with Mike. Where was Spencer? Why hadn't he come to see her?

Katy turned away and reached for the mop bucket. "I guess I better get busy scrubbing the kitchen floor or Ma'll have my hide."

Hearing a knock at the front door, Nona hurried to answer it, her heart speeding in anticipation. It seemed forever since she'd seen Spencer. She flung open the door but her greeting died on her lips. Libbie Custer stood on the porch with her brother-in-law, Tom.

"Oh, my dear!" Libbie cried. "I'm so pleased you feel

well enough to be up and about."

Nona gathered herself together and invited them into the parlor. Libbie settled herself in a rocker. After Nona was seated on the settee, Tom perched on the edge of a ladder-back chair. He looked as uncomfortable as Nona felt.

"What an ordeal you've suffered through," Libbie said. "I'm dreadfully sorry about your sister. A terrible tragedy."

"Terrible," Tom echoed.

Nona nodded, unable to speak. Every time she heard Helen's name, her throat seemed to close. Both Libbie and Tom watched her, waiting. What did they expect her to say? She swallowed and tried to clear her throat.

"Is there anything I can do to help?" Libbie asked.

"Thank you." The words emerged in a husky whisper, but at least she'd recovered her voice. "When I feel up to going through my sister's belongings, I'd appreciate it if you'd tell me of any women at the Fort who might be in need of—of clothes."

Before Libbie could respond, someone knocked at the door. Nona excused herself.

This time it *was* Spencer. Nona successfully fought her impulse to throw herself into his arms, but her hand reached out involuntarily and he clasped it.

"Nona," he said, "I—" He stopped abruptly and she saw him looking over her head into the parlor and scowling.

"Please come in," she said hastily.

By the time Spencer entered the parlor, he'd wiped all expression from his face. "Mrs. Custer," he said and bowed slightly. "Captain."

Tom, who'd stood when Nona left to answer the door and was now leaning on the mantel, nodded curtly.

"Why, it's our hero, Mr. Quinlan," Libbie said. "Everyone's talking about your brave deed."

"It was mostly luck," Spencer said.

"That's what the General always tells me," Libbie said, smiling, "but I know better. I'm so glad to see Nona is able to get around."

"She was badly frightened, of course," Spencer said, "but fortunately Miss Willard wasn't seriously harmed."

Almost the same words he'd said to Kilby. Nona recognized them now as a polite code he used to let people know she hadn't been forced by any of the Sioux braves. Would they believe him?

Is that what Libbie and Tom came here to find out? she asked herself bitterly. Is that what they were waiting for me to say? What would they have thought if I'd blurted out that the only man whose blanket I warmed was Spencer's?

Despite her agitation, Nona almost smiled as she imagined what consternation that particular truth would cause. She decided perhaps she was being too harsh on Libbie and Tom—they did seem sincere in wanting to help.

"Since I've caught you, Mr. Quinlan," Libbie said, "I'll extend my invitation to a small gathering I'm having when the General returns at the end of the week."

"I'd be delighted to attend," Spencer told her. "I'm looking forward to meeting your husband."

Libbie turned to Nona. "I know this is a sad time for you, my dear, but please do come by for a few minutes to say hello to the General if you feel able. Lieutenant Mead will be attending, I'm sure." Libbie rose and pressed Nona's hand in farewell.

"Thank you for inviting me," Nona said.

Tom took her hand and bowed over it. "Let me know if there's anything, anything at all I can do for you," he said.

"Thank you," she said. "I'll do that."

Nona walked with Libbie and Tom to the door. No

sooner was it shut behind them than Spencer exploded.

"You're a fool if you let that man anywhere near you!"

She didn't care a hoot for Tom Custer, but Spencer's tone and his words annoyed her.

"Kilby tells me Tom's a fine soldier and the best shot in the regiment." She paused to see how Spencer took this. He glowered at her, so she went on. "Tom does seem to be a gentleman when he's not drinking."

Spencer's hands clamped her shoulders. "I'm telling you to steer clear of him."

She gazed up at him, furious. "And just what gives you the right to choose my company?"

"This." He yanked her toward him and his mouth covered hers.

Chapter 14

Nona tried to struggle free of Spencer's arms but his kiss whipped through her like a windstorm, sweeping away her resistance. Whether she wanted to or not, she melted against him, a candle set too close to the fire. Never mind that she was angry at him, his touch wiped away her anger and everything else until nothing existed but his embrace.

He'd shaved off his burgeoning beard and she inhaled the clean scent of soap mixed with his man's smell, the most wonderful aroma in the world. She parted her lips and his tongue plunged inside her mouth, a teasing prelude to a more intimate union. Clinging to him, she throbbed with eager desire.

"Mine," he murmured into her ear.

At this moment, weak with her need, she couldn't deny she was his. Whether he was hers or not wasn't important. His hands cupped her bottom, pressing her against his hardness and she wished so many clothes didn't separate them so she'd feel again the thrill of his flesh against hers, the wonder of his nakedness.

The world narrowed to Spencer and her, the two of them suspended in their own magic kingdom where they were the only inhabitants. Nothing mattered except the two of them.

Someone behind her gasped and Nona was jerked back to reality. Spencer's arms fell away as she whirled to see who it was.

"Beg pardon, miss," Katy muttered, red-faced, her eyes shifting from Nona to Spencer.

"What is it, Katy?" Nona was surprised her voice didn't tremble.

"Ma said I was supposed to ask you if chicken's all right for dinner."

"Yes, fine."

Katy scurried from the parlor.

Nona looked at Spencer, denying her body's ache for his touch. This wasn't the wilderness, this was Fort Lincoln and she was a guest in Kilby's house. How could she have forgotten where she was?

He stared back at her, his dark eyes gleaming. "Well?" he demanded. "Do you deny it?"

Nona blinked, trying to gather her scattered wits. Deny what? That she was his? Coals of not-quite-vanquished anger flared into flame.

"I belong to nobody but myself," she snapped.

He took a step toward her and she moved quickly to put a chair between them. "Katy's sure to tell everyone she knows that she saw me in your arms," she said. "With the entire Fort already wondering if I'm hopelessly ruined by the Sioux, must you add to the speculation by compromising me?"

Spencer halted, staring at her. "I believe I prefer you in buckskins," he said.

She drew herself up. "I'm no Sioux! I hope I never see another savage as long as I live. Thank God I'm back among civilized people again."

"Are you implying I'm not civilized?" There was an edge to his tone.

"When I saw you dancing to those Indian drums,

211

there was little difference between you and the savages. I don't know quite what you are. You may be Spencer Quinlan on the surface but you're Buffalo Rider, too."

"And you don't like Buffalo Rider."

Nona bit her lip. That wasn't what she'd meant; she'd been referring to his unpredictability. "It's not that I don't like—" she began.

"Never mind, you made your point. You think I'm an uncultured savage bent on compromising you."

"I didn't say any such thing! But I can hardly afford gossip."

"No, of course not—what would Lieutenant Mead think if he discovered I kissed you in his parlor?" Spencer's smile mocked her.

Nona flushed angrily. "You're twisting my words."

"But that's what it boils down to. You're worried about the Lieutenant's opinon of you."

"He wouldn't understand—"

"What the hell do I care what he understands? What's his opinion got to do with you and me?"

Nona folded her arms across her chest. "I'm a guest in his house. Courtesy demands I do nothing to abuse his hospitality."

"So you're pretending that I, the uncouth westerner, need to be taught manners." Spencer shook his head. "I suppose it's too much to expect honesty from a woman."

Nona glared at him. How dare he accuse her of being dishonest?

"Admit it," he dared. "You enjoy being kissed by me as much as I enjoy kissing you."

"What I do or do not enjoy has nothing to do with the subject under discussion," she said frostily.

He raised an eyebrow. "It's clear you can take the teacher out of the schoolroom but you can't take the schoolroom out of the teacher."

"Making fun of me is evading the issue."

"My dear Miss Willard, the only issue is you and me. You're doing the evading, not me."

Goaded by her increasing anger, Nona snapped, "I don't care to discuss what happened between us."

"Neither do I. What I want is to *repeat* what happened."

Nona flushed. A gentleman would never dream of bringing up such a delicate matter—but then he'd assured her he was no gentleman. Did he expect her to admit she wanted him to make love to her? What gall!

"You'd better leave," she said coldly. "You've stayed quite long enough for a courtesy call, as I've no doubt the women along the Row realize."

"Do you think I care if they're peering at your door from behind the curtains, watching and waiting? Why should *you* care?"

"I care because I'm a woman with an already precarious reputation, thanks to my abduction by the Sioux. What else does a woman have except her reputation?"

He shrugged. "For some reason I thought you were less of a hypocrite than most women."

Nona put her hands on her hips and raised her chin. "It's all very well for you rolling stones—you never stay in one place long enough for your indiscretions to catch up with you. But what about the women you leave behind? The ones who remain to suffer the consequences? If anyone's a hypocrite, you are."

Spencer blinked. "No one's ever suffered because of me," he protested.

"Don't tell me you went back to make certain—that I don't believe."

"I mean I've never made promises I didn't fulfill."

"Yes, you've made it crystal clear you're not a man who makes promises." Contempt edged her words.

"Is that what you want—promises?"

Nona shook her head so violently, strands of her hair came loose from the knot at the back. "I don't want anything from you!" she cried.

Whirling, she ran from the parlor and up the stairs, slamming the door and shutting herself in her room. She leaned against it, tears burning her eyes. Spencer Quinlan was beyond doubt the most infuriating man she'd ever met in her life. In so small a place as Fort Lincoln, it was too much to hope she'd never see him again, but she would never, ever, let him touch her again.

When she was certain he'd had time to leave the house, Nona went back downstairs and found Katy rolling out a pie crust on the kitchen table.

"Thought I'd use some of them dried apples for a pie," the girl said.

Nona nodded, her mind not on baking, but on what to say about the scene in the parlor.

"I don't know if you've ever met Mr. Quinlan," she began finally.

"Ma washed some clothes for him. He sure is good-looking for an older man." Katy slanted a glance at Nona. "Guess you think so, too. You got no need to worry. I ain't going to tell on you, on account of you said you wouldn't say nothing to Ma about me and Mike lollygagging and all. What's fair is fair."

That puts me in my place, Nona thought wryly. Lollygagging is lollygagging whether it's in the parlor or on the back steps.

"Pardon me for mentioning it," Katy went on, "'cause I know you feel awful sad right now, but when you get ready to pack away your sister's things I'd be glad to help."

Katy's words jolted Nona from her preoccupation with Spencer, reminding her of what she should be doing. She thanked Katy, saying she'd let her know if she needed help and climbed the stairs again, determined to make a start.

Most of Helen's gowns hung in a second wardrobe in the guest room where Nona slept. Grief choked her as she took dresses down and folded them. Even if Helen hadn't been shorter than she was, Nona couldn't have borne to wear her sister's clothes—except for the gowns Dorothy had sent and Helen hadn't had the chance to wear. One of these was a black silk with thread-thin ivory stripes. Since it was unhemmed, Nona knew it would fit and she needed another black dress for the mourning period.

By the time Kilby came home for dinner, Nona had finished packing Helen's clothes. She greeted him with eyes red-rimmed from crying.

"Come into the parlor and have a glass of sherry with me," he insisted. When she'd seated herself and he'd handed her a stemmed glass of wine, he lifted his own and said, "We'll drink to Helen. She wouldn't approve of all this weeping; she'd want us to get on with our lives."

"She was such a happy little girl," Nona said, smiling reminiscently as she sipped the sherry.

"It's best to remember her that way." He set down his glass on the mantle. "Neither of us will every forget Helen, but we must remember we do have lives to lead." He fixed Nona with his pale green gaze. "I've always been fond of you, as I'm sure you realize."

Nona blinked. What was Kilby getting at?

"I mentioned this morning that I plan to rescue my daughter from those blasted Indians. Reno's agreed to consider my request for troopers. What I hadn't considered is who'll take care of the child after I return to the Fort."

"I'll be glad to stay on here for awhile and—"

Kilby cut her off. "I was thinking of a permanent arrangement." He smiled at her. "Marriage, in fact.

215

To you."

Nona's jaw dropped. Helen was scarcely cold in her grave. How could Kilby bear to think of marrying so soon? "I—I don't—" she began and found she couldn't continue.

"I thought you might have come to realize, as I did, that our marrying would be the perfect solution, but I see I've startled you."

Nona collected her wits enough to manage a coherent reply. "I—well, I must think about this."

"I understand." He crossed to her, took her free hand and brought it to his lips. "We'd do well together, Nona."

Thoroughly unsettled, she went in to dinner, served by Katy. While they ate, to Nona's relief, Kilby said nothing more about marriage but spoke instead of drilling the troops.

"General Custer returns in two days and he'll expect us to have our men conditioned to the saddle," he said over the apple pie.

"Conditioned? You mean you have recruits who've never ridden a horse?"

"We always get a few who can't manage to stay in the saddle. I count myself lucky if a recruit knows enough to aim a rifle. My job is to turn greenhorns and misfits into cavalrymen. General Terry reviewed the Seventh today and my men came through better than I expected."

"General Terry?"

Kilby raised his eyebrows. "He commands the three companies of infantry that will march against the hostiles with the Seventh—surely you've noticed the infantry tents south of the fort."

Nona had seen the tents when she rode in with the troopers who'd rescued her and Spencer, and it came to her now that she'd heard Kilby say the soldiers were under General Terry's command. She'd been so exhausted it hadn't meant much at the time.

"Three companies," she echoed. "Why that's hundreds of men."

"We'll march out of Fort Lincoln more than a thousand strong." Kilby's face shone with pride. "Led by the Seventh, greatest of them all, with General Custer at our head. We'll be meeting General Crook and General Gibbon with their men somewhere near the Yellowstone River. With three armies gunning for them, the hostiles don't stand a chance."

Nona thought of the Sioux village where she'd been a captive and the half-naked men dancing to drums as they prepared for the buffalo hunt. Kilby was right—no savages in breechclouts could match the fighting power of the United States Army.

"You won't be attacking the Indian villages, will you?" she asked, remembering Singing Reed telling her of soldiers killing Indian women and children.

"We fight hostiles wherever they are."

"But—the children—?"

"Haven't you heard General Sheridan's comment about nits making lice?"

Nona caught her breath. When she'd given the baby to Singing Reed she'd never once considered that Sioux women and children might also face Army rifles.

"Amanda Jean—I mean Martha—is somewhere out there with the Sioux." Nona leaned across the table. "Oh, Kilby, she's in danger. You must rescue her before the Army marches."

"I mean to," he said grimly.

Despite Katy's protests, Nona helped her clear the table and wash the dishes. She wasn't used to being waited on; besides, she wanted to delay a *tete-a-tete* with Kilby.

How could she possibly marry him? She still thought of Kilby as Helen's husband. Though it was true she'd once imagined herself in love with him, her time with

217

Spencer had taught her what she'd felt for Kilby hadn't been love.

Marriage would mean lying with Kilby as she had with Spencer. Nona winced, unable to imagine doing that. How strange to realize that only a few weeks ago she'd believed Kilby was the most wonderful man in the world.

"They're gonna be riding off pretty soon to fight the hostiles," Katy said, her voice jarring Nona from her reverie. "Mike says it's gonna be one goshawful battle. Mike don't have nothing against redskins. Why, he and one of them Rees—Three Crows—are buddies. So I asked him why is he going off to fight 'em then? He don't know. Just on account of he's a soldier, I guess."

"There's a difference between friendly Indians and hostile Indians," Nona pointed out.

Katy shrugged. "I don't like none of 'em. What I wish is that Mike'd maybe find a job in Bismarck and move across the river. Get out of the Army. Ma ain't gonna stop me from seeing Mike, but she's right about marrying a soldier. They can die on you real quick."

Nona pictured Spencer riding with the Seventh and shivered. Knowing him, he wouldn't stand aside while a battle went on, he'd be in the thick of it, even if he wasn't fighting. "I wish he wasn't going," she said aloud.

"Who?" Katy asked. "Lieutenant Mead?"

Nona blinked, and after a moment, Katy grinned. "You mean Mr. Quinlan, don't you?"

"Both of them," Nona insisted. "And Mike Grady, too, for that matter."

Katy's grin widened. "You're real nice for a school-marm," she said. "Prettier 'n most, too."

Nona had to smile. "Thank you, Katy."

When the dishes were finished and the kitchen clean and tidy, Nona had no reason to put off joining

218

Kilby in the parlor. If he persists I'll tell him it's too soon to think of marriage, she decided. Because it was. Though she shied away from an outright refusal, it might come to that if she was forced into a yes or no answer.

She found Kilby sitting beside the fireplace holding a partly-filled brandy snifter. The evening was too warm for a fire but he stared at the cold hearth as though watching imaginary flames.

"I've packed most of Helen's clothes," she told him, seating herself opposite him before he could rise. "If it's all right with you, Mrs. Custer is going to find some needy woman at the Fort to give them to."

Kilby waved a hand. "I'll leave it up to you. What use are Helen's clothes to me?" His tone was tinged with self-pity, making Nona wonder just how much brandy he'd consumed.

Not that she'd blame him for overindulging. Kilby had loved Helen and she'd died cruelly, so far away from him.

At least I was with my sister until the end, Nona thought. Poor Kilby was denied any last goodbye and now he didn't even have her body to grieve over. Or their child to ease some of the sorrow.

"It's hard to believe Helen's gone," Kilby said.

"Your daughter looks very much like her," Nona told him.

"Strange—I was so certain we'd have a boy. I'd even begun to plan his life—where he'd go to school, William and Mary, and—" He sighed and covered his eyes with his hand. "I'm overdue to be posted to Washington," he added after a moment. "If I hadn't written to my uncle that I wanted to wait until the Indian campaign was over, Helen and I would be safe in Washington."

Nona could think of nothing to say.

"Still, how could I know?" Kilby dropped his hand and straightened. "I'd follow General Custer into the jaws of hell if he asked me. He's a great leader, and I believe, may well be our next president." He swallowed the rest of the brandy. "The campaign against the hostiles is nicely timed, you know, since we're certain to come up with the great victory before the Democratic convention. I wouldn't be surprised to see the General nominated." Kilby smiled. "Neither would he."

President Custer? "I'm looking forward to meeting the General," she said.

"You will. At Libbie's party. We'll go, of course. Helen would understand." Kilby poured himself another dollop of brandy. "May I offer you anything?" he asked belatedly.

She shook her head.

Kilby held the snifter in both hands, staring at her over the rim. "Should think you could use some of those clothes." His words were slightly slurred. "That gown looks like you retrieved it from the ragbag. Helen dressed well. Prettiest girl I ever saw. Didn't have much sense, though. You got all the brains." He drank more of the brandy.

"Helen was smart enough," Nona protested. "For some reason she thought she had to conceal it."

"Stubborn as a mule, too. And contrary. 'S why she had a girl 'stead of my son. She knew I wanted a boy."

He'd definitely had too much to drink, Nona decided.

"That's the brandy talking, not you," she said firmly. "Don't you think you've had enough for tonight? I'm afraid you'll have a painful head in the morning."

"Got to keep a clear head. Set a 'xample for the men."

"That's right, you do."

Kilby put down the snifter. "Helen hated it here." Tears stood in his eyes. "Hated the place."

"She loved you very much," Nona assured him.

"She didn't understand 'bout Custer." He waved an arm, almost knocking the snifter from the marble-topped stand next to his chair. "I'd follow him anywhere. To the White House."

The White House? Was it possible General Custer really did have a chance to be the Democratic nominee for President? Nona wondered. Kilby obviously idolized him. Was he exaggerating?

"He's lucky," Kilby insisted vehemently, as though she were arguing with him. "Custer's lucky. Gonna smash the hostiles once 'n for all."

"I've heard of Custer's luck." Nona spoke soothingly. "I'm sure the Seventh Cavalry will acquit themselves with honor."

"Bet your boots."

Nona suppressed a smile. She'd never heard Kilby use slang before, though he undoubtedly did with his men. Nor had she ever seen him the worse for drink. She wondered how to suggest tactfully he go to bed and sleep it off. Finally she pretended she was covering a yawn with her fingers.

"Don't let me keep you up," he mumbled.

"I don't like to leave you down here by yourself," she told him.

"By m'self," he echoed plaintively, pulling himself to his feet. "All by m'self." Before she knew what he meant to do, he flung himself on his knees in front of her chair and laid his head in her lap, his shoulders heaving with sobs.

Nona stroked his hair gently, comforting him as she would a child. "You're not alone," she murmured. "I'm here, you're not alone."

Poor Kilby, she thought, her own eyes wet. He's lost

221

without Helen. I must do everything I can to make it easier for him.

But not necessarily by marrying him.

After a time he raised his face and, without looking at her, pushed himself upright. "Better get to bed," he mumbled, stumbling toward the stairs.

Nona rose and hurried to his side. "Lean on me," she said. "That's what I'm here for."

He sighed and put an arm over her shoulders, accepting her help without comment as they climbed the stairs together. Nona tried to leave him at the door to the bedroom he'd shared with Helen, but his fingers tightened on her shoulder.

"Goodnight, Kilby," she said levelly. "I'll see you in the morning." She attempted to pull free, but he wouldn't let her go.

Turning her toward him, Kilby put both arms around her and stared down at her. "I 'member when I used t' kiss you, Nona."

"That was a long time ago. Let me go, Kilby. You've drunk too much brandy and you don't know what you're doing."

"Gonna kiss Nona."

Realizing she couldn't avoid his kiss without a struggle, she turned her face so his lips touched her cheek.

"Now we'll say goodnight." She spoke with great firmness and ducked down and away from him. Hurrying to her own room, she slipped inside and closed the door behind her. There was no key so she stood waiting and listening to see what he'd do.

She was relieved when she heard his bedroom door close. Sober, Kilby was a gentleman, but she couldn't be sure what he'd do half-seas-over as he was. After a moment's thought, she wedged a straight-backed chair under the doorknob.

As she readied herself for bed, Nona pondered over the way she'd felt in Kilby's arms. Annoyed with him. Averse to being kissed. And guilty. The first two she could easily understand—after all, who wanted to be kissed by a man full of brandy? But why should she have felt guilty?

She hadn't done anything wrong. They were both upset over Helen's death and he needed comforting. Why had it seemed she was betraying Spencer? He had no claim on her; besides, nothing had happened except a brotherly kiss on the cheek. If Kilby had intended the kiss to be more than that, she'd thwarted him and likely he wouldn't remember in the morning.

She was slipping her nightgown over her head when the doorknob rattled. Nona tensed, hurriedly sliding her arms into the sleeves and tying the blue ribbon at the neck while she watched the door apprehensively.

"Miss, miss, it's me." Katy's voice. Why wasn't Katy asleep on her cot in the pantry?

Nona eased the chair from under the knob and opened the door. "What's the matter?" she asked Katy.

Katy eased inside and shut the door. "Oh, miss, I purely do hate to bother you but it's Mike. He's sick."

"Where is he?"

Katy flushed. "On the kitchen floor. He sure can't stay there all night, but I can't get him up."

Realizing she'd have to take charge since Kilby was in no shape to be responsible, Nona donned her dressing gown. As she was putting on her slippers, a sudden suspicion struck her.

"Has Mike been drinking?" she asked.

Katy nodded, growing even redder. "I know he shouldn't of come calling three sheets to the wind like he is. But he came round to the back door and I let him in, though I shouldn't of, either, and now he's passed out. Ma's gonna kill me."

"You had no business letting Mike in without Lieutenant Mead's permission," Nona scolded.

Katy hung her head. "I wish to God I never did."

"Wishing isn't going to lift Mike off the floor and whisk him off to the barracks. Let's hope we can rouse him."

"I sure am sorry to bother you, but I couldn't let on to the Lieutenant. Mike's in his company and the Lieutenant's always telling the men he's got no use for drunken sods. I hate to think of what'd happen to Mike if the Lieutenant sees him."

"Be quiet going down the stairs," Nona cautioned, not wanting Katy to know Kilby had taken too much brandy and was pretty sodden himself.

Mike lay flat on his back, his eyes closed, snoring. Nona tried calling his name, pinching his ear, and as a last resort, pouring cold water over his face. He didn't stir. He wasn't tall, but he was broad-shouldered and chunky. Together, she and Katy couldn't lift him.

"We can hardly drag him all the way to the barracks by his heels," Nona said.

"No, miss. Oh, dear God, Ma's gonna have a conniption."

Nona frowned at Katy. "You should have thought of that before you opened the back door."

"I just can't help myself where Mike's concerned. I have to see him. I'll die if I don't." Tears clouded Katy's bright blue eyes. "There ain't never gonna be no other man for me."

Nona felt both sorry and exasperated for her. What in heaven's name was she going to do about this young soldier? Katy was right. Mike simply couldn't lie here and sleep it off. Not in his lieutenant's kitchen. Especially since the pantry off the kitchen was being used as Katy's temporary bedroom.

"Don't cry, we haven't got any time to waste," she warned Katy.

If only there was a discreet way to reach Spencer. Unfortunately, she couldn't go looking for him without attracting undesirable attention. Nor could she send Katy without causing comment.

An idea popped into her head. Would it work? She wasn't sure.

"I'm not sure who commands what companies?" Nona said. "Is Mike under Captain Tom Custer?"

"No, miss. Mike's in Company G, that ain't Captain Custer's."

"Good. Here's my plan. You go along the Row to Mrs. Custer's and see if a light's on in her house. If so, peek in the window and see if Captain Custer happens to be visiting her. It's not too late. We may be lucky. If he's there, knock on the back door and ask to speak to him. If necessary, say that Miss Willard sent you with a message. Then bring the Captain to our back door as quickly as you can."

Chapter 15

Sitting on the cot assigned him in the officers' barracks, Spencer wiped his mouth with the back of his hand before returning the half-empty canteen to the captain who'd offered it to him.

"Thanks, Bill," he said, "that hit the spot."

Bill King shrugged. "Any time. Unless someone sends me decent whiskey, all I can get out here in the Territory is this rot-gut but it beats drinking water."

"I wonder how many of the troops carry whiskey in their canteens instead of water."

"Half, anyway. How the hell else can a man survive?" Bill took a long drink before putting the cap on and stowing the canteen away. He stretched out on his cot, his arms behind his head, and yawned.

Reveille sounded at dawn, rousing everyone, so it made sense to retire early, but it was barely ten and Spencer knew he'd never sleep a wink if he went to bed now. "Think I'll take a walk," he said.

The May night was cool without being chilly. Stars glimmered overhead, the moon was dying; soon there'd be a new one. A pungent stable aroma drifted on the river breeze, reminding Spencer he must see how Twisted Ear was faring in the corral. He planned to ride the pinto pony when he accompanied the Seventh on the campaign against the hostiles—the pony was almost as much of an old friend as Kaintuck.

Bill's whiskey warmed his stomach but not his heart. It was hell being so near Nona and yet not being able to be with her the way he wanted. The sooner he left from Fort Lincoln, the better.

Maybe he'd been out of line this morning, but he was damned if he'd admit it to her. Her mush-mouth words about how others expected them to behave irritated him past endurance. His brief time among the Lakota as Buffalo Rider must have altered his viewpoint, but since he didn't want to live like an Indian, he supposed he'd have to get used to civilized restrictions all over again. Such as not making love to a lady unless you married her first.

Damned if that applied to him! He'd never promised marriage to any woman and he didn't intend to begin now. Settling down in one spot with one woman had no appeal.

The trouble was no other woman had ever gotten under his skin like Nona Willard. If he wasn't ready to settle down with her, he wasn't ready to give her up, either. Not by a long shot. And definitely not to that blowhard Mead.

He hadn't meant to go anywhere near Officer's Row and when he found himself starting down the street he grimaced. He hated to think he was behaving like a moonstruck youth walking past a girl's house in the hope of catching a glimpse of her.

Face it, Quinlan, he told himself, you want to see her one way or another and you won't be satisfied until you do. So walk by the house and get it over with.

He sauntered past. Lamplight glowed somewhere in the back—the kitchen?—and from one of the upstairs rooms. He was turning to walk back when he heard voices speaking so softly he couldn't make out the words, but he knew a man and a woman were talking in the rear of Mead's. He had to know who they were.

Spencer drifted to the side of the house and eased along to the back where he halted and listened, hidden from view.

"Thank God you came, Captain," Nona's voice.

"Any time I can help you, I'm more than willing," Tom Custer told her.

"Please come in," Nona said.

When Spencer heard the door close, he clenched his fists. Why had Nona invited the Captain to her back door at this time of night? Because she was afraid of gossip if he came to the front? But why invite him at all? "Thank God you came," she'd said. What did she need Custer for? Where was Mead?

Damn it, if she needed help she should have asked me, Spencer fumed.

The more he thought about it, the angrier he became, until finally he stomped up the back stairs and pounded on the door. A flushed-faced girl opened it and stared open-mouthed at him. It took him a moment to place her as Katy.

"Where's Miss Willard?" he demanded.

Katy opened the door wider and gestured inside.

Tom Custer knelt beside a soldier lying on the kitchen floor. Nona, in a pale green dressing gown, stood beside Tom, her gaze fixed on Spencer.

"What on earth are *you* doing here?" she demanded.

Tom rose. "Just as well you showed up, Quinlan. I'll need help lugging this drunken lout to the barracks."

"Promise me you won't punish him, Captain," Nona implored. "When he wakes up and discovers the trouble he's caused, I'm sure that'll be punishment enough."

Tom frowned.

"Please!" Nona added.

228

Tom bowed slightly. "For you, Miss Willard, I'll break the rules this once."

With Tom holding the drunken soldier's feet and Spencer his shoulders, they carried him down the back steps. Spencer caught one last glimpse of Nona framed in the doorway, the lamplight casting a golden aureole around her, and then she closed the door, leaving him in darkness.

Spencer had noticed the poor bastard they carried wasn't even old enough to grow a proper mustache. The boy must be a recent recruit who was courting Katy— that would explain how he wound up on Mead's kitchen floor. But where was Mead during all this? After they'd dumped the soldier at the enlisted men's barracks, he asked Tom.

"Sleeping, or so Katy said," Tom told him. "That lout's in his company and Miss Willard didn't want to make trouble for him by rousing the Lieutenant. She has a kind heart as well as a pretty face."

True enough, but it irked Spencer to hear Tom say it. He was also upset because Tom had seen Nona in her dressing gown.

"Plenty of pluck, too," Tom went on. "It's a pleasure to be in her company."

"I suggest you keep that to a minimum," Spencer spoke between his teeth.

"Are you telling me you've staked a claim?" Tom demanded.

"Something like that, yes."

Spencer couldn't see Tom's expression in the darkness outside the barracks, but the antagonism in the Captain's voice was clear enough. "I'll believe it when Miss Willard says so. I notice it wasn't you she called on for help tonight."

Spencer's fists clenched. "Are you calling me a liar?"

"If the name fits—"

Enough was enough. Spencer swung, his fist connecting solidly against Tom's jaw and sending him staggering. Tom cursed, sprang forward, and landed a blow of his own.

Spencer stepped back, tripping in the darkness and sprawling on the ground. Tom laughed a derisive, cocksure laugh. Infuriated, Spencer leaped to his feet and hurled himself at the other man, swinging wildly. Tom warded off the blows with his arms.

Tom's fist struck Spencer's midsection, making him gasp. When would he learn? Spencer wondered. He'd been about to make a fool of himself over Nona; now he'd let Tom goad him into recklessness. He felt sure he could take Tom, but not unless he used his head.

He began to stalk Tom cautiously. All at once hands grabbed Spencer, pinning his arms, holding him despite his frantic lunge toward Tom. Someone held up a lantern and he saw other soldiers restraining Tom. A thin thread of blood trickled from the Captain's nose.

"Sir," one of the men cautioned Tom, "we been warned Major Reno won't stand for no fighting or carousing on account of General Terry being here. Best knock it off afore the guard sends for the Major."

Tom glared at Spencer. "We'll settle this later, Quinlan."

"Suits me," Spencer growled.

As he strode toward his quarters, Spencer recognized the salty taste of blood in his mouth. He tested his teeth with his tongue and was relieved to find none of them loose. He might hate the Captain's guts, but the man was far from all swagger. He was one hell of a fighter.

Katy brought the news to Nona with her morning tea. "Mr. Quinlan and Captain Custer, they got in a fight outside the barracks last night."

Nona, sitting on the edge of the bed, stared at Katy. "A fight?"

"I heard they was pounding the bejesus out of each other afore some soldiers broke it up."

"Why on earth would they do such a thing?"

Katy slanted her a look. "If you don't know, you ain't as smart as I figured. Didn't you notice last night in the kitchen how they was bristling like two strange dogs?"

Does Katy mean Spencer and Tom had a public brawl over *me?* Nona asked herself, shocked. How degrading!

"You must be wrong," she protested.

Katy shook her head. "I hear the betting favors the Captain on account of he's good with his fists."

"Betting?" Nona's voice was horrified.

"Most of the troopers figure the Captain's got the edge in all ways, being a Custer and all. 'Sides, the General's wife's been after Tom to get married and settle down."

Nona grimaced. The soldiers weren't only wagering on who'd win the fight, but on which man she'd choose, when the fact was neither of them had asked for her hand. Likely enough Tom had no more intention of marrying her than Spencer did. How humiliating to be the object of such gossip. She hated to show her face.

"Does Lieutenant Mead know?" she asked.

"Not yet. I heard it from Mike when he delivered the water and I sure didn't spill the beans to the Lieutenant afore he left this morning. But he'll find out soon enough."

Spencer had to be the one who started the fight, Nona told herself. Hadn't he been acting as though he owned her? His sudden appearance last night made her wonder if he'd actually been watching the house. That reminded her of Mike and she asked Katy if he was all right.

"Yeah, outside of spending half the night puking," Katy assured her. "I sure hope it taught him a lesson. Like Ma says—women, they got more sense than men."

Katy grinned. "'Course she don't think I got any sense at all."

Well, I have more sense than to involve myself any further with Spencer Quinlan, Nona vowed. Or Tom Custer, either, for that matter.

Nona, wearing one of Helen's aprons over the black dress with the ivory stripes, was dusting the parlor when Kilby came storming into the house at midmorning.

"Blast the man, he turned me down!" he shouted. "Had the gall to tell me there wasn't a chance in a thousand to find my daughter and I'd have to face up to my loss."

Nona realized he meant Major Reno.

Kilby paced up and down the parlor. "All I asked for was ten men. 'Can't spare a one,' he says. 'We'll be marching against the hostiles in a few days and we need every trooper. You included.' I've got half a mind to go alone."

"You can't do that," Nona pointed out. "Without an Indian scout you'd never find the camp."

Kilby stopped pacing and looked at her. "Quinlan could show me the way. He rescued you, didn't he?"

"Yes, but—" She paused, not quite certain why she was protesting. If anyone was capable of finding Amanda Jean, it was Spencer.

"There's no time to waste. I'll track Quinlan down and ask him," Kilby said, heading for the door.

Less than an hour later, Kilby was back with Spencer. Except for a bruise on his jaw and a scrape on his cheek, Spencer looked none the worse for last night's brawl.

"He's agreed," Kilby said in triumph, clapping Spencer on the shoulder. "We're riding out immediately. I've come home for extra gear." He raced up the stairs.

"I don't think there's much of a chance," Spencer said

232

in a low tone to Nona, "but I couldn't turn him down. Amanda Jean's not safe with the Lakota, not with so many troops going after the hostiles. I'll do my best to find her and bring her back."

All her anger and outrage against Spencer blew away like smoke on a windy day. "The Sioux won't trust you this time," she said worriedly. "You'll be in danger—you and Kilby both."

"I've got better sense than to risk bringing him into their village. Don't worry about me. I'll manage."

Nona bit her lip. She knew Spencer was riding into terrible danger whether he'd admit it or not. "Major Reno says there isn't one chance in a thousand of finding Amanda Jean," she said.

"One chance is better than none. I keep thinking of that helpless baby in a tipi with Terry's and Custer's troops charging through her village. Do you have any idea what a cavalry charge is like? A tipi's no protection against Army bullets."

Before she could respond, Kilby pounded down the stairs, carrying his gear. Moments later he and Spencer were gone. She controlled her impulse to run after them and beg them to stay, for she knew neither man would. As much as she longed for Amanda Jean's return, she feared they were on a hopeless quest, a quest that would end in their deaths. And there was no way she could stop them.

Holding back tears, Nona resumed her work, attacking the dust as though it were her enemy. She was polishing the brass andirons to a fare-thee-well when Kilby burst in through the front door. Without saying anything, he dumped half his gear in the entry.

"What's the matter?" she asked.

Kilby scowled. "Reno got wind of what I was up to. He ordered me out on overnight patrol. By the time I return to the Fort, General Custer will be here."

"You let that stop you?"

Kilby shrugged. "I can't disobey a direct order from my superior officer. Not if I plan to stay in the Army."

Only minutes before, she'd been eager to keep Kilby from going, but now she was upset because he'd let himself be stopped so easily.

"Once the General's here, we'll march," Kilby went on. "I haven't given up finding my daughter, but any rescue attempt will have to wait until the campaign's over."

Spencer's words about the baby's danger from Army bullets echoed in Nona's mind, reminding her of Singing Reed's terrible tales of Indian women and children killed in Army raids. She shivered. "God protect Amanda Jean," she whispered.

"I won't be back until late tomorrow," Kilby said. "With Katy here you'll be all right."

"Don't worry about me. I take it Mr. Quinlan isn't going?"

"He's a civilian, so the Major couldn't order him on patrol. But he warned Quinlan he'd arrest him for any unauthorized use of Army propterty, horses included. Quinlan meant to ride that Sioux pony you brought to the Fort, but he found it had escaped from the corral and was gone. Without a mount, Quinlan's more or less confined to the Fort. It's just as well—I don't know how dependable he is. I'd rather have troopers backing me up when I go after my daughter—it's the sensible way to go about rescuing her."

Kilby leaned down and kissed her on the cheek. "You know I hold you in high regard, Nona. I realize I drank too much last night and if I misbehaved, I apologize." He managed a faint smile, turned on his heel and left the house.

Nona picked up the gear he'd left behind and climbed the stairs with it. Kilby's apology for last night was acceptable, but it upset her to think about how he'd solicited Spencer's help when he was desperate to find someone to ride with him. Spencer had agreed to go at the risk of his own life. How dare Kilby turn around and question Spencer's dependability?

What had Kilby thought? That Spencer was a coward who'd fail him if the going got tough? Never! Spencer might have some annoying traits, but he was the bravest man she'd ever met. It was just as well Major Reno had put the horses off limits to Spencer or he'd be riding off alone trying to rescue Amanda Jean.

She'd no sooner reached Kilby's room than she heard Katy calling her.

"I'm upstairs," she called back.

Katy rushed up the stairs. "Ma sent the Leemo girl over with a message," she said breathlessly. "I got to go home and take over the washing on account of Ma's helping Mrs. Leemo have her baby and she don't want to get behind with the clothes."

"That's all right, Katy, I don't mind. I didn't realize your mother was a midwife."

"Ma can do just about anything. The only thing is, miss, you never can tell how long a baby'll take to get born. Chances are I won't make it back here afore tomorrow morning and I heard the Lieutenant say he was going on overnight patrol."

Katy didn't miss much, Nona thought. "I don't mind being alone at night," she said. "You run along and don't worry about me."

"I'll make sure Mike knows not to come by so he don't bother you."

"I'd appreciate that. I've seen enough of that young man to last for some time."

Katy flushed. "He's real embarrassed about what he did last night. I told him if 'tweren't for you he'd be in the guardhouse or worse and he ought to go down on his knees and apologize, but he's too ashamed to face you. He did tell me he was sorry and I said all right, but if he was gonna drink like that again he needn't come courting me, neither."

"Good for you." Nona was sure Mike wasn't really so bad and she hoped he'd profit by Katy's no-nonsense advice.

"I left a pot of chicken soup on the stove," Katy said, "and there's two loaves of bread rising, almost ready to pop in the oven. All right?"

Nona nodded. "Thanks, Katy. I'll see you tomorrow."

Katy hurried down the stairs; minutes later, Nona heard the back door close. She piled Kilby's things neatly on a chair in his room, then went down to take a look at the bread. She slid the loaves into the oven and was stirring the simmering soup when she heard a knock at the front door.

Spencer stood on the porch, hat in hand, wondering if Nona would even speak to him, much less let him in. By now she must have heard about the brawl and he had a pretty good idea she wouldn't approve. And since then there'd been the rescue fiasco.

To hell with Reno. He hadn't cared for the mealy-mouthed bastard from the first. If Reno were leading the Seventh permanently, Spencer just might place his bet on the Indians.

The door opened. Prepared to see Katy, he found himself gazing at Nona. Her amber eyes widened and her hands clutched at the skirt of her frivolous blue apron.

"May I come in?" he asked, hoping he sounded properly contrite. He wasn't too good at humility.

She hesitated and he held his breath until she moved aside wordlessly.

Spencer took a breath and stepped into the entry. A mouth-watering aroma that reminded him of his childhood filled his nostrils. "Bread!" he exclaimed. "You're baking bread."

"I'm baking it, but Katy made the bread," Nona said.

"It smells wonderful."

She smiled slightly. "Is that a hint?"

"You wouldn't turn away a starving man, would you? Army food leaves a lot to be desired."

"You're welcome to share soup and bread with me when the loaves are done."

"Thank you," he said fervently. "It's probably more than I deserve."

Nona frowned. "You're right."

"I've learned my lesson," he assured her. "If nothing else, I've discovered jealousy ruins a man's better judgment." He touched his bruised jaw. "To say nothing of damaging his hands."

"You do look a bit the worse for wear."

"Aren't you curious to know how the other guy looks?"

"I'm ashamed of you both." She turned and walked toward the kitchen and he followed. The striped black dress outlined her curves charmingly and quickened his pulse.

He looked around, expecting to find Katy in the kitchen.

"Katy will be back soon," Nona said. She lifted the lid off a large pot on the stove and stirred the contents, then opened the oven a crack to peer inside. "Another few minutes," she told him. "Would you like a cup of tea while we wait for the bread?"

"I can think of no one I'd rather enjoy a cup of tea with."

The kettle was already steaming on a back burner. He leaned against the wall and watched her rinse a blue and white teapot with hot water before dropping in several pinches of tea leaves and was reminded of his mother doing the same thing when he was a boy.

"When my mother was alive we always had what she called high tea in the afternoons," he said reminiscently. "Tea and cookies or cake or tarts."

"Was she Irish like your father?"

"Half-Irish, half-Welsh. She was very pretty." It occurred to him for the first time that Nona's eyes were the exact color of his mother's. In fact, if Nona's hair were black instead of auburn, she'd look a good bit like his mother. "As pretty as you are," he added.

Red crept into Nona's cheeks, a blush that charmed him. For all her schoolroom knowledge, she was an innocent in so many ways.

She set the filled teapot on a tray with a sugar bowl and two matching cups and saucers. After carrying it to the kitchen table she invited him to be seated.

"I'm afraid there's no milk," she said as she poured the tea.

"My father always claimed only lily-livered men used milk or sugar in their tea, so I learned young to drink it plain."

"*My* father wouldn't swallow even a sip of tea without both milk and sugar. He insisted it wasn't fit for human consumption otherwise."

"And you?" he asked.

"I'll only admit to one lump of sugar per cup."

Her smile, sweeter than the sugar she dropped into her tea, made him wish no table separated them. What he wanted more than the tea or the soup or the bread was to feel her warmth and softness against him.

Easy, Quinlan, stick to the rules or she'll toss you out, he warned himself. You're lucky she even let you in.

"How's Katy's boyfriend?" he asked.

"He delivered our water this morning, so he survived. He seems too young to be a trooper."

"Many of them are that young." He reached out and

touched her hand, then drew his fingers quickly away. "I'm sorry about Amanda Jean."

Nona shook her head. "I didn't want you to go. Not the way you and Kilby had planned."

"Major Reno put the kibosh on that. You heard Twisted Ear slipped away again?" When she nodded, he added, in a voice edged with bitterness, "I can't stomach the Major."

"General Custer *is* due back tomorrow. I can understand the Major wanting all the troopers near at hand."

"Reno never forgave me for taking Kaintuck the first time."

Nona's gaze held his. "Thank God you did."

He started to rise, not sure what he meant to do, knowing only he had to hold her.

"The bread must be done!" she cried, jumping up and hurrying to the oven.

Spencer sat back down. She wasn't going to let him near her; that was plain. It was just as well, because if he touched her he wouldn't be able to let her go.

He watched her remove the bread and set it on a rack. She ladled the soup into a blue-and-white tureen and he suddenly recalled the name of the dishes—willowware. From China, his mother had told him.

"The bread's too hot to cut," Nona said, "but we could tear off pieces to eat with the soup."

"Sounds good to me."

Savoring the chunks of freshly baked bread with the chicken soup, Spencer had a strong sense of *deja vu*. For all that this was Mead's house, it was as though he'd come home to a loved and loving woman.

It's because of the tea and the willowware and the fresh bread, he told himself. I'm reminded of my boyhood and my mother. But he knew he was lying to himself.

He finished his second bowl and the rest of the bread

before he decided what had to be done. Reaching across the table he captured Nona's hand, preventing her from escape.

"One way or another, I'm going to ride with the Seventh in a few days," he told her, "and I'm not leaving Fort Lincoln with ill feelings between us."

Nona bit her lip. "I don't have ill feelings toward you."

"You're angry with me for the way I behaved yesterday morning and last night. I don't blame you." He released her, rose and walked around the table, holding out his hand. He didn't breathe as he waited to see whether she'd take it or not.

At last she lay her hand in his. Spencer drew her to her feet, stifling his urgent need to pull her into his arms. Instead, he looked into her eyes, searching for what he so desperately wanted to see.

"Do you forgive me?" he asked.

Chapter 16

Nona gazed into Spencer's dark eyes. How could she refuse to forgive him? The fight must have been at least partly Tom Custer's fault. And yesterday morning, she'd invited what happened by not pulling away immediately from Spencer's embrace.

"As long as there's no more talk of ownership," she said, smiling. "After all, you've the name of this fort to remind you slaves have been freed."

"You're too strong-minded ever to be anyone's slave," he told her. "But slavery wasn't what I meant when I said you were mine."

She raised her eyebrows, waiting for his explanation.

"There happen to be some similarities in the behavior of stallions and men," he said. "I want to keep you to myself, I try to keep other men away from you."

"Stallions feel that way about every mare in sight."

He grinned. "I've no urge to be king of the herd; I've singled out the prize female and the rest don't interest me."

Nona pretended to frown, but in truth she didn't mind being compared to as beautiful an animal as a mare. When she was younger she'd often wished she were a filly racing across the spring fields, free and wild, without a care in the world.

"Will you take a stroll with me?" Spencer asked. "I'd like to visit Kaintuck at the stables and see how he's getting along, but if I go alone I'm afraid I might be reported to Major Reno for attempting to make off with Army property."

She slanted him a disbelieving look, at the same time realizing how much she wanted to be with him in the pleasant warmth of the May afternoon.

"I'd enjoy a walk," she admitted.

Because she'd lost her only black hat to Sky Arrow, Nona donned a small black beribboned straw of Helen's, sitting it forward to avoid her bun. The hat was more frivolous than she'd have chosen for herself, but the admiration in Spencer's gaze assured her he approved.

The houses along the Row faced the Missouri River, several miles to the east. Nona, her gloved hand on Spencer's arm, blinked in the bright sunlight as they sauntered along the road to the stables. She told herself the reason she felt so happy was because of the fine day, but she wondered if she'd feel quite so good without Spencer beside her.

Soldiers drilled on the parade ground—infantry, she presumed—while Old Glory with its thirty-seven stars snapped above them in the brisk breeze. She could hear the shouted commands as the columns marched left and right. A field of tents bloomed gray-white between the garrison and the river.

Though Nona had been aware since she'd arrived that the Army intended to march against the hostiles, it suddenly became threateningly real to her. Those drilling soldiers would soon be fighting, backing up the Seventh Cavalry in a war against the Sioux and Cheyenne. And some would die, as her brother Roger had died at Gettysburg. Kilby might be killed or Katy's Mike. Or Spencer . . .

She clutched his arm, gesturing with her free hand at the marchers. "They're soldiers, but you're not. You don't have to go with General Custer."

"I choose to go," he told her.

"Why?"

"Because someone has to report what happens."

"Why must that someone be you?"

Spencer shrugged. "It's something I want to do, something I have to do. Follow the campaigns against the Indians."

"What if you're killed?" she asked. "None of my family ever got over my brother's death at Gettysburg. Roger was everyone's favorite. My father will mourn Helen, but her death won't affect him the way Roger's did. General Custer fought at Gettysburg, too, but he didn't die. Not everyone has his luck." Her voice was filled with bitterness.

"I'll survive." Spencer spoke confidently. "I'm hard to kill—remember?"

"It's that old Minnesota medicine man of yours," she said fiercely. "His teachings make you follow the Indian fighting. It's why you rode with General Crook and why you're determined to go with General Custer."

"You may be right."

Nona realized nothing she said would change Spencer's mind—he would ride with the Seventh and that was all there was to it. Though the sun shone as brightly as ever, for her the day had darkened.

They found Kaintuck in the corral, his shining coat recently groomed. There was no sign of any swelling in his forelegs. The gelding's head came up as they approached and he watched them with interest.

"He recognizes us," she said. "Horses rarely forget anyone they've come to know."

"I expected him to remember me," Spencer said. "We're old friends. Now that Twisted Ear has run off, I hope they'll let me ride Kaintuck on the campaign." He offered the chestnut several lumps of sugar, saying, "Compliments of Lieutenant Kilby."

"You're pretty sneaky," Nona scolded. "I didn't see you palm that sugar. Don't you know it's not good for horses?"

"Kaintuck doesn't care. He likes the taste."

"Horses often don't know what's good for them."

"The same could be said for men and women. But it's never held me back from what I wanted to do."

Nona ignored what he said as she stroked the chestnut's nose, losing herself in memories of her travels with Spencer and Kaintuck. At the time it had seemed they'd never reach the Fort—but they had. They'd left hardship and danger behind for safety and security.

Why then did she long to repeat those days? Was it because something else had been left behind as well? Could she ever recapture what she'd lost? Never, without Spencer.

"How soon after the General's return do you think the troops will march?" she asked.

"Two days, maybe less."

"As early as the seventeenth?"

He nodded. "Terry and his men are already camped here. Custer won't waste time."

Nona decided *she* was wasting what little time she and Spencer had left. Though she wasn't certain what she meant to do, she knew she had to make a decision. She stepped away from Kaintuck, saying, "I'd like to go back."

As they passed Suds Row on their return to the garrison, Nona glanced between the small houses at the lines of freshly washed clothes flapping in the breeze. The Gradys lived in one of those houses and Katy would remain there until morning.

Nona's heart began to pound and her breath caught in

her throat. If she were brave enough, if she threw caution to the winds. . . .

She glanced involuntarily at Spencer and her face flushed. What was she thinking! But the idea persisted, fluttering inside her like a trapped butterfly longing to fly free.

They reached the house before she'd made up her mind what to do.

"I'll leave you here," Spencer said at the steps.

She was certain of one thing, that she didn't want him to go, and she cast frantically about for an excuse to keep him there.

"I'm sure you're thirsty after our walk," she said, forcing brightness into her tone and smiling nervously. "I think there's a lemon or two—I could make some lemonade. Providing you left enough sugar."

Spencer didn't smile. His dark eyes held hers in a gaze that took her breath away. "Are you sure you want to ask me in?"

Unable to speak, she nodded, aware she was promising more than the lemonade and half-afraid of exactly what the promise might mean.

They climbed the porch steps in silence and he opened the unlocked door for her. Once inside, she turned to him, and her words about making lemonade died on her tongue when he took her hands, lifting one, then the other, to his lips. She felt the brush of his lips all the way down to her toes.

"Nona," he said softly, her name a caress. Though he still held her hands, he made no move to take her into his arms.

The glow in his eyes pulsed warmly through her, heating her blood, burning away her doubts. She knew what she wanted as clearly as she'd known in the rain shelter under the cottonwood. She took him by the hand, and led him up the staircase.

Why worry about other people's opinions? What did other people matter? Why had she scolded Spencer yesterday for trying to make love to her? Why hadn't she been honest enough to admit to herself that nothing in the world was more important than being with him, being close to him, loving him?

This may be the very last time they'd ever be together and she meant to celebrate with love and joy the few hours they had to themselves.

He stopped outside the door to her bedroom and cupped her face in his hands. "Last chance to change your mind," he murmured.

She stood on her tiptoes and brushed her lips against his in reply.

He followed her into the room, and when she stopped, pulled her back against him. His hands cupped her breasts, holding her to him while her heart throbbed so violently she wondered if he could feel its wild beating.

Spencer released her, his hands going to her hair. Out came the pins and combs that fastened the bun in place, letting her hair tumble down her back, freed for his pleasure. He found the tiny buttons of her gown and undid them one by one. As he slid the dress from her shoulders, the sound of his ragged breathing in her ear sent tiny thrilling tremors racing through her.

He turned her so she faced him and she saw he'd shrugged off his jacket. Moments later his shirt was off, too, and she saw the angry red of the knife wound was fading to a healthy pink. She gazed in fascination at the black curls of hair on his chest, touching them with a tentative finger.

He eased her gown over her hips until it fell unhampered to the floor. She stepped out of the dress and kicked it aside. Underneath she wore only a lace-edged chemise and drawers and a muslin half-petticoat. It took Spencer little time to master the intricacies of removing these. Now she wore only her black silk stockings, held up by round garters, and black-buttoned boots.

"You're even lovelier than I remembered." His voice was hoarse with emotion.

Her breasts ached for his touch, her nipples peaking with need, but he dropped to one knee instead. He lifted her right foot to his bent knee and reached with both hands to the top of her stocking. Slowly and carefully he pulled it down, garter and all, his hands stroking her thigh, then her calf, sending delightful heat into her loins. He unbuttoned her boot and pulled it from her foot, then slipped off the stocking. By the time he finished removing the other stocking, Nona felt as though every bone in her body was melting. He remained kneeling, his lips against her inner thigh, seeking and finding her most vulnerable spot.

She moaned in feverish excitement, trembling all over, holding to Spencer's shoulders to keep from falling. He rose, lifted her into his arms and carried her across the room where, after sweeping back the covers, he lowered her gently onto the bed.

She watched impatiently as he pulled off the rest of his clothes. Her attention was caught by the way his body hair arrowed down from his chest and spread into the nest at the base of his erect manhood. She couldn't take her gaze away from his arousal until she heard him chuckle and realized he'd noticed.

"It doesn't retract, honest," he said as he slid into the bed beside her.

Nona blushed.

"I love the way you look at me," he said softly.

She longed to touch him, and remembering he'd liked it when she did, reached over and closed her hand around his throbbing hardness. He closed his eyes and groaned with what she knew was pleasure.

After a moment he eased her hand away from him. "I need time to savor you," he whispered.

He drew her into his arms and she clung to him in passionate happiness. This was where she belonged. He kissed her forehead, her cheek, her ear, before finding her lips. When his tongue sought entrance, she dared to let her own tongue explore the mysteries of his mouth, tasting his special flavor, wanting him to feel the same delicious excitement he gave her.

"If I could make this last forever, I would," he murmured into her ear. "I never want it to end."

His lips trailed down and she held his head to her breast, ravished with delight, her need for him flowering within her.

She had no more doubts; she loved Spencer completely and utterly, loved him with all her heart. If she refused to be his slave, she was certainly his in that she wanted no other man. Whatever happened, she'd never want any other man.

As for him, he was hers at this moment and nothing else mattered.

The skin on his back was warm and smooth, contrasting with the crinkly feel of his body hair. Touching him was wonderful. She could go on touching him forever.

His hands tangled in her hair, stroked her curves, caressed her everywhere, making her arch against him, fueling her desire until she burned white-hot.

She knew now that love between a man and a woman wasn't merely a romantic notion; love was fire and passion and need. Love gripped the mind and the body with desire as strong and fierce as eagle talons. Love consumed in a glorious burning. Love refused to be denied.

She longed to tell Spencer how she felt, but was inarticulate with rapture and could only gasp his name as he rose above her to bring them together, joining them in a wild throbbing rhythm that transported her to the magic realm where only Spencer's sorcery could take her.

She lay in his arms afterward, drowsy and content, and knew she'd never been so happy.

"How long do we have?" he murmured into her ear.

Forever, is what she wished she could answer. "Until morning," she said.

He raised himself on one elbow and looked at her, eyebrows raised.

"I realize there'll be talk," she said defiantly, "but I don't care."

He drew her closer. "There's no other woman in the world to match you, Nona," he said. "Not in any way."

She eased back a little and gently touched his healing chest wound. "I almost lost you once. I wish you weren't going with General Custer."

"Nothing's going to happen to me—even though you won't be around to protect me." He grinned and pulled her on top of him. "Remembering who and what I have waiting for my return is enough to keep me alive through any and all calamities."

"Calamities like bullets and arrows?"

"I swear I'll come back to you, Nona." All trace of lightness was gone from his voice. "I swear I will."

She sighed. "Then I suppose I'll have to reconcile myself to waiting."

"Isn't this worth waiting for?" As he spoke, he lifted her head and kissed her, long and deeply, fanning the embers of her desire into flame once again.

"Or this?" he asked huskily a few minutes later as he eased himself into her.

Nona's worry over Spencer was lost in the rush of pleasure that enveloped her—there was no room in their private world for apprehension or fear. No death birds circled; all was joy and delight and rapture.

Much later they went down to the kitchen, Nona in her dressing gown and Spencer wearing only his trousers. Because she'd partially closed the damper before they left the house, coals still smoldered in the black range. Spencer poked at them, adding kindling and opened the damper. Nona shifted the still-warm pot of soup from the back of the stove to the front burner.

Together they made supper—soup, bread, cheese and chokecherry jelly with tea.

Sitting at the table with Spencer, Nona looked fondly at him, wondering how it would be if she were married to him. Would they enjoy simple tasks together? Or would he be home enough to share much of anything with her? Wherever their home was. If they had one.

I don't care! she told herself fiercely. Wherever Spencer is, would be home enough for me.

But, though he'd vowed to return to her, he hadn't asked her to marry him. Nor was he likely to.

"So Katy's away for the night," he said between spoonfuls of soup.

"Yes. Her mother's the local midwife and was called out, so Katy had to do the laundry."

He smiled. "You were careful not to tell me that when I first arrived."

"I had to set my mind straight first."

He lifted his cup. "Here's to Nona Willard; may her mind stay straight forever but narrow never."

She laughed. "One of the first things I liked about you on the boat was your way with words."

"What? Not my way with women?"

"*That,* I mistrusted."

"I know, I heard about you drenching the cabin boy with water."

Nona's face flamed.

"Don't worry," he added, "I'm sure no one else aboard

250

realized you thought the poor lad was me."

"You frightened me," she confessed. "I'd never met a man like you and I found myself fascinated against my will. I couldn't admit to myself that I wanted to know you better."

He reached across the table and ran his forefinger along her cheek. "I think you've come to know me better than I know myself. And that scares me."

"I don't understand why."

"I can't explain. Perhaps it's time I tried setting my own mind straight." He shifted his shoulders as though they were under some invisible load. "Dancing Coyote would tell me to open my eyes."

"Back home on the farm, Jake would say you ought to use horse sense."

"What's your advice?"

Nona saw that something troubled him, but had no idea what. Had it to do with her? Or was it because Spencer rode with those who warred against the Indians, when, as he'd told her, he felt he was on the Indians' side. She had no answers.

"I don't know you as well as you seem to think," she told him.

"Forget me. Let's see how well *I* know *you*." His grin showed her that his mood had lightened. "I'll guess what you're thinking and you tell me if I'm right." He closed his eyes for a moment, pretending to concentrate. "Aha, I have it! You're wishing for a nice hot bath."

"The farthest thing from my mind is a—"

"Don't deny it; your secret wish is my command." He rose and strode to the stove where he added wood to the fire. "First we need to heat the water."

"Spencer, I don't really think—"

"I noticed a tub in the pantry, and luckily, the windows have shades we can pull." He examined a bar of brown soap on the counter and shook his head. "Too

251

harsh for milady's fair skin."

Nona shook her head. "I'm not going to—"

"Would you deny me the pleasure of helping you bathe?"

He ought to know she was incapable of denying him anything. A picture came into her mind of sitting naked in a tub of steaming water while Spencer soaped her back, sliding around to her breasts where his thumbs brushed teasingly across her nipples. She caught her breath, a frisson of excitement skimming along her spine.

"If you insist," she said, trying to sound resigned.

He slanted her a look that told her she wasn't fooling him one bit. "Of course, one good turn deserves another," he said. "I'd expect you to wash my back, too."

She blushed, feeling as though he'd been reading her mind.

By the time the water on the stove was hot enough, Spencer had pulled the kitchen shades and closed the connecting door. Nona found two towels and two washcloths and brought from her room the perfumed Paris soap she'd never opened. He used most of the stored water to half-fill the zinc tub. When it was ready he raised his eyebrows at her.

Nona kicked off her slippers and hestitantly untied the sash of her dressing gown. Her fingers fumbled at the buttons. It didn't make sense for her to be so shy, for Spencer had seen her naked after their lovemaking, but somehow she was. Taking a deep breath, she undid the buttons and slid off the gown. She wore nothing underneath.

Spencer drew in his breath sharply as the green robe dropped from Nona's shoulders and she stood before him in unadorned beauty. He was as aroused by seeing her naked as if it were the first time. With her auburn hair tumbling over her white shoulders and breasts, she was the loveliest woman he'd ever set eyes on.

He watched her step into the tub and settle herself into the warm water, her every movement graceful. She lifted her arms and twisted her hair into a coil, pinning it atop her head. Strands escaped and drifted down to frame her face, an effect that charmed him. He wanted to go on looking at her and at the same time he longed to run his fingers over her soft skin.

He knelt beside the tub and hefted the rose-shaped cake of *Le Fleuer* soap in his hand, an exotic perfume wafting to him as he dipped the soap into the water. Forcing his gaze from her firm, pink-tipped breasts, he decided to begin with her back because if he didn't, he might never get to it.

"A little soap goes a long way," she warned him, taking the cake from him and setting it aside. Her voice held the touch of husky sweetness which told him she wanted him and his hand trembled as his own need increased.

At this rate he'd soon be in the tub with her and it wasn't large enough for them both. As he slid the washcloth along the curve of her breast, the floral perfume surrounded him, overpowering his senses.

He had no idea why she'd changed her mind, why she'd decided to defy gossip and invite him into her bed, but nothing in his life had ever made him happier. Slowly and deliberately, he washed every inch of her exquisite body, teasing her and himself until he was ready to explode.

Suddenly Nona rose and stepped out of the tub. "It's your turn," she said, reaching for the towel.

He refused to let her dry herself, insisting on rubbing her gently with the towel. When she started to don her long-sleeved robe, he said, "You can't wash me with that on, you'll get soaked."

Nona dropped the dressing gown onto a chair. "I can't wash you with your trousers on, either," she informed him.

Because he was aroused, Spencer had some difficulty

discarding the trousers. He'd never stepped into used bath water with more enjoyment. As he sat down in the tub, he felt surrounded by Nona's wonderful essence, and when she knelt naked beside the tub and began soaping him, he thought he'd die of pleasure.

"I'm going to smell of French perfume for days," he complained and then felt a pang as he remembered he'd be leaving her soon, taking with him only the faint scent of her soap.

He didn't want to leave this woman, not tomorrow or the next day. The dread of losing her was like an arrow piercing his heart. But she'd promised to wait for him; he wouldn't lose her. She'd be here when he returned.

As she continued to wash him, his desire mounted until he could no longer wait. He sprang from the tub, toweled himself dry, scooped Nona into his arms and carried her up to the bedroom.

They tumbled into bed and he tried to take her into his arms. She held him off.

"Wait," she said. "I want to do to you what you do to me." She bent her head and touched his arousal, first with her lips, then with her tongue.

All but overwhelmed, Spencer groaned and pushed her away.

"Why won't you let me?" she asked.

"What you're doing feels so good that if you keep on I won't be able to control myself. I won't be able to make love to you the way I want to."

"Then you did like it?"

"Oh, God, Nona, you don't realize what you do to me. Just looking at you drives me so crazy I can't wait to make love to you. Even on the boat I knew I wanted you. I longed to be with you like this; your beautiful hair spread on a pillow and you in my arms."

"It took me quite awhile longer to realize what I wanted," she whispered.

"That's because you fought it and I didn't." He drew her closer, his hand sliding along the curve of her hip. He bent to kiss her and stopped a breath away from her lips. "When *did* you know you wanted me?"

"When I saw you leap from your pony onto the buffalo."

He laughed, a deep exultant laugh, feeling the same sudden surge of power he'd felt the day he rode *pte*. Nona had felt that power, she'd known then that she was destined to be his woman. The buffalo he'd killed had given him not only a name to be proud of, but his heart's desire.

The image of a white buffalo loomed in his mind, but this was not the time to ponder the mystery of spirit buffalos, not with the woman he desired most in his arms.

Spencer kissed her and the welcoming warmth of her lips drove every other thought from his head. There was only Nona and the all-encompassing web of passion that bound them together.

Chapter 17

Spencer left just before dawn, and by the time Katy arrived at midmorning, Nona had cleaned the kitchen and put away the tub.

"General Custer's home," Katy burst out before she even got her hat off. "Mike says the troops'll be leaving tomorrow for sure."

"Tomorrow," Nona echoed, her mind on Spencer. Would she have a chance to say goodbye? She could hardly bear to think of him riding away from the Fort and from her. She wanted to be with him, danger or not, but under the circumstances it was impossible.

She drifted around the kitchen, ostensibly helping Katy make dinner, for they expected Kilby home around noon. Katy chattered away, but Nona, reliving the wonderful all-too-short hours with Spencer, scarcely heard her until her voice sharpened.

"Miss? Miss?"

Nona blinked and focused her attention on Katy.

"You been taking so long peeling that one potato that the white of it's turning dark," Katy pointed out. "Ma'd say you was woolgathering."

"Your mother would be right," Nona agreed, finishing the potato. She dropped it in the pot of boiling water and picked up another. "I'd best tend to business or we'll never have dinner on the table."

"The Lieutenant's gonna be mighty hungry coming off patrol. Mike says trail food ain't fit for man nor beast." She took a deep breath and fixed her gaze on Nona. "You ain't gonna mind if Mike comes by tonight to say goodbye to me?"

"Not if he's sober."

"I swear he's learned his lesson. He told me whiskey did for his brother one winter and he don't want to end up the same way—freezing to death in the snow on account of being blind drunk. He says his mates carry rotgut in their canteens 'stead of water, but he won't no more."

Nona hoped for Katy's sake that Mike could stick to his vow.

"I suppose you and the Lieutenant'll be going to Mrs. Custer's party this afternoon," Katy said.

Nona had completely forgotten about the party. She no longer cared one way or the other whether she went, but for Kilby's sake, she'd go. There was always the off chance she'd see Spencer there.

"Yes, I think we will," Nona said.

"I was wondering if you wanted me to fix your hair. Twisting it into a knot don't do nothing to show off that pretty color. I'm good with hair. Even Ma says so."

About to refuse politely, Nona paused. Why not? If Spencer *was* there, she wanted to look her best.

"Thank you, Katy, I'd appreciate it," she said.

Shortly after Kilby arrived home, Nona sat down at the table to eat with him.

"You're looking very well," he said. "Rest is a great restorer."

She thanked him. If she did look well, it certainly had nothing to do with rest; she'd gotten very little sleep last night. She slipped into a reverie, recalling how wonderful it had been to wake to Spencer's caress, to feel his warm body touching hers, to soar with him as they made love. . . .

"Have you thought over my proposal?" Kilby asked.

She stared at him, for a long moment unable to understand what he was talking about. Then it came to her—Kilby had asked her to marry him. She couldn't possibly!

"I don't want to—that is, I don't believe we'd do well together," she said haltingly. "Just because Helen was my sister doesn't mean you'd be happy with me."

"What are you talking about?" he demanded. "I met you and liked you before I knew Helen. I thought you liked me, too. Am I wrong?"

Is that how he sees it? Nona wondered, old memories flooding her mind: How she'd met Kilby at a dance at the U.S. Military Academy in West Point when he was still a cadet; how they'd strolled along Flirtation Walk overlooking the Hudson River in the moonlight; how, when he'd kissed her, she'd been sure it was true love; how quickly he'd lost interest in her after he visited her at the farm and met Helen.

Because she'd idealized him and believed they had an "understanding," she'd been devastated at first. Helen's happiness and the wedding that followed had been hard to bear. Nona realized now her pride had been more damaged than her heart, but she hadn't known it then and she'd been miserable. Did Kilby suspect none of this?

"Of course I like you," she said at last. "But that's not enough."

His eyes narrowed. How pale a green they were compared to the rich, deep brown of Spencer's. "You've met someone else," he said. "That's what the trouble is."

How she felt about Spencer was none of Kilby's business. "I'm honored by your offer," she told him, "but I can't marry you."

"I imagine you'll want to leave Fort Lincoln before my

258

return, then."

Nona blinked. "I thought you wanted me to stay until the campaign was over and you rescued your daughter. Won't you need me here to take care of her when you bring her back?"

Kilby stared at her assessingly. "The man's at the Fort, isn't he?"

"I don't care to discuss that. If you don't want me to remain in your house while you're gone, say so."

Kilby smiled his usual charming smile. Why did she suddenly feel it was calculating?

"I didn't mean to upset you," he said. "Naturally you'll remain here if you wish. I'd be pleased if you did. And I will need you to care for the baby when I rescue her. At least until I can hire a trustworthy nursemaid."

He dropped the subject and attacked his roast beef with vigor and enthusiasm. "Katy's a good cook," he said. "You'd do well to keep her on while I'm gone."

Nona asked questions about his patrol. He answered, but absently she thought, as though his mind was elsewhere.

"Mrs. Custer's gathering is at three," he said when he finished eating. "I believe I'll have a short nap before we go." He rose and went up to his room.

Kilby took it for granted she'd go because he wanted her to. If she didn't hope to see Spencer at the party, she might be tempted to put a spoke in Kilby's wheel by refusing to attend. It came back to her how Kilby had ordered Helen to stay inside the house because of her condition and wouldn't permit her to go to the dance. How had her sister put up with it? Because she loved Kilby?

I'd never submit to unreasonable orders, Nona told herself. Not even if Spencer gave them.

She helped Katy clear the table and clean the kitchen.

"Lieutenant Mead wants you to stay with me while

259

he's off on the campaign," she told the girl. "Will you?"

"At night, sure. Daytimes, I might have to help Ma some."

"That would be fine. I like having you here."

Katy beamed. "Seems like we do get along." She looked Nona up and down. "I know you got to wear black, but ain't you got something a little fancier?"

The black gown with the ivory stripes, Nona realized, was somewhat the worse for wear. But her own dowdy black gown was even more so. "I'm afraid not," she told Katy.

"You might could wear something of your sister's."

"Oh, no, I wouldn't feel right. Besides, she was shorter and plumper than I am."

"It ain't for me to say, but I bet if she was alive she'd give you the shirt off her back. Did you know she once sent a beautiful white gown of hers to a Sud's Row girl who didn't have nothing white to get married in?"

Tears filled Nona's eyes as she remembered Helen's impulsive generosity. "Helen was never stingy," she said. "When she was a little girl she was always getting scolded for giving away her toys to other children. The only thing she wouldn't part with was her favorite doll, Amanda Jean."

Nona's tears overflowed and ran down her cheeks. What a terrible thing she'd done giving away her sister's baby. Amanda Jean must be rescued!

Katy put an arm around her. "I didn't mean to make you cry, honest."

Not wanting to upset Katy, Nona wiped her eyes. As she tried to compose herself, it occurred to her that there were some things of Helen's that Katy might be able to use—the larger gowns Helen had worn during her confinement. She mentioned this to Katy.

"I sure wouldn't turn down anything you want to give

me," Katy said. "Ma and me, we're pretty fair at altering clothes to fit."

"I left a box in the upstairs hall," Nona told her. "Take whatever you can use."

Katy wasted no time, carrying the box into the kitchen where she lifted out the dresses and admired them. Nona watched, her grief for Helen lightened by Katy's enthusiastic gratitude.

"Here's a nansook princess style with a train," Katy commented, holding up a black gown. "Wouldn't be hard to alter this to fit you. I notice you don't never wear trains, so I could cut off the extra material and make a ruffle around the bottom so the gown'd be long enough for you."

"Thank you, Katy, but I wouldn't dream of putting you to all that trouble."

"'Tisn't no trouble. Won't take me hardly no time. I wish you'd let me." Katy's blue eyes pleaded with Nona. "You been so good to me I want to do something nice for you."

Nona didn't have the heart to argue. At least the black nansook was a gown she'd never seen Helen wear, so it wouldn't remind her of her sister.

By three o'clock she was ready to set off for the Custers wearing the nansook with a tiny capelet Katy had contrived from the remainder of the train. Katy had also pinned the front sections of Nona's hair atop her head, leaving the rest to curl down her back. She'd settled the black straw onto Nona's head so curls showed to the sides and the front.

"You're very talented," Nona told Katy when she examined herself in the mirror over the mantle. "I hardly recognize myself."

"It ain't that you ain't pretty," Katy said earnestly, "it's just that you don't make the most of what you got."

Nona smiled at her, knowing Katy meant well.

Kilby came slowly down the stairs, yawning and buttoning his blue uniform jacket. When he caught sight of Nona he smiled. "How charming you look."

She thanked him, relieved that he didn't seem to recognize the dress. But then Katy's alterations had changed it considerably.

Kilby and Nona walked along the Row to the Custer house, her hand on his arm. She couldn't deny Kilby cut a handsome figure with the deep blue of his dress uniform complementing his fair coloring, but being with him didn't stir her in any way.

Other officers walked ahead, one with his wife who wore a Dolly Varden hat colorfully decorated with plumes and flowers.

"How Helen would have loved that hat," Nona exclaimed involuntarily.

Kilby slanted her a reproving look and she blinked indignantly. Did he think it improper to speak of the dead? She shook her head. More likely the mention of Helen upset him and he wished to be calm and collected when he greeted his commanding officer. She must watch her tongue.

Tom met them at the door and ushered them in, then pressed a cup of fruit punch into Nona's hands. The parlor was crowded with uniformed men and women in variously colored gowns, some in the very latest style, making Nona glad she'd let Katy talk her into the nansook. People overflowed into other rooms and Nona followed Kilby into what she guessed must be the General's study.

General Custer stood beside the fireplace talking to Captain French, Kilby's immediate superior and the commander of M Company. A large picture of the General and another, not quite so large, of General

McClellan hung on the wall to the right of the fireplace. A stuffed snowy owl perched on a rack of deer horns separated the two pictures. Mounted antelope heads hung to either side.

"You should see his trophy room," Kilby said. "The General's not only a fine marskman, but he does his own taxidermy."

Was there anything he didn't do well? she wondered. General Custer's looks were striking. His coloring was as fair as Kilby's but he had a lean hawk face that commanded the attention of everyone present. Nona had heard of his long flowing locks, but he'd cut them, his dark blond hair didn't reach to his collar. There was a marked resemblance between him and Tom, but somehow the General made Tom seem a lesser copy—even Tom's mustache wasn't as bushy as his older brother's.

General Custer bowed slightly over her hand when Kilby introduced her as his sister-in-law.

"I'm delighted to meet you, but I am so sorry to hear of the loss of your sister and your ordeal," he said. His voice was higher pitched than she'd imagined it would be.

She murmured politely, saying it was an honor to meet him. The General turned his attention to Kilby, repeating his condolences, but Nona scarcely heard him. She'd caught sight of Spencer standing under the trophies talking to the only other civilian in the room, a man of about forty, with graying hair. She drifted toward them, drawn to Spencer by invisible strings.

He was frowning as he listened to the graying man, but when he caught sight of her his expression changed. His welcoming smile warmed her.

"Miss Willard," Spencer said, catching her hand and drawing her closer. "Allow me to introduce a fellow correspondent, Mr. Mark Kellogg of the Bismarck *Herald*."

"How do you do, Mr. Kellogg?" Nona said. "Will you be riding with General Custer, too?"

"I'm happy to say I will be, Miss Willard. It's the chance of a lifetime."

After a few more words with Mark Kellogg, Spencer maneuvered her away and into a tiny nook whose space was taken up mostly by a rack of guns.

"I wasn't sure you'd be here," he said.

"How else can I say goodbye to you?"

"Aren't you coming out in the morning to wave farewell to us all—the gallant Seventh and the infantry, General Custer and General Terry?"

"I only care about you."

He grasped her hand, holding it between both of his. "I'll miss you, Nona."

The noise in the room faded as she gazed into his dark eyes; the people disappeared from view. Spencer filled her world.

"Nona." Kilby's voice.

She turned to see him standing behind her. Spencer released her hand.

"Mrs. Custer asked me to find you," Kilby said. "She wants you to meet Mrs. Calhoun, the General's sister." He nodded to Spencer. "I trust you can spare her, Mr. Quinlan?"

"I'm not certain I can." Spencer's smile was the one-sided smile she hated. "Miss Willard isn't easy to give up. Don't you agree, Lieutenant?"

Animosity vibrated in the air between the two men, but surely they had sense enough not to make a scene in front of General Custer. Glancing from Spencer's mocking smile to Kilby's clenched jaw, Nona decided maybe they didn't. She must do something to separate them, and quickly.

"I'd be delighted to meet Libbie's sister-in-law," she told Kilby. "Please do excuse me, Mr. Quinlan."

"I'll take you to Mrs. Custer." Kilby's voice was cool.

Nona cast a backward glance at Spencer's scowling face as she walked away with Kilby.

"Mr. Quinlan isn't the most popular man at the Fort," Kilby said. "If Major Reno had his way, Quinlan wouldn't be riding with us tomorrow."

"Why?"

"Civilians at Fort Lincoln are as subject to Army regulations as soldiers. Mr. Quinlan has gone out of his way to defy the Major."

Nona raised her chin and looked Kilby in the eye. "I wouldn't be here if it weren't for Spencer borrowing an Army mount and a Ree scout. Was that defying Major Reno?"

"Quinlan didn't bother to ask the Major's permission."

"Do you believe the Major would have said yes?"

Kilby shrugged. "Major Reno *is* human, after all."

What kind of an answer was that? Nona wondered. But she saw they were approaching Libbie Custer and decided not to pursue the issue—this was not the time or place to argue with Kilby.

Nona soon discovered that Margaret Calhoun was not only the General's sister but was married to the lieutenant who commanded the Seventh's L company.

"My brother Boston's riding with Tom and Autie," Margaret told Nona, "and so is our nephew, Autie Reed. He's the General's namesake, you know."

"The boys are so excited," Libbie put in. "They can't wait to get started."

When Nona discovered Boston Custer and Autie Reed truly were teen-aged boys and not men, she was horrified. "But surely that's dangerous."

Libbie raised her eyebrows. "The General will make certain nothing happens to them."

"I'm sure he will," Nona agreed, clamping her lips shut to hold back what she wanted to say: *In the midst of war, how can anyone be protected against arrows and bullets?*

On the other hand, if General Custer was bringing his young brother and nephew along with the Seventh, he must be supremely confident of a quick and easy victory. Thinking about this, Nona felt a little better about Spencer going.

"I was beginning to believe you'd slipped away without a word of farewell, Miss Willard."

Nona turned, noting Tom had a small scratch on his nose. A result of the fight with Spencer? "I never did thank you for your assistance the other night," she said, determined to be polite. "It was kind of you to help."

"Any time. I trust you'll be staying on until the Seventh returns in triumph?"

She nodded, cheered by his confidence in the success of the Seventh.

"Did you have some difficulty while I was on patrol?" Kilby asked her.

"No, of course not," Nona said.

Kilby looked questioningly at Tom.

"A minor problem," Tom assured him, winking at Nona. "Nothing of importance."

Margaret caught her brother's arm, and when Tom turned to her she leaned forward and said something about Autie Reed. Libbie was talking to another officer's wife. Kilby edged Nona away from Tom and the two women.

"You seem quite friendly with Captain Custer." He didn't sound especially pleased.

"Tom?" Annoyed with Kilby, Nona used the name deliberately, though she'd never dream of calling the Captain Tom to his face. "Why shouldn't I be? Isn't he the General's brother, a fine man and the best shot in the regiment? Doesn't he command Company C?" She was repeating the very words Kilby had once said to her but he didn't seem to realize it.

"Tom is all of those things," Kilby said solemnly, "but it's best you understand he's something of a ladies' man."

Nona almost burst out laughing. Could this be the same Kilby who'd urged Tom on her when she first arrived? Her amusement faded as it came to her what was different. Helen was gone and now Kilby wanted to keep her for himself.

She didn't want either of them—Tom or Kilby. The only man who interested her was Spencer Quinlan. Nona glanced around the crowded room. Where was he? She must say one final goodbye to him before tomorrow, but if she set off to look for him, Kilby might well follow her.

"Do you understand what I'm saying?" Kilby demanded.

"Thank you for warning me." She drained her punch and handed the cup to him.

As soon as he moved away for a refill, Nona slipped between the men in blue uniforms, searching for a man in civilian black. She didn't see Spencer anywhere.

A hand closed around her wrist, halting her, pulling her in the opposite direction. She whirled and stared into Spencer's dark eyes.

"I'll walk you home," he said, urging her toward the door.

Nona went willingly. Once outside, though her heart pounded and her skin tingled, she walked sedately along the road, her hand on Spencer's arm.

"I didn't have a chance to thank the hostess," she murmured. "Or say goodbye to anyone."

Spencer smiled at her. "Libbie will bear up under the omission. I'm not so sure about Lieutenant Mead."

She knew they'd reach the house all too soon and she

couldn't very well ask him in. There was no privacy in the house, and besides, Kilby was likely to come looking for her.

As though reading her mind, Spencer veered off the road and led her toward the rear of the house, then up the back steps onto the porch. He took her into his arms.

"I can't wait any longer to kiss you and this is as private as I can make it," he said as his mouth came down on hers.

Nona clung to him, lost in his embrace, wanting the kiss to never end.

"We said goodbye last night," he whispered into her ear, "but that wasn't enough. When I see you, I have to touch you, to hold you."

"I wish we didn't have to say goodbye."

He eased her away and looked at her. "The General predicts victory by the Fourth of July at the latest. That's not so far away."

Nona sighed.

"I'll leave you here," he said. "The Lieutenant's already hot under the collar and I'm not sure you'd forgive me if I got into another fight." He brushed his lips against hers in an all-too-brief caress and released her. "Let's say *au revoir* instead of goodbye. Because I *am* coming back."

She watched him stride down the stairs and around the side of the house. When she was out of sight, she opened the back door and hurried through the kitchen without a word to Katy, hoping to catch a last glimpse of him through the parlor window.

She'd almost reached the parlor when Kilby burst through the front door.

"You left with Quinlan," he said accusingly, looking around as though expecting to find Spencer there.

He must have just missed seeing Spencer, she thought gratefully. In Kilby's present mood, there'd surely have

268

been a confrontation.

Kilby's lip curled. "Or should I call him 'Spencer,' as you do."

Nona bristled. "And why shouldn't I? Spencer's my friend."

"What do you know about the man? He's a nobody, a roving journalist of no particular talent. Mr. Kellogg had never heard of him."

"Don't you think a man who risked his life to save mine and Helen's deserves my friendship? As for Mr. Kellogg—he's from Bismarck, a town that's not exactly the center of the universe. And how do you know Spencer has no talent? Have you ever read anything he's written?"

"No, have you?"

Nona had not, but she wasn't going to admit that to Kilby. "Since all of you—Spencer and Mr. Kellogg included—are leaving the Fort tomorrow, I fail to see your point." Anger edged her words.

Kilby caught her by the shoulders. "I've asked you to marry me and you've put me off. I'd hate to see you throw yourself away on a man who'll make you unhappy. Has *he* asked you to marry him?"

With Kilby staring her in the eye, Nona couldn't avoid the question. "We haven't discussed marriage," she snapped, twisting away from him.

Kilby nodded, as though this confirmed his poor opinion of Spencer.

Nona shook with fury. She wanted to shout that she loved Spencer and nothing else mattered, that even if he never asked her to be his wife, she'd still love him. She curbed her impulse with difficulty, reminding herself that Kilby was riding into battle tomorrow. What if he didn't return? What if all she had to remember was this quarrel on his last night at home?

He was Helen's husband and the father of poor lost

Amanda Jean. He deserved better than a shouting match tonight. He deserved her courteous consideration, whether or not she wished to give it to him.

Taking a deep breath, she eased it out slowly to the count of ten. "Let's not argue." With some effort, she managed to keep her tone pleasant. "After all, I consider you my friend, too, Kilby. Can't we behave like friends?"

Chapter 18

At five in the morning, Spencer, mounted on Kaintuck, waited near the Ree village while the Seventh Cavalry trotted through the river mist toward the parade ground. The Indian scouts headed the column, followed by the band on matching gray horses. General Custer rode next, flanked by troopers bearing the guidons, one the United States Army Cavalry's small swallow-tailed flag, the other the General's own pennant with crossed silver sabers framed by a red bar above; a blue bar below. Behind Custer came the Seventh's twelve companies.

Near Spencer, the Ree women wailed their melancholy farewell chants. He watched the Seventh pass Suds Row where the wives and children of the enlisted men lined the road. A motley company of small boys with flags fashioned from rags tied to sticks and banging spoons on tin pans, marched alongside the troopers. As if in response, the band struck up "The Girl I Left Behind Me."

The words of the song ran through Spencer's mind as he fell into place at the rear of the regiment:

> "The hour was sad I left the maid
> A lingering farewell taking

> Her sighs and tears my steps delayed
> I thought her heart was breaking . . ."

He didn't know if Nona's heart was breaking, but his felt like a lump of granite in his chest. He halted Kaintuck while the cavalry crossed the parade ground. The officers' wives stood on their porches waving. Two women were on Mead's porch—Nona and Katy. He quelled his impulse to ride along the Row for a last goodbye and contented himself with a wave, not sure whether she saw him or not.

The sun broke through the mist as Custer led his men away from the Fort to join the rest of General Terry's army. The band played "Garry Owen" and the horses stepped smartly to the spirited old Irish drinking song.

For a time Spencer rode at the rear of the cavalry. Behind him were the infantry, scouts, pack mules and horse-drawn artillery, followed by a long line of white-covered ambulances and supply wagons. The column, he thought, must stretch for at least two miles as it wound into the western hills.

Glancing upward at the lingering mist, Spencer was startled to see a reflection of the cavalry trotting above him. A sign, Dancing Coyote would say, that the spirits of the blue-coated warriors will soon ride the Spirit Path.

Spencer shrugged, dissipating his unease. It seemed to him the Army was well-nigh invincible. Over a thousand armed men marched against the hostiles, their strength multiplied by the artillery's three Gatling guns. The Gatlings, their ten barrels turned by a crank, fired four hundred shots a minute. Bows and arrows and single-shot rifles hadn't a chance against them. As for himself, he carried his Colt and Sky Arrow's Winchester rifle—though he hoped to hell he wouldn't be forced to use either.

They camped for the night on the Heart River where

the paymaster handed around four months' back pay. By Terry's and Custer's joint order, whiskey sellers were banned from the camp, but it was obvious from the men's drunken singing and raucous laughter, that somehow or other whiskey was available.

Rain began to fall before dawn, dampening the soldiers' high spirits. Libbie Custer and Margaret Calhoun, who'd accompanied the Seventh until now, were escorted back to Fort Lincoln by the paymaster and an infantry company. General Terry's army set off to the north.

For the next ten days, heading north and then west, each day's march was much the same as the one before. They saw not one hostile Indian; there were no alarms or excursions. On the thirtieth of May, the army reached the Little Missouri River. Terry commanded the entire army, Spencer knew, but by then it was obvious that Terry deferred to Custer. He could understand why— Custer was the Indian fighter; not Terry.

A week later, the Seventh camped on the Powder River, awaiting the slower infantry and wagons. Custer sent Major Reno and six companies to scout up the Powder River. Spencer begged permission to go along, but Reno balked.

"You're a troublemaker, Quinlan. I won't have you," he told Spencer in front of Custer.

The General eyed Spencer curiously, but said nothing until later that day when the rest of the army marched to set up a base camp where the Powder emptied into the Yellowstone.

Motioning Spencer to ride alongside him, Custer said, "My brother Tom doesn't much care for you either, Quinlan, but I didn't pay much heed because I know you two fell out over a woman. What did you do to rile Reno?"

Spencer told him about Nona's rescue and how he'd

273

appropriated Kaintuck and the Ree scout, Three Crows.

Custer shrugged as though he found it a trivial matter. "The upshot is Tom won't have you in his company nor Reno with his." He grinned. "It seems I'm stuck with you."

"*You're* the one the newspapers are interested in, General. *You're* the one I came along to write about."

Custer sat Vic, his blooded sorrel, with confidence and grace, but it seemed to Spencer as he spoke that the General drew himself even more erect. He was an inspiring figure in his buckskin shirt and gray-white plains hat—every inch a leader.

"You can be sure I plan to give you something to write about, Quinlan," he said.

By June twenty-first, the sternwheeler supply boat, *Far West,* was moored at the mouth of the Rosebud where Terry's army had linked up with General Gibbon's four cavalry and two infantry companies from Forts Shaw and Ellis in the Montana Territory. They camped there awaiting General Crook's force coming from Fort Laramie in the Wyoming Territory.

Spencer was impressed by the overall plan of the generals for a three-pronged attack and felt sure the Indians were doomed. He and Mark Kellogg spent that evening writing dispatches for the *Far West* to take back downriver; Spencer's reflected his growing admiration for General Custer.

After finishing his dispatch, Spencer left the boat and walked past the camp to the nearby Ree camp. The scouts preferred to stay apart from the soldiers and he knew at least part of the reason was Indians didn't like the smell of whites. The soldiers were happy with the arrangement —they thought redskins stank. Spencer had to admit he could tell a white from an Indian by his smell, but he didn't find either odor particularly offensive.

He entered the Ree camp, keeping an eye out for Three

Crows. Reno had returned to camp reporting that he'd seen no hostiles, although his scouts had spotted recent sign along the Rosebud. Spencer hoped Three Crows would tell him more about what the sign showed.

"Many Sioux pass. Big Sioux camp close," Three Crows said as the two men stood under a cottonwood.

"How many Sioux in the camp?"

Three Crows thought for a moment, then looked up and gestured at the star-studded sky. Spencer gazed up and wondered if the Ree was exaggerating.

"Cheyenne camp with Sioux," Three Crows said. "Arapaho camp with Sioux." Again he waved at the night sky.

Spencer knew the names of the most feared Sioux warrior leaders—Crazy Horse, Gall and Rain-in-the-Face—and he'd heard of Sitting Bull and his strong medicine. All brave and valiant fighters. But what good were valiant fighters, even though they might lead thousands of warriors, against three armies coming at them from three different directions, armies equipped with Gatling guns?

He decided he'd rise early and ride with the scouts to satisfy himself that there really were as many hostiles as the Ree seemed to believe. Besides the Rees, there were Gibbon's Crow scouts, mortal enemies of the Sioux.

As Spencer made his way to where he'd left Kaintuck and his gear, he caught snatches of the troopers' conversations.

"Up the Rosebud with fifteen days' rations, a hundred rounds of ammunition for carbines, twenty-four for pistols. How far we gonna be from the supply train?"

"You know old Iron Butt. He travels fast and light."

"If he's so hell-bent on speed, how come Terry's gotta review us afore we leave?"

"'Cause we're the best 'n he wants Terry to know it."

Iron Butt was Custer, Spencer knew, the nickname

275

given by his men because on long marches he never seemed to tire. So Custer was riding with the Seventh tomorrow. Another scouting mission?

Spencer knew the troopers would clam up if he questioned them. Many of the men knew Tom Custer and Major Reno regarded him *persona non grata,* and they spoke to him guardedly. What he needed was someone he knew, someone who'd talk to him without reserve. The only name that came to mind was Mike Jakes. Spencer looked around for the Company M tents. That was Mead's company, too, but he planned to avoid Mead.

"Uh, well, I don't know too much," Mike protested when Spencer found him and walked with him a short distance from the camp.

"Where's the Seventh headed?" Spencer asked.

"Up the Rosebud. We're following the trail Major Reno found."

"Scouting?"

"Uh, I guess so." Mike sounded uneasy. "Leastways nobody said different."

"Pinpointing the big Sioux camp for the generals."

"I hear tell it's a big one, all right. Three Crows don't like being near so many Sioux."

"You know Three Crows?" Spencer asked, surprised. Most of the enlisted men had nothing to do with the scouts, though Custer valued them.

"Yeah, we're sorta friends. Much as you can be with a redskin." Mike's voice was sheepish. "I got some medicine from Doc Porter for Three Crows' father once. Doc don't like to treat redskins, but I said the medicine was for me. The old man, he got better, and the one thing about them redskins, they don't never forget a favor."

Or an injury, Spencer thought, remembering Rain-in-the-Face's threat when he escaped after being captured by Tom Custer: "I will cut out his heart and eat it."

"Three Crows, he thinks the Sioux are camping behind

276

the hills, laying in wait for us. He don't want to ride tomorrow on account of only the Seventh's going. He figures we need the whole damn Army riding with us."

"But why, if this is just a scouting mission?"

"Well, sir, who knows that for sure?"

"General Custer, for one."

"*He* does, yeah. Me, I don't. Three Crows, he don't. Even you, sir, you don't. My Ma said Grandma Kelly, her ma, had second sight. I ain't claiming I got it. Far's I can tell second sight ain't something anyone'd want. But I dreamed last night 'bout my grandma, I did, and she warned me clear as a bell. 'Michael Kelly Jakes,' she says, 'you ain't coming outa this in one piece.' Grandma, she died seven years ago this month. Makes a man think."

Spencer suppressed a shiver. Dancing Coyote would call the dream a bad omen. But Mike wasn't a Dakota. And neither was Spencer Quinlan.

Whether he believed in dream visions or not, unease gripped Spencer. He clapped Mike on the shoulder in farewell, unable to bring himself to utter words of reassurance he had no confidence in.

By the time he was ready to turn in for the night, Spencer had overheard two officers of the Seventh discussing the next day's ride. Five days, they'd said. Scouting mission. Locate the hostiles. Wait for Terry. Wait for Gibbon. And Crook. But they sounded as uncertain as Mike.

The thin horns of the new moon rode over the camp, the Lakota Cherry Moon. Coyotes yapped from a distant hill, causing Custer's five elkhounds to howl in answer. I hope to hell I don't dream tonight, Spencer thought.

He fell asleep to fireflies dancing near the stream and to a chorus of frogs. His last thought was of Nona and their nights of camping together on their way back to Fort Lincoln. What was she doing now? Did she miss him as he missed her? He'd never realized he could feel about anyone as he did about Nona. . . .

The woman in white who stood sorrowfully over Spencer's sleeping body was tall and slim and beautiful. He knew he slept, oblivious to her, but at the same time he was somehow able to watch her and his sleeping self.

"Soon it will be too late to wake," she said softly. "You have ears, but you do not hear my words. Your eyes remain closed. Why will you not understand, my grandson?"

He tried to decipher her meaning but could not. Why did this lovely young woman call him grandson? He turned his attention to his sleeping form, struggling in vain to rouse himself. When he looked at the woman again she was nowhere in sight. There was nothing to be seen but a white buffalo disappearing in the misty distance.

"Pte!" he tried to shout. "Wait, don't leave me."

No words came.

But the buffalo paused and turned its head toward him. As it did, his sleeping self woke, and, leaping up, leveled a rifle at the white buffalo.

"No!"

Spencer woke with the word ringing in his ears. Around him men snored or breathed heavily in sleep. A nearby horse snuffled and stomped. He sat up, shaking the disturbing threads of the dream from his head. A man stood by the horses. Who was he? Slowly Spencer rose, one hand gripping his pistol, and made his way toward the unmoving figure. Before he reached the man he saw it was an Indian.

"Quin-lan." Three Crows' voice.

Spencer relaxed his grip on the gun and walked up to the Ree.

"We talk," Three Crows said.

"By the stream," Spencer agreed, not wanting to disturb the sleepers.

Fireflies still blinked in the darkness, but their intrusion silenced the frogs. Spencer said nothing when

278

they stopped by a cottonwood whose roots thrust into the water. Indians spoke when they were ready, they couldn't be rushed.

"Bloody Knife tell me go home," Three Crows said finally.

Spencer thought over his words. "Bloody Knife doesn't want you to die," he said at last, almost sure he'd made the right interpretation.

"He say too many Sioux, no good we all walk the Spirit Path. Some go home, some stay. I come tell you."

"Are you going home?"

"Bloody Knife my blood brother. I stay with him. Bloody Knife say to me, you stay, you no fight. Let soldiers fight. You no soldier, you scout."

"He's right."

"No like this place." With those words, Three Crows disappeared into the trees.

Spencer walked slowly back to his blankets, thinking to himself that he didn't like this place either. Why had he dreamed again of the white buffalo? She had warned him as clearly as Bloody Knife had warned Three Crows. But of what?

He rolled himself into his blankets but didn't sleep for the rest of the night, pondering both what Three Crows had told him and his own enigmatic vision dream. Whatever the warning, he, like Three Crows, would stay, would go on following Custer.

The Wolf Mountains lay between Rosebud Creek and Little Bighorn River—rough country with high ridges and deep ravines. Custer's relentless onward drive was hard going for the horses and hard on the men, too.

The Seventh numbered six hundred men, as well as forty-four Crow and Ree scouts and twenty guides, packers and interpreters, all hot under the relentless sun

279

and tired of the enforced marching.

And me and Kellogg along for the ride, Spencer thought wryly, as hot and tired as anyone else.

In the past three days they'd found more than one abandoned village. So many, in fact, that it looked like the hostiles had camped in the Rosebud's every bend. When they'd come across a sundance lodge where two buffalo skulls lay atop a pile of stones, the Indian scouts had turned sullen, muttering among themselves. The scouts had grown progressively gloomy as the Seventh passed from the pleasantly mint-scented valley of the Rosebud into the hills.

By the twenty-fifth, with dust pluming for a marker high above them, they reached a high bluff overlooking the valley of the Little Bighorn—the river the Lakota called the Greasy Grass.

At the foot of the bluff, Custer halted the Seventh and climbed with scouts to the top. Spencer stood with Kellogg watching the Ree medicine man, Stabbed, anoint the Ree scouts, chanting as he rubbed salve on their chests in an effort to protect them against the bullets and arrows of their enemies.

Spencer shook his head at the futility of salve and chants against bullets. The scouts had repeatedly told of a huge hostile encampment. "Too many Sioux," Bloody Knife, Custer's favorite Ree scout, had reported the day before. "Take many days to kill them."

"Oh, no," Custer had answered. "I guess we'll get through them in one day."

Spencer thought otherwise. He knew Gibbon had offered to send his cavalry with Custer and Terry had offered the Gatling guns. Custer had accepted neither. Why? Under the circumstances more men and especially more guns would be a godsend. Did Custer truly believe his phenomenal luck was enough to bring success? Was he too proud to admit the Seventh needed help?

Or did Custer mean to establish beyond a doubt that the hostiles were camped in the valley below and then fall back and wait for Terry and Gibbon, as he'd been ordered to do?

Spencer didn't believe that, either.

"We could be in St. Louis reporting on the Democratic Convention," Kellogg commented. "We could be clean and cool and comfortable."

Spencer nodded his agreement. "True. Would you prefer being there?"

Kellogg shook his head. "What, and miss this? Not a chance. Want to bet the Democrats'll nominate George Armstrong Custer? As soon as he hammers these hostiles into line, he's a shoo-in."

"Not as soon as. If."

Kellogg stared at him. "The man's the greatest Indian fighter in the country."

"I don't doubt that. But there are more Indians ahead of us than he's ever faced before. Too many. And this is no surprise raid. They know we're coming. They could see our dust for miles."

"Don't be a crepe-hanger, Quinlan," Kellogg advised. "Remember, we've got Terry backing us up."

How far back? Spencer wondered, aware the infantry and supply units couldn't march anywhere near as fast as Custer had driven the Seventh. He was afraid the answer was "too far."

They moved on after a grim-faced Custer came down from the look-out, dust rising above them, continually pinpointing their location. When they paused to rest, Custer divided the regiment.

Did he have a pincers movement in mind? Spencer asked himself as he watched Captain Benteen at the head of his H Company ride off to the southwest with D and K companies following.

Companies A, G and M formed ranks behind Major

281

Reno, leaving the rest of the companies with Custer, except for B, on mule pack duty. Kellogg and Spencer rode to join Custer's group.

Tom, next to his brother, leaned over and said something to the General. Custer waved an impatient hand, but Tom persisted. Finally Custer spoke to one of his aides, Lieutenant Cooke.

Cooke shifted his horse to block Spencer's advance. "You're to follow Captain Benteen," he said curtly. "General Custer's orders." Without giving him a chance to reply, he wheeled and rejoined his unit.

Spencer knew he had no recourse. He and Kellogg were with the Seventh only because General Custer had ignored a direct order that no newspapermen were to tag along. He was forced to obey the order. He watched resentfully as Kellogg rode off on his mule with Custer's and Reno's combined companies. Cursing Tom, he veered southwest to catch up to Benteen.

Nona sat with Katy on the back steps, looking up at the thin moon, just a few days past new. Tomorrow was the twenty-fifth of June and Spencer had been gone for over a month. She'd never missed anyone so much in her life. How long would it be before she saw him again?

"I got it all planned," Katy said, distracting Nona from her reverie. "When Mike's time is up, he ain't gonna re-up like Pa always did. We'll get married and move to Bismarck, Mike and me. He's clever with his hands, Mike is, and there's always work for a man who can make things. I'll take in laundry'n we'll do just fine."

Nona had heard all this before, Katy's plans for the future. When Mike returned. As, of course, he would. It didn't do to dwell on the possibility your man would be one of the unfortunates who didn't come back.

"Spencer thought it would all be over by the Fourth of July," she told Katy, as she had many times since the Seventh left Fort Lincoln.

"I was talking to Mary today—you know she's that Negro cook of the General's—and Mary said Mrs. Custer and that sister-in-law of hers, they plan to board the *Josephine* when she stops here next week on her way upriver. They're gonna surprise their husbands."

Could I go, too? Nona wondered, her pulse accelerating at the notion of being with Spencer. A moment later she sighed. Mrs. Custer and Mrs. Calhoun wouldn't want her along. In fact, they'd be shocked at an unmarried woman even thinking of such a venture and Kilby would be furious with her. Even Spencer might not approve. No, she'd have to stay here and wait. Dear God, she was tired of waiting.

"You ain't nothing in the Army less'n you're an officer," Katy said. "And Mike, he ain't what they call officer material. Me 'n him, we're better off over to Bismarck, 'stead of staying here at the Fort."

"I'm sure you're right," Nona said, scarcely listening to Katy's words.

She had no idea what Spencer meant to do when he returned or even if his plans included her. He was no Mike to allow a woman to arrange his future for him. What if he didn't want her in it?

Then I'll stay and take care of Amanda Jean when Kilby brings her home, she told herself. It's my duty. And marry Kilby?

She grimaced. No, she could never marry Kilby. How could she bear the touch of any man except Spencer? Spencer, who didn't want a wife. Nona sighed again.

Neither she nor Katy had spoken of what they'd heard today, almost as though bad news couldn't be true if you didn't dwell on it.

General Crook had sent couriers to report that the

283

hostiles had temporarily stopped his advance along the Rosebud and the telegraphed messages had been passed along to Fort Lincoln. General Crook had also said the warriors who'd turned him back had gone on to join Sitting Bull's Sioux somewhere in the Bighorn Mountains.

If not a defeat, it was a setback for the Army. Nona, remembering how Kilby had described Crook's planned three-prong attack, Terry with Custer and Gibbons, wondered what would happen now that Crook couldn't advance. Maybe a battle was going on at this very moment; how could she know?

"It doesn't mean the Seventh won't succeed," she said aloud.

Katy turned to look at her, and apparently understanding exactly what she meant, said, "It don't mean they will, neither. That Sitting Bull's got a slew of redskins gathering round him."

Sitting Bull. Nona had heard a lot about him since she'd come to Fort Lincoln, much of it conflicting. He wasn't a warrior, he was a medicine man; he was a great war chief. He was treacherous and weak; he was strong and powerful. All anyone agreed on was that the hostiles were all flocking to his camp in the mountains.

"One lost skirmish doesn't mean a lost war," she told Katy.

"Just as long as Mike comes back I don't care a hoot who wins."

Nona felt the same way about Spencer. All she really wanted was for him to return. . . .

After a restless night, Nona walked to Libbie Custer's on Sunday afternoon, the twenty-fifth. The officers' wives gathered there every day to sew and talk but she rarely went, preferring to be alone or with Katy. Since the news of General Crook's setback though, Nona felt a need to be with other women, to be reasssured that men

284

could ride out on numerous campaigns and come back—as their husbands had always done.

Nona joined a group gathered around Libbie at the piano, singing hymns. The old familiar words soothed her.

Everything would go right. Spencer would return to her and Mike to Katy.

Later, when Libbie left the piano to supervise the serving of the tea. Nona overheard a lieutenant's wife speaking in a low tone to a captain's wife.

"Have you noticed how despondent Libbie looks? It's almost as though she had a premonition."

"Nonsense. She's just upset about that steamboat we saw with all those piles of rifles meant for the trading posts upriver. And rightly so. Everyone knows the Seventh had only carbines, not the long-range rifles they're selling to the Indians. It's a crime, that's what it is."

The lieutenant's wife shook her head. "I think more than those rifles is bothering Libbie. She's just not like herself."

Later Nona, seeing Libbie Custer at close range, decided her face did look drawn, her smile forced.

That might be simply because Libbie has trouble sleeping, Nona told herself. God knows I do.

But though the day was sunny and hot, Nona felt a dark cloud of gloom settle over her as she walked back to Kilby's house. If the Fort had gotten word about Crook and his men, why were there no dispatches about the Seventh?

Had something gone wrong?

Chapter 19

As he rode with Captain Benteen and the three companies uphill, downhill, uphill, downhill through increasingly rugged terrain, Spencer became more and more tired and he realized the troopers and their horses must be as exhausted as he and Kaintuck. How well could tired men fight? Custer had driven the Seventh too long and hard without rest.

Spencer wasn't well acquainted with Benteen, a portly older man with white hair and ice-blue eyes, but he decided it was past time to ask him the plan of attack. They'd gone at least ten miles over this rough country and seen no sign of hostiles. No surprise, since any Indian in his right mind would avoid struggling through these inhospitable hills. He urged the lagging Kaintuck on until he pulled even with Benteen.

The Captain glanced at him. "Wild goose chase, if ever I saw one," he said.

Spencer nodded in agreement. "What's Custer's plan?" he asked.

Benteen shrugged. "Only he and God know. My orders were to hunt for Indians in the valleys and pitch into any I found."

"I haven't seen a good camping valley in this direction," Spencer observed.

"And we won't, not in these godforsaken badlands." Apparently coming to a decision, Benteen raised his hand and halted, shouting "Right oblique," to his troops.

A few minutes later the columns had reversed, riding back toward the Little Bighorn at a point south of where they'd split off from Custer and Reno, uphill, downhill all over again. Several of the horses gave out, forcing their riders to dismount and walk.

They'd gone about five miles when Spencer startled into alertness when he saw a trooper riding toward them. He recognized Martini, a garrulous Italian recruit who'd ridden off with Custer. A messenger? Benteen halted his men as Martini neared and Spencer edged Kaintuck into position to find out what was going on.

Martini handed the Captain a note, Benteen scanned it quickly, muttering the words aloud. "Come on. Big village. Be quick. Bring packs." He looked at Martini. "Where *is* General Custer?"

Martini's English was faulty but he made himself understood as best he could. Custer had looked down on the biggest Indian village that he, Martini, had ever seen and shouted, "Hurrah, boys, we've got them!"

Major Reno was not with the General, his men were already in the valley, charging the village. Martini would lead the Captain to where he'd left General Custer.

Damn! Spencer told himself. If I hadn't had that ill-advised run-in with Tom Custer, I'd be with Custer now, in the midst of the battle. If I'd kept my head that night, Tom wouldn't be my enemy, wouldn't have persuaded the General to shunt me away with Benteen.

Less than an hour later, the faint pop-pop-pop of rifle fire told Spencer the fight was still going on. Benteen urged his men to go faster, and as they climbed a final rise, the shots grew louder. They rode onto a flat-topped hill and saw two blue-coated riders galloping toward them.

One of them was Reno, minus his hat and saying words Spencer could hardly believe. Custer had disappeared, Reno's men had been routed by the hostiles in the valley and the survivors were now pinned down on this bluff by Indians firing from below. Benteen had arrived with fresh troops in the nick of time.

Where *was* Custer? Spencer wondered as Benteen deployed his troops along the ridge to aid Reno's men. He was looking for Martini to question him when he saw Captain Weir, who'd been with Reno, mount and ride north along the bluff. Spencer decided Weir must be searching for Custer and so he pulled himself onto Kaintuck and followed the Captain. After a moment he glanced back and saw what was left of Weir's company straggling behind him.

They rode for almost a mile before reaching a high enough point to view the entire valley. Spencer drew in his breath when he saw warriors beyond count swarming in the river valley below, some climbing the bluff.

"Good God, can that be the General?" Weir's orderly asked, pointing north along the ridge where, a few miles away, a cloud of smoke and dust obscured any details. The sound of spasmodic rifle fire convinced Spencer that Custer and his men *were* fighting there.

By this time Benteen and more troopers had caught up with them. Apparently Benteen suspected the distant smoke was Custer fighting, too, for he raised his hand and motioned his men forward. At the same time a bullet zinged past Spencer's ear as breech-clouted warriors leaped from hiding in front of them. The troopers milled in confusion, trying to wheel their horses to gallop back to the relative safety of Reno's defended position.

"Hear them goddam bullets?" a grizzled sergeant

called to Spencer as they rode side by side, urging tired horses to go faster toward the bulwarks of dirt and dead horses Reno's men had erected.

Spencer nodded.

"They ain't going 'zip' like they was earlier, they's going 'zing.' You hear?"

"I hear."

"Ain't rifles them redskins are shooting, it be carbines. Ain't nobody round here got carbines but the Army. Hell of a thing to get shot with your own guns."

Carbines. Spencer looked over his shoulder, hunching down when he saw painted warriors crouching to shoot. If the hostiles had carbines, whose were they? Those lost by Reno's casualties? Or weapons taken from Custer's wounded and dead?

Custer, it was plain, was cut off. Was he surrounded by hostiles as they very soon would be? Remembering the thousands of swarming warriors, Spencer realized with a shock that Custer might not even be alive. If Custer and his men were dead, there was no one to prevent the hostiles from overrunning the rest of the Seventh. Terry and Gibbon were too far away. He and the others might very well die on this barren ridge.

Was his own death what White Buffalo Woman had tried to show him in his dream?

He was no Dakota and he refused to believe in omens. He'd promised Nona he'd come back to her and he damn well would!

On Tuesday, the Fourth of July, Fort Lincoln held its Independence Day celebration Though the day was unbearably hot, soldiers chased a greased pig across the parade grounds and competed in wheelbarrow races. Every hour the cannons boomed salutes to the one hundredth birthday of the United States.

Nona watched the festivities with Katy, but her mind wasn't on the celebration. Spencer had assured her the hostiles would be routed by the Fourth of July and that day was here. Yet no one seemed to know anything about what was happening in the western hills.

Noticing Katy seemed as subdued as she felt, Nona suggested they return to the house for lemonade. When they arrived, they found Katy's mother waiting for them on the porch.

"I been down to the Indian village," she said. "I heard a lot of weeping and wailing this morning and went to find out why." She took a deep breath and let it out. "Maybe we ought to go inside, if that's all right with you, miss."

Nona led the way into the kitchen where Katy began squeezing lemons. Nona, though, watched Mrs. Grady anxiously, remembering that Ree scouts had ridden with the Seventh in May.

"What's wrong with the Rees?" she asked the older woman.

"You ever hear 'bout how redskins signal to each other from miles away?" Without waiting to discover whether or not Nona had, Mrs. Grady plunged on. "I found me one of the Ree kids who knows some English and I asked him what was up. He says the women are mourning for the dead and I says I can hear that but who's dead?" She paused and sighed. "It brings back bad times to me."

Katy, a half-squeezed lemon forgotten in her hand, stared at her mother. "What's happened?" she demanded. "What do they know?"

Nona waited tensely for the reply.

"The boy claims the village heard there's been a big fight," Mrs. Grady went on. "He says many troopers died and some of their men, too. Bloody Knife, for one—General Custer's favorite scout. He stuck to the General's side like he was glued there."

"But, Ma, how can they know?"

Mrs. Grady shrugged. "I seen it happen time and time again. I ain't no Injun, how should I know how they do it? But they know, all right. They know."

Katy dropped the lemon on the counter and stood defiantly, arms akimbo. "Mike ain't dead and no redskin's gonna make me believe he is."

Mrs. Grady's glance at her daughter was sad. "For your sake, child, I hope you're right."

Katy burst into tears.

Nona left Mrs. Grady comforting Katy and wandered into the parlor. From the open front door the shouts and laughter of the soldiers told her the celebration was still going on, but the happy sounds seemed to come from another world.

Spencer had told her enough about Indians so she couldn't dismiss what Mrs. Grady had said. It was possible that, by smoke signals or some other method, the Rees did have advance notice of what had happened to the Seventh.

Many dead troopers.

Spencer wasn't a trooper. But a hostile wouldn't distinguish between one white man and another. Nona had a terrible feeling Spencer would be sticking as close to Custer as Bloody Knife had. And the Rees claimed Bloody Knife was dead. She bit her lip. Spencer *had* to be alive, how could she bear it if he wasn't?

"I'm going to see if I can find Libbie Custer," Nona called to Katy and her mother.

But Libbie, at home, had heard nothing new and Nona hesitated to mention what the Rees were saying in case it was a false alarm. Smoke signals or not, how could the Indians know for sure what was happening hundreds of miles away? If anything terrible had occurred, surely the news would have been telegraphed to Fort Lincoln by now.

When Nona returned to the house, Katy had the

lemonade ready and the three women sat around the kitchen table without speaking, sipping from glasses etched with pine cones. Nona recalled the glasses were a wedding present to Helen and Kilby from the folks on the farm north of her father's. Until now it hadn't occurred to her that Kilby might be one of the dead troopers.

"Since there's naught we can do, we'd best leave it in the hands of God," Mrs. Grady said. She drained the last of the lemonade from her glass and rose. "I'll be getting on home."

When she'd let herself out the back door, Nona and Katy looked unhappily at one another. Katy sighed. "I don't dare breathe a word to Ma," she said, "but I got to tell someone. Me and Mike—" She paused and stared into her lemonade. "Seems like I'm carrying Mike's baby," she blurted out finally.

Nona gaped at her. "Are you sure?" she finally managed to say.

Katy nodded and gave a little smile. "I know what you do to get babies, if that's what you mean. We was gonna wait till we got married, Mike and me, but I was scared he might never come back and I think he was, too, so that's how it happened."

But are you certain you're in the family way?"

"Ain't had my courses since afore Mike left and that's a sure sign. Lucky thing I'm staying here or Ma would've caught on right away."

"Oh, Katy, Mike will come back to you. He must."

"I keep praying he does, but Ma's right. Only God knows and He never tells."

Nona reached for Katy's hand and pressed it. "Whatever happens, I'll do all I can to help you."

"That's right kind of you."

Nona realized that, though she wasn't pregnant, she could well be in the same unfortunate predicament as Katy. How would she feel if she were carrying Spencer's

292

child? Her hand slipped from the table to rest on her lower abdomen as she pictured herself cuddling a baby boy with Spencer's unruly black curls and velvety brown eyes. His son. She could almost feel the baby in her arms.

Perhaps Katy was the lucky one.

No news came the next day, but shortly after dawn on the sixth of July the water carrier came by to fill the barrel on the back porch and Katy ran out to ask him if there was any news. Nona stood in the open door, listening.

"Seen the *Far West* coming downstream, she ought to be at the dock by now," he said.

Nona tensed. The *Far West* was the sternwheeler that had carried supplies for the troops up the Missouri to the Yellowstone. If the boat had returned, did that mean the fighting was over?

Katy turned to look at her, a question in her eyes. Nona nodded, knowing Katy wanted to go to the dock.

"I'll go with you," she said, hurrying to find a hat.

They'd reached the front steps when Katy grasped Nona's arm, halting her and pointing toward the Custer house. "Look there."

Three men—Nona recognized one as Dr. Middleton— were outside Libbie's door.

"Something's wrong," Katy whispered. "A doctor always goes with 'em when the news is bad. Like when they come to tell Ma that Pa was killed."

They stood uncertainly on the steps, waiting, even after the men disappeared inside the Custer house.

"Let's go to the back door and ask Mary," Katy suggested. Without waiting for Nona's reply, she started for the rear of the Custer house.

Trailing after Katy, Nona bit her lip, afraid of what they might learn. Yet she had to know.

Katy tapped on the back door. It seemed an eternity before the door cracked open and Mary's round black face appeared. Nona swallowed apprehensively when she saw tears on Mary's cheeks.

"They's telling her now, them men from the boat," Mary wailed. "Oh Lordy, Lordy, the General, he's gone and got hisself killed."

Nona couldn't believe her ears.

"And Captain Tom and Miss Margaret's husband and the boys, they's dead, too," Mary added. "Oh Lord save us, what we gonna do?"

"No!" Katy cried.

"I'm sorry, I'm terribly sorry," Nona blurted as she grabbed Katy's arm and pulled her away, down the steps and toward the river where the *Far West* was docked.

They ran until their wind gave out, then walked as fast as they could. Nona kept her eyes on the twin smokestacks and white pilot house of the boat, visible even behind the screen of trees.

"If General Custer's dead—" Katy began but couldn't finish. She didn't have to, Nona had been thinking the same thing.

The General's luck had run out and he'd been killed. How many of the Seventh had died with him? Mary had listed Tom and Boston Custer, Autie Reed and Lieutenant Calhoun among the victims. Were there *any* survivors or had the hostiles killed them all?

She was somewhat reassured by the sight of several horse-drawn ambulances waiting beside the dock. She reached for Katy's hand. "They're unloading the wounded," she said.

Much as she'd hate to see Spencer hurt, wounded was better than dead. An injured man could recover.

Katy clung to her hand as they approached the boat ramp where soldiers carried the wounded on litters from the ship to the ambulances. She and Katy pushed

294

through the grim-faced onlookers until they could see the injured.

"Dear God," Katy whispered as they watched the procession of dazed and pain-filled faces. The stink of putrefying wounds fouled the air. Men with bloodstained bandages groaned and cried out as they were lifted into the ambulances.

Nona scanned each face in mixed hope and dread but recognized no one. The first ambulance, filled to capacity, pulled away and the second drew up to the ramp.

Tears blurred Nona's vision as the loading resumed and as she wiped them hastily away, Katy screamed out Mike's name and pulled free of her to fling herself at an approaching litter.

"Miss, miss, please step aside," the carrier begged. But Katy reached Mike and bent over to hug him, obscuring Nona's view of his face and disarranging the blanket covering him.

Nona drew in her breath sharply. Mike's left leg ended in a stump just below the knee, a stump wrapped in dirty bloodied bandages. Pulling herself together, she hurried to Katy's side.

"You must let them take Mike to the hospital," she told Katy firmly. "You can visit him there." Assisted by a soldier, she urged Katy away from the ambulance so the loading could resume.

"He's alive, Mike's alive," Katy babbled. "My prayers have been answered. Did you see him? He's alive, he's really alive."

Hadn't Katy noticed Mike's missing leg? Nona had no intention of telling her; she'd find out soon enough. And she understood it didn't really matter to Katy, any more than it would to her if that had been Spencer on the litter. Not as long as he was alive.

While Katy clung to her, weeping in relief, Nona

continued to scan the faces on the litters. She thought she recognized one or two troopers she'd seen at the Fort but Spencer wasn't among them.

"We can take one more on this load," the ambulance attendant called.

"We only got one more," he was told.

As the last litter came down the ramp, Nona leaned forward. She knew that face, that blood-encrusted fair hair.

"Kilby!" she cried.

He opened his eyes and looked at her. A moment later, as if the effort had been too much for him, his lids drooped shut. But it was Kilby and she was sure he'd recognized her. How badly was he hurt? Would he recover? She stared after the ambulance as it pulled away. Though she worried about Kilby's condition, finding Spencer was uppermost in her mind.

"Was that the Lieutenant?" Katy said, pulling away to eye Nona.

Nona nodded.

"Was Mr. Quinlan—?"

Nona cut her off. "I didn't see him. Maybe he was taken to the hospital before we got here."

She would not give up. Perhaps Spencer wasn't wounded at all, perhaps the space on the boat had been reserved for the injured, not the hale and hearty.

"I can't wait to see Mike. Let's ask if we can get a ride to the hospital." Katy pointed to a supply wagon beside the dock.

Nona didn't find Spencer at the hospital. Lieutenant Mead, the doctor told her, had a head injury as well as an arrow wound in his thigh. The doctor at the battle scene had removed the arrowhead but suppuration had set in and Kilby was gravely ill.

Nona visited him several times a day. Often he didn't rouse at all, but when he did, his eyes told her he knew who she was, though he wasn't strong enough to speak.

She always stopped by to say hello to Mike, too and, on the fourth morning after the *Far West*'s return, when she was certain Mike felt well enough, she asked him about Spencer.

"Me, I didn't see Mr. Quinlan after my company rode off with Major Reno," Mike said. "We wasn't with General Custer again, not at all. I'm sorry, miss."

Nona swallowed her disappointment. "I'm glad you came through, Mike," she said.

"Yeah." He stared down at his bandaged stump. "Most of me did, anyway. Katy says it don't matter, but it does."

Nona tried to think of something encouraging to say but couldn't. His time with the Army was definitely over and Katy's plans for him finding work in Bismarck would have to be reformulated. It would be difficult for a man with one leg to earn a living anywhere.

"You'll have the baby's arrival to look forward to," she said finally, seizing on the only positive thing she could think of.

Mike stared at her as though she'd lost her mind and Nona suddenly realized Katy must not have told him. She desperately wished she could call back the words—but it was too late.

"You're sure, miss?" he asked at last.

She had no choice but to nod. Embarrassed and unhappy about her gaffe, she said a hasty goodbye and left the hospital, even though she'd planned to visit Kilby.

"How's the Lieutenant?" Katy asked when she returned to the house.

"I didn't see him, I'll go back later. Uh, Katy—" Nona broke off, unsure how to admit what she'd done. "Mike knows about the baby," she finished in a rush. "I thought you'd told him. I'm sorry."

Katy sighed. "I guess he had to know sooner or later.

But he thinks it ain't fair to me to marry a man with one leg and I held off saying anything about the baby 'cause I didn't want him figuring he had to marry me if he didn't want to."

"I'm sure he wants to. He's worrying about making a living, that's all."

Tears filled Katy's eyes. "If we're together, Mike and me, we'll make out—don't he know that? I love him just as much with one leg as I did when he had two."

Nona hugged her. "You go and tell him so."

Katy returned from the hospital smiling. "I made him admit he still loves me. He's scared about the baby but sort of excited, too. We'll manage." Her smile faded. "Now I got to get up the nerve to confess to Ma. Guess I better run over now and do it. If it's all right with you."

"Go ahead. I think your mother will understand."

Katy shook her head. "Wish I thought so." She started for the door then stopped and turned. "I almost forgot. The doctor told me Lieutenant Mead was asking for you." With a wave of her hand, Katy left.

Nona pinned on her hat, preparing to return to the hospital. If Kilby was able to speak, he must be improving. She sincerely hoped so; with all her heart she wanted Kilby to live.

The Seventh had been practically wiped out by the hostiles; some of the companies had lost every man. She carried her fear for Spencer with her every moment. Was it possible he'd survived? She wouldn't give up hope, she'd never do that, but if Spencer had survived, where was he?

A short while later she was seated on a stool beside Kilby's hospital cot holding his hand. His skin was hot with fever.

"Nona." He spoke so low she had to bend forward to hear him. "It makes me feel better when you're with me."

"The doctor says you're on the mend," she told him. "I'm glad."

His sunken eyes held hers. "I'll recover quicker if you agree to marry me."

Nona bit her lip. She must be careful not to say anything to set him back, but they'd discussed this before and he knew she could never marry him, knew she loved another man. Loved Spencer. She'd do anything she could to help Kilby recover but not marry him.

Deciding to speak the truth, she said, as gently as she could, "Kilby, I care for you and want you to get well, but I can't marry you."

His hand tightened on hers. "You can. You must. There's no reason not to. Not now."

Her heart began to thud in fright. What did he mean?

"I fought with Major Reno," he said. "Most of us didn't make it out of that valley of death onto the bluff. I did. Up there—" he paused and a tremor ran through him. "It was a scene from hell." Kilby's voice was a thread of sound. "We hid behind dead horses to protect us from the bullets and arrows. Dead men lay with the wounded and there was no way, no one to take the dead away. The smell, my God, the smell—" He broke off and closed his eyes but he didn't loosen his grip on her hand.

Nona shuddered, imagining the horrors he'd been through.

"No water," he continued without opening his eyes. "Dying men pleaded for just one swallow of water and there was none to give them. Bullets tore into the rotting carcasses of the horses and arrows fell from the air like rain. We trusted Custer and waited for him to ride to our rescue, never dreaming he and those with him had been massacred, every man."

"Don't think about it," Nona begged, all but overcome by his words. "Don't speak of it."

Kilby's eyes opened, staring at her. "I haven't told

299

you everything."

A premonitory chill ran along Nona's spine and she fought an impulse to cover her ears with her hands. "No more," she said. She couldn't bear to hear another word, she feared what he might say next.

"You must face it." Kilby's voice gained strength. "I saw him lying dead, Nona. I saw Quinlan. Spencer Quinlan is dead."

Chapter 20

Nona didn't know how she got back to the house from the hospital. She reached the foot of the stairs leading to the second floor before her legs collapsed and she dropped onto the steps, her eyes closed, moaning.

Spencer's face flashed across her mind, smiling, his dark eyes glowing. She heard his voice, roughened by passion, murmuring that she belonged to him.

It wasn't true he was dead. It couldn't be true. Not her Spencer. Kilby must have made a mistake.

That's it, a mistake. Spencer was alive. He'd promised to come back to her and he would. He'd hold her in his arms again, kiss her, make love to her. Nona, her face pressed against the carpet runner on the wooden step, smiled, remembering how wonderful his lovemaking was. The rain shelter under the trees had been the first time she'd known a man. There he'd taught her the magic of love and she'd learned Spencer was the only man she'd ever want.

Her lips formed his name soundlessly as she recalled that time, detail by intimate detail. She'd taken down her hair for him, unbraiding it in the dim grayness of the shelter; he'd kissed the palm of her hand, his tongue tracing a warm promise. Gradually he'd drawn her to him, his caresses making her want more and more until their joining took her beyond wanting, beyond herself, beyond the boundaries of the world itself. How could such wonder be ended forever?

Nona shuddered, feeling herself floundering in treacherous water, being whirled deeper and deeper into the depths of despair. Spencer was gone and no one else could rescue her. . . .

"Miss Nona! Saints preserve us, what's happened?" Katy's voice. Nona heard her, but although she tried, she couldn't speak.

Katy grasped her shoulder and shook her. "What's wrong? Are you hurt?"

Katy's touch and her words penetrated the dark waters of misery surrounding Nona. She opened her eyes.

"Whatever are you doing on the steps?" Katy demanded. "Did you fall?"

Nona swallowed. "He—he's dead. Spencer's dead." She pushed the words past the lump in her throat and heard them echoing in her mind like a tolling bell.

"Jesus and Mother Mary, no!" Katy plumped down on the step next to Nona and put an arm around her.

This warm and sympathetic touch unleashed Nona's tears and she sobbed on Katy's shoulder. When she was all cried out she sat up, accepting Katy's offer of a handkerchief and was startled to see it was late afternoon. How long had she lain on the steps?

"I'm awful sorry about Mr. Quinlan," Katy said. "There ain't no mistake?"

"Lieutenant Mead saw—" Nona couldn't go on.

Katy nodded hastily, springing to her feet. "I'll fix us some tea and a bit to eat. Don't tell me no, you got to keep up your strength 'cause you got to go on. That's the way of it." She took Nona's hand and urged her to stand, then led her to the kitchen.

302

Though Nona couldn't force herself to eat anything, she swallowed the hot tea gratefully while half-listening to Katy's stream of talk.

". . . and so Ma says if I got a bun in the oven she guesses she don't have no choice but to get used to Mike as her son-in-law, one leg or not."

"I'm glad your mother is taking things so well," Nona roused herself to say.

"She is and she ain't. She never wanted me to marry a soldier, but she's sort of looking forward to having a grandbaby."

Nona's hand touched her stomach. If I were carrying Spencer's child, she thought, then I'd have a part of him to love. But I have nothing. Her hand rose to her breast in a futile effort to ease the ache inside, an ache she was sure would never end.

"Ma says you don't ever get over it." Katy spoke softly. Nona looked up in surprise at having her thoughts read.

"She lost Pa, you know he was killed," Katy went on. "She says you can't let down, you gotta keep on, one day at a time, and after a while, it gets bearable."

Does it really? Nona wondered bleakly.

After a sleepless night, she forced herself to rise, dress and visit Kilby in the hospital. Katy's mother was right about one thing, you had to keep living no matter how miserable you felt. Even though life had lost all purpose, you had to go on.

At the hospital, Nona was amazed to see Libbie Custer, in black, visiting the wounded men. But after she thought about it, she understood. Though she must be devastated by the General's death, Libbie was keeping on, too.

Dr. Middleton intercepted Nona before she reached Kilby's cot. "I'll be frank, Miss Willard. I'm worried about the Lieutenant. That arrow wound's gone septic—could be the hostiles poisoned the tip. Who's to say? What I do know is Lieutenant Mead's condition is worsening. He's not eating, so do whatever you can to encourage him to take nourishment. He needs all the help he can get."

Nona approached Kilby with some trepidation. First she'd lost Helen, then Spencer. She might not love Kilby as she did her sister or Spencer but she couldn't bear another death.

At the bedside, Kilby's weakness appalled her. He couldn't summon enough strength to even whisper her name. Before she left the hospital, though she couldn't coax him to take any food, Nona managed to induce Kilby to swallow a cup of water, one teaspoon at a time. As she returned to the house, she found she'd regained a purpose in life—to save Kilby. She'd bring him his favorite dishes and take the time to see that he ate, feeding him, if necessary. Kilby was *not* going to die.

A week later, his improvement was clearly visible. The thigh abscess caused by the arrow wound was beginning to show signs of healing and Kilby was strong enough to feed himself, eating only her homemade food.

"He's not out of the woods yet, but I have hope for him now," Dr. Middleton told her. "It's your doing, Miss Willard. I give you full credit."

Kilby said the same and more. "I felt myself slipping away more than once, but your face and your voice held me here. Don't you see our marriage was meant to be? I need you, Nona."

Two weeks passed and Kilby slowly grew stronger. When she came to see him on the tenth of August, he urged her to set a date. "Your saying yes will give me the incentive to get well, I know it will."

She looked at him propped up on pillows, at the new beard she'd neatly trimmed, his eyes no longer quite so sunken. "When you're fully recovered I'm sure the first thing you'll want to do is go off to find your daughter," she said.

Kilby nodded. "But what does finding Martha have to do with you marrying me?"

Nona took a deep breath. She'd anguished over this decision every night for weeks before finally making up her mind. Kilby *did* need her and she'd promised Helen to look after Amanda Jean. She meant to stand by that promise. While she could never love Kilby as she had Spencer—as she still did love Spencer—wasn't it her duty to marry Kilby and care for his daughter?

"After you come back to the Fort with the baby," she said, "I'll marry you."

Kilby smiled, clasping her hand and pulling her toward him for a kiss. She turned her cheek, unwilling to have him kiss her on the lips. Not yet, not until she had to. Not until they were married.

That night, when Katy came to the house to visit she told Katy the news.

"If that's what you want, then I'm happy for you," Katy said.

Nona looked at her. "It's what I have to do."

Katy met her gaze squarely. "You don't want to, do you? Not so soon after—" Her words trailed off.

Nona sighed. What she wanted to do didn't matter. Nothing really mattered anymore except bringing back Amanda Jean.

"How's Mike getting along?" she asked brightly, changing the subject.

Released from the hospital, Mike had gone to stay at Mrs. Grady's. The result was that Katy had gone home, too. Nona found she didn't mind being alone as much as she thought she might. In her heart she was always alone.

"He's doing good on crutches; he can even help me hang up clothes," Katy said. "'Course Ma, she makes sure we don't have no chance to be alone. As if it mattered now. But Ma says we got to behave till after the wedding. Only a week more. I can hardly wait!"

"You'll be a beautiful bride," Nona said.

"Thanks to you and Ma."

Two of Helen's white summer dresses had provided enough material for Mrs. Grady to make Katy a lovely wedding gown. Nona was sure her sister would have approved. Father Young from Bismarck was coming across the river to the Fort chapel to conduct the ceremony and afterward there was to be a reception at Mrs. Grady's.

Impulsively, Nona got up from the table and went around to hug Katy. "I'm so glad everything has worked out for you."

Katy hugged her back. "Me, too. Only I wish you and—" She stopped and bit her lip. "Well, I guess I'll be coming to your wedding in a couple of months."

"I wouldn't think of getting married without you," Nona assured her, forcing a smile. She knew what Katy had been about to say, that she wished Spencer would be riding back with what was left of the Seventh when they returned to the Fort from the western hills. God knows Nona wished it with all her heart but there was no use in wishing for what could never be.

The day of Katy and Mike's wedding dawned clear and hot. The ceremony took place at noon and the small chapel was crowded with guests and well-wishers. Some of the soldiers were, like Mike, on crutches and one was missing an arm. A sergeant friend of Katy's father, who'd remained behind at the Fort and so missed the battle, gave the bride away.

Mike, in uniform, stood straight and proud on his crutches, the left leg of his blue trousers neatly pinned

306

up. Katy stood next to him in her white gown with its veil of cherished Irish lace. Tears dampened Nona's cheeks when she saw the look Katy and Mike exchanged, their eyes beaming with love and hope.

Nona knew she was expected to attend the party at Mrs. Grady's, but she didn't know if she could bear it. She was sincerely happy for Katy but it was hard to keep smiling when her heart hurt from her own grief.

The sky was overcast when she emerged from the chapel, dark clouds promising desperately needed rain and relief from the searing heat of the August sun. Knowing she needed to be alone for a while, Nona decided to walk home first. To distract herself she wondered what the Sioux called the month of August. Probably something to do with wild berries or fruits. Blackberry Moon? Singing Reed had never told her.

Had the Sioux woman survived the battle at Little Bighorn? It seemed likely, since the soldiers had never reached the hostile encampment. If Singing Reed still lived, Nona was sure Amanda Jean was all right. But now, with Generals Gibbon and Crook and Terry chasing down the hostiles, anything might happen. If only Kilby could find Amanda Jean before the U.S. Army overran the hostiles' camps.

By the time Nona climbed the front steps, the day had grown ominously dark and thunder rumbled in the west. She hadn't locked the door; no one did because it was perfectly safe not to. When she came into the entry she didn't expect anyone to be inside, so at first she didn't see the tall figure in the parlor, not until he moved.

"Nona," he said, striding toward her.

She stared at him, unable to move or breathe or think. Her head whirled; her heart thudded alarmingly. All of a sudden everything turned black, blotting out the impossible sight before her.

Spencer knelt beside the parlor settee, his worried gaze

on Nona's ashen face. He'd managed to catch her when she collapsed and had laid her on the settee. He never dreamed his presence would startle her to faint.

Chafing her hand between his palms, he whispered, "Nona?"

Her eyelids fluttered and opened. She looked at him blankly, then recognition widened her eyes. Her lips parted, but no words came. He leaned forward and brushed his lips against her.

"Are you all right?" he asked.

She raised a shaking hand and touched his cheek. "Spencer?" Her voice was tremulous. "Is it really you?"

He wanted to gather her in his arms and kiss her with all the pent-up passion he'd carried these three months, but she looked so wan and fragile he didn't dare.

"Who else do you let kiss you?" he demanded, hiding his anxiety behind his bantering words.

"Oh, Spencer, I thought you were dead!" she cried, rising up and flinging her arms around his neck.

He held her as she shuddered with sobs. He closed his eyes, inhaling her essence, the intoxicating scent that was hers alone, feeling close to tears himself. There'd been times he'd wondered if he'd live to hold her again.

"I told you I'm hard to kill," he murmured into her ear.

Nona pulled away from him and sat up, fumbling in her pocket for a handkerchief. "Kilby told me he'd seen you lying dead," she said, her voice still quivering.

A bolt of anger shot through Spencer, driving him to his feet. "He was sure as hell mistaken." He sat beside her on the settee and put an arm over her shoulders.

She leaned against him. "When he told me, I wanted to die, too."

He pulled her closer, laying his cheek against her hair. "My sweet Nona, neither of us are going to die, not for years and years. Kilby's made his last mistake with me. If it *was* a mistake. I wouldn't put it past him to lie."

Nona turned in his arms to look up at him. "Oh, no, you mustn't blame Kilby. He was badly wounded, he could have been delirious with fever and seeing things that weren't there. Dr. Middleton despaired of his life. Kilby's still in the hospital."

Spencer grunted, unconvinced.

"Besides, why would Kilby lie? Since you aren't dead, you were bound to return and prove him wrong. No, I can't believe he did it deliberately."

Spencer disagreed but said nothing. He didn't trust Lieutenant Mead any farther than he could see him. Casting his mind back to the chaos and bloody terror of the troopers' stand on the bluff, he remembered Mead had been with Reno, so he'd either been wounded in the fighting there, or earlier on Reno's retreat from the valley to the bluff.

I never once ran across the bastard, Spencer thought, but then I was fighting, not tending the wounded.

He'd used Sky Arrow's rifle to fight alongside the remnants of Reno's companies and Benteen's men. He'd shot hostiles to save his own hide, his and the men trapped with him. Until Gibbon and then Terry arrived with fresh troops and the hostiles gathered their dead, folded their tipis and stole away in the night.

It was then he and the other beleaguered men on the bluff discovered that Custer and every last one of his men lay dead, their bodies stripped and mutilated by the Indians. Spencer had ridden to see for himself, ridden to the bluff north of Reno's position, to the place he'd tried to reach with Lieutenant Weir a day earlier. This time there were no hostiles remaining to drive him back.

The sight sickened him and he knew he could never write the truth of what had been done to the two hundred and fifty or more men who'd followed Custer into the jaws of hell and died there with him.

Hearing that Crook meant to pursue the hostiles, Spencer found the General in his camp on the Powder River and asked permission to go along. Crook was agreeable, but as time pased, Spencer realized the General had no intention of moving until reinforcements doubled the size of his command. God alone knew how much time that would take. Spencer left, planning to join General Terry on the Yellowstone. But there he discovered Terry was also waiting for reinforcements. No one wanted to tangle with the hostiles who'd killed Custer, not unless their troops greatly outnumbered the warriors.

Finally Spencer, who was missing Nona more with every passing day, gave up altogether. When Three Crows, also tired of waiting at the Yellowstone camp for scouting duty, offered to ride with him back to Fort Lincoln, Spencer had wasted no time setting off with the Ree.

Sitting on the settee with Nona, Spencer tried to recall who he'd told about his intentions of riding with General Crook. He'd certainly made it no secret. It was possible some of the wounded men being sent back on the *Far West* had heard what he meant to do. Kilby Mead could have known.

If I'd waited and gone with Crook, Spencer thought, how long would it have been before I returned to the Fort? October? November? Next spring? Plenty of time for Mead to recover from his wounds. Spencer gritted his teeth. Exactly what had Mead been planning?

A jagged bolt of lightning slashed through the darkness, followed by a blast of thunder that rattled the dishes in the next room and brought Spencer abruptly back to his surroundings. Nona started in alarm and clutched at him. His arms closed protectively around her. What did he care about Mead? With Nona here in his arms, nothing else really mattered.

310

Rain slammed against the windows as he kissed her; this time not a mere brushing of her mouth. The parting of her lips under his unleashed the desire he'd been holding at bay. He lost himself in the sweet depths of her mouth while the soft pressure of her breasts against him drove him wild with need. He couldn't wait to have more of her, all of her.

Shifting position, he scooped her into his arms, rose and carried her up the steps and into her bedroom where he stood her on her feet beside the bed. He put his hands on her shoulders and gazed into her amber eyes, eyes that glowed in the storm-dimmed room. Outside thunder growled and rain thrummed on the roof and windows.

"I can hardly believe you're here with me," she whispered, her fingers against his mouth. "I'm afraid I'll wake up and find I'm dreaming."

"I guess I've no choice but to show you how real I am," he said, his hands sliding from her shoulders to the back buttons of her black gown. He undid them one by one impatient with the tiny loops, until he could push the dress from her shoulders and down over her hips.

He touched his lips to the throbbing pulse in her throat while his hands cupped her breasts. "I was crazy to stay away from you one day longer than necessary," he said huskily.

She melted against him, murmuring his name. The feel of her in his arms pushed him past all restraint. In a frenzy of desire, he pulled off the rest of her clothes and flung off his own, tumbling with her onto the bed. It had been so long since he'd held her—too long. . . .

When his caressing fingers found she was as eager as he, Spencer poised himself over her.

"It can't be a dream," she gasped as he covered her body with his. "No dream could ever be so wonderful."

For long moments he didn't move, savoring the overwhelming intimacy. He wanted the joy and wonder

311

to last forever, holding her like this, being a part of her as she was a part of him. His intense pleasure was mixed with a sense of rightness.

He was where he belonged.

His lips found hers, promising, pledging, loving. Her ardent response told him clearer than any words that she felt what he felt, needed him as much as he needed her.

When she moaned deep in her throat, her hips moving against his in the most enticing of ryhthms, he could hold back his surging passion no longer. Moving with her, hard and fast, he soared once more, no longer alone but a part of a greater whole, the two of them bound to each other and to the earth that sustained them.

When they came to rest at last, he cuddled her to him, never wanting to let her go.

"What's the Sioux name for August?" she asked after a time.

He smiled. Nona, the ever curious. He wouldn't want her any other way. "The Lakota call it the Moon of Ripe Plums. Next to come is the Moon of Yellow Leaves."

"Do you think Singing Reed and Amanda Jean are all right?"

"For now, yes."

She eased away and raised up to look at him. "What do you mean, for now?"

"Crook and Terry plan to hunt down the hostiles. I'm afraid they won't distinguish between warriors and women and children."

Nona bit her lip. "Kilby's not anywhere near well enough to search for Amanda Jean. What's going to become of her?"

Spencer tensed at mention of the Lieutenant but forced himself to relax. "I'm sorry, but there's no way of knowing where Singing Reed has taken the baby," he said. "It depends on whether Lean Bear, her village leader, traveled on to join Sitting Bull's camp or not.

Lean Bear wasn't too keen on fighting bluecoats, though the young men of his village certainly were."

Nona sighed and nestled against him again. After a time she ran a finger over his chin. "You shaved off another beard," she said. "I can tell because your skin's lighter where the beard was."

"I stopped by the officers' quarters and shaved," he admitted. "I couldn't wait to get rid of the beard—I guess I'll never get used to having hair on my face."

"I rather liked the beard you grew on the way back from rescuing me. But then, I like you any way at all."

He hugged her, then slid exploring fingers over her breast. "I especially like *you* this way."

She drew in her breath when his thumb caressed her nipple and his desire quickened in response. He'd never get enough of this woman—the more she offered, the more he wanted.

As soon as possible he'd take her away from this damn fort and that conniving Mead. Maybe to St. Louis where she had relatives. She could stay with them while he went back to ride with Crook. Though he knew the campaign could only end in total defeat for the hostiles, he had to be a part of the final fight, had to be there, watch it happen and write the truth as he saw it.

At the moment he didn't intend to think about the Army or the hostiles or anything else but being with Nona and making love to her. She was gloriously unique and he doubted if any other woman could ever satisfy him again.

"You'll never know how much I missed you," he murmured.

"I thought I'd lost you forever." Her words were tinged with sadness.

He wished he could banish sadness and trouble from her life forever. He could throttle Mead for upsetting Nona. "When I tell you I'm coming back to you, I mean

313

it—never listen to anyone else. They won't tell you the truth."

"I still don't believe Kilby lied. He was so terribly ill when they carried him off the *Far West*, I'm sure he suffered some kind of fever dream where he saw you lying dead." Her voice quivered on the last two words and she clung to him, burying her face in his chest.

If he dreamed I was dead, it was because he wanted me dead, Spencer thought.

But to hell with him. Nona would never be Kilby Mead's. She belonged to Spencer Quinlan and no one else. He tipped her head back and kissed her, a deep, savage kiss, as though to brand her as his woman. His lips trailed to her breast to taste the sweetness there and she held his head to her as she made the tiny noises of delight that thrilled him.

"Nona," he whispered, "my beautiful Nona."

Her hand found him, caressing, stroking, pleasuring him until he throbbed with desire. As she guided him to her, she whispered something he didn't quite hear and then he was inside her and beyond thought.

Later, lying close to her, he watched the rain trickle down the window and sighed contentedly. Nothing could go wrong now.

"Katy will wonder what happened to me," Nona said. "She and Mike got married today. I was on my way to the reception when I stopped by the house and found you."

"I heard there was a wedding. I'm glad Mike survived the massacre."

"He lost a leg."

Spencer grimaced. Hell of a thing to happen to someone especially a man as young as Mike. He was little more than a boy.

"And Katy's carrying his child," Nona added. "I worry about how they'll get along."

"It'll be tough sledding, no doubt about that."

"I wish there was something I could do to help them."

Spencer smiled. "There speaks Good Heart." He turned onto his side and looked at her. "There's a downriver boat due tomorrow. I intend to take you to St. Louis."

Nona blinked and sat up, pulling up the sheet to cover herself. "To St. Louis?" she echoed.

He told her what he had planned.

She stared at him. "So I'm to stay with Cousin Henry while you ride west again?"

Did he imagine there was a slight edge to her words? Spencer sat up. "You sure as hell can't stay here."

Nona's mouth tightened. "Don't tell me what I can or can't do! I am not going to sit around making polite conversation in St. Louis while you're off getting shot at again. Go, if you must, but I intend to stay right here at Fort Lincoln where I can be of some use."

He bristled. "What do you mean 'of some use'?"

"I've been spending my time at the hospital feeding Kilby and doing what I can to help the other wounded men. Dr. Middleton says if Kilby recovers it'll be due to my care. I'm needed at the hospital. How can you expect me to walk away?"

Spencer tried unsuccessfully to control his flare of anger. Walk away from Mead, is what she meant. He spoke between his teeth. "I don't give a damn if Mead lives or dies. You're coming with me."

She gave him glare for glare. "No, I am not."

In a rage, Spencer flung himself from the bed and began pulling on his clothes. When he had his trousers buttoned he faced her again. "So he means more to you than I do," he snarled. "Is that it?"

The covers clutched tightly about her, she scowled. "You don't understand. Kilby's far from well. How can you expect me to turn my back on him? It isn't as though you need me—you've as good as said so. I'm far less

315

important to you than the campaign against the hostiles. What possible difference can it make to you whether I wait here or in St. Louis?"

'You're the one who doesn't understand. Sick or well, Mead's conducting his own campaign. His opening salvo was to tell you I was dead and you believed him. I'll lay odds the next thing he did was ask you to marry him."

Watching her eyes widen, he knew he was right. Fury tightened its coils about him. "Did you agree?" he demanded.

"I thought you were dead!" she cried. "I didn't want to marry him but there was Amanda Jean to consider and—"

"So you *did* say yes." Spencer grabbed up his remaining clothes, stalked to the door and flung it open. As he left the room he shot one final remark over his shoulder. "May I be the first to congratulate you and the Lieutenant. You deserve each other."

Chapter 21

"Spencer!" Nona cried as the front door slammed. Though she knew she was too late, she scrambled from the bed and ran to the head of the stairs.

He was gone. Numbly she returned to the bedroom and sat on the edge of the bed, staring at, but not seeing the raindrops beading the window. What was the use of going after him? She couldn't accept what he wanted her to do and he didn't even try to understand why.

Spencer was like a child with a favorite toy that he wanted to play with only at his convenience, she was that toy. But she was a woman, not a toy to be stored in a drawer or on a shelf until wanted again.

She hugged herself, rocking back and forth in misery. How could he just walk away from what was between them? Didn't he know how much she loved him? She'd done all she could to show him. It was as though her love didn't matter to him unless she did exactly what he ordered.

Anger seeped in to mingle with her pain. She stopped rocking and sprang to her feet. She would *not* hide herself in her bedroom and go into a decline because of one selfish man; she would go about her business. No matter how unhappy she was, others had more to complain

317

about than she did. She hadn't lost a loved one to the hostiles, nor did her man lie wounded in the hospital.

Of course, Kilby was there. Nona bit her lip. She couldn't believe he'd lie about seeing Spencer dead. It surely had been either a mistake or a fever dream. He'd be expecting to see her today, but how could she visit the hospital now? How could she face anyone, least of all Kilby, feeling the way she did?

You will do exactly that, she informed herself grimly, and you will do it now. You will not permit Spencer Quinlan to turn you into an embittered recluse.

By the time Nona had washed and dressed, the rain had stopped and the sky over the western hills glowed red and gold from the setting sun. Though she'd missed Katy and Mike's reception, that couldn't be helped. She meant to make certain that from now on she didn't evade any social or moral obligation.

Head high, she marched into the hospital.

Kilby saw her and he smiled broadly, sitting on the edge of his cot.

"The most wonderful news!" he exclaimed as she neared, lifting a paper from his pillow and waving it at her. "I'm being posted to Washington as of September first."

Nona was taken aback. The first of the month was no more than a week away. "But Amanda Jean—I mean Martha—what about her?"

Kilby shrugged. "With the hostiles fleeing every which way, we both know there was little chance of finding my daughter."

"*Was* little chance? Didn't you even mean to try?"

"Even if I chose to risk my neck, I could never have gotten permission for other troopers to come with me. I can't blame my superiors, not after what happened to General Custer."

Nona's temper rose. "You led me to believe you

318

intended to search for your daughter as soon as you recovered."

"Come now, you wouldn't expect me to go alone. That's what I would have had to do."

She stared at him, unable to believe her ears. "Do you mean you've given up ever finding her?"

He sighed. "Painful as it is, I've had to accept that I'll never see or know my daughter." He reached for her hand, but she stepped back.

"*I* can't accept that, Kilby." Her voice shook with outrage.

"Be reasonable, Nona. I know it's sad but there's nothing to be done about Martha." He glanced at his telegram. "You'll like Washington. That's where I've always wanted to be posted."

Nona shook her head. "I won't be going to Washington." Her words held a chill.

Kilby blinked. "But you promised to marry me."

"Marrying you was contingent on finding Amanda Jean." And, she added to herself, on Spencer Quinlan being dead.

No matter how angry she was at Spencer, his return had made her realize she couldn't marry Kilby, or, she greatly feared, any other man.

"That's unreasonable," Kilby sputtered.

She smiled coldly. "I've been told before that I'm an unreasonable woman. In Washington I'm sure you'll find someone else to console you. Goodbye, Kilby. I doubt we'll be seeing one another again."

Over his protests, Nona turned and hurried from the hospital, determined to leave Fort Lincoln as soon as she could; on tomorrow's downriver boat, if possible. Spencer wouldn't be boarding that boat now. If he planned to ride with General Crook he'd catch one going upriver. To be on the safe side, though, perhaps she should cross to Bismarck on the ferry and take a train to

319

St. Paul, then travel on to Chicago and New York.

There was nothing left for her at the Fort. She was through with Spencer and disillusioned with Kilby. Had Kilby ever intended to search for Amanda Jean? She thought not. She'd even begun to wonder if he *had* lied to her about seeing Spencer dead. He couldn't be trusted. Could *any* man be trusted?

At the house, she stripped her bed and put the dirty laundry in a canvas bag for Mrs. Grady. When she was through cleaning her bedroom, she began to pack. In the rear of her wardrobe, she found a rolled bundle she didn't recognize. When she pulled it into the light of the lamp, she discovered the Sioux buckskins and moccasins Singing Reed had given her. Immediately she was reminded of Amanda Jean. Cuddling the Indian dress to her as she had once cradled the baby, she began to weep, first for the lost child and then for Spencer.

No matter how he'd behaved, she still loved him and she always would. She cried all the harder because she knew she wouldn't change her mind and go after him. He was as lost to her as Amanda Jean.

Her sobbing lessened when the tiny glimmer of an idea lightened her dark spirit. Spencer was lost, yes, but was Amanda Jean? Could there be a way for her to find the child? Nona mopped her eyes and stared down at the buckskins she held.

No, she was crazy to think about it. She had no way of locating Singing Reed, especially, as Kilby had said, with the hostiles fleeing in all directions.

On the other hand, no one knew whether Singing Reed's band, under Lean Bear, had ever been with Sitting Bull. What if they hadn't?

Nona shook her head. Even if Lean Bear's camp was in the same place Spencer had rescued her from, she'd never be able to find it again. No one could except Spencer or an Indian scout.

An Indian scout.

Nona frowned. What was the name of the Ree who'd guided Spencer to that village? Something about crows— Three Crows, that was it. The scout must be in the Ree village, for she remembered Spencer saying Three Crows had ridden back with him from the Yellowstone.

Even if she convinced Three Crows to guide her and they found Lean Bear's village, the Ree scout would never enter a Sioux camp. She'd be on her own. Would the Sioux harm a white woman entering their village? Nona gnawed her lip. She didn't know. If Singing Reed was there, though, the Sioux woman wouldn't let anyone hurt Nona.

If she managed to get inside Singing Reed's tipi, how would she convince the Indian woman to give up Amanda Jean, her Light Of Sun?

I can tell her Light Of Sun is in grave danger if she remains with the Sioux, Nona decided. With the Army marching against the entire Sioux nation, every Indian man, woman and child not on a reservation risks being killed.

It was a risky venture, Nona knew, but she couldn't live with herself if she left Fort Lincoln without making an effort to find her sister's baby. If she didn't, certainly no one else would. It was true Three Crows might not find the camp, but in that case they'd return to the Fort and she'd go back to New York, disappointed and sad at her failure, but at peace with herself.

She had to try.

The first hurdle would be talking the Ree scout into guiding her. What could she offer him? Money, but she didn't have much and would have to save some for the trip home to New York.

What would appeal to an Indian besides money? Looking down at the buckskins, Nona recalled how Sky Arrow had forced her to remove her hat and then put it

321

on his own head. Would hats interest Three Crows? Helen had left a dozen hats.

Kilby had left it up to her to dispose of Helen's things—she could offer the Ree those hats. And what else? Setting aside the Sioux garb, Nona looked inside her wardrobe again. On the top shelf she saw the bolt of blue plaid taffeta she'd stored there.

Helen had set aside several lengths of cloth for new dresses that had never been made and Nona had given Katy all but this one bolt she'd planned to use for herself. Indians liked colorful cloth, didn't they? First thing in the morning she'd see if Three Crows could be tempted by the plaid taffeta.

As evening shadows lengthened, Nona planned for her journey. Blankets. Food that wouldn't spoil quickly. A canteen for water. A knife. Rope. She didn't have a gun, but she was certain Three Crows did. But once she reached the Sioux village she would need a horse—not a gun.

How was she going to get a horse? She didn't have enough money or tradeable goods to buy an Indian pony from the Rees, even if they'd sell her one. She'd have to use an Army horse.

Kaintuck knew her and he was the horse she wanted. She'd have to try to borrow him from the stables without telling the stablemaster where she was going. It was her only chance. Everything depended on finding a horse.

She could hardly arrive at the stable in the buckskins and moccasins, yet her only riding outfit had been left in the Sioux village. Since she doubted the Army provided sidesaddles, she'd have to divide the skirt of Helen's riding costume in order sit a horse astride.

Her supplies would have to be hidden near the Ree village so when she enlisted Three Crow's support she'd be ready to go. How could she manage that? It seemed impossible, but the most difficult task of all was getting hold of Kaintuck.

"Never plan to fail," her father had advised all his children. She wouldn't fail, she couldn't. She was Amanda Jean's only chance.

"Good morning, miss," Ned, the stableman, said with a tip of his hat. "You're up mighty early today."

Nona smiled her best smile. "I have some old clothes to take to the Ree village—I understand from Mrs. Custer that the Indians are in dire need of garments?"

He shrugged, denying any knowledge or interest in the Rees.

"In any case, I mean to take the clothes there. But I can't carry them, of course. I was wondering if I might borrow one of your horses?"

"I'd sure like to oblige, miss, but we don't stock ladies' saddles."

Nona tried for a blush—surprising how difficult it was to blush when you wanted to—and coyly exhibited her divided skirt. "I grew up on a horse farm so I'm accustomed to sitting a man's saddle. If you don't mind."

"*I* don't mind but I can't answer for the horses. They ain't used to skirts."

"But one of them knows me—a gelding named Kaintuck. I'm sure my being a woman wouldn't upset him." She approached the corral as she spoke, looking around for the familiar chestnut. To her relief, he came trotting toward the fence, evidently recognizing her.

Nona produced the last of her dried apples and fed him.

"It do seem like he knows you, right enough," Ned admitted. "Guess there's no harm in you using him to tote your stuff to the Rees."

"Oh, thank you, you're very kind." Nona produced another smile and hoped Ned wouldn't get into too much trouble for lending her Kaintuck. It wasn't as though she

323

was stealing the horse—she meant to bring him back as soon as she could.

The horse accepted her without fuss and Nona rode quickly back to the house. Tethering the horse outside, she hurried to gather everything she needed. Her supplies were jammed into canvas laundry bags so they'd pass for soiled clothes ready to be dropped off at Suds Row. She stuffed the bolt of cloth into a saddle bag and carried the hats in a handled box.

When she found Three Crows, he listened to her impassively while Ree children gathered round to stare at her. From the doors of their huts some of the women watched her, too.

After Nona stated her request, mentioning payment in gold, she gazed as calmly as she could at the Ree, who said nothing. "I brought this for you," she added, pulling the bolt of cloth from the saddle bag and unrolling a length. "Plus the gold coin." She offered him the cloth and he took it, feeling the taffeta with his fingers. She couldn't tell whether or not he liked it.

"And these," she went on, unlatching the hat box and lifting out the hat on top, a bright blue wool decorated with feathers, silk flowers, beads and bows.

Three Crows blinked, but remained silent. The Indian children edged closer, their eyes, wide with interest, on the hat. A small girl giggled, then covered her mouth with her hand.

Nona despaired as she watched Three Crows' unchanging expression. Why had she thought womens' hats would appeal to him?

He glanced at the children and motioned to the biggest girl. When she came close enough, Three Crows handed her the cloth and said something in his own tongue. The girl hurried to a nearby hut carrying the taffeta and disappeared inside.

Three Crows lifted the hat from her hand and turned it

over in his, examining it closely. Then he peered into the hat box. "All?" he asked.

"Yes!" The word burst from Nona. "All the hats. The box, too, if you want." She proffered the box, realizing the small huts of the Rees, like the tipis of the Sioux, made sturdy storage containers essential.

A half hour later, they rode away from the Ree village, Three Crows mounted on a pinto, she on Kaintuck. Nona had ducked into his hut where his wife supervised her change into the buckskins and moccasins and tucked her hair under an old wide-brimmed hat of Kilby's she'd appropriated. From a distance she hoped she'd pass for a Ree and not draw attention from any trooper.

Her buckskins certainly wouldn't fool a Ree. Three Crows had hissed, "Sioux!" when she came out in the Indian garb.

He didn't speak again until they'd put several hills between them and the Fort. "Maybe no Sioux," he said then. "Maybe all gone." He gestured westward.

"We'll search," she said. "Lean Bear didn't want to fight the bluecoats, so he might not have traveled west. His village may be no more than two days' ride."

She wasn't used to dealing with Indians, but she'd made up her mind to look assured and speak firmly—the way she always did as a teacher on the first day of school.

How far away those school days seemed! Protected by the safety of a schoolroom, she'd never dreamed she'd be riding into nowhere with her only companion an Indian man who was a stranger.

She refused to have second thoughts; she wouldn't permit herself to so much as glance dubiously at Three Crows. He's not Sky Arrow, she assured herself. He's an army scout; a friend of the whites. He has a wife and children. There was no reason to fear Three Crows. Mike and Spencer both trusted him. Spencer.

Nona's heart lurched at the thought of Spencer and

she admonished herself not to dwell on memories of him. It was futile to remember the wonder and beauty of what they'd had together. What she must keep in mind was the cruelty of his parting words—that she and Kilby deserved each other.

Spencer considered Kilby a liar. Spencer felt she'd betrayed him by promising to marry Kilby. She firmed her lips. It no longer mattered what Spencer said or did. Whether she was successful in finding Amanda Jean or not, one thing was sure—she'd never see him again.

"We ride three suns, no more." Three Crows' words startled Nona, bringing her back to the task at hand.

"Three days," she agreed.

"Me no go in Sioux camp," he added.

"I understand."

"Sioux no good. Sioux enemy."

"If we find the camp, I'll go in alone. Will you wait for me for one day?"

"No wait. Sioux find me, they kill me."

Nona bit her lip. If she found Amanda Jean, she still had to bring the child to the Fort. Singing Reed might help her but then again she might not. "Can you leave some kind of trail I can follow?" she asked the Ree.

"Leave sign," he agreed, but his skeptical look told her he didn't believe she'd be able to find her way back to the Fort alone, sign or not.

"You show me when and where you leave the sign as we go along," she insisted. "I'll remember; I'll find it."

"Sioux bad. Maybe better you not go to camp."

"I'm not changing my mind!"

Three Crows said no more.

Nona felt awkward and a bit fearful when they camped the first night. But Three Crows made it clear he wasn't planning to spread his blanket anywhere near her and she finally relaxed enough to fall asleep.

By the second night her mind had eased about him,

and without that to worry about, her thoughts shifted to Spencer and how exciting it had been when they camped together. When she closed her eyes she saw his face and his mocking grin.

You threw away what we had, he seemed to say. *If not for your stubbornness we'd be together now, sharing a cabin on a downriver boat.*

Yes, until St. Louis and then they'd part with no assurance she'd ever see him again. She'd done the right thing when she refused his offer.

On the third day, Three Crows, who'd become more and more withdrawn as the sun climbed the sky, stopped at midday.

"Sioux camp by creek," he said, pointing to the northwest.

Nona shaded her eyes, and by squinting against the sun's glare, perceived a faint shimmer of green. "Is that where Lean Bear's village was three months ago?" she asked.

"Sioux no can stay in one place three moons. Men go hungry; ponies go hungry."

Nona didn't want reasons for moving camps. She wanted to know if this was the right camp. "But is it Lean Bear's village?" she demanded.

"Same camp I show to Quinlan."

She didn't know how on earth Three Crows could be so certain. Was he as sure as he seemed or was he simply tired of the journey and eager to turn back? Was there even a camp in that thin line of green up ahead?

If she wanted to find Amanda Jean, she had no choice but to trust him.

"I go." Without another word, Three Crows wheeled his pinto and trotted back in the direction they'd come.

Nona stared at him, part of her tempted to ride after him. Now that her moment of truth was at hand, she was terrified. What-ifs spilled from her mind thick and fast.

What if it wasn't Lean Bear's camp? What if it was but Singing Reed wasn't there? What if—?

Stop it! she admonished herself. You've commandeered an Army horse, you've spent two and a half-days on a hot, dusty trail and you're not going to waste the effort. You're going to do exactly as you planned. You're going to take off the plains hat and let your hair down so Lean Bear's people will know you're not only a white woman but will recognize you as Good Heart. Then you're going to ride toward that camp and see what happens.

There was always the possibility the Sioux would kill her. Death was terrifying to face but, recalling her terror of Sky Arrow, Nona shivered. Though he was dead, there'd been plenty of other braves in the village and one of them might decide to claim her. Dying might not be the worst thing that could happen to her.

You're Amanda Jean's only chance, she reminded herself.

Dithering accomplished nothing. Facing west, Nona yanked off the hat and unpinned her hair so it tumbled over her shoulders. She thrust the hat into a saddle bag, took a deep breath, and head held high, urged Kaintuck into a trot.

After leaving Nona, Spencer marched from one end of the Fort to the other until he was near exhaustion. By the time he returned to the officers' quarters in the blue twilight, he'd walked off most of his anger. Bill King found him sitting morosely on his cot and offered to share a bottle of what he insisted was Kentucky bourbon.

The whiskey tasted like rotgut but Spencer didn't care; all he wanted was oblivion. He drank enough to finally reach his goal, but as a result, slept late and woke at noon with a pounding head. He spent a couple of hours trying to learn when the next upriver boat would arrive because he meant to be on it. The best guess seemed to be tomorrow or the next day.

Wondering how the hell he was going to occupy himself until then, Spencer concluded that he had to have it out with Kilby Mead before he left.

In the late afternoon he strode into the hospital, walking along the line of cots until he found Kilby sitting on the edge of his bed.

"What the hell did you mean telling Nona I was dead?" Spencer demanded without so much as a greeting.

Kilby smiled thinly. "We all make mistakes."

"We don't all lie."

Kilby shrugged.

Spencer restrained the impulse to jerk the Lieutenant off the bed and slam him against the wall. But Kilby was recovering from wounds and he had to control himself. He couldn't touch the bastard.

"You lied so she'd marry you," Spencer said. "Right?"

Kilby looked him in the eye. "If I did, at least I offered her marriage, which is more than you'll ever do. I know your type, Quinlan—love 'em and leave 'em."

Spencer clenched and unclenched his fists in frustrated fury. It didn't help to realize the Lieutenant had a point in his favor.

"In any case, I've been posted to Washington," Kilby went on. "I'll be leaving next week. Since Nona refused to go with me as my wife, I can only assume it's because of your remarkable resurrection. I hope she won't live to regret her choice but I wouldn't bet on it."

Spencer stared at him, digesting the words. Nona wasn't going to marry Kilby and the Lieutenant was on his way to Washington.

"What about your daughter?" Spencer asked.

"Trying to recover her is impossible, you know that as

well as I do. Chances are she hasn't survived the fighting. It's for the best if she didn't."

What a cold-blooded son-of-a-bitch, Spencer thought.

"I assume you'll be taking Nona with you when you leave Fort Lincoln?" Kilby asked.

"I'm heading upriver to the Yellowstone to join General Crook."

"Leaving her here?" Kilby's smile was mocking.

Love 'em and leave 'em. The words hung in the air between them.

Spencer, afraid he'd be tempted to take a swing at Kilby if he stayed any longer, spun on his heel and stalked off, not bothering with a farewell.

Damn the man, he thought as he left the hospital. And damn Nona, too. Hadn't he offered to see her safely to St. Louis? Hadn't he promised her he'd come back for her when the Indians were subdued? What did she expect?

Simmering with anger, he strode toward the Row but suddenly stopped short. He had no intention of going to her, hat in hand, and begging her to reconsider. Not that it would do any good if he did. Nona was as stubborn a woman as ever lived and she'd just refuse all over again.

Why, with all the women in the world to choose from, had he picked her to love?

Love.

The word reverberated through him, each echo driving the truth a little deeper into his heart. No matter how she infuriated him, he loved Nona.

"There you are, Quinlan. I've been looking for you." Bill King's voice startled him and Spencer blinked at the captain as though he were a total stranger.

"I just heard the *Lady Jane* is docked at Fort Rice and will be here by morning," Bill said.

"*Lady Jane*," Spencer repeated, unable to think beyond the boat's name. With dozens of boats on the river, why did it have to be the *Lady Jane*, where he and

Nona had met?

"You *do* want to go upriver?"

Spencer nodded, not caring to admit to the confusion that made him less and less certain of what he wanted to do.

Bill clapped him on the shoulder. "So you're all set. Tonight we'll have a bon voyage drink. Or two or three." With a wave of his hand, Bill went on. Spencer watched him cross the parade ground without really seeing him.

Nona. Why had he ever thought he could leave her?

Damn the woman! How was he going to convince her they couldn't part? Spencer sighed. How else? By going to her, hat in hand. He resumed walking toward the Row, rehearsing his speech. Nothing sounded right. Maybe he shouldn't talk at all. They did say actions spoke louder than words and God knows he badly needed to put his arms around her and hold her close.

Smiling in anticipation, he climbed the steps to the house and knocked on the door.

Chapter 22

When no one answered his repeated knocks, Spencer tried the knob. The door opened and he stepped into the entry.

"Nona?" he called. "Nona, are you here?"

There was no reply. Was she gone or was she refusing to answer because she didn't wish to see him? He wasn't having any of that nonsense.

Spencer glanced into the parlor, walked to the dining room and the kitchen without finding anyone. He hesitated at the stairs, then shrugged and climbed them. Nona wasn't in her room, or in the other bedroom. Her bed stripped of its covers unsettled him. Had she left Fort Lincoln?

He opened her wardrobe and was reassured at the sight of her clothes hanging inside. He stumbled over a full laundry bag and realized the bed covers must be waiting for Mrs. Grady to collect and wash.

But where was Nona? Not at the hospital; he'd just come from there. She hadn't been particularly close to any of the officers' wives—Katy had been more of a friend than anyone else. Perhaps she'd gone to visit Katy. Or if not, maybe Katy knew where she was.

Spencer strode from the house, determined to find

Nona and set things straight between them.

No one answered the door at Mrs. Grady's.

"Mrs. Grady ain't home," a stout woman called from the next yard where she was taking down clothes from the line.

Spencer walked over and introduced himself. After she told him she was Mrs. Penrose he asked if she knew when Mrs. Grady would be back.

"Can't say for sure," she said. "The whole bunch of 'em crossed over to Bismarck on the morning ferry—even that there one-leg that Katy up and married. They might come back tonight or they might wait till tomorrow, Mrs. Grady didn't know which."

"Did you happen to notice if a red-haired young lady was with them?"

"You must mean Miss Willard. Thick as thieves with Katy, she is. I couldn't say about her one way or the other 'cause I wasn't up and about when they left."

Spencer thanked Mrs. Penrose and set off for the dock to wait for the evening ferry's return from Bismarck. He was pleased to see it pulling in as he arrived but disappointed when the passengers got off. Nona wasn't among them, and neither were Mrs. Grady, Katy or Mike.

He'd have to wait until tomorrow to talk to Nona. If she *was* with Katy. But where else could she be? He'd stop by the house to see if, by chance, she'd returned from some errand, but he had a feeling she was no longer at the Fort. If she wasn't, she had to be in Bismarck; there was no other place to go. She couldn't have left for good, not with her clothes still in her room. She'd be back tomorrow. All he had to be was patient.

Easier said than done. He'd never been known for his patience. Besides, unease shadowed his heart. He had no reason to suspect Nona wasn't perfectly safe and yet he couldn't shake a sense of foreboding.

When he finally returned to the officers' quarters,

Spencer was in no mood for conversation. But he couldn't ignore Bill King, the only officer who'd remained friendly after his run-in with Tom Custer and Major Reno.

"A couple of swigs of Kentucky mash'll cheer you up," Bill predicted.

"No thanks," he told Bill, "I had too much of that forty-rod last night. My head'll never be the same."

"Since the fight on Little Bighorn I don't like being sober and that's a fact." Bill tipped the bottle and drank. "A goddamn disaster, that's what it was. Custer got all his men killed and Reno damn near did the same. Never thought I'd say I was lucky not to be with Custer, but by all the gods of hell, I guess I was. Reno's a bastard, but he got some of us out alive, which is more than Custer did."

Spencer knew Bill had suffered a head injury—a bullet had creased his skull—and had been sent back with the wounded on the *Far West*. He'd recovered quickly but his spirit remained darkened by his experiences on the day of the fight. He'd already told Spencer what had happened—twice.

"Did I tell you about Bloody Knife?" Bill asked.

Spencer nodded, but Bill either didn't notice or didn't care, for he plunged ahead.

"Bloody Knife was always Custer's favorite scout, but for some reason, he sent the Ree with Reno and the rest of us into that valley of death. The hostiles had us on the run, their arrows and bullets thinning us out, and I was riding up to the two of them, Reno and Bloody Knife, to ask the Major what the hell to do next.

"Bloody Knife's head exploded right before my eyes. You ever seen a man's skull shatter? Reno got splattered with the Ree's blood and brains and puked his guts out. I don't blame him. I hate the man but how can you blame him?"

Bill swallowed more whiskey. "The only trooper who had any luck that day was Benteen. Custer hated him, you know. He sent Benteen off on that wild goose chase on purpose; Benteen wasn't going to share the glory if Custer could help it. Later, on that bloody hill, it was Benteen who saved us all." He gazed at Spencer morosely. "Why is it I mourn Custer and don't give a shit for Benteen, the man who saved my life?"

Spencer had no answer. He didn't know who was to blame for the massacre of the Seventh and he doubted if anyone would ever be sure.

"That other scribbler, Kellogg, he died with Custer," Bill said. "Only reason you're sitting here is on account of the run-in you had with Tom Custer over Mead's sister-in-law. Tom made sure you wouldn't ride with the General and that saved your ass. Now Tom's dead and you got clear sailing with the girl. Right?"

"Does any man ever knows where he stands with a woman?" Spencer asked.

Bill laughed. "Giving you a hard time, is she? Redheads, they're feisty."

If only I knew where in the hell she was, Spencer thought, tuning Bill out as the Captain went on to brag about the women he'd known. If only I could be positive she's safe. . . .

After a restless night, Spencer woke early. First he stopped by Nona's house but it was still empty. Nor were the Gradys home. On his way to the dock to meet the noon ferry, he stopped at the stables to feed Kaintuck the lump of sugar he'd confiscated from the officers' mess.

"She ain't brought him back yet," Ned told him. "You can't trust women with horses and that's a fact."

The hair on Spencer's arms prickled. "Who hasn't brought Kaintuck back?" he asked, dreading the answer.

"That Miss Willard. She was toting some old clothes to the Rees and—"

"When did she take Kaintuck?"

"Yesterday, right about this time." Evidently sensing

Spencer's alarm, Ned grew defensive. "Ain't nothing wrong in her borrowing the horse."

"She was going to the Ree village?"

Ned spread his hands. "That's what she said."

Spencer spun on his heel and raced toward the village, afraid Nona had done exactly that—gone to the Rees. But for another purpose than delivering old clothes. She'd been to see Kilby so she realized the Lieutenant was abandoning his daughter. Knowing Nona, Spencer was willing to bet she'd decided to go after Amanda Jean herself.

Of all the hare-brained notions! Didn't she realize the danger?

As he ran into the village, setting all the dogs barking, Spencer prayed he was wrong. He halted in front of Three Crows' lodge where a Ree woman sat sewing. Spencer's heart sank when he saw that she wore a frivolous blue hat decorated with feathers and bows. Nona had surely given that hat to her.

"Three Crows, is he here?" Spencer asked, signing the same question as he spoke in case she didn't understand English.

"He go with white woman." She touched the hat as she spoke.

"Where did they go?"

"He find Sioux camp for her. Ride three suns, no more, he say."

Spencer's shoulders sagged. Why had Three Crows agreed to such a foolish plan? The Ree knew the dangers. Except it wouldn't be Three Crows taking the greatest risk. Nona was reasonably safe as long as she was with the Ree—until they found a Lakota camp. There lay the problem. If they located a camp, Three Crows still wouldn't be in danger because he'd hightail it for home without going near the Lakota.

Nona would be a different story. Spencer pictured her,

stubborn as she was, riding alone into the Lakota camp, ignoring her deadly peril.

And he was too late to stop her.

Expecting a challenge at any moment, Nona slowed Kaintuck to a walk when she neared the strip of trees that grew along the creek. When no scouts rode to stop her, she kept on, taut with apprehension. Remembering what Spencer had taught her about never riding into an Indian camp unannounced, Nona reined in the horse as soon as she caught a glimpse of tipis nestling between the cottonwoods.

Moistening dry lips, she shouted, "Singing Reed! Singing Reed, I'm here. Good Heart comes to visit you."

She waited holding her breath. No one in Lean Bear's camp understood English except Singing Reed. What if Three Crows was wrong and this wasn't the right camp? Even if it was, she couldn't be sure what might greet her. A bullet? An arrow? Mounted warriors?

Her fingers tightened on the reins when she saw movement between the trees. Moments later, her breath whooshed out in relief as she recognized Lean Bear himself, mounted on a buckskin pony, then behind him, afoot, Singing Reed. There was no sign of Amanda Jean.

Lean Bear halted his pony several yards away and watched Nona in silence. Not knowing what was proper, she waited until Singing Reed drew even with him.

"I come to visit you," Nona said to the Sioux woman. "To talk to you."

"You are alone?" Singing Reed sounded dubious.

"I was guided here; my guide has returned to the Fort. I am now alone."

Singing Reed spoke to Lean Bear in their language. He answered at some length, then they talked back and forth for long, stretched-out minutes.

337

"You get off horse," Singing Reed finally said to Nona.

Nona dismounted and Singing Reed took charge of Kaintuck. Lean Bear wheeled his pony and led the way to the village with the two women following behind, Singing Reed leading the chestnut.

"Not good you come," she told Nona. "Our hearts are bad against your people."

"I'm not a soldier," Nona protested.

"You welcome in *my* tipi," Singing Reed assured her. But nowhere else in the village, Nona thought.

"You help me take down tipi," Singing Reed went on. "Lean Bear says because you come, we move."

Nona realized they were afraid troopers might follow in her wake. About to insist this wasn't true, Nona bit back the words when it occurred to her that a search party might well be sent after her once Three Crows returned to the Fort. She didn't want to be responsible for what could happen then.

"I'll help you," she told Singing Reed. Then, unable to wait any longer, she asked, "Where is Light Of Sun?"

Singing Reed gestured the round of tipis. Fewer tipis than Nona remembered. Only seven now. Nona quickened her steps, eager to see her niece again.

The baby lay naked on a blanket under a tree, kicking her arms and legs, her eyes intent on a leather doll a young girl dangled over her. Nona would have known Amanda Jean anywhere. She was the picture of Helen. Hurrying to the blanket, Nona knelt beside the baby.

Tears pricked Nona's eyes when Amanda Jean looked up at her and smiled. How could Kilby abandon this beautiful child? Her eyes were blue as the Dakota skies, her hair the yellow of autumn leaves, her smile bright as the sun.

When Singing Reed spoke the girl ran off. The Sioux woman lifted Amanda Jean into her arms and carried her to a tipi. Nona followed her inside. Once Amanda Jean

338

was safe in her cradle, Singing Reed ordered Nona to take the cradle outside and hang it on a tree limb so they could strike the tipi.

In what seemed minutes the village was ready to move on. Nona was allowed to ride Kaintuck with Singing Reed on Twisted Ear, holding a lead rope connecting the two horses. It amazed Nona how the pinto had found his way back to Singing Reed from the Fort.

They traveled until the lingering northern summer evening blued into dusk and set up the camp on another creek miles to the south. Since Nona had expected them to travel west, she asked Singing Reed why they'd gone south instead.

The Sioux woman looked up from the fire she was kindling in the center of the tipi. "Lean Bear brings us close to reservation."

"He's taking you to the reservation?" Nona asked in surprise.

"No. He tries to keep us safe. Our young warriors rode into setting sun three moons ago, eager to fight and die. They do not return. Many times we go hungry. Still, we live."

"I know Lean Bear's angry because I came."

"He fears bluecoats will kill us all."

"It's safe on the reservation. Why don't you go there?" Nona asked.

"Reservation is cage. Slow death comes in cage. Better to die quickly." Singing Reed set the kettle over the fire, added water, and put in the small amount of dried beef left in Kaintuck's saddle bags.

"Hunger is also a slow death," Nona observed, realizing the beef she'd brought was the only meat Singing Reed had.

Singing Reed's glance was pitying. "You do not know. My people starve on reservation same like us. No more they hunt. Maybe we find buffalo and live."

Nona looked at Amanda Jean, asleep in her cradle carrier. "Light of Sun must not die," she said firmly.

Singing Reed sat back on her heels. "You came to take her," she accused.

"I came to save her," Nona countered. "Even if she survives the bluecoats, what kind of life will she have with you—going hungry, living in fear?"

"She is mine. I will look after her."

"How can you protect her against bullets?"

Singing Reed didn't answer. Nona also remained silent. She knew the Sioux woman wanted what was best for the child and decided to let her think over what had already been said. Surely Singing Reed would see the best solution for everyone would be to give up Amanda Jean to ensure her safety. At the same time, it would rid the village of Nona's disturbing presence.

When someone scratched the outside of the tipi flap seeking entry, Nona tensed, unsure of her welcome in the camp.

Singing Reed spoke a few words, Lean Bear pushed open the flap and entered, seating himself on the guest side of the fire.

Singing Reed offered him food from the kettle and Nona waited impatiently while he ate. She was certain he hadn't come to eat but it seemed to take Indians forever to get to the reason for a visit.

At last he set aside the bowl and, his eyes on Nona, spoke in his tongue.

"Lean Bear says council has met," Singing Reed told her without emotion. "He voted to kill you."

It was all Nona could do to stifle her gasp as she stared fearfully from the Sioux woman to Lean Bear.

He spoke agan and Nona's heart slammed against her ribs as she waited for Singing Reed's translation.

"Quiet Rain, he say not kill, you bring luck." The Sioux woman looked at her impassively. "When you